Denis Minns

The
Fisherman's
Ring

novum 🔺 pro

This book is also available as e-book.

www.novum-publishing.co.uk

© 2018 novum publishing

ISBN 978-3-99048-750-1
Editing: Rachel Jones, BA (Hons)
Cover photo: Ilyach | Dreamstime.com
Cover design, layout & typesetting: novum publishing

www.novum-publishing.co.uk

1.

ST THERESE L'ENFANT, SOUTHERN FRANCE

It is said that 'To whom you gift your secret, you surrender your freedom.' Until that hot August day when she was just 10 years old, Maria Anna Temoin had not thought of freedom; nor had she known of any secret worthy to gift. But when one came to her that day at twilight, she held a secret so sacred it placed on her a burden she would have to share. The freedom she was to surrender was the sacrifice of her young life.

That was 36 years ago in the village of St Therese L'Enfant. A small group of square, rendered houses, their faded white walls soiled with the passage of time. Homes that cower under dark grey tiled pitched roofs scattered sparsely on a bleak hillside in the lower Pyrenees. Narrow lanes separate them, winding through the undulating rock. Small groups of silver birch and poplar valiantly cling to the thin soil and low stone walls mark boundaries in random lines that follow the contours of the landscape. The modest buildings are loosely linked by sagging cables running overhead, and on poles by the roadside; a straggling loose connection to the world beyond. To the south, the Pyrenees Mountains rise magnificently away over green fields wetted by low cloud and dried by the constant sun on cloudless days.

This village has nothing of the beauty of those that nestle within the deep valleys among the mountains above. The mountain villages are the hosts of winter skiing, their pretty buildings, cafes and bars are for the carefree fun of the wealthy. St Therese is a settlement of the foothills. She provides the homes of the poor, the agricultural labour that ekes out an existence from the bare but magnificent landscape. These are the homes of the faithful and fearful. The docile and the dammed.

In the village centre stands the small church of St Therese, her square tower pointing to heaven with its pinched grey roof formed like some modest spire. Her entrance door, narrow and austere, is coloured dull blue from some ancient paintwork and sheltered by a low roof centred at the foot of the tower itself. On her faded white rendered wall one can only just make out a clock face that tells a time that all who look to her already know.

The early August sun had been full in a wide blue sky throughout a summer of long days and endless evenings. A summer of children's games, swimming in the cool stream by St Therese and running and ball games in the open fields. Of eating with friends around open fires, roast vegetables and cheese on torn slices of rough bread, and fresh fruit from the sparse garden plots. A summer of careless innocence. A season of laughter when the menfolk could idle and the women taunt them in good humour and toast them in good wine. It was that rare joie de vivre, captured in that simple season of summertime before nature turns her temper to the rains the winds and the bleak dark seasons so harsh a feature among those beautiful peaks.

Maria Anna sat on the bank of the stream and watched as two younger children played an endless game of splashing one another in the water by bringing their sticks down upon the surface with shrieks of delight. They had crossed the fields to the woodland some distance from the village that was the children's playground, where nature invited the adventure of her discovery. Her ever changing pallet that grows and fades and changes with the seasons. They had spent a long day there by the stream. There were the games that drew on the mystery of this silent space and swimming, running, exploring, a brief picnic of bread and cheese and the indolent slumber in the cool shade of a pine tree that overtakes the excitement of the morning.

She looked to the sky where two young buzzards sailed the soft warm currents of air squeaking like kittens as they drifted to and fro, and high in that azure infinity above the spectral peaks the lone flight of the lammergeyer, the bearded vulture circled watchfully for some prey fallen victim of the steep and perilous slopes below.

At first it was no more than a murmur in the air that Maria Anna thought she had imagined. Something she might have ignored perhaps but then it was more, almost a presence of something, or even, someone. She thought she heard the sound of a voice in the air carried on a soft and sudden chill breeze.

She could hear it more clearly now.

'Watch closely my child' she was sure it said. Maria Anna looked around her shrugging her shoulders as she felt a chill as she did so but seeing nothing.

'It's time we went home now' she shouted out to the Esterre siblings feeling an apprehension.

'Come on we had better get back'

Swiftly, she gathered the young ones together impatient now feeling an uneasiness. It was as if someone was watching them from somewhere out of sight. Briskly she started back towards the village looking around her as she ushered the giggling children with an increasing impatience. Then she heard it again, the voice in the air was following them.

'Let's run' She instructed now with some anxiety and the three children began to return to the village in haste the younger two oblivious as to the urgency she demanded of their pace.

Madam Temoin looked over towards the mountains as far as the woodland at its foot and awaited the return of the children. The light was now fading and there was no sign of their return. Stay together she had always told them. They understood how important that was, she was sure that their delay would be no more than some incidental tribulation. Something forgotten and returned for, something lost to be looked for, but now dusk gathered a tangible apprehension and the watch grew stronger.

Madam Temoin had been joined by Madam Esterre and old Madam Veux. A series of enquiries and suppositions exchanged between them. Of theories and assurances. Confabulation was mixed with silent pauses as the three women looked out to an increasing darkness.

It was something then that Madam Veux said, perhaps through the transparency of her faith or out of habit and her advancing years that seemed quite natural but held in retrospect, a significance well beyond that intended by her.

'Holy Mary mother of God' she entreated under her breath by way of concern for the safety of the children.

It was almost at that point that the three women saw across the landscape a light so bright that the mountains were revealed in all the detail of their splendour. A beam of light that fell into the woodland like something had fallen from the sky. It was a vision that was unaccountable to them and they watched it in awe and trepidation.

The three children had come to a small opening in the woodland where the rock surrounded a small enclosure as if it were an opening to a cave. They could hear now the voice above them in the air. Soft, confident but unclear. They felt a movement above their heads as if something was shaking in the trees. The fear gathered in their eyes as they looked up to see the crowns of the surrounding trees swirl in frenzy. The light was blinding to them and they could feel the presence of something or someone, close to where they stood. Maria Anna reached out to hold the Esterre children as if to protect them from the unseen presence.

Then, they saw Her. There on a piece of rock, sat the figure of a lady. She was clad in a blue robe falling to her ankles, with a white sash at the neck and blue headscarf. She wore no jewellery but her golden hair shone in the bright light and her eyes a piercing blue as the summer sky itself. On her feet were simple sandals that looked unworn and unsoiled and in her hand she held a rosary.

The children looked at her paralysed with fear. They stood in silence waiting for her to speak, for they knew who she was and that she had come to speak to them for they had heard of such things before. It neither seemed unnatural nor unbelievable to them, nor was there excitement but the simple obedience of faith as they realised that they were in the presence of the Holy mother.

They saw the shadows of her eyes, long with sorrows but now, those eyes were shining the strength of resolve fixed upon the frail trinity standing in sullen wonder before her, and as she spoke her voice was strong and clear and a light smile lifted it to a level of tenderness.

'I have come here' She began 'as I came before one century ago.'

'To repeat to you the warning I gave then. That you might tell of the comings that will befall those who have questioned the word of God that all might praise God and live in righteousness.' There was the simple elocution of Her speech that respected the youth of her audience.

'There are two among you who will soon join me in Heaven.' She began. They will be taken on the same day that the Holy church had its temporal powers taken from it in the Eternal city.'

She looked at them to see that they were concentrating on Her words and said:

'There is to be a sign. A fury will come from the bowels of the earth to run a red rage of destruction that will destroy large numbers of humanity. When the sign is given the Antichrist will place his servant in the Holy church to seize the souls of men through their avarice and greed. The Holy roman empire will rise again with unparalleled riches and the Antichrist will seize power to control it. From the blue people will come the blue eyed child to show the way to freedom'

I must tell you now the second part of the secret prayer which you may only say to God, for within it is great power. Where it is spoken there will be reconciliation and where it is written there will be protection to those who hold it in their grasp. I declare that you will not forget this prayer for it will be part of you that you should one day join it with its first part to give the blessing of unequalled power.'

The Holy Mother then recited a prayer for the children and Her message delivered, her image faded into the stillness of the evening and there was a quiet to the surrounding trees. It was dark now and as she led the children in silence to return to the village Maria Anna felt curiously serene and comforted as if the power of the presence of her holy mother had held them in some warm embrace.

In his modest lodgings by the church Father Etienne Pierre Petit had lifted his gaze to the sky outside his window. The brightness of a light such as he saw had caused him to look out with curiosity. He had not long been the priest in the village and assumed that had he been so, he would know the identity of the brightness in the sky and thus did not take much account of it other than to resolve to ask one of the villagers for an explanation.

Father Etienne Petit was not in any event the most welcome priest ever appointed to the village. There was an inbred suspicion particularly from the older folk, as he bore the pale skin of a northerner, an outsider the kind of who were not always appreciated in the closed circles of the contrite community of St Therese, who from time to time would exclude him from their conversations and confidences by their Occitan exchanges.

This evening an expedient fate would see to it that he was to feel the full authority of his ministry. A feeling of intense satisfaction of his powers that would extinguish the doubts of his flock. His judgement would now be required to fulfil the expectations of all villagers and there would forever be reverence and respect in the hushed whispers that carried his name. For shortly after dark he was visited by three of the village children. They brought to him the most extraordinary story for his interpretation and counsel. It was no less than the report of a Marian revelation.

Father Etienne Petit well understood the superiority of a Priest in a region where poverty and ignorance drove respect for authority and contrition for indiscretion. He knew that he alone had the important task of deciding what truth there might be in the revelations. He had been given the authority by Almighty God himself, that of governing the souls and consciences of his flock. He would hear what had to be said, carefully write it down and he would consider whether to pass it on to higher authorities.

He sat in his sitting room in stern silence as the three small figures stood in a line before him.

'What is your name child?' He asked the eldest of them.

The slim pretty girl was about 10 years old. She was dark skinned and well formed with an incipient sensuality. She wore her hair in a dark tussled mane that hung below her shoulders. Her eyes were full and there was an excitement in them that gave them an unusual beauty.

'I am Maria Anna.' She answered softly.

'Tell me.' he started with a contrived softness to his gravelly voice 'Tell me what you heard' He looked into her eyes and felt their eagerness.

'She said that she had come just as she had come one century before. She said two of us would soon join her in Heaven and it would be on the day that the Eternal city lost its temporal powers.'

The priest narrowed his eyes in his failure to quite comprehend the message.

'Was that all that was said?' He asked seeking clarification.

'She said that there is to be a sign and that fury would come from the bowels of the earth to run a red rage of destruction and at the sign, the Antichrist would place his servant in the holy church.'

The child affirmed seemingly unconscious of the meaning of the words.

The Priest's eyes narrowed. He could hear that these words were not the invention of a child who might have the audacity to fabricate a story 'What else did she say my child?'

'She said that the Antichrist would rise to rule over the Holy Roman Empire and that from the blue people would come the blue eyed child to lead the way to freedom'

'She recited to us the second part of a prayer that we may speak only to God. Where it is spoken there will be reconciliation and where it is written there shall be protection.'

Father Petit took up his pen and began to write as he listened to the child recount the revelations the children had been given by the Holy mother and bade her recite to him the prayer in the name of the Lord. He marvelled at this young child, with limited education giving her account with extraordinary articulation. He was in awe at the precision with which the revelations were conveyed to him and becoming increasingly aware of the notoriety that they might bring to his parish, the recognition that might bring to his ministry, and to himself, a lowly Priest who might hope for a more exalted position in which to serve.

When they were finished their recount, and he had questioned them as much as he could and wrote down the evidence, he invited the children's parents into the room and held up his hand to give his verdict.

'I may need to speak to the Holy See to report these revelations' He advised.

'There must be no telling of these matters.' He announced solemnly. For it is written that if anyone shall take the words of prophesy away from the book then God shall take away his part in the book of life.'

As the parents nodded in complicity, he turned to the children.

'You children are sworn to secrecy regarding everything you have heard today and by that will you be judged when the final judgement is upon you.'

Father Etienne Petit could see in their eyes the firm resolution to secrecy born of fear. He did not doubt that he alone now held the words of revelation in his grasp. As he blessed the children one by one and thanked their parents for bringing them to see him as they left his cottage in silence and as he stood by the window looking out into the darkness, he felt that he might have been gifted a revelation that might bring to him immeasurable advantage.

It had been the night of the great storm. Thunder had crashed overhead among the deep black clouds. The wind whistled wildly, shrieking a judgement among the eaves of the small houses. The rain fell fast and furious on the hard ground in terrible and torrential anger. Lighting revealed the spectral peaks in vivid white outlined against the night sky. A number of small goats sheltered where they could, shaking with fear at the sound of it and dogs whelped helplessly unable to comprehend the savagery of the tempest that lashed them like a cruel master.

The small houses of the village rocked at the usurpation. Somewhere a roof leaked rivulets of rain down an inner wall. Somewhere a window rattled madly at the overwhelming power of it, and everywhere drains choked at the deluge, spitting out what they could not swallow into the ditches by the small lanes, now rivers, running wild with water.

At dawn the single church bell of St Therese L'Enfant was ringing out a low toll sounding in the thin air as if a distance away. Father Etienne Petit had crossed himself when he heard the tragic loss of the Esterre children. He stood and watched the silent work of menfolk extracting bodies from the small and fallen cottage and listened to the dismal sobs and cries of women's grief.

While the great storm had raged, both children had been taken by falling masonry in their home. A wall that had come crashing down on their bed while the small ones slept. It was devastation for their family, a great sorrow for the entire village. The bell of the church of St Therese L'Enfant would ring today the solemn toll of death. Today the faithful would go about the business of clearing the storm debris in hushed reverence and bear the wounds of sympathy for the loss of their children.

For Father Etienne Petit however the significance of their loss was not to be ignored. It had placed upon him a duty that he alone was qualified to execute. From the bookcase in his room he selected a large leather bound volume. He fingered through the pages as if he knew what he was looking for. Not for something new, but to confirm something that was lodged somewhere in a mislaid memory. Something that had stirred in his mind since he had heard the evidence of the small troika of children before him. It was something that he could hardly bear to read such was his excitement. Something that he had dreamt of before coming to St Therese L'Enfant but never dared hope for.

He spread the opened book on his desk and searched the list of Marian revelations reported to the church that were recorded in the pages before him. He stopped and read out loud the details of a revelation to some young children at Aix en Bairn almost exactly one hundred years ago. First, two of the children had died shortly after the revelation was given. There was a prediction that the sign that would herald the coming of the antichrist was thought to be a volcanic eruption and the reference to the blue eyed child. There was reference to the first part of a secret prayer given to the children and the promise to return with the second part. There was nothing further. Clearly the full details were a matter only for the highest authorities in the church, but it seemed to him to be too great a coincidence.

Here before him, the gift of the second part of the secret prayer that had been prophesised would give protection to those who held it written. He murmured to himself as if to give an assurance.

'Surely there can be no doubt.'

Quietly he picked up the letter he had composed from the writing desk in his sitting room. The letter he had written to report the event to the highest authorities in the Holy See. An event that he knew had to be the second edition of a revelation given one hundred years ago close to this village.

This was an event that would make his exiled parish known throughout the world. 'Notre Dame de St Therese L'Enfant' he whispered to himself in awe to comprehend the perceptible consequence of the action he was to take. For he was sure that he alone was aware of the significance of the date of the great storm and the death of the two children. It was the twentieth day of September. The day that the temporal powers of the Holy church were taken was the date on which the children had been taken just as the revelation had said.

He read out again the final words of the letter he was to send as he carefully signed his name.

'I can respectfully advise Monseigneur Dufour, that the deaths of the children predicted in our lady's revelation have come to pass.'

2.

LONDON, ENGLAND

It was eight o'clock in the evening and the party at the Connaught held by the Architects Fisher Holt and Fitzroy was already in full swing. The trio of musicians hired for the occasion, were playing a lively medley that gave a feeling of optimism that was felt by all present. It was, in the words of the senior partner Sir Clement Fitzroy, an event to celebrate an outstanding achievement.

Marcus had been looking forward to his share of the acknowledgements and congratulations that would inevitably come his way. He felt perhaps for the first time in his life a feeling of pride in himself, standing champagne glass in hand at the side of the room dressed in black tie and dinner jacket searching the room and recognising so many of the elegant invitees ready to target them when the opportunity arose.

'Mullen.' He exclaimed on being surprised by a figure at his side.

'I just had to say Marcus old boy, fantastic and well done'

Marcus acknowledged the comment as if it had been unexpected with a polite.

'Thanks.'

'I heard that you won on all counts. There was a lot of emphasis on renewable energy and that blessed affordable housing requirement always gets in the way. You used it to your advantage I gather. Tell me, how did you achieve it?' Mullen placed a hand upon his shoulder.

'Well we at FHF had known that our competition design of the new Gelco headquarters was exciting but then so many of the entries would be. We went for a more traditional building and this was a risk. The planning authority was looking for a strong

15

emphasis on renewable energy which often implies more futuristic design. It was unwilling to give up on its affordable housing requirement.' He began by way of an explanation that he was sure to have to repeat throughout the evening.

'The usual approach is to opt for the financial contribution to the council, a sort of 'buy off' but we elected to make the provision onsite. We struck a deal on a basis of Gelco offering employment to local residents who would qualify for affordable housing on site.' He finished draining his glass.

'Yes something grandly described by Fitz as a 'win win' approach I gather' recalled Mullen happy to quote Marcus illustrious colleague in the knowledge that it would raise a smile.

Another small group of familiar faces approached him to apprise themselves of further details.

'Marcus, Good evening and well done with the Gelco job' Said the chap who worked with Sidler and Davies who Marcus was sure had never so much as acknowledged him before.

'Fantastic solution mate.'

'Yeah. Nice one Marcus' Came from a pair of brothers from Camberwell.

The comments were coming like an applause. The air was full of compliments and congratulations as Marcus moved between guests modestly acknowledging them.

It was for Marcus Graham a bit of a 'first'. Never before had he designed a scheme that had won such admiration, never before had he been so celebrated. Never before had Marcus Graham felt the warm glow of success.

Fitz had called it 'the winning', that coming first in front of all others that Fitz understood so well. For Marcus there was something about 'the winning' that he knew to have been a stroke of good fortune. It was just as likely that the judges would have favoured another of the proposals, but there was something now in having won that he had never felt before. 'The winning' held his scheme up as the best most inspirational stroke of genius available. It questioned the adequacy of those that had merely come second and third. It was almost as if they had missed something.

'The winning' felt good but it was only for today. Tomorrow saw the start of a fresh race in which he would be seen as a favourite and he already knew that he could not win again, for that was not something that he had been accustomed to.

He had learned to know his shortcomings within the harsh confines of a cold Edwardian boarding school near the north Kent coast. A minor school academically, where sport was held in an esteem calculated to overcome the intellectual inadequacy that had long been acknowledged to be part of the school's ethos. Here he had grown up with the rigid rule of self-improvement that imposed the notion that it is for the individual to achieve things in life. Nothing is set out for him; it is he who must create it himself. Marcus had retreated to his books from the earnest cry of sporting competition that had resulted in modest academic success and entry to Blackfriars college Oxford. It was here that he eschewed Theology and discovered himself more in love with the old stones of the city. He had resolved to be an Architect. To discover how such buildings were put together.

Marcus's mother never quite recovered from the requirement to retract her boasts about his Oxford education when he came down without a degree midway through his second year. It had been the core of her conversation among her friends ever since he had been accepted at Blackfriars to study Theology. He had felt that the disappointment had soured their relationship throughout the later part of her life. If only she could be alive to see him now, the move was surely now fully justified. The warmth of 'the winning' would be here waiting to embrace her.

He could see that across the room Fitz was obligingly giving his account of the whole affair tinged with the usual embellishments to a group of young ladies. Among them Marcus caught the eye of the personal assistant who worked for him and Fitz. Emma Dreyfus smiled knowingly at Marcus. She was clearly amused by Fitz version of the events which would inevitably record details of the advantages to be gained by clients in using FHF. Marcus was certain that Fitz too would be well aware of the subjectivity that had resulted in 'the winning' but that that he would be portraying it as inevitable, the result of careful analysis, unique professionalism, teamwork, commitment and all the other Fitz vocabulary that was brought out whenever he was in company.

From behind him a young woman approached Marcus wearing a simple black dress without any hint of accessories.

'Hello, you're Marcus Graham aren't you?' Marcus turned to see that the enquiry was from a petite intelligent faced young woman who looked at him as if she knew precisely who he was.

'I'm from the Southwark Chronicle. Lulu Pierce. I was looking at the plans of the flats that will be let within the scheme. I have to ask you. Are they intended for families?'

Marcus toyed with his answer to this question. The truth was he thought that there had been a good deal more to consider about the project than exactly who would occupy the flats. They were two bedroom flats they complied with the housing standards for rent and that was as far as he had considered them. Miss Pierce was clearly about to launch a follow up question. She was a journalist ... He had to consider his answer carefully.

'Well that will depend on demand. I mean the flat residents will be employees of Gelco.' He blinked evasively behind his round framed glasses.

'My point Marcus is, that there is no external space at all with them and there are bound to be some families'

She was not about to give in. Nine months of solid graft designing and submitting against some of the finest architects in London and he was being quizzed as to why subsidised urban housing was not afforded the Arcadian attributes of a rural idyll.

'I would like a quote from you Marcus' She pressed.

'But let me ask you. Do you have a family yourself?' The instinct of the journalist had been to go straight to the weak point. To unveil the hidden truth. An architect with no family of his own could not possibly be expected to understand etcetera ... He could see it in print.

'Let me explain.' He responded politely though a little ruffled by his preconception. He paused. The explanation was bound to be unconvincing. He would be portrayed as a pompous bachelor architect who had so catastrophically missed the point of that part of the scheme that was of key interest to local people.

Marcus was thinking as quickly as he could and sought to divert her.

'Er do you live nearby?' Marcus questioned seeking justification for her interest.

'Yes. I have a small flat in Cable street that I use during the week and at weekends I try to get away to see my parents. It's just me so no need for external space.' She smiled anticipating the reprisal.

He smiled at her with relief at this revelation and the impression that as she had been so forthcoming in her admission perhaps it was not after all her purpose to skewer him on the absence of amenity space. Indeed Lulu went on to reveal a far less intimidating character than her initial questioning suggested.

'I have to confess that I know little about the Gelco scheme. I hadn't realised that there was such a need for employment in the area and that had been central to the debate around the site's development. Perhaps I should make a point of emphasising that.' She said in a tone less questioning than conciliatory.

Marcus detected that for the first time in his career that he had put together a scheme that seemed to please even the hardened journalists of the local press.

'Yes. I should say so. Quite.' He blurted.

'Speaking personally Marcus. I did feel that the FHF scheme was the best in the competition. I liked the traditional design approach which I guess was your own idea. But there will be those who have questions, particularly those who were against the development of this site in the first place. I have to examine all issues' Lulu explained with a sternness that was now unconvincing.

Marcus felt more relaxed and that he was on secure ground, he turned the conversation to a more personal line.

'So 'just you' you say. You have no family?' Marcus questioned in order to drive home the point that she was perhaps no better qualified to speak for families than he was.

'No. No family' With this she looked at him wistfully. Marcus had the impression that Lulu was a young women who had come to the point where she would prefer to give up a career to settle down with a home a family somewhere in the countryside. Organising schooling. Cricket for the boys and ponies for the girls. He could quite see her in this role. Her aspirations for that rural idyll were manifest. Her charm tangible. He had her on the run.

By way of completion of the rout, Marcus was able to play his trump card. An introduction to his well-known and illustrious colleague Sir Clement Ambrose Fitzroy and while conscious of the certainty that Lulu had not heard of Fitz either, it nevertheless seemed to ensure that the article that would feature in the Southwark chronicle the next day would be favourably disposed to the Gelco scheme.

He was awaiting the Chronicle to arrive at his desk the following morning when Fitz fixed a friendly hand on his shoulder.

'Let's catch a coffee Marcus.' Fitz announced loudly.

'We've been blessed with a little sunshine out there, we can sit outside.'

The offices of Fisher, Holt and Fitzroy were sited on the first floor of a building that faced the return frontage of a cute coffee shop that was entered from the Kings road in Chelsea. F.H.F Staff all knew the quieter times of day for coffee breaks and for whatever reason it was generally possible to get one of the two tables on the side street at just after 10am.'A great place to sit for a chat away from the office.' Fitz would say.

'We can have a frank and confidential exchange without interruption.' He would add. In practice it had been generally observed that it was possible to hear every word delivered in Fitz distinct and eloquent voice with the window of the office partially open. A significant drawback to the facility, the recognition of which Fitz had recurrently failed to make.

Marcus was dressed in his usual casual style. A light tweed jacket over a bright blue shirt and a tomato red bow tie, moleskin cotton trousers and brown suede shoes all chosen not to impress, but for comfort. His small round frame glasses completed a persona that in the eyes of many identified his profession.

Fitz ordered coffee and sat back under a warming sun of early spring at the table by the overgrown Jasmine and the large pot with some yellowing plant left over from last year. He swept the table top with the back of his hand as if something had been left there. He brought with him the optimism of one who will always believe that anything is possible. This expressed itself in a confidence and certainty that was rarely open to contradiction.

This morning he seemed excited and unusually animated. The usual format was that Fitz imparted the information, he would then outline how he intended one to react to that information, then seek the agreement of his colleague by way of immediate response sealing the 'exchange of views' with a triumphant confirmation that agreement had been reached, an emphatic endorsement of the 'like-minded professionalism to be found at F.H.F.'

'Now I think we have something coming up that will interest you.' Fitz began.

'South of France small ecclesiastical job. How does that sound?'

Marcus had learnt not to jump at any suggestion Fitz made with alacrity. Often ones over enthusiastic response would be met by a condition or circumscription such as 'just one small thing' or 'mind you there would not be scope for.'

He responded nonchalantly.' Could be interesting Fitz. Where in the south?'

'Avignon. Renovation of a small chapel. Part of the palace complex. Came through our Catholic church surveyor chap. He felt we could do something having seen what you did around the St George Cathedral I must say, in my view.'

Fitz's words tailed away. Marcus felt his heart skip a little, his mind thrown back to a distant past.

'Avignon' Marcus interrupted' I haven't been there for years. Did you know that was where my wife and daughter died Fitz?'

Fitz looked down at the table a little uncomfortably.

'Well yes, I knew it was somewhere around there. I don't know the area at all myself. I am sorry' He managed with a clumsy insincerity. 'Does that make it difficult for you?'

Marcus leaned back in his chair and paused, more for effect than reflection.

'No, not at all Fitz. I think it would be good to go back. I always meant to sometime. It's been over 20 years now. It seems like another life.'

As he spoke Marcus felt his words promote a resolve. He had often meant to go back to Avignon and reflected that he remembered little of his brief life in France. The hastened marriage. The birth of a daughter at which he was not present and the shock at the news of their death shortly after the marriage that reached him when visiting his home in Tunbridge Wells.

'Yes, not at all' he repeated. I think it is time I returned to Avignon and it would be good to have such a splendid reason to do so.'

Fitz had not anticipated any alternative reaction to his suggestion. Generally the response to any suggestion or offer made by him was expected to be positive. It was in the manner it was put over. A favour from Fitz. What more could one want.

Marcus knew his old friend well. He had worked for him for 20 years since qualifying as an architect and it was Fitz who had given him the opportunity to work, first on his own stately home in Somerset and then on a variety of the houses of the titled, the good and the great whom Fitz knew socially or from his various activities and appointments in high places. Fitz's contacts didn't provide the bulk of the work of Fisher Holt Fitzroy but they certainly provided some of the more interesting commissions.

FHR had become for Marcus all his permanence in an uncertain life. In a life strewn with unfulfilled promise, it was his reference, his endorsement, his identity. It was the nearest thing to a family that he had and the fulfilment of this commission would be his pleasure.

Over the next few days more details emerged on the commission that was to be his assignment. Marcus began to look forward to the opportunity that Fitz had assigned to him. He had always liked the ecclesiastical restoration work so much a part of the FHF portfolio. Perhaps it was his year at Theology college at

Oxford where he had no more than toyed with the idea of graduating in Theology but had gained his admiration for buildings and an affection for ecclesiastical architecture.

Success, he reflected, can open so many doors that one must choose judiciously which one to enter, for failure will follow success with an alacrity and the greater the success, the greater that failure can be. This French commission would withdraw him from the limelight of the Gelco project that he had lit up successfully but in its heat, he now felt an apprehension as to his ability to carry it out. Avignon, a small chapel renovation and sunshine beckoned and perhaps even the memories that had wounded him would be given a chance to heal.

3.

PROVENCE, SOUTHERN FRANCE

Madame Collette Temoin looked out from the front window of her small stone house just outside the town of Eyragues in Provence. A light drizzle of rain had just begun to fall onto the narrow street lined with square buildings clad in broken grey render, their windows framed with worn duck egg blue shutters hung on rusted hinges and random plant boxes teeming with coloured flowers. Outside on a concrete forecourt shared with neighbouring houses, was parked the family's Citroen.

The uncertainty that she felt each time her daughter had taken out the car was a visceral one. No logic of mind could support her apprehension nor condemn the prospect of her daughter's independence now that she had a child. It would be important to her to gain the mobility afforded by the car. To meet friends, to take the child to the clinic and then to nursery and eventually to school. The Catholic school at St Remy de Provence that had gained such praise from the community. It was an apprehension that Madame Temoin was sure she would learn to put to one side, and perhaps in time she would come to terms with the shock of her daughter's pregnancy and inevitable sudden marriage.

She smiled gently as she watched Annie carefully place her baby carriage onto the rear seat of the Citroen careful to strap it, to avoid it falling forward were she to break suddenly. She saw her slip her slight body gracefully into the front seat an felt the small warmth of pride a mother feels at the sight of a daughter's new confidence. Annie glanced towards the window instinctively feeling her mother's watchful eyes and smiled at her briefly.

Madam Temoin looked on as her daughter reversed the car carefully and drove away with a decisiveness that gave her some reassurance as she glanced at the clock face on the wall. It was 11.34am the time of Annie's departure. It was the last time she saw her daughter smile. The last time she saw her alive.

The road south to St Remy is a flat, straight and narrow carriageway. Deep ditches and high hedges form unkempt boundaries on either side. The countryside to the south of Eyragues is strewn with overhead cables and by the sides of the road there were plastic buildings for the growing of fruit and vegetables formed in vast regimented rows that sparkle in the sunlight, appearing from a distance like some vast water filled ditches hewn from the landscape. The beauty of Provence lies all around, but here the buildings are built for function. Local stone held together with crumbling jointing, concrete block faced in faded render or sometimes left bare and those oceans of plastic tunnels.

Marie Segolene was asleep in the baby carrier strapped on the front seat beside her mother. The rhythmic squeak of the car's windscreen wipers was the only sound Annie could hear above the low hum of the small engine. She travelled carefully along the wet road conscious of her passenger beginning to sleep in the carrier beside her.

The fruit lorry parked in the exit of a track way by the road leading south to St Remy was not a sight that attracted her attention. It was typical of those that transported the harvest of fruit grown under the plastic poly tunnels in the area and a regular sight on this road. She passed it by without a glance at a young woman of about Annie's age sitting in the driver's seat with hat pulled down to cover the dark eyes that narrowed as Annie's car passed by.

Annie could not know that the fruit lorry had been waiting there for about half an hour, its driver looking with expectation along the road for the arrival of another vehicle throughout that wait and she could not know that it was Annie's car that she was waiting for. It was just before midday when the Citroen drove past. The fruit lorry had pulled out to follow it, its engine revving wildly to catch up.

It was not long after that it happened. On the clear straight section of the road the lorry begun to pass the Citroen. It swerved vigorously to the right forcing the small car off the road immediately where it turned wildly as it skidded on the verge losing its front wheel and swinging violently across the rough ground by the side of the road and smashing into a tree where in came to rest, battered and overturned.

Annie had not seen the lorry coming. She had no time to brake evenly and had fallen first forward against the steering wheel and then as the car tumbled over she had been crushed under its crumpled roof killing her instantly. Her baby had fared little better surrounded by the baby carriage but thrown to the roof of the overturned car as it came to rest. It was small mercy that the vehicle had not burst into flames.

The road had been quiet that day, there had been no one to witness the incident and the only evidence were the tyre marks and part of the lorry's cargo of lemons that had been split across the road as its driver had sped off. That was over 25 years ago but Marcus remembered the road to Saint Remy de Provence etched upon his mind after just one visit having hastily returned to France following the news of the accident.

It had been a grey morning dull with the threat of rain. The car's tyre marks had been heavy on the tarmac surface half way along the straight stretch several kilometres outside the northern limit of St Remy. The earth was torn where it went to ground. A twisted relic of a dull chromium plated bumper lodged in the hedge and some unrecognisable debris, part buried where it met its end and that was all. The rest had been taken away, except the lemons that had fallen from the lorry that had hit her. Lemons scattered all around marking the scene of death with the unreal scent of rotting citrus.

What was the simple truth? A motor accident. Perhaps a momentary distraction from a crying baby. Perhaps a dog on the slippery road. He would never know and he had never been told. If only he had been there. He felt the guilt of his absence even now. The landscape is indifferent to the events of yesterday. Time and nature work together to repair the scars. For Marcus too, now upon his reflection, the passing of 25 years had erased the details and left just a vague and incomplete memory.

He had felt empty, but not for the loss of his wife and child on that day but because he literally felt so little at all. Regret and guilt were the more superficial emotions that haunted him now. In that tragic moment after their death he had felt the relief that this was for him some form of release of his responsibility. He would now be free to own his life. Free to take his time. Free to choose his lovers. The uneven hand of fate that had cut them down had turned the key to his freedom.

He had met her in a small café in the Place du Marche Ste Catherine in Paris. Marcus was travelling with a group of Architectural students visiting a restoration project in the Rue du Vieille du Temple. She was just nineteen and had not long been in the capital having travelled up from the south. She had been a waitress in the Café he and his friends frequented. A cheerful pretty waitress who had dreamed of visiting England, flattered by the attention of that group of young Englishmen.

'Go on' urged Joe 'I dare you to ask her. If of course your French is up to it' he teased.

'Mademoiselle. Excuse moi. Je suis Anglais' He started to the amusement of his friends. Marcus had managed by use of his less than impeccable French and his dubiously exotic English credentials to secure a date. It had been a source of some ribbing of him but it soon turned a great deal more serious when her pregnancy was discovered. He remembered Joe asking.

'What will you do?' in a way that expected him to know the answer. The decision had been made for them by her parents. No child could be born out of wedlock. It was the simple decision to take. It was all somehow so uncomplicated then. The future was to be constrained by convention. Life's possibilities had until then rambled around a disparate geography and vocational variety. Here was the violent requirement of decision the heavy yoke of responsibility, the shackle of commitment all thrust upon his habitual uncertainty.

For Marcus Graham the tragic failure of his marriage to Annie had little but bitter memories underpinned by guilt and regret He often wished it were only the sweet delicious guilt of indulgence and the wistful regret of its passing but it was more that of failure.

His brief time with her had been the best thing in his life but now it was just a dream. For now Annie appeared to him on lonely nights and lost moments as if a fantasy. The warmth of her embrace. Her hair between his fingers her skin between his teeth. Her scent a thousand fragrances in one breath. The softness of her breast in his grateful hand. Her taught belly firm under the spread of his fingers. The joy of willing limbs in ecstasy of urgent energy and sighs that became moans. The motion of her hips half undressed in the morning light. Her declarant words, slow, fresh, caressed by soft uncertain lips.

In quiet moments of selfish contemplation his mind was filled with her. His tongue ran wild in her thighs like the weaving of an artist's brush. The joy of her was the best of her. Sweet ephemeral moments. On cold nights skin to skin huddled in intimacy under patchwork. A hot day by the river at their ease, her in soft cream linen, open to bare shoulders and skirts above her rounded knees. Him peering into the gaps left by her loose dress in mindless and tormented curiosity. Now their souls were parted. The briefest romance that had ended in her pregnancy, their marriage, their child and the death of two of them in a car accident close to her parent's home.

He had been married to Annie just three months when she died. His daughter, Marie Segolene, had been just one month old. A daughter who had so nearly survived, rescued from the car but lost later in the hospital at St Remy.

He had often thought of how life would have been different had Marie Segolene survived that crash. How she would have grown up with her Grandparents in Eyragues. How they would have in time forgiven him for his hasty liaison with Annie. How they would have mourned her death together, celebrated the growing child's experiences and achievements and how by now, the greatest mistake of his life would have been repaired and those good God fearing people rewarded.

Instead her parents had not accepted his sympathies after the deaths. They had considered it a retribution, a punishment for the sin of her pregnancy and he would have no part in their lives now that she had gone. Their staunch catholic terms had been imposed on the young couple. They had insisted on marriage to avoid the disgrace of an illegitimate birth.

Yet Marcus and Annie had not really known each other, so short was their relationship. Her French and he English there had not been the easy confidences that define a close couple. Perhaps a life together had been doomed to disaster from the outset. Perhaps her mother was right. It was God's punishment for their sin.

4.

CHELSEA, LONDON

As he entered the office Marcus interrupted Emma Dreyfus sorting some paperwork and was keen to convey the news.

'Fitz has offered me a delicious assignment Emma' He began in a chirpy tone.

'Seems I am going to the South of France for my next job. Not sure whether this is Fitz ploy to get me out of the way now that the Gelco scheme gets serious or some sort of reward for getting us across the line'

'I heard something about it Marcus and I am delighted for you and yes, he sees it as a reward not a rebuke of course. You need to get away after the work you have put in on Gelco.' She was both reassuring and somehow convincing. Marcus valued her judgement which seemed always to be so well grounded.

'Excuse me for saying this Marcus. There was one thing I was a little unsure about. I mean … well Annie your wife.'

'Yes Fitz and I brought that up. The truth Emma is I look back at those days as if they were from a different life. One not even my own. The reason I cannot bear to remember her is because each memory brings the guilt of my not being with her and Marie Segolene at their death to mind.'

'I wondered if perhaps you need to bury the mistake you feel you have made. Perhaps to visit Avignon again?' She left the question unfinished but it was clear that she had raised the point with Fitz prior to the meeting and clear too that she felt the assignment would be a restitution.

Perhaps it had been contrition that had led him to remain unmarried, to live alone, enjoying only the company of close friends in his small flat in Chelsea or at the cottage he kept just outside Tunbridge Wells for weekends to experience the fresh air of country walks and local beer. It soothed him a little to believe so.

The truth was that he had the time to spend in indolent isolation, time that was his own to spend as he pleased. His work as an Architect gave him the outlet for his creativity and innovation among those with similar aspirations. He was able to travel abroad, and particularly enjoyed visiting the cities of Europe to see their Architecture. His life suited him, how it would have been different.

'You know Emma' He said.

'I have of course questioned why fate singled out my wife and child but I also wonder if I will ever know more about the mystery that surrounded the fruit lorry that had hit her car. I never heard that it had been found. I guess her parents must have been told but they never said anything to me. Maybe I will find out more about that when I am there.'

'I imagine that the action of a reckless driver was to blame for the deaths of your wife and daughter' Emma suggested not wishing him to dwell on the possibility in her mind that it may have been the fault of the young mother distracted by a crying baby.

'Perhaps' She added 'All these years later it does not matter. The cause of their deaths has been buried by time.'

His mind was now focussed on something that he now knew had bothered him all these years. Questions that had remained unanswered about the death of his wife and child. He would now be working in Provence on a project that would keep him engaged for some months. He now resolved that part of this assignment would be to find answers to those questions. To find out why they died.

5.

LONDON, ENGLAND

Marcus had slept well. He had woken with a momentary confusion from his deep sleep. The bright rays of an early sun that probed deep into the room had taken his mind back to the comfort of his childhood. It made him feel that he was in the attic room with the window that faced east over the river, where the sun would wake him in time for school before the fresh voice of his mother could be heard from downstairs calling him to get up, and where the mass of pink flowers of the Japanese cherry tree tapped at his window in soft effusion to tell him it was spring. He was happy then, before the burden of adulthood had weighed so heavy upon him and he often returned there in his dreams. To that blissful innocence, that easy, simple existence of his boyhood. When the ships horns sounded on the river in the night the low drone in the thin air that would settle him in contentment in his bed.

Lulu opened her eyes and looked at him from the pillow, a sleepy knowing smile on her mouth. It was the first time she had stayed over, the first time she had allowed her urge to sleep with him to be gratified. It had gone well she thought, some evident compatibility in conversation and physical expectation.

'Good morning Marcus' She murmured slowly feeling the satisfaction of being in his presence as intimately as she had been. It was not a role she often played, the seductress. That was a play that required after all, the reluctant protagonist and she had found that most men of her acquaintance were only too keen to instigate any move of a purely sexual nature. Marcus had been different. His apprehension of anything that might imply dissolute conduct had clearly needed her to make the first move.

Perhaps that is why for Marcus Graham the stability of a relationship had proved elusive. There had been an attempt to settle down but it seemed that together with this apprehension, the spectre of responsibility was one that would forever haunt him.

'I saw you had eggs, bread, butter and milk' Lulu suddenly exclaimed leaping from the bed with a determined mind on domesticity.

'I'll get breakfast' She added, and with that she made her way to the small kitchen wrapping her nakedness in Marcus's old blue dressing gown and humming something from a musical. She clearly relished the role of girlfriend and was determined to show what she could do.

Marcus lay back in his bed his eyes fixed on the mirror across the room. His thoughts turned involuntarily to the last time he had experienced a woman like this, and how he had left her on a morning just like this one. How he had just up and left her without explanation or notice. How he had run from the a responsibility that had brought the incipient burden of duty to haunt that relationship.

It seemed like spring had arrived too soon. Too early, it brought only a pleasant warmth of sunshine and a small chatter of songbirds in the naked boughs of the trees that remind one that it was still February. A pale sun in a blue sky caught the frost where it could and dissolved it to a damp dew. Towards noon, the day would swell to an illusion of April.

Sara had sat at the breakfast table. She set about her simple fare with determination. A blue and white ringed dinner plate laid with a single slice of well browned toast; buttered, hot. Fruit marmalade, spread with precision by the knife with the broken handle. A careless twist of peel sucked briefly from busy fingers. The ceremony of her ritual needed all her concentration. The stirring of hot dark tea. The cutting of toast into four quite equal pieces.

Her eyes had turned to the window as she started to eat with measured deliberation. To the small bare garden. To that early spring, its wasted promise. Sara had spoken, a patois of mono-syllables through teeth and broken toast. A casual collection of words. A comment on the weather perhaps. Who cared. He answered 'Yes'.

She finished both tea and toast. They sat in a silence broken by the strike of a clock that agitated her.

'I must go now. Can't hang around'

'Course not' He confirmed.

She was still lovely. Her dark hair ran in ringlets to her shoulders. Her olive skin a lucky break at birth that others always envied. Her features retained the beauty of a younger face. The soft look her eyes had once. The line of her body untainted by time, nor faded by fortune. The curves of her hips that moved to accentuate her perfect shape were shrouded by the thin and formless coat she threw around her.

They had been residents of suburbia. Dignified by red brick, semi-detached, tiled roof in faded red clay. Worn pine in the kitchen, clock in the hall. Walls painted in a colour suited to a grander style were spread with pictures. Lives, travel, intimacies. Sunsets over Windermere, painted by her cousin and two prints of horseracing and a harbour scene. A plethora of knickknacks on the shelf romped from Venetian art to a hideous tribute to Roy of the Rovers. This had been her life. Her house. Her memories. They had predated him, and they had held no fascination for him. Not then. No interest, no enquiry, He knew that he would one day leave her.

Sara had packed a bag with homemade soup, fresh fruit some cheese and other comestibles. She stopped for just a moment and then made for the door.

'I'll be back around four. Jean will be coming round then'

He knew that Jean would not be coming round to this house. Not to her home. She meant that Jean would come around to Paul's, to take over his care. To be there for Paul as Sara had been every day. Being there for her brother, looking after him just as she had done as his elder sister when they were children. Their parents now passed away, Sara was his only relative, watching his decline and weeping for a life that had never really begun. Poor Paul, it had always been poor Paul. A victim of in built and protracted decline.

Five years of his life, a relationship that had been overtaken by the selfless devotion she had shown to Paul and the pessimistic picture of life that the experience had painted for her. What might she be doing now he mused? First beauty, gaiety optimism and fun had faded and then, overwhelmed by the hypnotic call of filial duty.

A light rain now began to fall on an April morning cleaning away his memories of that February morning under the pale sun when he walked out of her life, quite sure that he had failed. When he had walked away from that declining relationship and its unbearable responsibility, to his solitude. He knew not for what but something he could manage. Something if not better, something he could bear.

How had it been for him? No partner no children. No family of his own. How Lulu had been right to challenge him. No understanding of the needs of families.

He was standing now in the bathroom in front of the wash basin when her arms closed around his waist shaking away his daydream.

'Better come quickly. Scrambled egg never likes to wait'

'No, no. quite right' He responded part in gratitude for her culinary preparation and part to affirm the sure truth of her comment.

'It just has to be slightly under cooked' He added with enthusiasm.

She smiled at him eager to understand his preferences. She thought that there is something wholly delightful in eating breakfast with her new partner that cannot be measured by the quality of its presentation nor the effort of its preparation. It is the affirmation of a relationship. A relationship that she now knew she had longed for.

'I am going travelling' Marcus began emphatically as he sat at the small kitchen table.

'Fitz wants me to supervise the refurbishment of an old chapel in France. Either he wants me out of the way or it's his way of thanking me for the Gelco award. I will know when I get there I suppose'

'It sounds marvellous' Lulu replied, surprising herself with how enthusiastic she sounded. It seemed to her that her new relationship could slip from her hands.

'How long will you be away?'

'I am not sure exactly' He answered preparing to calculate time but then looked at her in realisation of what the better answer would be.

'I'm expecting to come back regularly. Can't spend too long in some dull hotel room.'

Lulu smiled in gratitude. She would not plan for the future for the future had always failed her. The present basked in the sunlight of a new morning. Joy was always ephemeral, it cannot be harnessed, for to do so will surely destroy it. Here was the comfort of one sublime hour in which to savour a companionship that could permit her mind to dream.

It was only some days later that Marcus prepared to leave for Avignon. The advantage of living alone is one of certainty. That when one leaves one's flat one knows that one will return to it exactly as it is left, tidy and ordered. His small flat was always kept just so and he reflected that he had never needed amenity space himself in fact he had never really thought about the necessity of it. There was plenty of opportunity to walk and take in the air close by in the open spaces around his home. Imagine he thought, having to concern oneself with the tending of a garden and the cutting of a lawn while one is away.

Carefully and methodically, he ensured that all services were turned off for his period of absence. As he locked the front door of the small flat and made his way to St Pancras, Marcus was thinking about something that Emma Dreyfus had said to him the day before. Emma was quite a one for astrology he reflected with a smile. She had often explained that her horoscope had accurately predicted the events of her week. It was not as if he would be taken in by celestial speculation, but he could not help thinking about a prediction she had insisted would come true.

Marcus' horoscope she had assured him, had confirmed that in a foreign country he would find something he thought had been lost.

6.

AVIGNON, FRANCE

The TGV arrived at Avignon right on time. It was not the station at Avignon that he thought he remembered but further south of the town. Cloud had hung obstinately over the journey all the way from Lille but now the brilliant sunshine of the Midi would be with the train as it travelled on to Marseille. Perhaps the sunshine was an omen that heralded the fortune of his stay. It was certainly an inspiration for it Marcus thought, as he disembarked the train with spring in his step carrying his superfluous trench coat over his arm and his suitcase in the other hand.

This city is the ancient crossroads between the north and south. The now broken bridge famous for the trade that travelled across the Rhone east and west north and south through the middle ages. The ancient city was home to the Popes during the 14th century when the papal city was changed from Rome. Today, it was the weather that had changed at Avignon.

He felt the curious feeling that one does when alone in France. The simple realisation that to communicate one has to speak French. He reflected that the French are not generally a people disposed to speaking any other language on their home soil and while one can travel in silence on the TGV from Lille, the locating of taxi, Hotel and any supplementary conversation requires some facility in the French tongue. For Marcus that was agreeable as while his French was not that good, his enthusiasm to improve his use of the language would, he was sure overcome any shortcomings. He hailed a taxi.

'Pour Hotel des Papes si vous plait.'

During the brief journey from the TGV station to the Hotel the taxi driver exhibited a determined silence that demanded little of Marcus' French and the receptionist at the Hotel des Papes was Dutch, a citizen of a country where English is spoken to greater perfection often than in England itself. He arrived in his room fresh and content after a satisfactory journey. He washed himself and hung his clothes and then plugged in the lap top computer. There was time to dispatch a brief email message to Emma Dreyfus.

From Marcus Graham

I have arrived at the Hotel. All is very pleasant here and the sun is shining. I plan to report to the client tomorrow morning. For the moment I may just go about town and find some supper. Steak frites? Moules? A glass of Chateau neuf du Pape. Mmm.

From Emma Dreyfus

Sick!!! It's raining and there's a tube strike!!!

He chuckled at his good fortune comforted by Emma's feigned envy and prepared himself for a modest supper in the town.

The following morning after a breakfast of toast and coffee Marcus could not wait to step out into the street and it seemed to him that his clear destination was to be the Palais where he might identify the building on which he would be working. The papal palace of the Papes d'avignon dominates this beautiful city on the Rhone the ancient part of which is surrounded by medieval ramparts with substantial towers built at intervals into its walls.

By the square he found himself standing by a group of tourists complete with a tour guide who was addressing them in English.

'The Palace was built mainly in the 14th century when Pope Clement established Avignon as an alternative to a Rome in decline and disorganisation. There were Popes in Avignon recognised by the church and when the office of Popes moved back to

Rome the papal tradition at Avignon remained. Those that followed bore the title Anti Pope, a title seemingly given to leave no uncertainty among the faithful of the identity of the true pope in Rome.' The guide spoke fluently and in the manner of a recital that indicated that she had said all this many times before.

'The city remained a Papal possession until the French revolution of 1791 when it became part of France. The temptation to use its massive walls as a prison was not lost to the revolutionaries. There are accounts of the torture of many counter revolutionaries and the height of its buildings was used to great advantage in casting off delinquents.' At this the guide had invited the response of her audience with a tone to her voice that suggested there might be some retrospective humour in the notion of bodies falling from above the high walls of the tower.

He moved away looking up at the magnificent building. The Palais rises up beyond even the Cathedral of Notre Dame des doms close by. Its buildings are a collection of the most outstanding medieval architecture.

'We will visit the Chapel Clementine in the Palace Noveau where college of cardinals met to elect a new pope.' The guide continued.

Marcus often tried to imagine the work of building such edifices in the cities he had visited, the toil that went into their creation the conflicts they had witnessed. Here was a symbol of Catholicism and a seat of power bearing the gravitas of history in the same way as the Vatican in Rome.

At last he came across a small Chapel located just outside the Palais area. It was, he could see straight away of a much later construction than the Palais buildings themselves. It was in a poor state of repair and he could see why he had been told that it had not been used for worship for over one hundred years.

As Marcus stood gazing at the building he was approached by a small figure of a friar dressed in a black and white habit. He hurried quickly towards Marcus with an exaggerated shuffle and Marcus could see that he was old by the white beard that protruded from above his cassock.

The old friar greeted him in English.

'Mr Graham?' He asked unexpectedly.

'Why yes' Marcus answered surprised by the recognition.

'You will be working on the Chapel renovation?' He inquired.

'Why yes. I am the supervising Architect. I am with Fisher Holt and Fizroy in London. We are Ecclesiastical Architects.'

'Yes. I thought so' the Friar confirmed with a smile.

'I was expecting you to come by today. One cannot resist these beguiling walls and besides, it is a lovely day to be strolling about the city.'

The friar sensed that Marcus wished him to explain his hurried introduction.

'I spent some time in England' he explained.

'Just outside Canterbury. I am Father Gabriel Fidel Rocher. I have been asked to meet you and show you to your quarters.'

Marcus hesitated. He was unaware that he would be staying on site. Emma had been careful to select the hotel des Papes and had indicated to the receptionist that the stay might be for the duration of his time in Avignon though she had been careful not to confirm a booking for this period as she was too aware that Marcus bachelor existence inclined him to be particular and that he was quite likely to wish to change the arrangements were some small matter to be found to be unsatisfactory.

The old friar led Marcus away from the Palais to a short and narrow path leading from the Rue Bertrand to a row of stone terraced houses and stopped outside the first of these. Father Fidel Rocher turned the key in the heavy door of small cottage that fronted straight on to the path. It opened directly into a delightful drawing room, small but cosy with an open fireplace, and a window to the front that let in a stream of sunlight. The room was well furnished with seating, low tables and pictures on its walls that were not as one might have expected of an ecclesiastical dwelling. There was a musty but pleasant smell that added a homely atmosphere to the place. A small galley kitchen immediately to one side of the entrance door had an exit door to a courtyard at the rear and a small flight of stairs ascending from the drawing room accessed two bedrooms and a bathroom.

'I say' Marcus exclaimed 'This really is quite splendid. I really did not expect to be accommodated so well.'

Father Fidel Rocher smiled. He was most flattered by the very genuine nature of Marcus reaction to his quarters.

'These are not the quarters customary to a cleric' He joked perhaps keen to emphasise the first principle of his calling. That of poverty.

Marcus had observed a box on the mantelpiece that contained a fine chess set of elegant Staunton pieces.

'Do you play?' Father Fidel Rocher asked.

'Oh rather' he confirmed.

'Though not too well' he was quick to add not wishing to proclaim an expertise that he may later regret.

'When you have made yourself comfortable I will return should you wish and we can become acquainted over a game of chess.'

It was a friendly gesture that Marcus was quick to agree to. He spent the next hour or so transferring his temporary belongings from the hotel des Papes to the cottage and settling the account for his foreshortened stay at the hotel.

The chessboard was placed before them on a low table that demanded the players hunch over it in obsequious fashion. Marcus habitually played white. Feeling more sure on familiar ground he had been glad to have drawn his choice. He straightened his posture and studied the small cleric. The thought process in the Friar's mind was almost tangible. It seemed to exclude all else around him. He lifted his right hand repeatedly only to rest it again as he thought better of the move he had intended to make. The silence was palpable.

Father Fidel Rocher examined the pieces on the chess board in front of him intensely. He had never been highly skilled at the game but it had always fascinated him. The parallel opposition that gave no favour nor advantage to either black nor white. The hierarchy of the pieces. The paths that were set for them to follow. The outcome of the game that depended on the wit of the player alone. Not the greatest skill, only the greater skill. That a player be more skilled than he whom he opposed. The comforting reality that one has only to rise to the opposition one faces and no further until the next game is laid out.

Marcus had suffered the clumsy loss of his queen early in the game and had sensed defeat, but that defeat was taking a time to materialise as Father Fidel Rocher missed several opportunities to capitalise on his early success. The old Priest studied the board for inspiration and at last as if to fill the space between his moves, murmured an observation.

'The Bishop, my friend. He moves through his life on the diagonal line in order to travel the path of black or of white. He never changes that path. His path in life is pre-ordained.

The King is well protected from the affray. He directs it but will never suffer the consequences of his failure. In victory he will be heralded for his heroism, in defeat he is preserved for the next confrontation. But who are the pawns that their sacrifice is of such little consequence?'

He laughed as he said this and grasped his king's Bishop moving right into the heart of Marcus defence. He had by the manoeuvres of his bishops secured a very real advantage. It allowed him to move the black queen in for the kill.

'I think, my friend that you will find that it is check.'

The move at least gave Marcus the ability by the penultimate move of the game to take the black queen but she had been dispensable. What followed was inevitable.

'Check mate' said the old priest with satisfaction.

It came as no surprise. The clumsy loss of his Queen so early in the game does no man credit. He is by such carelessness, hostage to doubt, fearful of failure and vulnerable to destruction. Hunted by the black bishops, who had their paths set for them to follow. And haunted by a black queen.

'Let me pour you another glass of wine' Said Marcus, relieved that the inevitable had eventuated.

A smile spread across the old man's face. He somehow ascribed the offer of wine to the reward for his success. Marcus sat with his new friend feeling very content. Companionship is enormously comforting when preparing for a new challenge. He was to value the companionship of Father Fidel Rocher well beyond the mutual imbibing of wine.

The old priest paused as he held the black bishop in his grasp and reflected.

'Our path through life is preordained by God my friend. It is a pathway set out for us and it takes us across a chequered board. Some of us are mere pawns, some kings, some queens. Some are the rocks of men dependable, solid. Some take the paths of wisdom gifted by their service to God. There are some heroic knights that move in curious directions to flirt with circumstance but all of us, all of us play our part however small to win or lose the game.'

He held the chess piece in his hand and lifted it towards Marcus to emphasise his point.

'But the outcome. The outcome my friend. It is the grand master who will determine what the moves will bring.' He chuckled at this in a childlike manner that was endearing.

Marcus listened with amusement and interest at his new friend's perception of life. He wondered for a moment which piece best represented him.

'I'm sure that I am just a mere pawn in the great game and I console myself with the prospect that I might just reach the final square.' Marcus confirmed.

'Well' Responded the old friar.

'Life paints black and white the vision of he who hesitates. We must grasp opportunity and bear responsibility within the subtleties of circumstance. For this has been ordained for us by God.'

That evening Marcus sent a brief email to Emma Dreyfus.

From Marcus Graham
To Emma Dreyfus

Your much appreciated efforts in booking the Hotel des Papes have been found to be unnecessary. My kind hosts have put me up in a cottage next to the Chapel. It will serve as a useful base as well as a comfortable lodging. I have settled in very well and

have established a friendship with one of the Friars here. We played chess. He won.
Sun is still shining. Hope it is there too.

From Emma Dreyfus
To Marcus Graham

And I thought you would envy me getting all the drawings and environmental reports ready for the Gelco pre project presentation next week! Et, Il toujour pleut.

7.

AVIGNON, FRANCE

The pretty streets of Avignon begin to crowd in spring. Tourists from everywhere bring with them a cosmopolitan atmosphere and search for excitement, history and beauty. The city has not the importance that it had in medieval times. Today its appeal lies in its location and its past. An appeal that will increase as summer arrives due to the blessing of its climate and its historic beauty.

Marcus had decided on a brief excursion to acquaint himself with the city and he took delight in walking those streets and feeling the energy of the atmosphere as it went about its business. He found himself looking up above the shop fronts at the varied architecture of the upper parts of the buildings as he often did. France sometimes fails to offer the variety that is offered in England but here the centuries have woven their contributions into a delightful tapestry of time.

In the Musee Calvet Marcus found himself examining a bronze bust that read that of Paul Claudel. As he studied it, he was approached by a young woman curator. She turned to Marcus with a light smile on her face.

'You are English Yes?', She questioned.

'This sculpture is the head of Paul Claudel the well-known poet. It is the work of Camille Claudel his beautiful younger sister. You may know, she was mistress to Rodin.'

The R was perfectly rolled and the final syllable struck him with a lively inflection which was infinitely attractive and his attention was hooked.

'I did not' Marcus confessed 'I only knew that she was a sculptor.'

'She was a most interesting and talented artist but she was incarcerated in a lunatic asylum by her family after her affair with Rodin.' She continued.

'It is a very sad story. Her mother did not visit her in the 30 years that she spent there.'

'My goodness' Marcus replied. It sounded so terrible to spend 30 years in an institution without a single visit from ones mother.

He began to think of his own detachment from responsibility. What would be said of him when he passed on. He lost his wife, failed a second relationship and stood in the shadow of his mentor afraid to show his face. It was a discomfort that visited him when confronted with situations like this. Some small words of little relevance could resonate upon the brittle frailty of his guilt, and leave him in retreat from the world quite unable to do what might mark him out as contributing something that he could be proud of.

A brief tour of the city undertaken, Marcus made for the Café Zizi Jean maire just off the Place de l'Horloge. He had noticed that the local people appeared to use this establishment rather than the more expensive tourist cafes overlooking the Place and it was always busy, its customers less inclined to sit for too long at its tables. A pair of small trees overhung its small forecourt filtering the sunshine to a dappled light on its tables. At this time in the early afternoon, shade was at a premium and those establishments able to provide shade were those better subscribed.

'Pour un suilment' He emphasised.

The waiter looked around him in the 360 degree way that waiters do to holding his arms out at each side to illustrate that the café is full and shook his head.

'C'est bien. Je chercherais autre part'

He was still conscious of his use of French. Was that right? Was his accent acceptable? He wondered?

As if to answer his concerns a small laugh was heard from the table behind him to his left. He turned instinctively to see if the laugh was directed at him.

She was looking at him with her eyes raised towards her brow as if by way of enquiry. Her head was crowned with a large pair of sun glasses. She had been reading something insubstantial, a journal that she placed in front of her on the small table in response to his glance. She was stylishly dressed in a light blue sleeveless dress that revealed her tanned shoulders and complemented her shapely arms. A small leather hand bag was laid in front of her on the table and Marcus noticed that it matched the shoes she wore. She was stunningly beautiful. Her fresh face lit by a sideways smile and eyes that were full and focussed directly on him.

'Would you like to join me?' She asked.

'What sit here?' He answered looking at the second chair at the table.

She smiled as if to say 'where else' but was more polite.

'Yes, It would be good to have some company. Perhaps we can talk. You visited the Palace yesterday didn't you. I saw you there. What did you think?'

Marcus felt the slight awkwardness that an older man feels at an unexpected invitation from such a beautiful young woman. He could hear Fitz say.

'Don't knock it old boy. I'd swap with you anytime.'

He decided to respond in a light casual style. A young woman like this could not possibly appreciate his detailed analysis of the buildings even though he now recognised her as one of the guides at the Palais.

'Big' He responded with schoolboy humour.

'Big! Is that a word that English Architects use to describe buildings like this? It sounds very technical.'

Marcus was taken aback. While in retrospect his response had been slightly demeaning he hadn't expected her to require a full exposition.

'You know that I am an Architect? I didn't mean. Well no I'm sorry I didn't mean to.'

'To be condescending' She finished.

'That's Ok. I do know a little bit about the Architecture of the palace myself. It goes with the job'

Her voice was soft but strong. Her confident use of English was exemplary but she considered the words she selected with care correcting those that were not quite right. After each phrase she smiled a cute pirate smile as if to dispatch it completed to perfection, as one might an email.

'I am Segolene' she said thrusting her hand forward in a bold Gallic style.

'I am a tour guide at the Palais.'

'Oh and I'm Marcus. Marcus …'

'Graham' She finished again as if to taunt him and laughed at his surprised expression.

'I know who you are you were on my manifest. I know too that you have come to Avignon to work and to look at the architecture of the Palais and to carry out some remodelling of the old chapel building.'

'Who told you that?' he asked.

'You did Marcus. When you were queuing for the Chapel, we spoke.'

This time they both laughed. He had of course explained his interest to her yesterday. He was flattered that she had remembered.

'Well yes' he began to expand.

'I have the good fortune to be posted here by my firm to oversee the 'remodelling' as you put it.'

There was a contrast between these two that had played to her advantage. His formality that seemed more pronounced when uneasy in company. An awareness that he was an Englishman abroad and aware too that all would recognise that. Her casual and relaxed, in control and on home ground.

'Do you live here in Avignon?' He asked.

'I grew up here. I lived in the city with my Grandparents after my Mother died, until I was 19. Then I went away to live in Italy and now I am back to work here. I started at the tourist agency a few weeks ago.'

'Are you back with your Grandparents?'

'No they are both dead now. I am sharing with a friend for the moment.'

The waiter stood unnoticed behind him.

'Deux café. Au lait?' she questioned looking at Marcus for his response.

'Oh Oui. lait pour moi.' Marcus now felt more comfortable and would have been happy drinking anything in this appealing setting with his delightful companion. They were sitting at a table that was somehow closer to the action of the small café. The one used by the staff to rest a dish on, or strip off one of its chairs for the tables further away. Marcus thought it might well have had a sign on it saying 'reserve pour les Francais.' He had that feeling of being part of the locality, absurd of course, but with so many tourists in the town there has to be a certain knowledge and conduct that defines 'them and us' and its always more satisfying to be part of the established order.

'Your English is exceptionally good.' He remarked without any need to flatter her.

'I watch too many movies I expect.' was her modest response.

'We always had two languages at home. My grandparents would speak in Occitan with each other. They had come from the mountains south of Toulouse. Then there was always French and in school I learned English and Italian.'

'An impressive record. No wonder you make a good tour guide' He said by way of compliment.

She was unsure whether she was a good tour guide but it was useful to have had the assumption made.

'I have always been interested in the history of the city and its architecture' she affirmed as if to convince herself. She appeared interested in the work that Marcus was undertaking at the papal chapel and to his delight an interest in him too.

'What made you come to France to work in Architecture?'

'I did some of my training here, well in Paris. My mentor and now colleague Sir Clement Fitzroy is well known in Parisian architectural circles. He was involved in some of the restoration work in Marais. He is well known in England too, a delight to work with. Everything is possible with Fitz. He knows everybody and will never accept no for an answer. It was he who asked me to come here and work after I won an Architectural competition in London.'

His description of Fitz delighted her particularly and not for the first time Marcus good see the more humorous side of his friend. The patrician, a caricature of the English aristocrat, born to a ruling class but born too, to an expectation of a life of service and achievement that he had never sought to avoid.

'You won a competition. That sounds impressive.' She flattered.

'Well not so much really.' He answered modestly.

'But it got me to come and work here'

He was now at ease as the conversation flowed freely. Marcus felt the common ground of mutual interests under his feet.

'You are staying in Avignon?' She enquired.

'Yes. I was rather lucky. I was booked into the Hotel Des Papes but my clients have provided me with a small cottage on site. It really is convenient and rather lovely. I can see myself quite at home there.'

'My arrangements are not quite so satisfactory. My friend works as a chef and is often living at whichever Hotel he is working. It makes him less concerned about our domestic arrangements, but Avignon is not a place to stay at home in during the summer. There is plenty to get out and see' Segolene suggested.

'Yes, I visited the Musee Calvet earlier. I had not realised that Camille Claudel spent much of her life in an institution unvisited by her mother. Imagine that, some desertion' It somehow made him feel better to hear himself recount the parental detachment he had learned of earlier as something more terrible than his own absence of feeling for a loss that had happened so long ago.

'How awful' she said flatly. Then, changing the subject to what for Marcus, might have turned to an uncomfortable conclusion she asked him.

'Have you been to this part of France before?'

'Yes, but I can't say I know it' Was as much as he cared to answer.

'One can get here so quickly now on the TGV service from Lille. Just ten hours from London.'

'Do you know I have never been to London. Perhaps I should. Or perhaps it rains too much.' They laughed, at the cliché, though Marcus reflected that his last communication with Emma Dreyfus had confirmed that it was indeed raining in London.

They discussed the local food and their culinary preferences. They talked of her love of American films. Their quick coffee had lasted some fifty minutes. Marcus thought briefly of the loss of his daughter here in Avignon and how she might now be a young woman such as this had she survived.

'Well' She said finally.

'I guess I have to go.' More than once her use of English indicated that she had indeed learnt it from American cinema.

'Well it has been very lovely chatting with you Segolene' he said rather formally.

'I hope we bump into each other again sometime.'

'I am sure we will' She said with certainty with a look direct into his eyes.

She turned her head as she walked away towards the Place de l'Hologe and smiled at him again.

8.

AVIGNON, FRANCE

Marcus was certain that the light knock on the cottage door was Francois the assistant Archaeologist come to return the Chapel keys. He hastened across the small room and opened the door, turning in the same motion with a flourish intended to convey a light hearted welcome. Then he stood back startled.

She stood there head to one side, same smile. Eyes looking up directly at him her head slightly bowed. She looked radiant. A soft silk trouser suit in taupe with matching cardigan. Light sandals in leather and gold. Her hands held together in front of her rounded her shoulders as if in some form of apology and in them she clutched a tan leather handbag.

'Je suis seule.' she teased, pleading admission.

'It's you' He said incompetently.

'It's good to see you. What brings you here?'

'I was around the Palais. I thought I would come to see how you have settled in. We all have an interest in the chapel restoration you know' she finished with mock indignation.

Segolene entered the small drawing room and stood with her back to the fireplace still clutching her handbag with both hands. She had an appearance of unease, strongly in contrast with their last encounter.

'Café?' He suggested buoyantly.

'Thank you' She answered slowly, rounding her vowels wistfully like a shy schoolgirl.

'Did you have an interesting day?' She enquired regaining some composure.

'I really have been very busy' Marcus replied.

'Identifying and dating some of the structure so that we can source materials mainly. There will be a lot of that to do.'

He fussed around the process of the preparation of two cups of coffee swapping with her some dialogue that chronicled the events of his day and re-entered the room with a full cup in each hand placing them on the small table by the fireplace.

She was now looking across the room in an uncertain manner wishing to avoid his eyes.

'You know' she began.

'You know, why I came to see you?'

'Well I had hoped that it was not business. A social call? Or am I to be disappointed?'

Segolene took his light hearted response as an opportunity to respond in like manner.

'Oh yes she smiled at him.' You are going to be very disappointed.'

He was intrigued but not yet disarmed. He had no idea of the gravity of what she was about to announce. The sheer impact of a few simple words would dumbfound him. They were so unexpected. Yet in a way they were obvious. He had even in some brief and wild moment imagined the reality those words portrayed before she uttered them. Those words.

'Marcus. I am your daughter Marie Segolene.'

It was not disbelief that rendered him speechless. It was a kind of confusion, the need to rapidly assimilate his thoughts, process emotions, doubts, joys, recall facts, dates, ages, and appearances. It was the impact of these words on his life. What would happen now? What was expected of him? What should he do?

'But' he said incredulously,

'Marie Segolene is dead.'

'No I am alive' She sung theatrically, attempting to lighten the moment.

'I knew that you always felt that I had died with my Mother. My Grandparents wanted you to think that. They did not want you to take me to England. They said I was dead so that you would not come and claim me. You could have you know.' She looked up at him as if to question whether he might have done so had he known and then returned her gaze to one side.

'We lived for a while in Eyragues before moving into the city. My Grandparents were very strict with me and when I was 19 I left to live in Italy for a while where I could be independent. I am sorry now that both died while I was away. I did not have the chance to say goodbye. I really regret that now.'

Marcus could understand why she had felt it necessary to move out from her Grandparents house. He too had experienced their uncompromising attitude and strict morality. It would have been difficult for her just as it had been for Annie who had moved to Paris at the same age for the same reason.

'So Italy, You were there for, how long?'

'For nearly six years. I lived in Guardia Piemontese. I was a waitress most of the time. Just like my Mother.'

He was taking this all with considerable calm. A beautiful young girl had entered his life in a foreign land and befriended him. He had even allowed himself to imagine her as his daughter, the daughter he had never known and lost in infancy. She had now told him, that was exactly who she was. It was fantastic and unreal, but as he listened to her story he became convinced that she was indeed Marie Segolene.

'What happened to your Grandparents house?' he asked attempting to fill in some of the detail.

'Oh. It was not theirs. They rented it. If they had owned it I would have been lucky. It would have been mine.'

There was no regret in this from Marie Segolene. It was the voice of acceptance not of resentment. She was not of a class that owned property and she was aware of that. It was difficult for him to see anything of Annie in her far less of him. Only the dark eyes and tanned skin of the Midi and the extraordinarily pretty face. Had Annie had such beautiful eyes? He was ashamed to say, he could not remember.

'Tell me Marie Segolene. How did you know that I was here in Avignon?' He inquired.

'I knew you were an architect. My Grandparents had at least told me that and I knew that you worked for Fisher Holt and Fitzroy.

As you say, Sir Clement Fitzroy is well known in Paris for his work there. I had looked him up on Google. You make him sound an interesting man. When I saw that your firm was to work at the Palais I wondered whether Sir Clement would be coming here. It was really only when I saw my visitors manifest that I saw that it was you. I was so excited, I could not resist speaking with you then.'

'By George no. Fitz coming here to work?' They both laughed. She felt she knew by now that Sir Clement Fitzroy was someone special in her father's life and was sure that his character would always engender some humour.

She broke the small silence with a question.

'So are you pleased with me?' She ventured timidly.

'I would certainly say so' He responded emphatically.

'It's just Segolene by the way'

'Oh yes of course. I am, well, just Marcus'

They both laughed nervously at this. He poured two glasses of wine by way of distraction and they sipped in silence each considering where the conversation was going to go. He felt a peace, a comfort in her company, a strange closeness that he had never felt before. The closeness of kinship that permits the silent pauses between words. The filial bond. He was completely overtaken by her.

9.

AVIGNON, FRANCE

Sunday breakfast had been served in plain English to placate the demands of a viscera abandoned for six weeks to the French alternative of croissant and coffee. He had found a white cloth for the breakfast table and enjoyed laying it with the fine Pillivuyt crockery he had found in the carved oak sideboard under the window by the staircase. He had searched for the condiments that would complete the indulgence. Salt, pepper and a little mustard. It was a leisurely enjoyment of fried egg, bacon, mushroom and toast, and the tea had been brewed in a grand tea pot, the discovery of which had inspired the feast.

He had notified Emma to report the extraordinary discovery of Segolene on her private email to ensure confidentiality being sure to complement her on the astute prediction she had extracted from his horoscope. It was good to sit back in a snug chair after breakfast and reflect, update and plan.

The air was sweet as it wafted through the window and he could hear the uncertain call of a blackbird that reminded him of the home he was brought up in, where summer was the only season he truly remembered. Where not the slightest tribulation ever reigned, where he was always happy and where his mother took upon herself all responsibility and protection. Perhaps now he had a child of his own he could offer her the same. This afternoon perhaps he would meet with her and view some part of the town he had not yet seen but this morning he would idle at home.

It was early afternoon when the knock came on the heavy wood door. He had been dosing in the chair but quickly realised that it was her. She had come accompanied by a young man of around about her own age.

'This is Luc' she said with a smile as he opened the door to her. 'He is my handsome friend' She added with a laugh having emphasised the word handsome.

Luc looked at him with a less than sincere interest and offered a smile that was little more than a sneer. He was a good looking fellow but one who perhaps was too aware of the fact. One whom men envy and detest at the same time. A man with the ability to attract women with little or no effort. Marcus instinctively felt that Luc was someone he had to protect her from. He could not permit his daughter to associate with such a man. This was absurd of course as he had only just met him and not long met her, she had presumably known him for some time and had grown to trust him. Besides, he reflected that of course Luc did not speak English as Segolene did. Perhaps that was the reason for his dismissive reaction. Perhaps he did not wish to engage in conversation that was to be stilted by a lack of fluency. Perhaps he felt uneasy with his failure to match her linguistic ability. Whatever, Marcus told himself he was being too harsh in his judgement of Luc.

'Luc has to move out of his flat next week Marcus. He is working at a Hotel in St Remy de Provence for a while, until they find a new Chef. He will stay there at the hotel.'

Marcus felt a tinge of pleasure at the news. Perhaps Luc was to be too busy to associate with Segolene. He was unsure whether Luc was the friend whom Segolene was living with. He did not have to ask.

'Marcus, when Luc moves out I will have nowhere to stay for a while. Well until he comes back to Avignon. I wondered.' She paused to allow Marcus to catch up.

'I wondered if I could move in with you for a short time.' She looked at him with enquiring eyes that demanded only one response.

His instinctive reaction was to say. 'Yes, move in, forget Luc, we are family' but sensibly he paused. He would have to clear such an arrangement with Father Fidel Rocher who would he was sure be content with it, but also he had to consider his ability to work from the cottage with Segolene in residence.

'I would love that' he replied.

'I will need to speak with Father Fidel Rocher however.'

She beamed a full smile at him. She did not consider that Father Fidel Rocher would object. Segolene would be moving in.

From Emma Dreyfus
To Marcus Graham

Marcus, I just can't believe that, You mean that you have discovered your daughter? Did she know that you were going to Avignon? She must have; I reckon she was aware you worked here and somehow knew you were going to do the Chapel job. Hey that is what your Horoscope meant. I won't tell anyone at work but make sure you tell me all your news. I am dying to hear more. Emm.

Marcus did not see Segolene for the next few days while she moved in as he was busy in the Chapel and spent his lunch times there over a sandwich. She certainly did not as he had expected, spend much of her time at home in any event and he supposed that some of her time might be spent at the hotel in Remy that Luc had moved to. He had to be realistic as to the time she would wish to take up with him. What young woman he asked himself would wish to have the company of her father? He probably saw more of Emma Dreyfus than her own father did. He was content as he reflected on the arrangements.

It was late in the afternoon of Monday just after Marcus had returned to the cottage when Segolene came bounding in the front door with evident excitement.

'I'm going to be an actress Marcus' She announced theatrically.

'I have a part in the Felibrigian festival play, it's a Son et Lumiere. It's great isn't it?' She demanded.

'Why that is wonderful' He exclaimed, unsure as to what was involved but caught up by her enthusiasm. He reflected how many times in the past his colleagues at the office had spoken of going to see their son or daughter in a play. Now he would have that opportunity. He would offer advice, compliment her costume, rehearse with her, her lines.

She threw herself back into the armchair by the fire and stretched her long legs forward.

'The play is a re-enactment of an historical piece that tells how an attempt was made on the life of the first Anti Pope Clement VIII.' She begun as Marcus looked at her with an interested smile.

'The great schism of the west saw the appointment of Clement VIII the first Anti pope in Avignon in 1378. He was by birth Robert de Geneve and by reputation the butcher of Cesena.' This revelation was uttered with mocking malevolence as if to give it a greater note of authenticity.

'It was he who gave the order to slaughter some 3000 innocent souls who would not recognise the Patrimony of Peter. He was spoken of by many to be the antichrist' Segolene informed him, in a manner that convinced him, would not support any request for further more detailed information.

'He sounds a pretty rum one to me. I can see why they would want him assassinated.'

'His would be assassin was a putain who surprised him dressed as a Cardinal. She poisoned him with hemlock but he survived.' She continued.

'He successfully repelled the assassin who was taken to some rather unpleasant torture' These final words hissed for further emphasis.

'And where do you come in to this piece Segolene? I mean what part do you play?'

'Her' She sung in a mischievous way, her eyes lifted to his with her tease, anxious to see his response.

'You are to play the assassin?' He questioned in disbelief.

'Luc has shown me how the medieval assassins made poisons of hemlock. It grows by rivers and on wet soils and when made into a poison it causes the brain to swell and convulsions occur. It was a favourite way of killing people off in those days'

She clearly relished the opportunity of playing the assassin's role but Marcus felt some of the disappointment a parent feels at his daughter cast in a role that is out of character. He did not stop to think how much more edifying it is for an actor to be cast in such a role. Surely great acting is just that, acting, not merely playing a carbon copy of oneself. Strangely, such is lost on parents. Their daughter should always be the princess for that is her role in their lives, and Segolene was fast assuming such a role.

There followed several evenings of rehearsal, but it appeared as if the putain assassin had little to contribute aurally to the piece. Her entrance surreptitiously made under a copious cloak was all too shortly ended by a dramatic arrest and scuffle followed by a hasty departure.

It was shortly before the play was to be staged that some preoccupation had caused Marcus to wake soon after retiring and go into the sitting room to check that he had papers he would need first thing in the morning. As he switched on the lamp on his desk he started as he became aware that there was someone else in the room.

He turned suddenly to see standing silently in the shadow a child before him. Her face powdered in white was beaming a bright smile that resembled a leer in the half light. Her costume was formed of a black full length dress smothered by a crimson gown accentuating a certain grandeur by its ballooning sleeves. Some gubernatorial chain of dubious historical accuracy was draped around her neck.

'She is only pretending to be a Cardinal. She is not actually a Cardinal' She emphasised, seeing him fix his incredulous eyes on the chain.

His doubt was not assuaged. Her beautiful face was shaded a pale chalky white. Her hair the most deviant distortion of all was dark black. Her head crowned by a scarlet skull cap. Marcus beheld a contrivance no doubt of great skill and accuracy, but he had longed to see his beautiful daughter in her more natural guise. His princess, upon a stage adored by all, not the comic villain that stood before him.

'Absolutely stunning' He found himself saying. The deception was quite complete. Her beauty suffused in slapstick face paint and wrapped in a comedic gown.

'I just thought that I would see what it looked like' She offered by way of explanation for her unexpected presence. As she stared vacantly to the window she added mystically,

'Just to see what it feels like to be her, inhabiting the darkness.'

It was a curious comment that held an uncertain silence. Marcus felt an urge to enquire further but contented himself with the acceptance that this was something that an actress would need to do and besides it was late and time to return to bed.

'Don't leave it too late then' He said flatly, in a manner that sounded parental.

Segolene turned her head deliberately to fix her eyes on him still acting her part. A cold serious stare made the more malevolent by the costume she wore.

'I won't' She drawled in a low tone, and shrieked with laughter.

Parental expectation is dashed by disappointment no more sharply than the realisation that youth views its beauty with too casual an assessment and so often fails to make the best of it. Now it was more than that. He felt a detachment, a feeling that what had stood before him was something silent and almost sinister, a feeling that he could not explain with rationality.

His uncertainty was on his mind the following morning when he saw Father Fidel Rocher sitting under a low arch on a small wicker chair.

Marcus stopped to greet him.

'Good morning Father'

'Good morning to you.' He answered without looking up from his task.

'Do you know anything of these Felibrigian festivals? I expect you do, they're something of a local feature I understand. Well Segolene tells me that she will be playing a part in the Felibrigian festival play' He said.

The old man nodded.

'Oh yes' He acknowledged.

'She's playing the part of an assassin no less.' He explained seating himself on the low stone wall.

'She showed me her costume last night. Quite a concept. I seem to have inherited a beautiful young daughter who wishes to conceal her beauty behind whatever less attractive means she can. It seems a such shame to me.'

He could see that Father Fidel Rocher was shelling nuts. He was seemingly quite accomplished in this activity. As he squeezed lightly with a small steel implement an audible snap responded, allowing the nut to spring into his hand. He answered Marcus without looking up at him.

'I have known many virtues. Grace, goodness, charity, self-lessness and obedience. Beauty never really understands itself. Is that not what Goethe said? While she requires no sacrifice beauty reigns supreme. Her reign is short, cut down by the toll of time or battered by the bitter wind of circumstance. You must decide my friend what price you put on beauty and how you value the virtues that God has gifted to mankind. For they all have a value. Not only those that shine the brightest in our eyes, only to fade away.' He continued to break open the nuts with his admirable dexterity.

Wisdom, Marcus reflected, was it not that that is precious? It is so often sealed within a shell of ignorance. The words of an Augustan friar could prize open that shell with one light squeeze. Father Fidel Rocher turned to Marcus as if to add something to his observation.

'I am a man of the cloth my friend. Mine is the promotion of mystery not of spectacle. Of the realm of the divine not of the superficiality of the secular.' He paused as he heard himself begin to preach.

'Forgive me' He said looking at Marcus with his head to one side.

'An old man is circumscribed by convention and prey to foolishness. I am of course delighted at the whole idea and you know, I am rather looking forward to it.' With that he laughed to lighten the moment. It meant a lot to Marcus at that time that his friend should approve of the concept.

His email to Emma necessarily contained requests for dating materials and designs against the vast library held at Fisher Holt and Fitzroy. He had not included any reference to Segolene. This she read as she opened the mail in her private email address.

From Marcus Graham
To Emma Dreyfus

Emm, Just to say my daughter Segolene has moved into the cottage for a short time as she is temporarily without accommodation. I will be seeing her acting skills shortly as she is playing in something called the Fellibrigian festival. I am not sure about the part she is playing but she seems very keen.
Hope all is well with you Emm.

'So she has moved in with him' Emma exclaimed out loud.

'A lost daughter who turns out to be an actress? I wonder why she is playing this part.'

10.

LONDON, ENGLAND

It was another dull wet morning in Chelsea when Emma Dreyfus flicked through the inbox on the screen at her desk in the offices of Fisher Holt and Fitzroy. She had been shocked to receive the email from Marcus telling her of his daughter's move into his cottage. There was definitely something not right about this and she was far from convinced that Segolene was truly Marcus daughter. Why would she say she was? Clearly she had been convincing. It was something that had Emma's inquisitive mind searching for answers.

Among the usual accumulation of unsolicited emails on her screen was the daily email attachment from Marcus in Avignon. Photographs and details for dating and matching that would put together the patchwork of history and sew together the years of the old building he was working on. Panelling, decoration, glazing and stained glazing, it all had to be identified as she knew Marcus would not wish to introduce anything into the renovation work that was out of place or untrue to the original.

It was just before lunch when she spotted something intriguing in one of the dozens of photographs of panelling. At the top rail of the panelling at equal intervals, the carving was raised in the shape of an eye with a groove carved around it to make it stand out. One might imagine that this effect was deliberate to create the notion that those who knelt at prayer were surrounded by a series of eyes, protective perhaps, judgemental even, or merely watchful. What had caught her attention was that someone had taken the trouble to paint onto one of the eyes a vivid blue pupil that was eerily realistic and underneath it, carved into the panelling some words in Latin.

'Memento minima maxima sunt.' Swiftly Emma Googled the phrase to decipher a meaning. There were several variants but all meant much the same. The best she could get was: *Remember the smallest are the most important.*

She paused to reflect. What could such an inscription refer to? A number of vague possibilities presented themselves. Could it refer to the smallest eyes being blue? Did it suggest that one should look out for the smallest? She could make no sense of it and dismissed her theories after brief consideration of each until she was distracted by a colleague and thought no more about it.

Emma Dreyfus had all the attributes of a first class personal assistant. A girl without pretention she was the no nonsense type who liked to get things done speedily. She knew no ceremony nor acted any pretence. She was particularly methodical in her recording of each detail so that information could be retrieved if necessary. She was forensic in her analysis of problems and preparation of reports. She challenged the assumptions made by others, not so as to demean them, but often revealed matters that had been overlooked.

She was the kind of person who was fiercely loyal to those she worked closely with and for Marcus Graham that was to prove to be a great advantage. She had been personal assistant to Marcus for six years and while she also fulfilled the same role for Sir Clement Fitzroy, his frequent absence from the office, his aloof manner and elevated status led her to respect him, but not to have the same affection as she had for Marcus.

Emma knew that today was to be busy and rewarding. Her natural energies would bring her satisfaction in her work and she would meet someone with whom she might become, romantically involved. She knew this because she had read it in her Horoscope. She had always had belief and fascination in the predictive qualities of Horoscopes such had been their success in reflecting the expectations and events of her life. For every enterprise she sought celestial confirmation and her confidence was often attributable to the astrological assurances she read on a daily basis.

This morning however, there had been something else. It was not in her own horoscope but Emma could never resist looking into the horoscopes of friends and colleagues and had habitually read that of Marcus. The fact that he never took any notice of it at all simply gave her the feeling that she was one step ahead of him. Knowing what lay in store. She reached for the newspaper and read again the horoscope under the sign of Virgo.

'The past has revealed herself to you, but do not let your future rise from that past'

Emma thought straight away of the daughter who had so recently moved in with Marcus. She was sure that his horoscope referred to her and was now sure that she was an imposter.

She put her thoughts aside hearing her mobile phone buzzing. The message that appeared read: 'See you for drinks tonight at Gong.'

Emma's heart jumped a little on reading the text. She had arranged drinks at Gong in the Shangri La with a man that she was sure would be interesting. Rick Brown was a man she had met briefly at an evening dinner with friends two weeks previously and now he was confirming a date.

At 7.30 that evening in the flat at Earls Court, Emma Dreyfus was nowhere near ready to depart for her evening at the Shard. She was still drying hair and fixing makeup and she decided that she would need to treat herself to a taxi as she was running late. She was not ready for the taxi as it arrived which had to wait while she shouted to the driver words confirming her imminent arrival without that arrival actually eventuating for a full ten minutes.

The hurried journey to London Bridge was however made just in time to provide the expectation of a successful evening. Emma took the two lifts up to the 52nd floor and was shown to a table by the window. Here she thought, was the sophisticated atmosphere that provided the ideal setting for a first date. The magnificent view over the capital and beyond is unrivalled, and Emma had discerned a favourite cocktail following her last visit here with clients.

The man who had walked into Gong at 20.15 hours was in every sense a prospect. He wore his hair a little longer than what was conventional, a dark charcoal suit and light blue shirt open at the neck. He had said that he was in property, a valuation surveyor with a large London practice which she was certain sounded rather dull and while she had hoped that he be engaged in something a little more interesting, this evening she reflected he looked more than acceptable.

She was ambivalent concerning her liaisons with men. She had a healthy disregard for the majority of them finding them too concerned about themselves and their image and interests. Rick had seemed a different proposition. He had the willingness to admit to his shortcomings and the humour to laugh at them and to appreciate her priorities and inhibitions. She had found this to be a most engaging trait that made him contrarian among a cohort of potential suitors.

Rick came over to her lifting his eyebrows on seeing her and raising his arms to draw her into them in an extravagant greeting. His warm smile and generous mouth spoke of the potential for a relationship to come.

'What will you have Emma?' He asked decisively as the waiter came over to them.

Emma responded with a request for vodka and orange. It was upon reflection, not the time to ask for anything more indulgent. There would be occasion to indulge her love of more exotic cocktails. This was not it.

'So, you've been at work today Emma I guess. Anything interesting?'

'I work for a firm of Architects in Chelsea remember. We don't do interesting.'

Then she remembered the horoscope.

'Do you follow your horoscope Rick?' She asked.

'Can't say I do.'

'Well the most interesting thing that happened to me today came from my Horoscope. I always find my horoscope to be uncanny accurate. That's why I follow it.'

'Do you believe then that life is set out for us? I mean that life is pre-determined?' He inquired conversationally.

'I guess I do. I hadn't thought of it like that.' Emma looked at him as if he had discovered something about her she had not realised and found that quite attractive.

'Yes I think I do see life like that. We are born to a role in life there is not much we can do to change that is there?'

'Some would disagree. They would say that there is nothing one cannot do to reshape one's life. It is in our own hands so to speak.'

'What about you? Is that what you think?'

'I suppose I do. We cannot possibly imagine that we are stuck with what we have been born to with no ability to alter course can we? It is not merely chance or some pre-ordination that dictates we follow one path or another.' He ventured.

'It had not occurred to me that believing in a horoscope is the belief in an order of things. The pre-determined inevitability of our existence. Actually it sounds rather dull.' She laughed as she said this as if she had just uncovered a flaw in her philosophy.

'How come mine is always so accurate?'

'Well' He said slowly as if thinking through his response. 'Probably because you are programed to live according to a certain pattern set out by some invisible big brother being, who is sending you messages through your daily newspaper.' He looked at her with intense seriousness of pursed lips and a frown and they laughed together.

'Put like that I see that it all sounds a little, well, implausible. I am sure that I am not the first though to believe in horoscopes am I?' She enquired wishing to justify what she now doubted.

'No Emma, there are many who believe in predestination of some kind. They might see some significance in the flight of birds or the constellation of stars. I think it could be something to do with our premonition. They say that the brain is some 25 percent premonition. If one follows an omen, prediction, horoscope whatever then perhaps the human has the power to act out that prediction thereby bringing about the consequence predicted. Does that sound plausible?'

She was finding his analysis appealing as he seemed to be wanting to understand her in some way that indicated an interest in her. He wasn't merely dismissing her beliefs as mere nonsense.

She sipped her drink and continued.

'So anyway, the interesting thing I found was that my horoscope said something about a friend of mine abroad being introduced to someone from the past. My friend Marcus is abroad at the moment and has just met a young woman who says that she is his daughter. Imagine that. Now come on, that is surely extra ordinary isn't it?'

'I wonder if one's own inner consciousness can respond to the prediction. I mean if one has a strong impression that something is going to happen then there might be a way in which a person can fulfil that prophesy.'

'So how does that work? He didn't know what the horoscope said.'

'That's true. Fifteen love to Mystic Margery Emma.' Rick conceded. He thought for a moment and then pronounced with humoured formality.

'The Dorsorlated Prefrontal Cortex is that part of the brain that simulates the future. It is the part of the brain that focusses on intuition. Some say that it represents a significant part of the brain and one has to believe that it is better developed in some than in others. Perhaps that would explain the median, she who sees the future. We all process known information and reach a conclusion as to how it may affect the future. We are after all instinctive animals.'

Emma laughed at his pretentious pedagogy. She was happy to allow some scepticism as to her conviction but she was at the same time committed to her belief and had an addiction to the daily horoscope despite enjoying hearing Rick's theory on intuition.

'You sound as if you have thought this all through. Did you ever study psychology?' She asked him.

'No, I was at Cambridge reading natural sciences. I loved it. One cannot help loving Cambridge but, when I finished I decided I needed to do something more vocational. So I went on to train as a Surveyor at the University of Reading.'

All evidence was that the life spent as a student had not been wasted on Rick. He had the appearance of one highly educated who had worked hard and achieved well. He was now a surveyor and although Emma considered that to be rather dull it at least allowed him to mix with some more interesting people.

'Do you ever get to travel?'

'Occasionally, in fact I am away next week visiting a bank in Frankfurt.'

'Is that Deutsche Bank?' she guessed wildly trying to sound knowledgeable.

'No, It's a small local bank over there Drexell Hesse. They have become a client of ours. We are seeking to set up a continuing service to them. It's just a courtesy visit.'

'I will have to check your horoscope to see how things will turn out for you.' Emma teased.

Emma looked down at the city through the wide windows that surround the bar. She could pick out the buildings below with ease. Tower Bridge almost beneath them and city hall close by. It was possible to see the passengers on the platform at London Bridge station.

'What a fantastic achievement this building is' She heard herself saying.

'Who could ever have predicted it?' Rick added.

She smiled at him almost unconsciously an inviting smile and looked into his eyes.

'There's a pizza restaurant on the river down by the Globe theatre' she suggested, finding her mouth close to his as they rose to leave.

'It's a short walk from here'

'You read my mind' He said, returning the smile.

11.

AVIGNON, FRANCE

Under the magnificent gold statue of the Madonna that crowns its tower, the bells of the Cathedral of Notre Dame des Doms tolled the dull measured voice of time. A toll that announces beginnings, a toll that confirms ends. It strikes each with the same sonorous sound. An equanimity, that the lowest labourer and the mightiest marquis alike must heed.

Father Fidel Rocher smiled as he leaned back in his chair clasping in his hand the glass of Perrier et Mint that he sipped almost surreptitiously listening to that sound outside the Café Zizi Jeanmaire in the dappled shade of a plain tree.

'All creatures are time's issue.' He reflected as he looked up at the bells.

'To all he grants the lease of life. Its term, its conditions, its obligations, the extent of the demise, the certainty of effluxion, the fear of forfeiture.'

As Marcus gazed across at him he responded as if it were an enquiry.

'The world was never intended to be all goodness. Evil has been with us from the beginning of time. We are told are we not, that it was an act of Satan that brought about humanity. Still there are some who do not believe in God. Surely they do not believe that there is no God. That would be absurd. No living soul can possess the evidence that would contradict the teaching of two millennia. They say that God cannot exist because there is evil. That he would not allow evil. This my friend is the philosophy of the fool.' He allowed himself a small chuckle.

'Everything has its opposite. Yet we know that the co-existence of opposites is what make them exist. Light and dark, man and woman, law and equity, life and death. All are interdependent they cannot exist without their opposite and so too good and evil.'

He paused for a moment and went on.

'Remember that the line between good and evil runs through the centre of every human heart my friend. We are all of us capable of either good or evil in equal measure. It is our choice. That is what faith is for my friend. It is our faith that helps us choose the right path. Or the wrong one.'

The last sentence was delivered with a questioning tone. He added.

'It depends perhaps whom you serve.'

'Out of failure will come success.' The old Friar said wishing to lift the conversation with a slightly more optimistic slant on the subject.

Marcus stared at the sky in reflection at the introduction of this subject for it came close to his preoccupation. He felt his failure, his fear of responsibility, his lack of success and in the presence of the old cleric he felt the need to confess.

'I have known more failure than success.' He said looking vacantly upwards.

'You know I only once loved a woman. My marriage failed from the moment it started and the only real relationship I ever had failed because I could not face it when it got too tough. When responsibility loomed it was just as if it became unbearable.' He admitted feeling the small relief of confession.

Marcus began to recount the details of his brief marriage, the death of his wife and the subsequent relationship with Sarah whom he had deserted when she had chosen to take the responsibility to look after her brother.

'But you have been successful in your work have you not, I see your skills here making a great difference. We know that every advance is complemented by retreat and every rise a fall. So it is too in reverse.' The friar assured him in an attempt to make him feel better.

'Me no. Look at Fitz. Now there is someone who has succeeded'
The old friar shook his head with slow deliberation.

'Even God cannot change the past my friend. We carry the guilt of history only if we do not learn from it. Only when we face our shortcomings can we go forward to face the world. Guilt my friend has a way of preserving memory, you must let it pass.' He paused.

'The past can inspire regret and bitterness. It is sometimes better to forget, and always to confess. The open heart heals itself.' He took a handkerchief from his breast pocket and wiped his brow.

'You see!' He exclaimed.

'When I sat in this chair I was in shade. Now the light is on my brow. The shade and the light traded places with each other revealing what was obscured and obscuring what was revealed. So it is that from failure will come success.' He chuckled mischievously at his metaphoric observation and slapped his hand upon his knee to emphasise it.

Marcus was becoming well versed in the conflation and oscillation of opposites that inhabited the mind of the old friar. It was simple and convenient to see good and evil as black and white as the pieces on a chess board, but the world turned on the light and the shade trading places with each other. The enemy becomes the ally, the loved the hated. All things on earth will change as waters ebb and flow.

He now understood that to go forward he had to face his past. He had not realised the pain that a journey down memory lane could bring. The hard knot one feels in the viscera at every corner one turns. For Marcus it was not the pain of loss, it seemed worse, it was the pain of lost opportunity.

He felt that strange realisation that the places of the past now have new owners, new occupiers. They have the same energy the same noise but it is other people's noise. He is now just an onlooker. The places of the past are now transformed and he is left behind them, in some distant long forgotten part of those places. Here after 25 years he would seek to discover some part of that past and the closure that might bring.

They sat in silence and reflection. If the past had wounded Marcus, so too had it his companion. For Father Fidel Rocher the past had been at times a harsh existence. Oblate Rocher had been a supplicant to St Denis en Seine; a Holy Order of abject domination and suppression. It had been a harsh and frugal life that had imposed contrition and obedience as its virtues. The temptation of evil was ever present and its incipient manifestation was to be exorcised with vigour and determination. There was no room for doubt or discussion. No room for favour or forgiveness. The curse of evil threatened those who did God's work with greater veracity than those who had accepted sin.

In times of introspection he allowed himself to grieve for the agony of his defloration. The brutal loss of innocence and dignity. The hurt and humiliation that had informed his contempt for the equanimity of justice.

It had been a day like any other for the Oblates of his order. A peaceful day of charity and prayer. The accusation had come before vespers. The nomination of three young boys of just thirteen years old as the thieves who had stolen a number of treasures from the monastery such that they had been found for sale as relics on a traveller's market stall in the town.

'We are all to be grateful to Father Dominic Dufour.' It was announced.

'He has retrieved the treasures and saved us from the indignity that the sale of such treasures would have brought upon us.'

Father Dominic who been such a welcome presence in the order since his recent arrival. Father Dominic who alone had elected to undertake the just and necessary punishment of the perpetrators of the theft in the name of the Holy Father.

So it was that the three Oblates were directed to the private rooms of their accuser, judge, and punisher. The vindication of their sin would be completed by their introduction to the outcome of the sin of man. Their recognition of such was an essential prerequisite to their understanding of the hidden urges that can invade a man's soul and dominate his being.

The humiliation necessary for the repentance of their sin was contrived by the requirement to stand naked in line on the cold stone floor while the priest studied them, handled them and with the slow deliberation of some kind of ceremony, squeezed their genitalia in his cold hands entreating the stir of incipient manhood that would decide for him his first victim.

It was to his eternal shame that such a stir evinced itself in the young Oblate as much as he had tried to resist it. A rush of warm blood answered the Priest's encouragement. A stiff response from a wilted will. The priest's eyes looked at him in excited agitation. His disingenuous smile that of a predator seeing the weakness of its prey.

The cold metal bed frame was his cross. Father Dominic strapped the naked boy with arms outstretched and legs parted in brazen Vitruvian reflection turned to face the cold frame. Then, in full view of the second and third accused in order to alert them to their impending fate began the blunt rut. The gnarled grimace on his face contrived an agony in his action. The violent vindication punctuated by the wholesome expressions of exorcism as he shouted for the Devil to depart. In the finish the limp reduced avenger, suspiring like a spent athlete. The purity of a child sacrificed for the banishment of evil.

The act fulfilled, the victim deposed, the honour of the righteous had been restored. Its interlocutor satisfied. Father Dominic had patted his head in a playful manner, had said they would all be friends now he was sure that they all understood that to steal was wrong. He had vindicated the sins of the second and third of his larcenists in the same manner at his pleasure over the following days. The younger Oblates had become aware that a new initiation to adulthood was awaiting them in the licentious and vengeful loins of Father Dominic Dufour.

On the victim falls the crushing guilt of his usurpation. Father Fidel Rocher had been haunted by that evening, even though he had subsequently endured rape of the same kind, it was this first unjust introduction to buggery that had so affected him. His innocence lost, his body impaled, his faith impaired. But there is a great strength that emanates from injustice and adversity. It is the strength of faith and of the limitless optimism of hope. The resolution for endeavour and sanguinity of endurance. It is the power of prayer.

Father Fidel Rocher turned to Marcus and said:

'You will turn failure to success as surely as change is inevitable. You have tasted it now with your winning. It is only a matter of time. You must trust in God my friend for He has cleared the path for you and He will light your way.

Nothing is impossible. Events are only improbable. We have seen how the improbable becomes reality, the black swan that for centuries was deemed impossible until the western world made new discoveries. All the time it was it was not impossible merely improbable and it became reality. Events that seem improbable are often those that can have huge consequences just because we have assumed them to be impossible and acted according to our limited knowledge.'

Marcus reflected how the old can be imbued with a wisdom often rejected by the young. Surely wisdom and old friends are the compensation for old age. The one serves to help us better appreciate the other.

That evening the city of Avignon opened up to a delightful spectacle. The medieval son et Lumiere and the felebridgian play that Segolene was to make her mark in, playing the role that Marcus felt so inappropriate. The role of the assassin disguised as a cardinal. It seemed that everyone in sight wished to take the opportunity to dress in medieval costume and everywhere was busy with the rush and enthusiasm of those intent on festivity.

There were the vendors selling everything from cheap jewellery, pottery, clothing and hot food, their stalls lit in the most imaginative of ways. Mime artists on every corner portraying a range of guises. Colour of costumes and scent of candles. Sounds of laughter and surprise. It was an evening of excitement and colour that set the scene for a medieval drama.

The play began with an announcement that Marcus had to confess he did not understand. It was probably an introduction to the background of the piece but it seemed from the response that there were many others who found it equally difficult to understand. Father Fidel Rocher however seemed to be listening with intent and Marcus felt sure that he would be apprised later of the details of the introduction should he wish.

This medieval theatre was clearly an excuse for the most voluminous costumes in the brightest of colours, embellished with extravagant embroidery. Faces made up with paint added a dramatic and almost sinister touch to many of the players. It was difficult for him to imagine that all the revelry on stage was truly part of the performance and it seemed that a good deal of improvisation was to be part of it. He had already seen the part of the assassin with its limited exposure to the stage but this evening there was something more. Something he had not expected.

It was as if the crowd were imbued by the mystic atmosphere, taken back in history by the splendour of light, sound, scents and colour to a time when this city had been the centre of culture. This city, the wilful sycophantic mistress of a French monarchy determined to rival Rome. It was an evening that paid homage to that past. A time that treasured the title of its puppet papacy that saw itself as rival to Rome. That revelled in the power of its commerce and the grandness of its palace. It was all there again that evening. In the sounds and light of a mystic night the city rose from its past.

It was in a narrow alley close to the Palace Marcus attention was caught by a slender dark bearded man wearing a long green smock with yellow cuffs to its sleeves and a crimson cloak and skull cap. He was carefully weighing out what appeared to be small quantities herbs onto and old weighing machine.

'He is the apothecary' Father Fidel Rocher explained raising his voice above the hubbub of excited energy around them. He dispenses potions and medicines and in the medieval days he would try his hand as the Physician. He was also the provider of hallucinating potions and poisons to those who chose to use them' He chuckled.

'Costume told of the vocation of its wearer in medieval times. That is why he wears the green smock with yellow cuffs to the sleeves. It says little of the competence of its wearer in that vocation however' He laughed.

'So often that was highly suspect. The apothecary became a chemist following the professionalisation of all branches of medicine. You can be sure that a remedy was less certain in medieval times.'

It was then that Marcus attention was diverted. As he turned around he saw a man talking heatedly to the apothecary and appeared to be buying goods from him. There was something furtive in the transaction. The man's head covered with the dark hood of the cloak he wore. The glance from side to side as the sale was made. The way that he moved away swiftly pulling the hood forward to cover his face. Marcus reflected on the words of the old friar.

'Do you expect that he is buying a potion?' He asked Father Fidel Rocher in a hushed whisper.

As spoke he saw the wide sleeve of the man's cloak fall back down his arm to reveal a distinctive tattoo on his arm.

'Did they have tattoos like that in medieval times?' Marcus joked to his friend in a light hearted manner.

It was that light remark that would make that tattoo stick in his mind. What he could not know is that he would soon see that tattoo again, but only later would he come to learn its ominous significance.

12.

AVIGNON, FRANCE

Marcus returned late to the cottage, carefully opening the front door and entering quietly to avoid waking her. He had spent a blissful afternoon on the Pont Saint Benezet exploring the Saint Nicholas chapel for inspiration and had come to the conclusion that he would need to work hard to achieve the standard of restoration that he had witnessed there.

Now he stared into the drawing room shocked and speechless at the scene in front of him. She was straddled naked across a writhing man who moved inside her with slow and deliberate motion his hands firmly holding her hips. Her hands held Luc's bare buttocks while she sucked on him with hungry energy as he stood in front of her. They hadn't seen Marcus enter such was their absorption in their ménage a trois. Their desperate grunting and agonised moans of satisfaction were entirely uninhibited.

He backed silently into the kitchen doorway and stood in its shadow. The fire in the grate behind them crackled loudly to announce that it had been freshly lit. Its flames were burning brightly among the small sticks licking across the logs in quick and hungry flashes. He could see the mounting ecstasy in her body as she moved it in an uncoordinated movement like a rag doll. Her mouth empty now, emanated a viscid discourse of rhythmic panting and random syllables, her hair swirling from side to side, her fingers digging deep into his buttocks, her taught tummy, her breasts moving from side to side. At last, she sighed a long loud sigh of ecstasy throwing her head first back and then down hard onto Luc's belly.

Luc took her in a firm embrace and held her in a moment's silent rapture. Her passion defused into his muscular nakedness, his arms wrapped around her, his hand gently stroking her hair. Segolene drew her hand up Luc's sated body and hung upon his shoulder her head upon his chest. The man who had been below her was quickly gathering his clothes and dressing himself, preparing to leave the room without word.

The extravagance of the action was fast defused to a quite comfort of serenity. Marcus prepared to edge back into the inanition of cool shadow that was the small kitchen. It was then that he saw clearly the tattoo mark on Luc's tanned arm, the mark of a saint slaying a beast that could almost have been St George. It was something he was certain he had seen before.

He drew the back door bolt in slow silence to affect his surreptitious exit, his mind racing with confusion and uncertainty.

His had been a childhood of innocence. A sheltered existence unused to prurient inquiry or licentious endeavour. Just one moment had haunted him. It seemed one brief split second from his youth that had opened his eyes quite literally to the potential of the sexual relationship. He and Stocky were employed to cut the wide lawns around a large bungalow owned by a Mr and Mrs Driver who lived there with Mrs Driver's younger sister a Miss Court, who had been generally known as the younger Mrs Driver. Perhaps it was those post war years of deprivation that so liberally tolerated such cohabitation, though Marcus had been let into the secret of that liaison one late afternoon in the half light.

They had gone to collect the few shillings that were due to them. He had seen Stocky frozen at the window of the bungalow gazing with intent into the half lit room. Marcus joined him and stood by his side. It was a sight to delight any schoolboy. As Mr Driver lay unclothed on the bed the naked figure of the younger Mrs Driver was riding him with energetic enthusiasm. The elder Mrs Driver was sat across his chest her mouth clenched on that of the younger, her hands fondling her breasts. She dismounted casually on being aware of the voyeur's presence to come to the window to close the blind and end the spectacle. The viewing had been momentary, but permanently captured in his young mind is if a photograph, recollected throughout his years with wonder, delight and satisfaction.

There was not the same satisfaction in seeing ones daughter's simultaneous servicing of two lovers though he tried to rationalise his reaction. Why should she not enjoy her beauty and natural inclinations with the energy and imagination of her youth? Was this not a Gallic rite?

It was a conclusion that eluded him no matter how much he tried to convince himself. Now though, there was another preoccupation that set his mind to question. He had remembered where he had seen the tattoo on Luc's arm. It was the tattoo he had seen on the furtive purchaser of potions from the apothecary at the son et lumiere.

The furtive man was Luc. It was the same tattoo. But what did it mean?

13.

CALABRIA, ITALY

Tate knew that he was victim of kidnap within a short time of waking from the drugged sleep that had left him with a splitting headache. Had he not done so already it was now clear to him as he sat in a dark dungeon within stone walls and with a barred window in the roof that admitted a rare ration of sunlight. He was looking at the unkempt figure that sat opposite him barely visible in the darkness. His shirt once white was creased and grey, open at the neck. His trousers dark formal and inappropriate to his incarceration. In fact, much like Tate himself but with a dishevelment that bore the signs of longer detainment.

He looked at Tate as if he had just been waiting for him to regain his consciousness.

'I am Alberto Viscoli.' The captive explained in a gravelly voice.

'I was taken from my office in Milan and brought here. I don't know how.' He looked down at the ground.

'I think that they will want a ransom.' He followed softly.

The explanation had been delivered in a plain and matter of fact way with little trace of an Italian accent. No hysteria, more resignation. The speaker seemed almost convinced of the reason for his captivity. Tate needed to know more. Did he know who was responsible? What sum of money might they be seeking? Had Viscoli spoken to his captors since he had been here? Why might they have taken him?

There were no answers to these questions. Only that, the captors had said nothing. Tate had only Viscoli's suppositions and subjective convictions born of his longer internment. He knew nothing factual. Tate's story was similar to Viscoli. Abducted on leaving his Hotel room in the piazza Portia. A short taxi ride and he remembered no more.

Viscoli had become convinced by his kidnap theory on the basis of historical evidence.

'It happens a lot in Italy.' he explained.

'We are no doubt being held in the Aspromonte in Calabria. It is the hiding place of the Calabrian Mafia. They are well known for kidnap and ransom. They will keep us here until our families pay.'

Viscoli was a quiet unassuming man who Tate learned, owned a chain of stores in north of Italy and in Monaco. He was clearly wealthy and that he assumed, was the reason for his captivity. He had family, a wife and grown up children but his captors had not spoken to him about contacting them in any way for a ransom. Tate reflected that his companion was the kind of man that he might befriend, but not here. This was no place for forging friendships. They may break at any time or enforce a morality that eschewed self-preservation.

Two weeks went by in the sweaty heat of that cramped cell. A jug of water was provided regularly and a crude kind of risotto and fresh fruit provided for sustenance. A latrine had been set up in a dark recess connected to the outside wall. A tap above it delivered fresh cool water, something approaching luxury in their condition. One morning the door of the cell opened and Viscoli was taken away. That was the last that Tate saw of him.

Tate had been careful to do some calculations. He had been taken on the third of June. If he had been unconscious for 24 hours then the first day of his captivity was the fourth. The sky had darkened over the small window seventeen times when the cooling of the cell had allowed him to sleep. It was the twenty third of June. He had had no communication with anyone. He had had no clean clothes. No newspaper or reading matter whatever. He still did not know where he was other than what Viscoli had surmised. He would stay alert. He would record every small detail. If the opportunity arose he would make an escape.

On the 20th day by his calculations and with such an opportunity in mind he welcomed the dull thud of the approaching jailer and the clanking rustling sound of the door being opened. The jailer motioned for Tate to go with him.

Tate moved awkwardly and apprehensively along the narrow corridor towards the light. He was rehearsing some dialogue he had invented for his kidnappers. Stay calm he told himself. Do not appear to give in easily. They need my cooperation. Tate felt that his family would have remained calm. They knew they had the money to pay for his release. It was just a matter of negotiation now.

He was turned right in to a room with stone floor, stone walls and considerably more light than his own.

'Mr Tate?' The voice had clear English and the intonation of a question.

A thin man in a dark suit was sitting in front of a wide table. His collar unbuttoned at the neck revealed a rough tanned neck around which a striking gold chain hung, matching a large gold ring on his finger. His eyes were cold and grey, betraying the pretence of conviviality in his greeting.

'We apologise for keeping you for so long but we are now ready for you.'

Tate was ushered to sit on a chair at a wide table in front of the man. He looked down briefly at the table and the papers that were assembled carefully in front of him. Suddenly he jumped visibly. He could see that the address on a letter in front of him referred to a building in Dulwich that he owned. He was confused. What connection could there be between a property in south London and this remote hideaway. He looked further. The man said nothing but watched his reaction with a casual indifference. Tate reached out and spread the papers so that he could read more. All of them were related to property owned by Tate. The effort of his confinement and absence of anything to stimulate his mind made his situation all the more incomprehensible. His hand wandered among the papers turning them picking them up. His eyes stared captivated, confused, frightened by his inability to comprehend.

'We have brought you here to sign away your property Mr Tate. We are advancing you a considerable amount of money. You must of course extend to us the necessary security.'

Tate was baffled. How could this have come about? These properties had been owned by his family for years. There were no mortgages or borrowings against them. He had no need for borrowing. These were properties worth some seven million pounds. Tate looked up at the two heavily built men standing behind his interlocutor. He could see now that each carried a revolver. Each looked at him in a menacing manner. Tate began to remonstrate aware that it would be to no avail.

'Now look. There is surely some misunderstanding. I do not owe any money. I never have.'

The thin man smiled a thin smile.

'Mr Tate. You are being advanced a considerable sum of money to buy your freedom. You will sign the security papers.'

Suddenly it made sense. Creating mortgages on his property was the manner with which the payment of a ransom was to be made. Viscoli had been in the same position. He had no doubt signed the papers at considerable cost, but now, he would be free. Tate looked again at the papers he could feel his resolution to sign them growing.

There was his letter to Dortman a Swiss finance broker seeking a loan for business purposes and asking them to make arrangements on the best possible terms. A letter to Sandersons Chartered Surveyors in London informing them that he had applied for a mortgage advance from Drexel Hesse bank in Frankfurt and that the bank would be contacting them to arrange valuations of property. There was a Mortgage Deed to be charged by way of first charge on his property at Dulwich. A letter to a firm of solicitors in London asking them to act for him and informing them of his intention to obtain a mortgage advance from Drexel Hesse and confirming instructions for them to cooperate with solicitors for the bank in the perfection of the banks security. There was even his solicitor's client care letter setting out the numerous terms and conditions to his instructions and confirming that they had examined his passport and documents by way of identity check. It was all complete. What could he do but sign. At least in doing so he would pay the ransom and be free from the sweaty cell. At least he could be free to see his family again. Tate signed all the papers.

'Thank you Mr Tate.' said the thin man on casting an eye across the papers.

'You may now remove your clothes. They must be filthy. Place them down by the door and go with my colleague.'

The prospect of a shower and fresh clothes and that of imminent departure from this place inspired Tate to strip as quickly as he could and turn towards the door. As he walked from the room the thin man did not acknowledge him go. He was sorting into order the papers that Tate had just signed.

He did not even turn his heard on hearing the sound of the two gunshots fired into the back of Tate's head as he stepped out naked into the bright Calabrian sunshine.

14.

AVIGNON, FRANCE

That single soft sweep of breeze that comes from nowhere to lift the first fall of leaves and lay them by the kerb or side wall, brought with it the sweet chill of autumn. The brightness of summer had finally faded but the river Rhone has a beauty that does not fade with the seasons. It is an enduring beauty at all times of the year, though starker now in the quiet shadows of a still morning lit by the pale sun of early October.

The plane trees stand proud against her banks, the grass verges wide along the path are spread with the early mist that evaporates into the sunlight. Walkers with small dogs call them and throw sticks for them to chase with their endless enthusiasm and tireless energy. A pair of lovers find fresh morning air lift them to laughter as they walk hand in hand and an old man studies the scene intently as if he wishes to cherish a recollection of it to take with him to eternity.

Along this path walked two teenage girls arm in arm talking and laughing together. They were firm friends. Both had come to this town in recent years and therefore had none of the established family relationships that were common here. Both had come from the south west and both had, unknown to each other, been compelled to flee their pasts. Pasts that were now unspoken of, set aside by new experiences and youthful exuberant discovery.

For them now the old city was their place to visit away from the domestic routine of the small towns they lived in nearby. It had the excitement of life, Cafés, clubs and parties and visitors in the summer months that had promised romance and flirtation. There was always much to discuss between them that would follow a familiar pattern. It was there by that river pathway that they sat to exchange nouvelles.

'You left early last night. Did you see Sipo?' Annie enquired knowing the answer. She had known that Elise was manipulating a relationship with a handsome Spanish boy working at the café Marche. She had seen her leave a late party at Le petit bouche with him and her question was not so much an enquiry as to the facts, as a wish to hear a detailed account of any incipient sexual encounter that might serve by way of substitution for her own lack of indiscretion.

A radiant though mischievous grin was her response.

'Shall I tell you a secret Annie? You mustn't tell anyone' Elise asked clearly anxious to reveal it but keen too to be entreated to do so.

'We went back to his place. Well you know the place he shares with that Pablo guy who works with him at the back of Café Marche. He had some stuff to smoke and we sat around smoking for a bit'

'Was it just you and Sipo?' Annie enquired seeing the opportunities that might arise from their being alone together.

'No; Sipo, me and Pablo' Elise confirmed. With this she shrieked with laughter. Annie looked confused and clearly had no idea of the outcome of this revelation. Elise was enjoying the suspense.

'Did anything happen?' Annie felt compelled to ask feeling now that she was missing the point.

Again another shriek of laughter.

'Yes, Yes Annie. We all stripped off together and did it between the three of us. I'll tell you Annie that Pablo is huge. I just couldn't believe it. You ought to get off with him Annie. Really. It felt, well awesome. We were all so high on the weed stuff and some brandy they were drinking, it was so wicked Annie.'

The revelation had left Annie speechless. She had anticipated restrained procrastination and incipient intimacy between Elise and Sipo. Here was the revelation of an orgy between experienced protagonists.

Annie had been made to reflect on the inadequacies that her sheltered life had ingrained in her. She now questioned her ad-

herence to a rigid structure of conduct that could never have foreseen the potential for the revelry that Elise had enjoyed so liberally and without regret or contrition. She questioned whether
she was to abandon the faith that she had adhered to all her life
in order to enjoy these collective carnal joys.

She felt that she had no equal secret of her own, but she knew
that she was holding the greatest secret of them all, a secret that she,
Maria Anna, had been sworn to keep at the penalty pronounced
by father Etienne Petit on the day of judgement. It was a secret
that her parents had been sure that she should keep. They had,
moved away from their home soon after the death of the Esterre
children in the great storm that had convinced them of the truth
of the revelation and the need for her to keep the secret prayer.

Now Annie felt betrayed. Her friend was gaining notoriety
from her willingness to disclose information and Annie the hold-
er of the greater secret enjoyed no credit nor currency.

If Elise's secret did not hold its value for long it was only because it was superseded by updated revelations of the tripartite
relationship that had developed between her and the two Spanish
waiters. Scandal travels with fluidity. It gains momentum as it
goes and is augmented in its detail to satisfy the predilections of
its listeners. Elise had gained notoriety that if not envied for its
content, imbued to her a celebrity that was the fascination of the
entire town.

One evening the two young girls were alone in Annie's room
at the small house in Eragues that was home to Annie and her
parents. It was not as if Annie had made any resolution to herself
more a response to another boast from Elise regarding the secret
that she had asked Annie to hear. It might have been the weight
of secrets accumulating in her young mind that broke through
the wall of her discretion. Whatever, it was the first and last time
that she made the revelation.

'You won't tell Annie, I know you won't' Elise began. 'Sipo
took some money from the restaurant yesterday and we went
out to the Café Zizi Jeanmaire for supper. He doesn't think anyone will find out. Anyway I stayed the night with them after

and we all got. Well they both wanted me and I wasn't going to complain …'

'Elise!' Annie raised her voice to stop her.

'Well it's not right you giving me all the details.'

'If you had secrets Annie you would want your best friend to know' Elise teased.

It was like a challenge. Elise had assumed that Annie had no secrets to reveal and while she was not at that point thinking beyond the prurient, Annie felt for the first time in her life the urge to break her vow to Father Etienne Petit and tell of the revelation.

'It's just that, well you don't have any' Elise stabbed.

It could have stopped there and then, but Annie heard herself saying,

'Actually, I do' immediately she said those words she felt a power developing inside her. Knowledge can imbue power, but it is only at the point of its release that the power is truly felt. The eyes of her friend turned to enquiry. A hesitation that almost anticipated something more revealing than her own indiscretions. It was an expectation that held the moment in an exaggerated pause.

'It is something that I am sworn not to tell' She began.

'Something that I have never told to anyone'

'Not even your Mother?' Elise asked certain of the exception.

'No Elise, not even my Mother, only the priest.'

It was following a cold silence that Annie began her account of the revelation that she had held since her childhood. A revelation from the Holy Mother herself that she had told to Father Etienne Petit to whom she had sworn secrecy upon the sentence of judgement. What did it matter now. To tell her best friend who would be trusted to maintain her silence. Why should she not share the burden and at the same time deploy its currency, one equal and more than Elise's indiscretions.

Elise listened in awe of her friend's account. She had been brought up in the same kind of community as Annie. She knew the magnitude of a Marian revelation and there was no disbelief in her mind as she listened to the detailed account.

'What will you do?' She asked under her breath.

'Nothing. I mean I don't have to do anything. I have told the priest at that time. He holds the secret too. It was him who told me not to.' she halted.

'Not to tell' Annie finished, staring in silence contemplating some far part of the room while Elise studied her looking for something in her friend that she might not have seen in her before.

'That is awesome. An awesome secret to keep' she whispered.

The low light flickered, casting a shadow on the wall. A small gust of wind rattled the window pane in a small protest. A silent contemplation devoured their youthful humour as darkness fell and as night drew further in, the girls held each other in quiet embrace under the covers of her bed to await the sleep that was soon upon them.

Morning broke on a new day with new rules. The reinvention of a hierarchy, a relationship reversed. Annie now held the upper hand. The beneficiary of a secret so profound that no sexual indiscretion could ever hope to hold the trump card. It was a miracle, a revelation from the Holy Mother. What could ever defeat it.?

Annie returned from the bathroom fastening her hair behind her head with a band as her towel dropped to the floor revealing her slim figure naked as truth, to which she displayed not the slightest inhibition. She was now in control. She bound knowledge greater than any other; she had been entrusted with a revelation.

There was a silence in the room as Elise shuffled her way to the small bathroom covering her body with a blanket from the bed. There was an envy that was palpable but Annie was enjoying her moment.

Some minutes later Elise stood in the door dressed and clearly ready to leave, her small bag tucked under her arm. It was her eyes that Annie was drawn to. Her eyes that betrayed a silent enmity for the way in which she had been upstaged. The room was caught in a moment of stillness and as Annie looked again into those eyes she caught sight of something she now recognised. Something she had not seen before in Elise. Something remembered from a distant past that was now fast coming back to her. Something cold and disturbing and with it, Annie could feel a fear that she had not felt since she was a child. It was the feeling of terror. For as she looked into those dark eyes she saw, not for the first time, the penetrating stare of evil.

Without words and in silence Elise departed the house leaving Annie trembling with the vivid recollection of those eyes that had flooded back to her, choking her senses to dysfunction. For she had felt in that short stare, the stab of a dagger that cuts into the soul and opens the wound that lies there dormant, the wound once cut, that lasts a lifetime.

It was at the Ecole Saint Vincent Madelgarus convent school just as she had started there as a small child. She had been given a new identity. Her name would now be just Annie rather than Maria Anna and no one would know the secret of her past. She was to receive instructions on the measured trinity of hard work, obedience and education. She remembered the austere cavernous dining hall. It's cold hollow space, its high ceilings, the two lines of tables one on each side and the top table raised on a platform where the nuns would sit in a line overlooking their flock.

She remembered how, before they dined, the girls stood in enforced silence awaiting the entry of elegant sisterhood. Nuns in their white robes and cornette headdresses, walking in silence to the top table through the hall. She remembered Sister Henrietta, the novitiate, who would always bring up the rear of the line sweeping her glance around the hall to look out for dissidents. To reprimand the dissenting smile, question the furtive glance and punish the muttered word.

She remembered the small frail figure that followed that awesome line to a solitary table laid for one diner, placed in the centre of that hall within full view of all. Head bowed the dishevelled gamine was made to stand barefoot on the cold floor until all others were accommodated. Made to wait until last for her meagre meal. The Brebis galeuse; the black sheep. That was what she had been known as. She who by some unknown and uncertain act had betrayed the Holy Mother.

She recalled those awful times when penance had been extracted from the Brebis galeuse. When she was made to bow over her solitary table to face the mother superior, her body held down firmly while her skirts were lifted by two nuns, one each side of her and the flagellation of her naked buttocks. Humiliation that Sister Henrietta carried out in front of the school with a birch wood cane in four furious strikes to the gasps of all who witnessed it.

'To sit upon the sting of retribution will surely bring her to contrition' she had heard Sister Henrietta confirm with confidence to the other nuns.

Annie had first felt an overwhelming sympathy for the Brebis galeuse and empathy for the abject humiliation she suffered daily. It was said that she slept at the foot of Sister Henrietta's bed like a dog but that was surely untrue. She had been discussed in hushed whispers of wonder and trepidation among the students in both pity and admonition. What was it that she had done? How awful it was to be treated so. Was she really evil? It was said that she served the devil. She should repent her sins.

It was a morning like any other, except it was the morning after Sister Henrietta died. She had been found with her throat cut lying on the floor of her bare room her hands clasped together in one last desperate prayer. Her soul had that day made its inevitable ascent to a Heaven that would find no reason to reject its admission, its liberator identified without any precursory investigation.

Annie had been last in line moving in haste to a lesson when she met at a doorway the Brebis galeuse being led away between two officers of the Gendarmerie. It was a momentary glance between them. A glance that could confirm friendship or fear in an instant. For Annie that glance had relinquished all her sympathy. She was sure from that one glance that the Brebis galeuse indeed wore the cloak of evil that she had been ascribed. Annie had not to this day seen her since and had heard that she had been incarcerated. Now she saw with clarity and a shock that crept through to her bones. How could she have not seen before? Elise had been that energumen. Elise had been the Brebis galeuse.

Some mornings she would awake in a start with cold wet skin when the nightmare ended, but she never saw her again. Not to speak to. For a time she sometimes caught sight of her in the town but shortly after it had been confirmed that she had moved to Spain. But Elise would not forget Annie. Neither would she forget the secret that Annie had injudiciously revealed to her one October night, the last night of their friendship.

15.

KIDAL, MALI, WEST AFRICA

It was the week that the travelling theatre artists came to town. When the sun drove its fierce heat into the dry dusty ground of that flat barren land, the theatre artists came to Kidal, that lonely desolate town deep in the heart of the northern Sahel. It was the one special week in June when life was lifted to joy by artful expression and the riotous colour of the travelling theatre. The sublime performances of mime and of comedy and music that united and excited them all and the dancing that raged in the street that went on into the early hours of sunrise under the acacia trees hung with candle lights, streamers and coloured sweets.

For Bintou Diabarte this had always been the highlight of her year. The travellers' theatre came from the south west of the country. They were the people she grew up with as a child. Her people, the dark skinned Bambara people who seemed always happy and laughing. People who did not stand in the sun pounding millet nor clean their master's soiled clothes at the river bank. These were her people from whom she had been taken, to be stripped of freedom and gladness and condemned to her life of servitude among the blue people of the desert. The nomadic Tuareg tribesmen with whom she had lived in slavery since childhood.

For many years she had dreamt of joining the theatre people on their return south. To be free among her people away from the drudgery of her servitude. Now, she had resolved that this was the week that she would escape her captivity.

Her enslavement had started as a child when she was taken by a grim young northern Tuareg who had claimed her through

some kind of feudal fidelity as his property due to her grand-
mother's death in his family's service. In a country where poverty
runs deep in many differing guises, de facto slavery is commonplace as such obscure customs can provide a convenient means
of support for the destitute. The indifference of the state provides acquiescence to such perverse rights and Bintou Diabarte
was, at just seven years of age an innocent and defenceless victim.

She had been raised serving a master not much older than herself, living with his family a nomadic life around the arid Sahel
of eastern Mali and Niger. First there were the domestic chores
of the household, washing and cleaning and then with the cooking and even the receiving of guests when they returned from
the Mosque towards midday. The preparation of flat bread, yo-
ghurt and coffee to sustain the men over which they would converse without acknowledgement or communication with the
plain young black girl who served them.

In fact the blossom of her beauty must have opened late in
her, for it was not until just after her 17th birthday that it had inspired in her master something more than the cold indifference
that had hitherto been the limit of his interest in her.

She had noticed the low studied gaze of his lust as she bent
down to feed the goats. Her long dress drawn tight into the curves
of her body as she stretched to cast the animals their feed. The
eyes that followed her lifting her dress above her knees at the
water's edge on wash day. She had wretched at the soiled under-
garments and wondered whether the ejaculation had occurred
as he looked her up and down. And when she had showered in
the low light of evening she had sensed his distant presence and
hard stare at her ebony body glistening under the thin drizzle of
water that was all she had to cleanse it.

The rape came soon after that, and it was as no surprise or
shock to her. Just the inevitable result of his growing attention.
What had shocked her was the sudden appearance of his father, the
Amghar, who had astutely read the signs that the time was right
for him too to enjoy the young body that had come of age. He
had exhausted his limbs in a frenzied fit of lust early one morn-

ing just after she woke, rolling from her body, limp and gasping for air, grappling for his clothes and gathering himself hurriedly to go to prayers.

These episodes had lasted for just a few months until it was clear that she was to bear a child. The uncertainty of parentage did not trouble her as she was unable to relate to either man. She preferred in her quiet moments to reflect on the possibility of Immaculate Conception as to contemplate the usurpation of her body was more than penance for her. It was better to believe that she had given it freely, although she knew that in reality her body had not even been hers to give. From this invasion of her young body was to be extracted the one treasure in her life. Nyeleni would be her only child. The damage of disease to her after that birth that had guaranteed her a barren future but that was of no concern nor consequence to her as she had Nyeleni, the child that was to be her life.

Nyeleni spoke no words to any human being other than her mother. She was the silent child to whom day and night appeared the same as she had the curious ability to see in the dark. This unusual feline facility was established to be due to her right eye which was coloured completely blue and radiated a reflection of green light in the dark. For Nyeleni the dark held no fear and she would often rise after nightfall and wander the black silent spaces surrounding the compound stroking the animals and feeding them small treats by way of affection.

The child enjoyed a quiet existence without education spending much of her time with the donkeys in the yard with which she enjoyed an affectionate and close relationship and which she would frequently rename in order to give the impression that her friendship group had been extended. She had favoured names that were French much to her mother's approval as it seemed to show her regard for the French lessons that she gave to her daughter. For Bintou Diabarte had resolved to speak always in French when she could be understood as that she perceived, was to be the key to her freedom and she ensured that she did so with whomever she could find when the family were in Kidal.

She collected whatever French journals she could and it was one of these that had inspired her resolve to be free. It was an article about a group named Maliberation in Bamako. A group who sought the freedom of all slaves in Mali. It was something that she had only yearned for before, not really believing it was possible and not really knowing what freedom meant. She had from that moment resolved to make her way to Bamako and contact Maliberation to declare herself free. This week she was sure to be the week that she would have the opportunity to escape this life for freedom.

It was late morning when the open flat backed truck of the theatre artists pulled away noisily from the by red earth wall by the mosque and along the dusty dirt road heading south for Bamako passing the occasional merchant with a donkey loaded with wares and the camel caravans that drifted along in slow silent steps in the fierce sun.

Bintou Diabarte held her child in a joyful embrace. She could not believe her good fortune. She had dared to escape but feared the retribution that would inevitably follow if she should be caught. If she were to be found out she would be taken back to the house and beaten for desertion. She would surely suffer her severance from Nyeleni and banished from seeing her again. That thought had been enough to dissuade her against this mission in previous years. Only now had she dared to risk life for liberty.

Now here she sat with Nyeleni among the friendly faces of the Bamana people who passed around cooled fruit to quench the thirst. Now she felt not just the warmth of camaraderie but the strength of her faith. There would surely be those here who would not allow her to be taken back. Surely God had decreed that this was her hour of freedom.

It was towards afternoon that the truck came to a halt by the shelter of a group of acacia trees. It was an opportunity to disembark. To stretch legs and to look out at the vast silent Sahel stretching far into the distance, empty save the few patches of acacia trees and grass that punctuated the red ground. Bintou Diabarte looked at her child and felt the strange feeling of solitude. For the first time in her adult life she was free to run. She could spend her time at her own pace and as she pleased. It was an overwhelming feeling that she swiftly resolved not to spend with profligacy.

As the rising heat played with the still air distorting the shapes of things in the distance she looked out at the road they had come down and she felt the pain in the pit of her stomach as she saw something she recognised traveling fast towards them. It was the battered pickup truck of her master's father, the Amghar. He was coming to reclaim them.

Her heart turned heavy at the thought. She had dreamt that she had got away and now he was almost upon them. Absurdly she thought of how they might drive past unaware that she could be part of this party but soon she knew the danger as the truck swung into the side of the road and she could make out the figures of three Tuareg men.

Led by the Amghar the three Tuaregs strode purposely towards the party dressed in their tagelmusts, the blue turbans and loose veils that kept out the desert sand. They stood in a line in front of the artists and the Amgar addressed them in French.

'The woman with the child. You have her with you. She is our property. It is the law we will take her with us.' He said sternly.

The men they addressed seemed unconcerned sitting without recognition or concern. At first she thought they may not care perhaps waving a hand in her direction and saying. 'Go on take her' but then she heard one of them say:

'She is with us we are taking her to Bamako. She stays with us.' It was a bold response.

The Tuaregs moved uneasily as if to anticipate a confrontation. She saw them look at each other uncertainly as if unsure how to respond. She knew that they were not young men, the Amghar was in his early fifties while his companions were not much less. Surely they would not start a fight, they were outnumbered by younger men. Bintou Diabarte's heart pounded as she watched the slow dialog that would decide her fate.

Then the deciding card was drawn. From under his blue robe the Amghar drew a gun.

'We will take the child now. She is my daughter.' he said.

There was a cold authority in his voice. It was a confidence that had the strength that emanated from truth and there was the gun he held in his hand to support that truth. There would be no denying his right to take his own daughter. The artists stood to one side and beckoned to the shaded spot where Nyeleni was sleeping. The Amghar stooped uneasily to pick up the child and held her to his chest as he would a possession, devoid of affection. Bintou Diabarte froze in terror as she watched on. They were taking her child in the knowledge that she would not wish to be parted from her. That she would return to them like a scalded dog eager to please her master. She would be made to pay for her desertion and there would never again be the opportunity to flee.

She trembled as she watched Nyeleni taken away. There was a desperation she had never felt before. Was freedom worthwhile she asked herself. Momentarily she reached for the comfort of certainty, the security of servitude, the knowledge that while she was of value she was safe. She saw the truck drive away, her hand to her mouth biting at her fingers in cold distress. Then she let out a wail of pain and anger. They had taken her away. They had taken her Nyeleni.

'We could do nothing' explained the short dark man with wide eyes who now stood at her side.

'She was his daughter. He is allowed to take her. But he won't harm her will he' He added attempting to comfort her and re-assure himself.

When the heat passed and theatre people moved on Bintou Diabarte was not among them. Uncertain what to do she remained there by the roadside her grief countering her resolve. Should she go back and confront the Tuaregs and to take her daughter? Perhaps she should travel to Bamako to see the people at Maliberation first and enlist their help. She felt the torment of indecision.

Dark came upon the Sahel like a silent shroud and the cold under the empty sky was sudden. She tried to sleep but her troubled mind distracted it. Then as light began to break in the early hours of morning she found herself waking from a slumber under an acacia tree still unsure what route she was to take.

Sometimes, as if by some deep mystery a tough decision is set aside as if it has been decided for one by some divine intervention. It was almost before she could compose her thoughts to decide her next move that she found it decided for her. For there, riding towards her down the road alone on a small donkey was her child Nyeleni. Bintou Diabarte could not contain her joy she ran forward to embrace her child but found herself instead on her knees thanking God for the child's return.

The child had escaped from the camp at night leaving her bedclothes in a manner that suggested that she was still among them. She had recruited the assistance of one of her donkeys to ride south in the pitch dark to meet her mother. Her absence would by now be discovered and it was essential that they could hide themselves away somewhere perhaps until nightfall and travel on in darkness. She looked nervously along the road but could see no movement. She was sure however that they would come and that day she Nyeleni and the donkey walked south to freedom.

A day had passed when Bintou Diabarte looked to the horizon as the sun set in the western sky. At first she thought that the cloud of dust was part of that sunset but then she could see the movement of shadows within it moving rapidly toward her. Her fear grew as she began to count them and stopped when she got to five. Horsemen riding fast towards her. She knew that they would certainly be bandits and although she had nothing for them to take from her she understood that in the Sahel the value of her and her child was quickly earned from their sale as slaves to one of the nomadic tribes who passed these barren lands. It would be a race between their inevitable encounter and the arrival of darkness.

Bintou Diabarte did her best to conceal the three fugitives within a small thorn bush and prayed that the riders pass. The wait seemed eternal until she could not prevent herself looking out again toward the western horizon. It was then she saw it. The dust she had thought to be thrown up by the riders was now wide across the sky and was rolling towards her a dense cloud of sand, grey against an evening sky that hung above it lit by the last rays of the sun. She watched the shadows of the riders circling in disarray, caught by the sand storm. They had been saved by God's own hand and as darkness fell their escape was made.

It was the following day when she saw again the same dirty white truck turning up the dust along the road around midday. The truck she knew to be that of the Amgar who she knew to be searching for her and their child. There was something less threatening about the truck today. It was travelling more slowly as if wounded by the rough track. It was almost as if its occupants had given up their search believing her to have escaped and at last she saw the vehicle turn and head back north.

They moved by night and hid by day snatching their broken sleep in what shade they could find by the roadside. The week of travel south to Bamako was hard, it was the road to freedom and for Bintou Diabarte the road to freedom was the hardest road to travel.

They relied on the generosity of strangers for scraps of food always aware of the chance of an informant as there were many who would seize the opportunity of returning her to her northern masters for a suitable recompense. Then, as they neared the green undulating land around Bamako their spirits lifted. Now she was sure that she had had her last sight of the Amghar and that her life of servitude was over.

Bintou Diabarte had kept the page of the article about Maliberation although she knew the address off by heart. It would not be long now until they were in safety among the anti-slavery people who would give them food shelter and perhaps a little money to make their start in a new life.

Bamako is a city of two million people straddling each side of the river Niger. It is a city growing through the prosperity brought by trade and manufacture and the influx of Mali's rural population to the cotton industry. It is an ancient settlement of Islamic scholarship and learning and of trade and it has about it an energy from which Bintou Diabarte smelt the sweet scent of freedom.

It had been a long journey from Kidal to Bamako. The Maliberation address was close to the city centre by the artisanal zone and Bintou Diabarte and Nyeleni would find their way there through bustling streets such as she had never seen before. Stalls with women selling tomatoes and fruit. Craft works with large earthenware pots surrounding their doors and metal workers weaving coils of steel wire into shapes she could not determine.

She walked along by the roadway avoiding the seething mass of sotrama, taxis that moved skilfully among the pedestrians carrying their prosperous passengers between business engagements that she would never understand.

The address took her to a heavy wooden door via a stone archway that led into a small yard where leather was being fashioned into goods that she assumed to be shoes. Above a heavy wooden door she read the single word painted on a faded sign, Maliberation. Bintou Diabarte looked at the door in disconsolation. The building was clearly deserted.

'They gone some six months ago' she heard from behind her. It was the neighbour.

'They was the French women, Maliberation. Went back home. Family business, new grandchild I think it were.'

Bintou Diabarte stood in silence and looked at her child. She had been hoping for some guidance, some assistance perhaps. The abolition of slavery was clearly not important enough for these foreign women. They had their homes to go to. Their own families. Their own problems. Now Bintou Diabarte would have to find her own freedom.

They spent some five days in Bamako and they turned out to be five days of energetic preparation. The chance sale of that donkey had blessed them with a small amount of money, and Bintou Diabarte had heard of a way that she could escape the retribution of her northern masters and find safety in a foreign land.

It was the third day she spent in Bamako that she met the fortune teller by the vegetable market.

'My child, there is your future in this picture book and I have seen it' she had shouted out to her as she had passed. Bintou

Diabarte had reached for her money as she had seen how it was a necessary part of every transaction.

'There is no price to pay to me' the old lady confirmed as she spread the tarot cards upon the fruit box before her that served her as a small table.

'For these cards implore you to listen to the words they whisper.'

'You will find happiness in Europe for your child. There is nothing here for her but misery and servitude. The world waits for your child in Europe. She will achieve greatness there.' The old woman looked at her kindly.

'It is the will of God' she added as if to dispel any doubt.

'You must travel north now to the sea. It will be hard but you must go to what your child has been born for.' She smiled courteously in a way that conveyed wisdom rather than friendship. Her wrinkled black face torn to contortion by her years under the fierce sun.

Bintou Diabarte had led a life without kindness and counsel. It was for that reason that such advice bore for her significance beyond what it may have done for others. It was for her as if a direction had indeed been given from God.

That night as she slept beneath the stars of Amancar, the constellation they call the warrior of the desert, holding Nyeleni close to her breast, she felt a strength, a comfort that was new to her. For innocence is prey to the reckless certainty of promise. It was the strength and comfort of optimism, the feeling that freedom would release her from her bondage and the expectation of opportunities for Nyeleni that drove her now.

She smiled as she heard the busy bustle around her that would continue into the night. Sounds of energy and optimism way beyond the sounds of the caravanserai that break the bleak silence of the western desert. Of animals coughing in the cold of morning, of travellers voices heard through the stillness that grips the hollow air of evening. Here was the hubbub of the city. The sound of freedom. This she imagined would be something like Europe. A word that held a hope for her that now became a dream and tomorrow she would begin her journey north to the sea that would take her there.

16.

AVIGNON, FRANCE

Work on the Chapel restoration was proceeding well. Much of the preconstruction efforts were spent in ensuring the identification and dating that of historic value. A process necessary to plan its incorporation into the refurbished structure the history of which it had been decreed, would be as visible as possible to visitors. Construction in such circumstances can be discontinuous but now Marcus could see real and gratifying progress as his plans took shape.

Father Fidel Rocher was a frequent visitor to the site. His interest in the chapel had been secured by the discovery of what had appeared to be an old relic. A diary of a nun had been discovered five years prior to Marcus's arrival. She had almost certainly stayed in accommodation above the Chapel sometime in the past, indeed the last entry in the diary was over 50 years ago and it was thereby credible to assume that she had moved away, or perhaps passed away that year.

It was perhaps the possibility of further finds that drew the old priest to the site of the renovation, and he appeared one morning with a look that gave Marcus the impression that he was about to explain more his interest in the chapel.

'It was here in this Chapel that a discovery was made some years ago.' He began casually. There are those who hope that some further discovery may be made from within these walls.' He announced as if to disown any such interest on his own part. Then after a pause he said.

'It is something that interests me.' As if reflecting on the implausibility of his disinterest.

'It was the diary of Sister Beatrice who wrote how she witnessed a revelation of the Holy Mother when she was a young oblate in Aix n Bearn. These things always fascinate those who search not for truth but for conspiracy my friend.' He laughed to disguise his fascination in the matter.

There was however something about this revelation that cannot easily be dismissed. It was St Bernard who declared the Holy mother a mediator between man and God. It seems that revelations such as these might be her way of communicating the word of God.

This revelation like others in the past was just part of a whole. The first edition so to speak. It is not well known that just 36 years ago the second edition of the revelation was reported to the church at St Therese L'Enfant a village in the Pyrenees almost exactly 100 years after the first. It referred to that first revelation described in the diary. The intriguing thing about it is that the diary was at that time undiscovered. So the children to whom the second revelation was made could not possibly know of the first revelation to Sister Beatrice.' The old friar furrowed his brow looking puzzled at this as if to invite Marcus to provide an answer.

'That sounds fascinating.' Marcus responded continuing with the task of labelling his paperwork but appearing less than fascinated himself.

'Though I rather think that you were right first time. These things are of more interest to those who seek conspiracy theories.'

The old priest looked as if he was to add something more.

'Well there is one interesting part. The diary shows the Beatrice revelation talk of a second revelation to come and also the second revelation refers to the first revelation one hundred years earlier.' he went on enthusiastically.

'There was in each, a part of a secret prayer that offered protection to those who would put the two parts together'

'And what did that say?' Marcus enquired.

'Oh no one knows that detail. That has been kept quiet by those who need to know, but it is generally thought that the two revelations go together just as the prayer is two parts of a whole.'

'Presumably then' Marcus replied thoughtfully.

'Both revelations must be true as they sort of, well prove each other.'

'Oh certainly my friend. Why certainly they are true.' Father Fidel Rocher exclaimed with a relief that his friend had come to that conclusion as he clearly wished to believe the two Marian revelations to be true, and he was grateful for an affirmation endorsed by Marcus's lay logic.

'So these two revelations add up to something? But we don't know what.' Marcus suggested.

'Well not exactly.' Father Fidel Rocher confirmed unable to hide his excitement.

'Mankind is being warned of something terrible to come. It is God's way of telling us what is to come.'

The notion sounded a little improbable to Marcus but he could see some interest in the fact that two revelations had occurred, they confirmed each other and were unknown to the recipients of the other. Both had apparently been similar and the notion of a secret prayer seemed interesting in itself. Interesting enough for Marcus to refuse to dismiss this altogether.

'I imagine' continued the old priest enthusiastically wishing to furnish further detail.

'That the secret prayer was a series of quatrains.'

'Quatrains' Marcus questioned.

'You have I am sure heard of the mystic Nostradamus.' The old priest began to explain.

'He was actually an apothecary in St Remy de Provence and I am not certain whether he was a good one at that, but he is thought to have used hallucination as a means of divination. He produced his prophesies in an interesting manner, as Quatrains, you are familiar I am sure with quatrains my friend, four sentences put together like a little rhyme. I suppose that at that time, without the written word, it was easy for people to remember them that way. He produced a large number of these over the years and it is well known that there are many people who care to believe that any event that happens in the world has been predicted by him. What is interesting is that one of the Quatrains coincides with the Beatrice prophesy.

The mighty rock will pour forth a new red rage. This shall be the signum of a new evil the last line of a Quatrain of Nostradamus it is generally agreed the mighty rock almost certainly refers to Vesuvius.'

'In fact' He continued. 'The revelation given to Sister Beatrice in 1882 referred to a number of calamities that were to befall the world. It spoke of a volcanic eruption, a date that coincides with one in the more recent revelation and the rise of an Antichrist. It says that this Antichrist would place his servant to wear the fisherman's ring.'

'The fisherman's ring?' Marcus enquired with uncertainty.

'Why yes.' Confirmed the old priest.

'The Holy Father wears the fisherman's ring my friend. Every new Pope will have it newly minted for him. Imagine if some force of evil were to control the very church itself, to command the beliefs of its followers and the sanctity of its word. Oh and there was something else, something about his seizing the Holy Roman Empire.' He added as if unsure of the precise words.

'You don't believe it Father but you would like to be able to explain it. Is that what you mean?' Marcus asked generously of the old priest.

'Why yes exactly.' The old Friar exclaimed glad to be attributed a sound and logical reason for his interest in the matter.

'It would be most gratifying to have an explanation.'

'You say that the revelation at St Therese L'Enfant was made to children. They must now be adults. What do they say about event now?' Marcus asked.

'Well, it appears two died shortly after the revelations as had been predicted and just as had happened after the first revelation, as predicted by that revelation and the third child, we just don't know what happened to her. They say she was taken away by her parents to avoid the potential of enquiry on her young mind. I don't believe even those in the church know of her whereabouts.'

'I have to admit that I am not one to want to believe in prophesies Father. I would however be interested to see the diary and to see exactly what it says.' Marcus invited, hearing the interest the old priest had tried in vain to disguise.

'Well I can show it to you yes. It is kept securely of course but there is one thing I overlooked.'

Marcus looked up at the old priest as if something significant were about to be disclosed.

'It is of course written in Occitan. You will not be able to read the original.' The old priest smiled widely before adding.

'But I have translated it.'

Marcus smiled back at him. He had not thought that it would of course be incomprehensible to him if it were written in anything other than the most modern French, but it amused him to think that Father Fidel Rocher had taken the trouble to translate the work not withstanding his doubts about its content. He admired the old priest's facility for languages but more his determination to translate a work he considered only of interest to conspiracy theorists.

'I shall then, be very interested to see the diary and your translation.' He confirmed.

Later in the day Marcus had almost forgotten his conversation with the old friar and was therefore surprised to have been visited by Father Fidel Rocher that evening such that at first he wondered what the nature of his visit could be.

'I have them here.' Announced the old priest with satisfaction.

Father Fidel Rocher produced a battered leather bound book together with two transcripts. They were of each of the revelations written in his own hand.

'You see, they may not be complete but this is what I understand them to say.' He started with excitement.

First he spread out the diary and its translation. Marcus quickly appreciated that the original would be of little use to him nor indeed most people. Even the handwriting was difficult to decipher let alone the words themselves. It was clear to him that it must have taken some time for Father Fidel Rocher to complete his translation of the work. It then occurred to him that he was reading it in English. Father Fidel Rocher had taken the trouble of translating his French script for the benefit of his friend.

He read it out aloud:

'There will come a time soon when two of you will join me in Heaven. That time will be the day on which the Antichrist took the Western Schism. And there will be a thunderous eruption south of the eternal city that will announce the coming of the Antichrist. He will place his servant in the Holy church to wear the fisherman's ring and he will seize for himself the Holy roman empire from which he will rule the world with wisdom of lies. By his cursed divination he will know that coming and from the blue people will come the blue eyed child to show the way to freedom. I will give you now the first part of a secret payer that you must recite only to God for when it is recited it will bring harmony and where it is written it will bring protection. I will come again in one hundred years to warn of these again.'

'My goodness' Marcus remarked uncertain as to quite how to respond.

'The Antichrist who took the Western Schism is generally agreed to be Robert de Genevre' Father Fidel Rocher added anxious to fill in the detail. 'He took the western schism on the 20th of September 1378 and it is reported that two of the young children who received the revelation died on the 20th of September later the year they received it …

… The second translation is what I understand it to be from my enquiries, though no one knows exactly.' He went on excitedly.

Marcus turned to the second translation. This time it was a translation provided by Father Fidel Rocher from the French version.

'I have come to you now 100 years from when I came before. First I must tell you that two of you will soon join me in Heaven. The day will be the same as that when the papal state lost its temporal powers in Europe. Again that is the same date you understand. The 20th of September' He added enthusiastically.

'The volcano will announce the coming of the antichrist who will place his servant in the Holy see to take its power and take for himself the Holy Roman Empire from which he will conquer the world but not by war but by wealth. That wealth will create misery and destitution but for the few who shall reign with untold riches across every part of the earth.'

Father Fidel Rocher looked at Marcus his eyes bright with enthusiasm.

'You see the dates referred to are the same. The date when the Antichrist took the western schism is the same as the Risorgimento. The 20th September. No one believes that the children who witnessed these revelations would have known that.' He looked at Marcus as if for confirmation of his believe in the revelations and added.

'She went on to give the second part of the secret prayer which she confirmed gave protection to those who possessed it written.

These predictions relate my friend to what many Christians believe to be the second coming of Christ. It is said that the antichrist will reign before that epiphany. He will comfort mankind with wisdom of lies untruths that are told to deceive us and bring contentment to the oppressed for his own advantage.

It is said that the English physicist Sir Isaac Newton accurately predicted by mathematics and biblical interpretation the date for the return of the Jewish people to Israel. He suggested that this return would herald the end of the world and that the world will end in 2060. Given that the second coming is widely thought to be preceded by the Antichrist is likely that we are coming to a point where these events are about to take place.'

Marcus looked at the old priest quizzically.

'Newton was a scientist. Surely science does not align with religion.' He suggested.

'On the contrary. Science can only be created by those who are imbued with the aspiration toward truth and understanding' The old priest confirmed as if reciting the words. These are the words of Einstein my friend. We should not contradict such a mind.

He said that 'science without religion is lame. Religion without science is blind' These words are so true my friend. It is science that will reveal the sign of the return of the antichrist. The eruption of the volcano that has long been predicted to herald that coming. It is the ambition of the antichrist to seize the power of the economic entity that rules the Holy roman empire. At the same time he will control the church that is sworn to silence for the confessions of mankind and offers forgiveness for their sins.'

'Though surely' Marcus started.

'Surely real power is in the hands of politicians?'

'Power derives from the currency of wealth and from the mystery of belief. It pays little tribute to the posturing of politicians. They will weaken and wither with fate and are but ephemeral in time's eye. Power and secrecy are the enemies of freedom, and they are bound together like brothers sworn to vengeance.'

Marcus knew something of the cult of the virgin. He recalled that several cathedrals in France are dedicated to the Holy mother. He recalled his visit to the magnificent cathedral at Chartres during his time studying theology at Oxford. It is the cathedral of the virgin more than any other as it is Chartres where the most famous relic of the virgin has survived. The tunic she wore at the annunciation. It has been said that the relic has been responsible for many miracles and Chartres influenced the spread of the cult of the virgin within Christianity.

The Cathedral is described in architectural terms as a bridge between two styles. The Romanesque and the Gothic. It is the bridge between the Romanesque artistic towers on the west front and Gothic order of the new church with its clusters of columns supporting the huge pointed arches and ceilings under the ribbed vaults that make the stone appear weightless and its spaces spiritual. Perhaps Marcus thought, the Virgin is the bridge between the spirits of man and God. It would certainly be wrong to dismiss the notion of Marian revelations, especially in a country where the virgin is such an important part of man's relationship with God.

It was dwelling on that architecture that suddenly brought a thought to his mind. He had provided Emma Dreyfus with some samples of wall panelling for dating and matching. Some of the panelling had a peculiar feature. The carving of eyes on the rail and Emma had commented on one of these eyes which had been painted blue with an inscription 'memento minima maxima sunt' Could this, he thought, be some sort of reference to the blue-eyed child mentioned in the revelation? Perhaps it could even have been Sister Beatrice who had painted and carved this for posterity.

Marcus found that his doubts regarding the prophesies dismissed so unconvincingly by Father Fidel Rocher were receding. Indeed as the days went by he began more and more to think of what Father Fidel Rocher had told him and to believe that the revelations did indeed hold a truth. A truth that was waiting to be discovered.

17.

AVIGNON, FRANCE

It was a bright summer morning. A clear blue sky invited the spirit to carefree optimism and the mind to restrict itself to absorbing only those less demanding and unchallenging tasks. Marcus worked alone at the old desk by the window of the cottage sifting through and selecting a number of designs for panelling the walls to the lobby of the chapel building.

His mind was not concentrating on the task before him. It was preoccupied by something it found difficult to resolve. He had seen a delightful young woman dressed with the flair and sophistication of a Parisienne. She had intelligence, charm, a chic and panache. She dressed in the most elegant manner spoke fluent English, Italian as well as her own French, was astoundingly beautiful and yet she had rallied round the ruse of portraying an assassin, a putain, dressed in the cloak of a Cardinal. A role that to his mind demeaned and ridiculed her.

Now he had witnessed her naked lust before him in his sitting room, there was an uncertainty in his mind. Should he judge her by his own conventions or should he admit his shortcomings and embrace her creativity and her willingness to disregard the femininity and beauty that were gifted her and use her body with expediency to satisfy her carnal lusts.

He had planned to take her with him to her mother's resting place but now felt an apprehension. Would it mean anything to her at all? What feelings might she have? His were hardly driven by contrition. He had never visited the cemetery before and only planned to do so because he was here in Avignon. It was more a matter of closure for him. For her it may well be meaningless. Besides he did not know whether she had been before. Or even frequently. He decided that this was a personal visit. One he should make alone, indeed perhaps it was one that could be put off for the time being.

He had almost convinced himself that he should in some way confront Segolene. That he should set out his concerns. She had not had the direction of parents she might appreciate the guidance he might give to her. Again he dismissed this. What he had found in her that was perhaps to his distaste was only a small part of the whole. She was after all delightful, beautiful and accomplished. His mind had been taken with this debate for too long. It was time to set his concerns to one side.

That evening Marcus found himself in the company again of Father Fidel Rocher outside the Café Zizi Jeanmaire. He was attempting to translate the inscription above the door and at last he felt he had done so. Of course he suddenly recognised, they called the café 'The dancer' because Zizi Jeanmaire was a dancer and its walls were filled with pictures of dancers. Impressionist paintings by Degas and more modern photographs of ballet and contemporary dance. Yes he had it now. It read,

'We should consider every day lost that we have not danced.'

He turned to the old priest who sat beside him. Somehow he did not deem it appropriate to inform him of the scene he had witnessed on the sitting room floor. He had tried to tell himself that he should accept her boisterous energies and that her willingness to portray herself as something opposite to herself was somehow creditable but he had failed to do so. It did not cross his mind that her proclivities might portray her more accurately than the softer vision of her that had become embedded in his mind.

'Father Rocher' he ventured wishing to seek the counsel of the old priest.

'Do you believe we should be free to follow each one of our preferences to exact our desires?'

The old man smiled glad to have been posed the question.

'Our lives are not our own. We are prisoners of our culture our prejudices and our time. We follow the path that fate has cut out for us.' He answered.

'Sometimes that path will divide and sometimes we will reach a crossroads. Sometimes that path is paved and sometimes it is strewn with obstacles to block our progress. But all paths lead to certainty and there is no turning back.

Man is born to see this world as black and white. Of good and evil. He sees virtue in beauty and villainy in ugliness. He thinks within the limits of his knowledge and dares not to comprehend what he does not see. He praises celebrity and fortune and derides wisdom and endeavour. Celebrity and fortune are idols fashioned by the hands of fools. We know that they mean nothing in times great plan.

Truth is shrouded in a grey mist that hides its face and moves on the wind like a leaf, transient, fickle, impetuous just as the beautiful young girl the youth has put his faith in. But she is surrounded by so many suitors, she is uncertain to which one to submit herself.' Father Fidel Rocher lifted his gaze to him, his face lit with the small mischievous smile that finished his observation almost as if he was aware of the incident that had preoccupied Marcus.

'By doubting, we come to question and by questioning we come to truth but truth is the disloyal mistress who will desert you my friend, just when you are sure you believe in her.'

Perhaps it was the reference to suitors that made him think of Luc. The handsome friend that Segolene had introduced him to. He remembered the email he had folded and placed in his pocket just as he left the cottage. It was from Emma Dreyfus answering his enquiry as to the identity of the tattoo on Luc's arm. The picture of an Angel slaying something with a sword on the ground. It seemed possible that it could explain something more about Luc, Segolene's silent handsome friend who seemed so willing to share his lover.

Marcus could not empathise with those who saw any attraction in bearing tattoos. He was unlikely to understand why Luc should wear this image. It could be however that he belonged to some religious sect and that he was somehow obliged to wear it. That Marcus rationalised, would be acceptable.

Casually he unfolded the sheet of paper and read the message from Emma Dreyfus. It confirmed the tattoo to depict St Michael the Archangel slaying Satan but it was not quite as he had imagined. It was not only an image used by the church but one that infamously represented another quite different organisation. With a jolt he read again Emma's message in front of him, now with a cold dread.

'This sign is the mark of an Italian Mafia known, as the Ndrangheta.'

18.

SARORIO, CALABRIA, ITALY

As a small neatly dressed man left the fruit store by the Via delle duo Chiesa, he paused to turn and look towards the sea. He was standing by the small lemon grove he had known as a child. It was as unchanged by time as the lemons themselves, still the finest. The rich people of the North had always sought those lemons.

Scalfero recalled how as boys they would steal them to sell to tourists and suffer the occasional beating for their troubles. The distractions and imprecations of early adulthood suffered heavy reprimand from those of the order to whom dignity and obedience were the foundations upon which its continuance depended. It had sometimes felt as if an inquisition had been established for the discovery and extirpation of heresy.

He had gone from fruit vendor to the vendor of ecclesiastical relics of remote authenticity. The experience had an enlightening effect on him for he had found that the wearing of the cloth promoted a greater success in this simony that augmented the sales of his indulgencies. It was this early revelation as to the potential of deception and the willingness of the righteous to be deceived, that had opened his eyes to his future. He would live his life the actor. He would be who people expected him to be. He would play the leading role in his life and he would take charge of his own direction.

As a young man he worked as Picciotti d'onore, persuading shop owners as to the merits of insurance for their businesses. He took pleasure in seeing those businesses thrive with the growth of tourism and the protection of the Onorata Societa, his customers were content, his sanction rarely brought to bear.

Those were days of certainty. He worked to instructions. Life had been straight forward then but now age imposed the burden of responsibility, and with responsibility a harsher imposition of conformity. The brutal extinguishment of opposition or failure that bought instant resolution and earned him the fear and respect his position required.

Through narrow eyes he gazed out across the blue bay his lean figure cooled by the soft breeze that blew in from the west. He wore the burden of his mandate with a quiet and respected authority. His dark suit, plain shirt and patterned tie the modest dress of conformity. His dark hair now thinning and receding from his brow was brushed back over his head in an uncontrived manner and his tanned face was lined with age beyond his years.

For him there had been no offers, no opening. No mentor to look out for him. No Alma Mater to look back on. Only the tortured hand of fate that had reached out for his kiss. He had ridden the cycle of change and felt the turn of its wheels. The times of blessing, the times of judgement. He had played the cold card of vengeance and felt the widow's bitter reproach. His had been the routine of monastic rigor. The self-denial. The dread of perdition. He had lived under the code all his life. The code of consensual silence borne of the bond of consanguinity and raised under the blessing of the Archangel to bare the sword of judgement.

When he spoke his words were never contradicted, but he had been inclined to admonition rather than the ruthless disciplines that his sanction allowed. He bore few hallmarks of wealth or position. Only the large gold ring on his finger that bore the engraving of the Archangel, the one trinket that confirmed him as the Mammasantissima.

Now there was to be a new path to follow. The success of his endeavours would allow him to stand apart from his order and build an empire without recourse or observance other than that dictated by him. He had learned that the winner of all wars is the side more committed to ruthlessness. The player without conscience nor pity who will not only destroy his enemies but disregard the bystanders to achieve his ends. He had learned that in the end violence and immorality are rewarded by positions of power and that repentance earns forgiveness from those too weak to begrudge. A new order based in the eternal city itself and with powers both temporal and spiritual. The power and sanction of life or of death.

Scalfero had lost the family he could have called his own. Now the conscript of celibacy had made its barren bed in the house of his calling. Fifteen years had passed since Elise had died, gunned down in a fire fight with the Guardia Seville in Bilbao. Their union had yielded one daughter. A child with Elise's temperament. A wild angry child who he had become convinced was beyond sanity and whom he had committed to a lunatic asylum outside the Guardia Piemontese. He had not sought to see her since then. He had told himself, there was no time for love in this bitter world, and he had not had the time nor the inclination to bear the burden of her disability.

He drew satisfaction from Elise's memory. She had been a French girl from the Basque country who had moved across the border to Spain following some years in Avignon. They had met during the years that his order was working with Euskadi Ta Askatasuna in the supply of small arms. It had been a time of great excitement. She was the most angry and resentful young woman he had ever encountered. Clever, animated, her huge spirit and endless energy had craved action and her confused politics led her efforts to overthrow the state for any reason that presented itself. She died a hero's death working for Basque freedom. The last words of resistance uttered from her lips were those of the Pasionaria.

"Il vaut mieux mourir debout que de vivre a genoux."

What he treasured above all was what Elise had confided to him that had the power to change his life. Something that had confirmed his resolution to instigate what he was to call his 'grand plan'. It was some years ago that Monsigneur Dominic Dufour, a cleric who was stipendiary to the order, had told him of a Marian revelation reported to him by a priest in a small village in the Pyrenees. It contained the second part of a secret prayer that offered power to those who spoke it and protection to those who wrote it.

He had often thought of that sacred secret. What if he could own that prayer? Then one day Elise had told him of the revelation to Annie her childhood friend from her years in Avignon. Annie who had confided to her friend the secret of the revelation that she had had made to her at St Therese L'Enfant and the second part of the prayer.

It had excited him as he knew that even the Holy See did not have the full revelation as Monseigneur Dominic Dufour had not been so unwise as to reveal it to them in full. He, Scalfero, had been blessed with the coincidence of hearing it. It was clear to him then that he must now use the segreto to be in a position to take advantage of its eventuation. It is that which he now planned for.

Elise had assured him that she alone had been afforded the privilege of hearing the revelation from Annie who had been under some pressure to measure up to some secrets she herself had been revealing at that time, and that no other person would have heard it. Not even her mother. It had been prudent then to see to it that the possibility of further indiscretion was extinguished. A traffic accident had been arranged close to Annie's parents' home which had resulted in the necessary confirmation that no further revelation was possible, but he had heard that Annie's husband an English Architect, had recently arrived in Avignon to work on the very chapel in which an earlier version of the revelation had been discovered. This could not be coincidence. It had to be that this Architect had been told of the revelation and was seeking the first part of the secret prayer. He had dispatched Luc to find out what he knew and to report any further discovery.

Scalfero was convinced that soon the time would come for great works. It would be the time to put in motion the plans that would realise the ambition that had excited his mind for so many years. The events he had planned and prepared for. An audacious plan that would see him take control of an empire once the most powerful on earth.

19.

BATH, ONTARIO, CANADA

It was a good day to have been born. A good day to rise early and wash in cold water in the small cubicle in the shared cell. A good day to pull on the hi visibility suit that never fitted. A good day to stand in that breakfast queue among the sodden smells, the howls of complaint, the pushing and jostling and suspicious eyes, and a good day to look out of the window to wish for the pale sun's promise and the fresh open air. It was a good day for all this, because it was the last day of all this. The last day of a ten year stretch at Millhaven maximum security prison. It was the day of his release.

One always hopes for the sinner's redemption. Prison as a deterrent, the endurance of which promotes the recognition of moral and ethical deficiency. A time for reflection that incites the mind to change. To seek the pursuit of goodness and to resign evil.

Perhaps Jacopo was in a better position than others to make the change. His brother Father Simeon was a priest back in San Luca in Italy. The land of Jacopo's birth and where he lived until coming to Canada in his late twenties. Strange, a hood in Toronto with a brother who is a priest in Italy. Jacopo had devoted himself to the church for his past 12 months in prison since Father Simeon visited him for the first time, and he had worked well in his duties at Corcan themselves a privilege only for those in putative reform.

He had almost become the prison authority on Catholicism. Attending prison mass and reading whatever he could. He had dressed the walls on his side of the cell with pictures of the Pope and of the Virgin Mary.

'Next you'll be takin' confession' They humoured. The sinner had come to God.

'You know what he's in for?' The surly prison guard asked his colleague.

'He's was with the Mafia. Running drugs and guns that kinda thing.'

'Can't believe it can you. Swapped guns for God'

The guards laughed a cynical laugh. Guns meant more to them than God. There was no mercy for the meek. No second chances for those who did not grasp the gambit. They knew. They stood in stewardship every day. They saw the wretched debris of mankind, the residue of the Homo Sapien. The scoria of humanity. No God could resurrect goodness from this evil. No God could mend bones beaten by daily drudgery, nor clean fallen souls soiled by fear and ignominy. It was the way of the world. The undeniable truth.

Cometh the day, cometh the hour. The last order of his sentence and the first delivered with a smile.

'It's your time Jacopo. Get your things together and we'll go down and get you signed out.' As casual as that.

'God needs you more than we do here' a laugh followed the cynical taunt.

Jacopo remembered that Father Simeon had bought fresh clothes for his release. A suit, shirt and shoes. Smart stuff to meet the world with respectability and assurance. The warden passed over to him the three stylish carrier bags that contained them.

'Looks like you'll be meeting some lady dressed up like that. Here take a few loonies. That's on us boy. It'll buy you a bath a beer and a bus fare.' The warden laughed at his joke. He had probably laughed at that joke many times before. Jacopo signed the release form.

'That's that boy. You're on your way.'

It was almost midday as Jacopo took in a breath of the clean air outside the prison walls. Freedom championed opportunity. Without freedom there was only servitude. He had spent 10 years in servitude and it had taught him the value of freedom. He had longed for this day but all the more since his visit from Father Simeon. With him had come the opportunity to change his life. He would go back now to the land of his birth to fulfil the role which had been ordained for him ever since Father Simeon's visit. His brother, who had recommended him and made his new vocation possible. His brother, the priest from San Luca. The youth from his boyhood who would never steal or injure. Who would study and help his mother. The one with compassion. The one they all had always admired and respected. Soon Father Simeon would revere Jacopo and kiss his hand.

The black Lincoln saloon crossed the Canadian border to the states at 100 islands bridge and sped along the Interstate 81 towards Syracuse. It was a fine journey, as Jacopo sat back in the lush leather seat feeling good saying little, looking out at the sky the freshly greened trees the free world. Relaxed he opened the brown paper parcel lying on the seat beside him and studied its contents. Passport, a recent photograph of him with collar and tie. Something he had not worn for ten years. He chuckled. A flight ticket from Newark to Gatwick England and a second ticket from Gatwick to Leonardo da Vinci Rome. A wad of United States Dollars and a further wad of something that looked like monopoly money.

'Euros?' He gasped. Hey. It was all the same to him he reflected. So long as it was legal tender he mused. Well, not so much legal. What did that matter. He smiled at his thought.

Wrapped in a small envelope on which was written the number 920 was a locker key. Jacopo rolled the small key in his hand and memorised the number. It would be as well to know where to get a gun and ammunition when he got to Rome.

The call of the cloth could be more compelling than the call of a woman. It is the promise of the Eternal life to he who might capitulate not the ephemeral carnal pleasure that follows the invitation from a woman's lips. Jacopo revelled in the authority and licence that would be attached to his calling. The adulation of a kneeling congregation. Souls stripped bare to beg his forgiveness. The sycophants flattery. The widow's trust. And the unquestioning faith of the feckless that had sickened him as a child. This was the call that moved him to his groin.

He had slept the journey east across the Atlantic waking to the sight of English countryside passing swiftly below him. It was much greener and more open than he had imagined. Fewer roads and towns on this small island, less buildings, more trees and fields. Its beauty enthralled him. Another country he had never been to. Another world he had never known. Another life was down there, a life of innocent endeavour. Of comfort and conformity, a protected pastoral existence secure without apprehension or unease. It was the land of aspiration. England.

It was a budget airline from Gatwick to Leonardo da Vinci. The airport busy and well organised, the flight prompt and efficient with all the courtesies and a captain who spoke good Italian. Jacopo had surveyed his fellow passengers noting their characteristics following their exchanges and guessing their identities as anyone might often do when travelling alone. Would any of them remember his face when it became the most famous in the world? It had been a long journey but a relaxed one. Hey. He thought with satisfied grimace. Better spending time here than doing time there.

As he walked along the platform at Termini he was smiling the smile of a returning hero, wearing the laurels of a legionnaire. The sun was a welcome warmth on his face and he decided to walk to the Piazza Barberini where they had booked his hotel room. Challenged by hopeful cabbies as he strode along the Via Giovanni north towards Repubblica he felt the exhilaration of freedom, heard the language of his youth, smelt the city in its bustling and frenetic energy saw the beauty of its buildings. Here, in the Eternal city he would live like an Emperor.

The cell phone rung in his pocket.

'Prego' He answered instinctively.

'I understand that you have arrived. Go straight to Bernini and book into your room. I will meet with you there tomorrow morning. We have much to arrange.' The voice was clear, the message brief. This was to be no ordinary meeting.

The dining room of the Hotel Bernini in the Piazza Barberini gives a view over the eternal city to the Vatican and the hills beyond. Scalfero was looking out for a man who had arrived from Canada to take on a special task for him. It was the task of deception that he had known as a boy. The work of the imposter. Scalfero had seen how the cleric's word is trusted in the minds of the faithful. The cloth that makes the perfect cloak for deception.

As he sat at his table alone, watching the door he became aware of someone at his shoulder. The man was looking at the ring he wore or his right hand. Then, he looked into his eyes as he turned to him.

'Signor Scalfero' He said with reverence, sure that Scalfero was the man whom he was to meet. I am Jacopo and I am here to serve you.

He examined the man who now stood in front of him before bidding him to sit at the table. He was surely an excellent likeness. Father Simeon had been right. This would be the man who would act as his agent in the Vatican but first he would speak with him to ensure that he would be reliable.

'Father Simeon. He is your brother? You are close to him?'

'Well yes. Hey, I have only seen him once while I was banged up. When he came to see me but sure we've always been close.'

'Father Simeon is a most trusted and most discrete member of our order. He has recommended you for the most prestigious and important task. He has spoken of you with the highest regard' He paused to allow Jacopo the opportunity to digest the commendation.

'Our order places the greatest reliance on the position you are to take. While you have only to play a part and you will receive every assistance it will be necessary to for you to know how to conduct yourself at all times. We require that there be no failure on your part. Such would be most unfortunate.' He looked Jacopo straight in the eye at this point to emphasise his understatement. It was clear to Jacopo that failure would result in his death. He had already accepted that was the price he would pay. Sure it went with the job.

'You can rely on me Padrino' he faltered in his emotion.

'I will not let the order down.'

Scalfero was not sure about this man. He looked precisely the part. The image of the new Pope that he was to replace but he was certainly not a man with the intelligence of his brother. He might have every intention of carrying out the deception but one false move, carelessness or remissness could create an uncertainty among those who would serve him, and have him revealed.

There is a quality in certain men that is denied to most. The ability to make a decision in an instant that might torch the toil of a lifetime or light the beacon of future triumph. He who lives by the sword, carries at his belt an implement that demands such a quality and it was a quality that Scalfero possessed.

'You are to join us then in our mission' he confirmed.

'I will inform Father Simeon that you are ready to start your training.'

Jacopo bowed his head in gratitude. He felt a resolve within him to fulfil this task and not to allow the mission to fail.

He, the hood from Toronto, who had suffered 10 long years' incarceration would be free to wear the fisherman's ring.

20.

FRANKFURT AM MAIN, GERMANY

Lufthansa flight LH 1618 from Naples touched down at just after midday on Thursday morning on a hot runway in July at Frankfurt am Main airport. It was the day before the strike that was to keep its aircrew out of work for ten days and disrupt the freight and passenger services at one of the busiest airports in Europe. It was not a day that anticipated any further disruption but unwelcome events are so often like wolves that hunt in a pack to better bring down their prey.

Among the arrivals was a group of bankers from the Frankfurt-based bank, Drexel Hesse returning from a business trip to the south of Italy. It was a trip that they made frequently and they swiftly found their way to the baggage hall to collect their suitcases. There would be no question of anything irregular in the cases, just a small quantity of clothing in each; a business suit and a few casual clothes for downtime. There had been little time for frivolity or leisure on their trip.

It was the day of the holiday circus. The clowns and jugglers on the visitors' terrace were attracting the crowds and an itinerant magician was proving most popular with the families watching the circus clowns on their stilts. A fortune teller was reading palms in a small boldly coloured tented cubicle and it was a day of innocence.

Then it changed so suddenly. It was the group of bankers leaving the arrivals hall wheeling their bags behind them, their jackets draped over their arms. Fumbling for parking tickets, wiping brows with white handkerchiefs, winding past the large couple who stopped to look around oblivious of the thoroughfare they blocked. There were the clowns who had come to greet the arrivals with mock applause, clapping and laughing at them to gain their attention.

Then there was the roar of gunfire as two assassins, dressed in their clown costumes, let rip with sub machine guns into the bewildered group of bankers tearing them apart in a hail of bullets. They stood no chance. One after another, and in swift succession, seven out of seven fell to their death on a blooded stone floor.

There was the shock of bystanders frozen in disbelief. The screams of terror sounding in the hollow hall. The confusion as onlookers threw themselves to the floor. The cries of 'terrorist attack get down.' Almost as soon as it had begun it was over and the assassins had left almost unnoticed in the confusion. A strange stunned silence held an air heavy with the acrid smell of cordite.

Peter Beck was up before the sun rose over his low rise block of flats in Geraur Strasse in Frankfurt am Main on the Friday morning following the airport slaughters. It was bright as it shone low through the kitchen window as he finished his brief exercises and began to eat a bowl of cereal while listening to the transistor radio on the kitchen table and its report on the latest about the slaughter at the airport. He had taken the call around 5.00am, a call that had ejected him from his bed. It was Serge; did he ever sleep? Always first to get the tip off. Two teenage girls found by the Main river bank, dead. It seemed that some fantastic ritual killing had taken place. He intended to get to the crime scene before the corpses were taken away. He would take his own photographs, there was no time to call a photographer and besides he liked the idea of his name being attached to the prints as well as his article. That would not have been possible when he had been a reporter at the Frankfurter Allgemeine Zeitung but at Hesse Heute it was accepted practice.

There was a soft cool breeze as he walked briskly towards Theodor Stern Kai but the sky promised that the day would be hot. It would take him just 25 minutes to make the walk if he stepped out. Practically in his back yard he thought, a rare bit of luck for a news reporter. He swung the camera on its strap and broke into a whistle. Then he reminded himself that he was going to see the corpses of two young girls in their early teens Serge had said it looked like some form of satanic killing. Hardly something to whistle about.

As he rounded the corner at the path that ran by the river bank he could see the presence of the police in the distance. There was no one else about. Just as well he thought. He would need to find out how they had been discovered. There would be a medic here to give an opinion as to what happened. A police officer to tell him who they might be looking for. Would he be a serial killer? That would be a great story he allowed himself to think briefly.

As he reached the scene he was pleased to be recognised by the older of two officers that stood by the path preparing to ask bystanders to move on.

'Hello Peter' The officer said flatly.

'You won't want to see this' The retort was made seriously. The officer looked genuinely affected by what he had seen.

'Couple of kiddies ripped apart by some devil worshipper it looks like to me.'

There was shock in the air, and a silence while two forensic officers went about their work. A common kind of response to horror that binds people together. Even police officers rarely see this kind of thing.

'You don't mind' He said quietly. 'If I take a photograph?'

The officer stood to one side.

'We have taken ours earlier. Go ahead. They are an awful sight I warn you. Pretty little girls too. You just can't understand who could do this kind of thing.'

There was little to retrieve from the murder scene but the horror of it that burns itself to the memory. The two young teenagers had appeared to have been subjected to ritualistic killing their viscera having been removed and as the officer had suggested that was possibly the cause of death not a consequence of it.

'What you mean they had their guts taken out while they were still alive?' He had asked.

'Seems like it' Was the flat reply.

The photography was easy. He just didn't care to look too hard. There was something unreal in the stillness of death he thought. So much life just brought to halt here by a riverbank.

'Were they murdered here?' He thought to ask.

'Unlikely. We think that the bodies were almost certainly dumped here having been already slain' Responded the officer confidently.

'Oh when I said the guts had been removed, I meant removed. They weren't left here with the corpses.'

'Any clues as to who was responsible?' He asked finally.

'Maybe when forensics are complete. We will let you know Peter.'

He was on the way to the office now. It was churning in his head. He was trapped between the shock of the deaths and the need to capitalise on the story. Should he question in print whether this could be a serial killer? It would certainly move some papers. There had been no other similar killings in Frankfurt, in fact murders had been rare until only yesterday when a mass killing had taken place at the airport. He would soon have the identities of the young victims. There would be some photographs of them provided by their families that would allow him to describe two pretty young girls who had everything to look forward to in life. Two young girls hideously cut down and mutilated by some unknown demon. His mobile rang.

'We have some details on the victims.' said a voice.

'Both reported missing last night. We are getting photographs. Hey these girls really are nice girl next door types. No drugs or late nights. They appear to have been picked up as they left dance class at about 21.00.'

This was unusual. There was usually a contributory cause. The girls who were out of their depth trying out some new experience. Drinking, out late, a misjudged acquaintance, an invitation to an after party, but tiny dancers? It seemed more shocking and somehow brought the horror closer.

'I'll be back shortly' Peter confirmed. 'I've taken some pretty awful shots at the scene'

'Did you get any clues as to who did it?' Shouted Matias at Peter by way of a greeting as he entered the news room at around 09.00.

'Nothing'

'We're getting a front page. Photographs from the families. We have some information on the girls but it seems nothing on the killer.'

'Hey. You know that you're competing for the front page Peter? We had some more on yesterday's killing down at the Flughafen. Seems like it was a gangland mass execution. Never rains it pours Hey?'

Peter sat at his desk in silence for a moment on auto pilot tapping his password on the keyboard in front of him. It seemed as if some of his younger colleagues were enjoying the excitement of their news gathering and that it had somehow gained a fresh impetus. He could not stop thinking of the horror of it. Yesterday, gangsters killed by gangsters; that was good news. Today, tiny dancers killed by devil worshippers that was definitely bad news.

'I can see this one has cut you up' said Mizzi standing by his chair as she passed him a cup of black coffee.

'Not surprised. Do you think it had anything to do with yesterday's killing at the Flughafen. Seems incredible that we should get two multiple killings in two days.'

'I don't know' He said pensively looking across at his screen.

'But I have a strange feeling that this is only the start of something. This city is about to know what it is to feel fear.'

He was staring at his screen now looking at the images that the search had thrown up.

'What the hell is that?' Asked Mizzi following his gaze.

'My pal at Reuters information site. I'm getting the background to demonic killings. Seems like there have already been some just like these'

The site showed and described in detail the deaths of young girls in Italy. They had mainly been immigrants from north Africa some apparently there illegally.

'Perhaps it was assumed to be some African cult but why would something like that come to Frankfurt? There is no great north African community here.'

'Speculation should be left to others. We report the news.' Growled Matias quoting the much used saying of the paper's editor Hans Klempner and grinning as he did so.

'I don't know.' Peter responded thoughtfully, ignoring the jocularity of his colleague.

'I don't know but I intend to find out. Mizzi, you and I have got some work to do. Get me the details of that gangland killing. As you say, It seems strange that it should happen around the same time. Maybe there is a connection.'

'I sent an email to lieutenant Swartz.' Mizzi confirmed.

'He doesn't think there is any connection. Just coincidence.'

It troubled Peter. Murder like this in his city. It lowered the tone besides everything else.

'OK, ask Swartz when he thinks there might be an official report on the causes of death.'

The story was coming together the 'tiny dancers' description was thought a suitable description to seize attention but as yet there was little more and the press was waiting. Peter looked at the family photographs that had just come in. It was difficult to judge who was the prettier he felt Monika or Ulrike. He chastised himself for making any judgement at all.

As he wrote up the story Peter Beck felt a numbness that derived not from an absence of the knowledge to write the whole story but a response to the tragedy of the event that had shocked him so deeply. He did not know then that what he had observed that morning was merely an event that would lead him to be involved in a much bigger story. One in which Peter Beck was himself to play a tragic part.

21.

AVIGNON, FRANCE

Father Fidel Rocher was in a pensive mood as he sat looking over the small rose garden surveying the meticulous geometry of a square planted with yellow and white blooms that came together like the colours of a giant flag laid out on the freshly cut grass. On his knee he loosely held a book which he appeared to have been reading and he held his thumb within its pages as if he meant not to lose his place. A wicker basket lay beside his chair, which showed him to have been dead heading the roses.

'Voltaire' He announced without looking up as Marcus approached him. 'Said that the Holy Roman Empire was neither Holy, Roman nor an Empire.' He stated without changing the direction of his stare.

'It comprised some 300 or so small states and cities at its height in the 16th century all virtually self-governed but under the titular leadership of King of the Romans in Vienna. The Holy Roman Empire included part of modern France, Switzerland, Austria, Luxembourg, Italy, Poland but all of Germany. It was the state of Germany.'

His eyes still studied the roses as if the bold variety of blooms in his garden were giving some insight into the variety of colour, attributes and allegiances of the many states and cities that made up that empire.

'Power was in those days in the hands of dynasties not of countries. The Habsburg hands held much of Europe in their grasp. Vienna was their capital.' 'Austriae est imperatura orbi universo' was its motto.

'Today that seems impossible does it not?'

Marcus listened to this history lesson with interest.

'So is this why the revelation speaks of the Holy Roman Empire spreading through Europe. It was, in its day, much of Europe and the areas in its control are the richest in Europe. It will re-establish itself as an economic force and if the revelation is correct the states within it will fragment in the way they were when the Empire reigned'

'It is all very plausible my friend. Look at what happened in the Balkans. A nation that compromises its morality will be hostage to anarchy. Europe is today bound together in economic union that punishes the poor and rewards the rich. It is the nations of the Holy Roman Empire that have the power. Power from wealth just as in those days. The threat it appears to me lies in the control of this power. The revelation speaks of the Antichrist. The last Antichrist to emerge from Austria was Adolf Hitler. We do not wish to see the re occurrence of that episode' He followed this observation with a short chuckle.

'I have often wondered why it is that mankind seeks to impose his will by force when he has proven so often that by economic pre-eminence a nation will bring all others to its heel, but only the dead have seen an end to war my friend. War will return to haunt the living, to taunt them with their triumphs and praise them for their victories, till the tide turns and fortunes fade and there is nothing left but futile valour.' He shook his head as if to affirm his observation and added.

'The early church provided civilisation with stability. It gave the learned a democratic institution that allowed them to thrive. It was neither partial nor territorial. Its power was benevolent its riches beyond the imagination of its followers. Civilisation is bound to the church and it maintains itself through the rigours of devotion and constancy. Power from wealth and commerce is envied, from strength and conquest it is detested my friend.

Perhaps that is what our Lady reveals to us. Wealth will rule us. Wealth from economic strength and the exercise of power to create more power to create dependency from the masses, to command the loyalty of the feeble minded, to enjoy the service of the sycophant. The power not of a nation state but of a dynasty. Power like this in the hands of one man, such is the power of life and death. This is what will be sought by an Antichrist'

'It is' Marcus acknowledged briefly.

'But for some submission to a despot can be rewarding. A life of ease without challenge but with material benefits.' He added.

The old priest looked at Marcus with determination.

'He who surrenders his soul to greed will live in eternal servitude my friend. I have seen how the guilty flourish. Avarice is the fuel of their advancement. The greedy hand that is ever stretched out to take and not to give, will seek out the venal soul and discover it like a dog does the buried bone where no one knew it lay. I have seen how it will gnaw that bone until every morsel is devoured.'

'So this revelation is saying that the person who seizes economic power through control of something akin to the Holy roman empire will be an antichrist dispensing evil?' Marcus asked.

'Saint Paul, in his letter to the Thessalonians, warned us of the Antichrist. The son of perdition who opposes and exalts himself above all that is God or religion so that he sits in the temple of God affirming that he is God. So we learn that the Antichrist will place his servant into the heart of the Holy See. To assume control over the Holy church. It could bring the end of the civilisation to which mankind clings so desperately to, of that I am sure.'

He stepped over towards the effusion of flowers. First of the white and then of yellow blooms that covered the two beds under a large low window. Marcus watched the old priest as he saw between the yellow and white roses one single blood red thistle.

Carefully Father Fidel Rocher pulled up the thistle and held it by its stem in his closed hand.

'You see' he said turning to Marcus with mischief in his eyes.

'The creeping thistle has an awesome beauty that attracts our eye does it not? Yet we must uproot it from among those blooms of yellow and white and it will wither and die.' He smiled broadly, pleased with his metaphor.

'The servant of the Antichrist must have no place in the Holy see. He must wither and die, just as does that thistle and we must see to it my friend that that is his fate.'

22.

AVIGNON, FRANCE

Marcus had been supervising the installation of electricity cables in the chapel all morning. He was checking the positioning of points and switches against the furniture layout that had been prepared by the interior designer. The quiet of this occupation was broken suddenly when Segolene rushed in.

'Marcus. You haven't by any chance seen Luc?' She enquired, sounding now more English than she had ever done.

'He has disappeared. He left the hotel he has been working at and gone without a word to me.'

She sounded as if she might be under the impression that he may have left for good and Marcus could see a tremble on her lip that signalled what he read to be her feeling of rejection. The opportunity to capitalise on the betrayal presented itself as tempting but he resisted, saying only.

'I expect that he is out with a few other chaps. A drinking weekend perhaps.' He added innocently knowing that his explanation was wholly insufficient to assuage her concern and incipient wrath.'

'He is not like that, you don't understand. He would only have left if something serious had happened.'

'What you mean if he had to return to his family for an emergency?'

'No, if he was going to his family he would have told me. I think he might be in trouble with the police or something like that.'

With that she looked at him enquiringly to see that he had comprehended the allegation.

'He is a little unreliable in that way.' She added by way of explanation and understatement delivered with a small pirate smile.

Marcus felt vindicated. His suspicions and instant dislike of Luc had been justified. Not just branded with tatouage as part of an Italian mafia organisation but now Luc had probably been responsible for some petty crime and moved on. He allowed himself for a moment to imagine the kind of offence that Luc might have committed, theft, fraud or perhaps even an assault.

'I believe I may know where he may have gone' she said thoughtfully.

'I feel that I should find him he may need my help.'

Marcus could not understand her and protested violently at the idea.

'So he commits some petty crime here in Avignon and you feel that you have to go and find him to bail him out. That sounds extraordinary.' He responded raising his voice in agitation. He could see from her passive reaction that his remonstration would get him nowhere. He did not know what history there had been between his daughter and Luc and it was clear that she had great affection for him.

'I will be leaving Avignon now for a few days Marcus. I am sure that it will not take too long to resolve.'

If he wished to debate the matter further, the opportunity was lost in a curious coincidence of timing as there was a knock at the chapel door that suggested impatience. Perhaps the fugacious Luc had returned. Marcus hoped he had not.

As he walked towards the door the knocking became more urgent. He opened it to reveal a young cleric moving from foot to foot in agitation.

'Please' He implored.

'You must come quickly. It's Father Fidel Rocher. We think that he has been poisoned.'

Marcus was in a daze. He was so taken aback he had not fully understood the young friar's entreaty.

'Poisoned?' he repeated unconsciously.

'It is you to whom he asks to speak' The young friar confirmed.

'He has said that he has something of great importance to ask of you.'

Swiftly the friar led Marcus across the courtyard into a side door then along a dark corridor and up a flight of stairs that led to the small bare room that was the lodging of Father Fidel Rocher.

The heavy door was swiftly pushed open to reveal a room lit only by a narrow shaft of light from a high window. Marcus crossed the floor in a few short strides to where he could see the old priest lying on a narrow bed under the high window.

As Father Fidel Rocher became aware of his presence he drew him close and whispered to him purposefully.

'The diary my friend. It is gone, and I its keeper, have been the victim of poisoning.'

Instantly the significance of Luc's departure became apparent. Luc who Segolene described as unreliable. Luc who had instructed Segolene in the use of medieval poisons when she played her part of the assassin in the play and it was Luc he had seen with the apothecary acting suspiciously. He could see quite clearly that Luc had poisoned Father Fidel Rocher and stolen the diary probably to sell off to some dubious collector of such items, but as the old man spoke he realised that there was much more at stake than the theft of an artefact.

'Be aware that this theft means more than the loss of some words of revelation for it is said that he who bears the words of the secret prayer will have protection. If the Antichrist were to gather the two parts of that prayer then he would be immune from justice forever. I have kept the diary for this reason my friend.

I have to give the warning, to the Holy Father, to expose the deception that is sure to occur as it is written in that revelation. I must go to Rome to warn of the dangers that are faced by the church and the world my friend, for there are those close to the Holy Father who are evil and who will destroy any message that I send. Now I see how weak I am and that I may not survive to do so.' Marcus could see what was implied in these words.

Father Fidel Rocher looked into his eyes purposefully.

'I know that what I ask is a great sacrifice, but perhaps my friend it is your destiny to be my proxy, to warn of the deception that is to occur.' With this Father Fidel Rocher managed a small flicker of a smile as if he was teasing his friend but Marcus could see that there was nothing of the old man's endearing tease in his obsecration.

'Whatever befalls, nature has either prepared you to face it or she has not. If something untoward happens which is within your powers of endurance do not resent it, but bear it as she has enabled you to do. Should it exceed these powers, still do not give way to resentment; for its victory over you will put an end to its own existence. Remember, however, that in fact nature has given you the ability to bear anything which your own judgement succeeds in declaring bearable and endurable by regarding it as a point of self-interest and duty to do so.'

At this he sighed and took breath before adding,

'These are not my words my friend but those of Marcus Aurelius he who through stoicism insight and intelligence long ago has seen that mankind is born to bear the harshest of circumstance by conquering each travail one by one.'

The energy of his exhortation laid him back on the bed exhausted. Marcus could see that it was now clear that this attempt on his life meant that someone suspected that Father Fidel Rocher knew of something and was correct in his interpretation of the Marian revelations that he had spoken of with such enthusiasm.

'Nature has given you the ability to bear anything which your own judgement succeeds in declaring bearable.' The old man repeated in a whisper by way of assurance as he closed his eyes again.

'It is written, that to everything there is a season, and a time to every purpose under heaven. The time has come my friend for you to bear that which God has ordained to you.' He swallowed a small mouthful of water poured into his mouth by the young priest at his side.

'You who have confessed to failure in your life will see that from failure will come success for with everything in life there is an ebb and flow and it is the destiny of mankind to find fulfilment.

'Will you do that for me?' He asked suddenly with a gravity of purpose.

There had been no time to consider the request. It had never been in Marcus nature to agree to anything without considering it fully.

'Sleep on it' Fitz would say. 'You always get a better perspective after you have slept on it.' This was different. A decision that had to be made now by the bed side of a frail friend. There was at this point no hesitation or uncertainty in the response that Marcus would give.

'You can rely on me.' He confirmed without thinking through his response.

Father Fidel Rocher squeezed the hand that had brought him the assurance that he had craved. In some way he could reach out to save his church and in Marcus there could be the messenger who would deliver the message and alert of the danger. He felt a warmth and satisfaction as he drifted to a sublime unconsciousness.

Marcus now felt something he had not felt before. Surely God had given him a chance with 'the winning.' Perhaps, He had demonstrated that there really was a life predetermined and he could see now his destiny set out before him and he would rise to it. Failure would now turn to success as the old priest had assured him. He now had a sense of purpose. He was now determined to fulfil this mission and he felt the passion of his friend as he knelt by his bedside, but there was something more. Marcus felt the guiding hand of certainty that would guarantee his success in this mission. It was a mission that had been preordained for him.

23.

FRANKFURT AM MAIN, GERMANY

Messe Frankfurt was quiet. The crowds that gathered for the exhibitions it famously staged were absent today and the bar in the hotel Kunsthaus was staffed by just one barman who strove to look busy wiping glasses and rearranging the line of spirit bottles. Rick was looking at the girl sitting on her own by the bar as she shook back her long blond hair and seemed to snatch a glance at him. It was perhaps not surprising he thought. He was the only other person there, sitting conspicuously on his own behind a large glass of local beer.

He tried to imagine what it might be like to go over and talk to her. Would she simply dismiss him he thought. Would she invite him into her life? He stopped himself. She was surely German and that was likely to lead to long silences, particularly on his part given his lack of understanding of the language. Besides, he was now interested to develop his new relationship with Emma Dreyfus. There was no shortage of conversation with Emma, she always had something to say.

He reckoned the girl was waiting for someone. He could see that now. She had looked towards the door several times only to be disappointed by a member of the staff entering with a tray of glasses and an old couple who hesitated turned and left no doubt put off by the low level lighting that threw a soft haze of blue and red across the room. Yes she was certainly waiting for someone. It had to be a man he surmised. He allowed himself to imagine the tall tanned blond man who was keeping this beautiful young woman waiting alone at the bar. He was wealthy for sure. Busy of course, he was keeping her waiting because he was concluding some deal, something to make him mega bucks. She would be aware of this. It had happened many times before and she would not mind.

It was at this point when his phone bussed with a message from London. It was something instantly forgettable. What was of more interest to him now was the arrival of the companion. Would he confirm Rick's preconception? Now he was arriving and Rick could see that he was not as expected. Tanned certainly but a dark slender man, shorter than he had imagined with a head of unkempt hair swept back across his head. He was dressed almost too casually, his shirt hanging outside his trousers, his jacket sleeves rolled up to reveal his tanned arms. Rick felt that he had more a southern rather than a northern European appearance.

Rick looked across with an inappropriate fascination as the suitor placed a tattooed arm around the girl's slim body and pulled her toward him in an embrace. Her lips caressed his check, her eyes fixed on him as if she had longed for this moment.

He continued to look over at them intrigued by them perhaps in the absence of anything of alternative interest in the bar. He found himself observing something that he at first found curious. He could see that they said little to one another. Surely he thought he could have managed this level of dialogue himself, and then it struck him why. The suitor was foreign too. They did not speak because they could not speak fluently in one another's language and it became clear that they had only recently met.

His distraction by the two lovers was interrupted by a telephone call from a colleague in London.

'Hi Simon. Yes I am meeting tomorrow morning with the bank's people. My hotel is just around the corner from the bank. I am in the bar at the moment killing a bit of time. I won't be leaving it too late tonight and I guess I will be back at London City airport early evening tomorrow if the airline strike permits.'

It was just before 08.30 the following morning when Rick arrived at the Drexell Hesse bank. His meeting was scheduled for 09.00 and he knew how Germans felt about punctuality so he had allowed himself plenty of time. After all, it had been absurdly easy for him. A good breakfast at the hotel and a five minute walk. Now he was in the waiting area absorbed in an article in a copy of Forbes magazine.

The slim attractive receptionist on the front desk tossed back her long blond hair and flicked her eyelids to focus her beautiful blue eyes behind the contact lenses she had placed just minutes before. She wore a dark navy business suit over a white blouse, unbuttoned to appear inviting rather than revealing. It was a style that had attracted several admiring glances from the staff who had entered the building from around 08.45.

She allowed herself a brief daydream while she shuffled the post into a number of small piles. A recollection of her sublime submission to the young Italian man, who had spent an energetic night in her bed at the hotel Kunsthaus. She had not got his surname, but Luc was an easy handle to remember and one she had hoped she would receive a call from later that day. Pity she thought, that she had not been able to find her cell phone this morning. She would have to call round to the hotel to pick it up later to find out if he had messaged her.

Rick was engrossed in the copy of Forbes when she addressed him.

'You have an appointment with Herr Meyer?' She said in a soft voice in perfect English.

'Yes, that's right' he said and as he turned to look up at her. He stopped.

He was looking into the eyes of the girl who had last evening drawn his fascination at the bar of the hotel. He felt embarrassment at his having studied her so assiduously but quickly reckoned that she probably did not even recognise him. Rick put down the magazine and rose from his seat.

'Yes' He repeated feely clumsy.

'Herr Meyer at 09.00.'

She smiled at him and simply said:

'This way Sir' and showed him into a well-lit and inviting meeting room in which stood a middle aged man dressed in a check business suit white shirt and blue tie.

'Good morning Mr Brown I am Gustave Meyer.' Herr Meyer appeared in jovial mood as he greeted his guest.

'I trust that you were accommodated well at the Kunsthaus. It is one of several hotels owned by the bank in the city. We like to think that our guests are well looked after.'

Rick was pleased to confirm his host's expectation. He had not appreciated that the hotel was owned by the bank but he recalled, it had of course been selected by them. That must have been why the receptionist was there. She probably had an account at the bar. He tried to imagine Sandersons owning a hotel in London to accommodate their visitors. Pretty unlikely he thought.

'We have a number of private clients willing to let us lend them money secured upon assets in England.' Herr Meyer began by way of introduction.

'Our rates are of course most competitive Mr Brown, and our service is well ...' Meyer laughed as he gestured to Rick to seat himself at the table.

'We aim to provide a unique service'

Meyer had learned his business from the frenetic Investment banks that he had worked with in New York city. The sale of securities held by the bank at overvalued positions to susceptible and trusting clients. The creation of derivative products from stale and awkward assets that churned commissions. The manipulation of share prices through bulk buying and selling and the persuasion of weak wills with payments and other considerations that suckered loyalty.

It was Real Estate that was Meyer's passion. The security of its permanence, the feeling of authority in its ownership. His route to buy real estate was to buy the debt that supported it. When the debt is not serviced by interest payment or a breach of banking covenants occurs then foreclosure is inevitable. Meyer would buy the debt at a reduced price use any means necessary to improve the value, and pursue the original borrower for breach of the banking covenants. His success in this activity, had secured him significant financial benefit.

Rick had a well-rehearsed presentation to make. Sandersons organisation and staff, fee structure, insurances, reporting, presentation and turnaround times and he spent about forty minutes running through it with little response from Meyer other than the occasional nod of his head. Indeed Meyer seemed relaxed on all these matters. It was quite different from the detailed strictures laid down by some of the British clearing banks as to the content of their reports. Rick sometimes felt that those clients should write the reports themselves and just have him sign them.

'That is all very satisfactory Mr Brown' Meyer said by way of response when the presentation had been concluded.

'Drexel Hesse will be pleased to instruct Sandersons for its valuation work in the UK, and of course any disposal of repossessed property. Though I am sure that there will not be much of that.' He added with a broad smile and turned as the telephone rang.

'Excuse me Mr Brown' he said and made for an office to the side of the meeting room to take the call.

As he answered the call Rick could not avoid hearing him change his demeanour audibly. The conversation was in German, that he was unable to follow, but he could detect a distress in the voice of his host far removed from the convivial conversation he had just had with him. It appeared as if he was being related details of an accident of some kind. He heard him repeat the question 'All seven? But all seven?'

There was a word that had been repeated several times in that conversation. It was a word he did not recognise but one he felt could be from a language other than German. He made a note of the word on the back of a business card in his pocket and was sure that he had misspelt it. The word was Ndrangheta.

It was a very different Herr Meyer who briskly bade him farewell following the telephone call and as he left the offices of Drexel Hesse. Rick reflected on the meeting. No problem with the client he thought but clearly something had occurred in the life of Herr Meyer that had caused him distress. He did not imagine however that it was a life soon to be taken. That very evening Herr Gustave Meyer would be dead.

Rick could not have appreciated the gravity of the telephone call that had changed the jovial demeanour of Gustave Meyer that morning. The pretty blond receptionist had sought to have the caller ring later.

'Herr Meyer is with someone at present she had said. Is this urgent?'

The caller had made a clear impression that the call was indeed very urgent such that she had put it through direct to his office by the meeting room. Meyer had excused himself with Rick, entered his office from the meeting room and stood by the window to take the call from Arnwald one of his lieutenants. He had been sure that it would be something routine, or even something inane, where did you say to take it boss? Or what time was it? Arnwald could do with a lesson in listening to his instructions the first time.

'Guten Morgen Arnwald. You have taken me from a meeting. I hope you have good reason for doing so.'

'Herr Meyer?' The voice inquired with hesitation as if uncertain of the identity of the voice on the line.

'We have a problem. Some of our operatives have got into some difficulty.'

'What kind of difficulty do I need to speak with them?' He enquired.

'Not possible. They have been shot at the Flughaven as they came in from Italy. Bullet holes in all of them. I just heard from Jeager'

Jeager was trusted. He was an inspector of police who was the bank's stipendiary in the local police force. It was his job to provide inside information.

'All of them shot you say. Are any dead?' He asked.

'All seven of them.' Came the answer.

Meyer sat down in his chair unable to respond coherently and shocked at the news.

'All seven. But all seven' He questioned.

He was not usually concerned about the loss of operatives but seven dead was a blow. The inquiry into their activities that would inevitably follow their deaths was of clear concern. Even more so however was the realisation that someone with the capability to take out his men was now acting in the city.

Meyer finished the call after briskly demanding that Arnwald come around straight away. He was confused. Perhaps there would be an explanation. Maybe his men were involved in something and this was a revenge. Maybe this had nothing to do with his organisation.

'It was, almost as soon as he had bade goodbye to Rick Brown that he took the second call.

'Who is this?' He enquired of the receptionist with genuine confusion.

'He said that you would know. He delivered you a message this morning at the Flughaven.' The blond confirmed innocently.

'OK put him on.' Meyer barked clearing his throat in readiness.

The voice was low and gravelly. It had an accent that could almost have been from Meyer's homeland but he was not sure.

'My organisation is moving into your city and will take over your operations. You have only to agree to my terms to retain your position in the very profitable business that you have enjoyed.'

'Who is speaking?' He enquired uneasily.

'That is not of concern. You will shortly receive full instructions.'

Meyer would never know that the voice was that of Michaelangelo Scalfero.

As he put down the receiver Meyer felt a signal discomfort. Life had always gone to plan. He controlled his bank and its multi layered activities and did not necessarily concern himself with the business of others. While the structure and possibilities of the material world had excited him far more than those of faith, he had not been without faith. The recognition of man's predestination that ascended from grace bestowed at birth was the purity of the Calvinist vision that he had ascribed to. Grace and predestination the ultimate fate of each soul whether for Heaven or Hell is foreordained by an all knowing God and a man is born either with or without grace. It was this that would define his destiny and he had been confident that that destiny was for him secure.

It was therefore almost bewildering for him to receive a telephone call informing him quite literally that his reign was now over. If it was the receipt of funds from organised crime in southern Italy that had fuelled the bank's activities, it appeared that those who generated those funds were ready to take over their distribution into the commerce of legitimate enterprise through the connections of Drexel Hesse.

It was around 22.00 when he reached home. A large house by the Leiter Strasse 35 minutes from town. A quiet and peaceful spot. That's how he liked it to be. All that is except his family. Three noisy girls always laughing and larking around. Two had boyfriends who seemed to have nowhere else to go but that was fine it somehow added to the atmosphere a little. They all sat around in the kitchen while Paulina made pasta and baked bread. It always smelt good. They were German but not so. The Italian in them was too hard to supress and besides they were from the south. That part of Italy that produces the closest families.

This evening Meyer felt a signal apprehension. It was the uncomfortable numbness in the viscera, the feeling that his whole world was about to cave in. It was the discomfort he would feel when his family asked him questions as to why? Inquiries as to matters he should have known about. Actions he should have taken. The accusations from his loved one's of blame that life had gone wrong. He had let them down. He knew now that somehow life had been too comfortable. Too easy. What he had seen as wrong or misplaced had been overlooked. Remedies suspended. Failures forgiven. If only he had been more astute, more ruthless. It was too late now. His weaknesses had been spotted. His reign was over. The future now belonged to the low gravelly voice he had heard on the end of his telephone.

That evening alone in his study, Meyer threw the runes that would tell of his fate; the small pieces of nut wood marked with the blood red letters of an ancient alphabet that he had always used to tell of his future. They told of the end of his reign and he could see the disaster that would befall him in the message they conveyed. He felt a cold panic as he threw them again only to read the same terrifying result. It was that moment of panic that made Meyer pick up the telephone to dial a local number. The fatal call that he should have known would be intercepted. The call to Peter Beck the journalist at Hesse Heute.

Luc looked into the mirror on the wall of the bathroom in his room at the shitty motel outside of town that he had been allocated where no questions would be asked. Where cash was paid and no identity required. He examined his naked torso and flexed the muscles in his chest. He smiled with satisfaction at the conquest he had made. The girl he had met at the Kat Kat club. The beautiful blond girl who worked at Drexel Hesse whom he had enjoyed so vigorously in her bed and who he had tricked into giving him the very address of his victim last night in the Kunsthaus Hotel.

He stroked the large tattoo on his arm and muttered to himself the pledge he had given at baptism.

'As the fire burns this image so will you be burned if you stain your honour.'

It was an honour he would not betray. It was the bond of consanguinity that held him from birth to the order of the Ndrangheta. It was the trust that had been placed in him to be the assassin at the word and whim of Scalfero. For him there was no need to question, no need for explanation. Only the callous clear direction to kill.

He splashed on some aftershave and pulled on the china blue shirt and short leather jacket. He packed the small roll of wire that was to accompany him and with which he would carry out the strangulation of his victim. He placed in his pocked the cell phone he had taken from the blond girl, combed his thick dark hair and left by the door that led direct to the outside of the building. It was a fine dry night to go visiting and he felt good as he mounted the small Kawasaki that was to take him to Leiter Strasse.

Approximately 1200 kilometres away, Scalfero relaxed in the leather armchair in his study waiting for his cell phone to ring. His informant had reported Meyer's call to a reporter at Hesse Huete which confirmed that he would give information regarding the elimination of his men and the intentions of the Scalfero Ndrina. Scalfero had needed to have one of his most able assassins ready to swiftly despatch to Meyer's home to control the situation. Luc had been transferred to Frankfurt from Avignon to address just such a mission as this should it prove necessary. A new bank director would need to be found and he would inevitably be required to know the source of the funds he would need to distribute. It would be a difficult appointment, it was a pity that he could not have relied on Meyer.

Luc found the house on Leiter Strasse with ease and pulled the Kawasaki onto its stand by the kerb on the opposite side of the road. It was a gated house but it was easy to gain access between the gate pier and the hedge to the side. Clearly he thought to himself Meyer had never needed to expect intruders. He crossed the lawn and looked into a window on the ground floor. He could see Meyer sitting at his desk. He seemed to have been casting dice onto a white cloth in front of him. It would be easy he thought to himself as he swiftly moved to the rear of the house surprising a small black cat feeding from a bowl of its food outside the kitchen door. He tried the door, it was unlocked.

Swiftly and silently Luc made his way to the front of the house. He could clearly hear Meyer's family talking loudly in front of the television in the drawing room. They were completely unaware of his presence.

Meyer spun round in his chair as he heard Luc enter the room. He raised his arms to protect himself but it was too late. The wire was around his neck and Luc's practiced hands were in control. Meyer choked, his eyes widening as the breath was squeezed out of him. He drew his hands to his neck and grasped at the taut wire in hopeless defence. Then he slumped forward onto the floor. It had just taken a few short minutes. Luc knew that his instructions were always to exit immediately after the job was done and he was able to leave the house unnoticed retracing his route of entry and moving swiftly back to the Kawasaki.

Before starting the bike, Luc pressed the button on the cell phone he had taken from the blond girl to send the text message he had typed earlier. The brief message of confirmation of Meyer's death.

On the table by Scalfero's chair a cell phone buzzed a moment later.

24.

FRANKFURT, GERMANY

The search for evidence as to the deaths of the tiny dancers Monika and Ulricke had found nothing. Peter Beck felt the frustration just as much as his contacts in the police, surely the severity of the crime would lead to some clue as to who or what was responsible. All there was to report had been conjecture. A coven of witches had apparently been discovered operating from a house to the north of the city but this story had soon lost momentum given the advanced ages of the ladies who were apparently involved. Rumour had suggested that there had been no gangland killing, just one murderer of the all those deceased, but no one had yet the imagination to complete the theory.

He was sitting at his office desk reviewing his file when the phone rang. It was Mizzi from reception.

'I got a guy on the phone for you wants to pass on some information on the gangland killings. He rang before when you were out. Shall I put him through?'

It was the burden one had to bear. Cranks ringing in with theories, looking for some recognition or perhaps genuinely delusional. The problem was, one had to hear them out, just in case.

'Hello. Peter Beck speaking. What do you have to say?' He asked in a frustrated voice.

'Mr Beck I am Gustave Meyer. I have some information regarding the killings at the Flughaven. I can tell you who is responsible. I think that we should meet up.'

There was something in this voice that told Peter that this was no crank. No theory expounded. No questions as to what Peter knew already. No deal as to the identity of the caller being printed for all the world to praise. Just the confirmation of a lead and a simple request for a meeting.

'Yes. Sure, I could do that. When and where? He questioned instinctively.

'Under the hammering man at 21.00. I know what you look like' came the response followed by a phone being cut.

It was easy to agree. A lead on the murder of the seven gang members was an exciting move forward. Maybe this would lead to something that would answer the murder of the tiny dancers. To date Peter understood from friends at Reuters that the police had nothing on either crime. He looked at his watch. It was 18.00. The best lead he could have hoped for could be just three hours away.

It would have been around 20.30 when he got the call from Swartz at the local police.

'Peter, we have just been to Lieter Strasse. Another killing. We think that this one is linked to the airport killings'

Peter's mind raced. He might soon be finding out the truth behind these killings. Should he say anything or keep quiet. It was again his instinct that drove him.

'I had a call about an hour and a half ago.' He volunteered.

'Can't say what to make of it but some guy wants to meet up to give more information on the airport killings.' He confirmed wishing to sound as if he had not reported it as it was not of great importance.

'Where are you to meet him?'

'Under the hammering man at 21.00.'

'OK. Well someone else got to him first. The deceased had called a taxi to take him there just before he died. The taxi driver reported the body. His family had thought that he was working in his study someone got in and strangled him. My bet is that the guy you were to meet was Gustave Meyer?'

Peter cursed under his breath. He had been speaking to an informant who would have led him to the truth. Now he too was dead. Killed just about one hour before he was due to spill the beans.

'Sure. That's the name he gave. So at least we know that he knew something about the killings and that there is someone out there who didn't want him to tell. What do you know about Meyer?'

'We have quite a lot on the guy. We never took him in for anything but it seems that he was on the fringe of a lot of organised crime in the city. Ran the bank Drexel Hesse near the Palmengarten.'

'Drexel Hesse? The bank the seven gangland members worked for. So the whole thing was involved in organised crime?'

'We can't say for sure but there have been a lot of suspicions over the years. Money laundering, price fixing, distressed debt stuff, financial crime really. We think that Meyer stretched the boundaries a little, drugs prostitution.'

'Maybe someone felt that he was overstepping the brief. Treading on someone else's toes'

'We think so. We're investigating that line now. I will keep you up-to-date'

Peter Beck put down the phone thoughtfully. He felt now that he was more deeply involved in this case than before. The deceased had rung him to potentially reveal something. He cursed again the coincidence of fate that had lost him the lead.

'What do you make of it Peter?' Mizzi invited having overhead his call.

'Well Swartz rang me from the crime scene. He clearly knew Meyer had contacted me that's for sure. Either came up on his phone or my number was written down in his study. Swartz was thinking maybe I knew something more. I guess the killers were already on his tail. They can't have killed him to stop him talking to me as they killed him within hours of his call.'

'Maybe not, don't you remember?' said Mizzi.

'I mentioned that he had rung previously. They had clearly tapped his phone and a call to a journalist had alerted them to action. You don't think they had some kind of tip off? Someone at the police perhaps. It's some organised crime gang if they had the ability to monitor phone calls.'

'Swartz said they had been following Meyer for some time. quite possible they had a trace on his phone line.'

Peter understood that Meyer had been operating his clandestine activities in the city unhindered by the police for some time. It had to be the case that someone in the police force was an insider keeping him informed. But how could such a protected figure be assassinated in his own home?

There was a light rain falling as he walked home to Geraer strasse. The kind that clears the head with a sweet freshness and almost washes the mind to think more clearly. Now he began to piece together the events of the last few days. Meyer had operated a criminal operation from his position at Drexel Hesse, possibly with the knowledge of someone in the police. Someone had taken it over, but it was not to be operated in the way that Meyer had done. This was someone far more ruthless. Someone who would stop at nothing to reach his goals.

Try as he might however, he could not piece together these gangland killings with the macabre ritualistic slaughter of two young girls whose bodies had been found by the bank of the Main. For the time being, the tiny dancers deaths would go unanswered.

25.

NICE, SOUTHERN FRANCE

The tall Canadian stood in the queue waiting to be called for the flight to Rome. He could not take his eyes off the girl just six steps in front of him. Her dark tanned skin was covered by a light printed cotton sleeveless dress and on her feet she wore leather sandals. Over her shoulders was draped a loosely woven black cardigan and her head was crowned with designer sunglasses. She carried a woven bag which she swung lightly to and fro as she waited.

He had been conscious that he was staring at her taking in the shape of her extraordinarily beautiful face but not wishing to catch her eyes for fear of an embarrassing admission of his pre-occupation. It had been an outside chance, perhaps the power of a crudely muttered prayer or something less spiritual like coincidence, but on taking his seat on the aircraft he had found that he had drawn the one next to her.

Tom Royal had stumbled into the seat that was to accommodate his tall figure on the flight to Rome with enthusiasm. As he went to sit he saw a passport on the seat. It was certain to belong to the girl in the seat next to him but he swiftly and astutely recognised an opportunity to open a conversation with her. He held the passport in front of him and opened it to reveal the name inside.

'Segolene?' He announced with confidence causing her to turn towards him.

'I believe this is your passport' He smiled and followed with a chirpy laugh.

She knew that she had an admirer the moment that he sat down by her. He was not bad looking and that was a good start.

American possibly, one could always tell the American from the English from the shirt collar. Buttoned down American, no buttons English. The shirt collar test made him American. Also it was denim and while that fabric is universal it leads one to think American. Another indicator was the fact that on picking up her French passport from the seat of a French flight he did not hesitate to speak to her in English. Definitely American she thought. This would be a flight with conversation and opportunity. She smiled at him a small pirate smile.

'Tom Royal' He announced in a way that anticipated gratitude.

'Je m'appelle Segolene. Je suis Francesse.' She replied timidly.

His smile evaporated at the response and a forlorn Tom Royal said simply:

'Oh.'

'I do however speak English if you would prefer me to do so.' She teased innocently.

'Hey you really had me there' he was smiling again.

'I do have a bit of French myself though. I'm from Canada. We have French folk there too.'

Segolene had good reason to be careful not to reveal too much of herself, least of all to strangers. She kept herself at distance by playing the small game of inviting her interlocutor to make suggestions and suppositions. This had the potential of allowing the supposition to manifest itself as reality should she wish it to by a neat non-committal confirmation. By such means was she seen more as people wanted to see her than whom she actually was. She had found out early in life that for many men, the more superficial and less complex the image she portrayed the greater their interest was.

She was aware of the power of feminine beauty. It was not for her the manifestation of vanity nor did she use it in rivalry. She had found that a perfect mix of beauty and charm could unlock each door she wished to enter. To flatter the gullible, to incite expectation and to reward its supplicants. Beauty is the trump card that must always be played with precision, but now she saw the potential to use it to great advantage.

Royal would never have thought that the passport he had picked up on the seat next to her so gleefully was a forgery. Not only was it impossible to detect as such but he could not begin to think that she had reason to hide her true identity. In fact Segolene had a very different identity to that Tom Royal was introduced to. He would in his short time with her, experience the consequence that her true identity was to bring upon him.

The Tom Royal that she learned about was a travelling salesman aiming to sell hydraulic pumps to machine manufacturers throughout Italy. Rome was just a stop on the way of a journey that was to take him north. He was not really expecting her to show much interest in his vocation. He had clearly failed at that level before. So he stuck with anecdotes about fishing and hunting trips suitably embellished with insights to his prowess with gun and line. He came across as boyish not manly, playful and athletic rather than rugged. She listened with amusement and attention. He was a fine companion for a short plane flight.

It was with regret that Royal saw the seat belt sign was lit and the stewardess was busy ensuring that seats were in the upright position in order to make the descent. Then she surprised him.

'Do you have a hotel booked in Rome?' she questioned as they caught the views of the west of the city from the window of the descending aircraft.

Tom Royal reached in the breast pocket of the jacket lying on his knees.

'Let's see hotel Londra Piazza Sallustio. Home to Americans in Rome I understand.'

'That sounds good. Quite central. I am sure that they would not have a problem with one more guest.' She looked at him impishly. The intention was clear. She had not suggested that they should insist another room be made available, only that they would not object to one additional guest. Tom Royal could barely contain his excitement.

She awoke early in his bed in the hotel Londra. She remembered that she had drawn the curtain to look out onto the side street just before retiring and now the sun's first rays penetrated far into the room. She looked at the naked figure next to her. Tom Royal had not been that bad a choice and a night in this bed was a small price to pay for the service she was to extract from him. Besides, it was good to have company in Rome. It was difficult being a woman on one's own with all the attention that followed one and to eat Gelatto on one's own was indulgence, to share it was benevolence.

She smacked his rump playfully, turned him still half sleeping onto his back and spread herself across his chest, eyes meeting his, waiting for them to open. The delight in awaking with her naked body spread on his caused him to laugh at his sheer good fortune.

'Segolene' He croaked 'You are just the most beautiful ...'

She held her hand over his mouth to stop the flow of sentimentalism.

She said 'Let's get breakfast. I'm hungry.'

They were late for breakfast owing to his shameless mendicancy and her not unwilling participation in its satisfaction. Pastries and hot coffee, strawberries and laughter were shared among the usual predominance of American guests in the Hotel dining room.

'What do you have on today?' She enquired at last.

'I gave myself the day off. First appointment is tomorrow morning. Thought I would get to see the city. You seem to know it well. What do they mean when they call it the eternal city?' He asked boyishly.

'That it will last forever. It will never die. Not like us we are only here for a short time.' She looked at him thoughtfully and added.

'What would you do if you knew you were soon to die? Plan your death or live your life? We must live every day as if it were our last for to fail to do so is to fail ourselves.'

'Seems to me we should get out there and enjoy it.' He laughed.

She wondered if Tom Royal was not acting as if he misunderstood the deal. The smile on his face was that of a newlywed. Surely he realised that this was a transactional relationship. An exchange of bodies, a bed for the night? If he did not understand the headline then how could he ever understand the small print? In fact, the price he was to pay for the enjoyment of her body was the risk of losing his own.

She looked into his eyes with a firm fixed assurance that brought him back to reality.

'Do you know Tom, in a way I too am a salesman. I have something valuable I wish to sell in Rome.' She confided in a hushed and confident tone.

'My problem is that I will not be able to get its full value.'

His interest was immediate. Something of value? Perhaps she was implying that he could help her.

'It is a relic and there is one person who will pay the price I need for this relic. But he will not pay it to me.' She begun by way of explanation.

Royal was intrigued: 'Why not if it is so valuable?'

'Because the buyer is my Father.' She looked him in the eyes inquiringly. There was no mistake now. She intended that he intervene in this transaction in order to negotiate an 'arm's length' deal.

'I get you.' he said.

'What is it that is so valuable and how much is valuable?'

Two questions at once seemed to display an interest in her proposition. She smiled her soft smile and lifted her eyes again to his.

'The relic is a diary and my father will pay one million euros for it.'

'One million euros Hey. What do we do get hold of a lawyer and meet up in his office?'

Segolene stifled a laugh.

'No that is not how he will do it. We will arrange to meet him in a public place and exchange the goods.'

'What if he doesn't have the money?' He questioned reasonably.

'Oh he will. I am sure of that.' Indeed she felt that there was little risk of her father not having the money, what was less certain was whether Tom Royal would leave an exchange of this kind alive. It was not a potential outcome she wished to reveal. She was certainly not about to tell him that her father was the head of one of the most ruthless criminal organisations in the world and that in addition to that he had had a mad vision of world domination ever since her mother had told him of a revelation that told of the omens that would announce his elevation to some kind of superman.

She had no alternative but to attempt the exchange by Royal's proxy and there was by doing so the likelihood that Scalfero would not suspect that anyone would dare to approach him unless they acted for a professional organisation. It was the simplest of plans that therefore had the reasonable prospect of success.

'So' said Tom Royal enjoying the prospect of some excitement.' I meet up with this old guy and swap the relic with one million euros and that's job done?'

It had not occurred to him that he would be dealing with the Mafia. Had it, his reaction would no doubt have been very different. Any member of the Ndrangheta would find it difficult to tolerate the sheer audacity of an amateur such as Royal casually demanding one million euros from them for an antique book.

She looked at him with a measure of affection in her eyes.

'More or less' she affirmed calmly.

'So you will help me?'

'Sure thing' Royal confirmed and smiled at her broadly. She smiled at Royal in gratitude for his cooperation looking at him over a slim glass of lemon juice. Suddenly she got up to go.

'I have to go out to buy some clothes.' She said.

'Something from Via del Corso. I will be back in a couple of hours.'

It was a short taxi ride via Piazza Barberini to the elegant stores at Corso and the small Hotel that Segolene felt she had selected well. Its entrance was visible from the small window to the front and a larger window to the rear looked over a small path that led from the kitchen service door that gave access to Crociferi should she need to make an escape. Room number thirty seven was the first floor twin room she had booked in the names of Mrs and Miss Beck, the name taken from a musician she once admired. She paid a deposit for the room sure that the balance might be settled from cash she would soon be in possession of. She returned to the room at Salustia with a glamorous shopping bag to endorse her reason for departure.

Tom Royal looked at her with a puzzled expression as Segolene passed him the diary of the old nun Beatrice. It held the words of the 1892 revelation that was made to her, words that were corroborated in the revelations of St Therese L'Enfant exactly one hundred years later, confided by the Holy mother to Maria Anna Temoin.

'So is this it?' Royal asked.

'One million euros for this?'

'Yes this is it. One million euros for this' She repeated mimicking his accent with a smile.

'We will make arrangements to make the exchange.'

If Royal was doubtful as to the value ascribed by her to the artefact, Segolene was not. She knew precisely how important it was to Scalfero to own it and how much he valued it. Together these two revelations would complete the secret prayer that gave its possessor protection. A protection he believed would give him great power.

To him it was a secret so perfect and of such immeasurable consequence, that he had instructed Elise to kill Annie to prevent her further revelation of it on a road close to Eyragues 25 years ago but when Marcus arrived in Avignon to work in the very Chapel where the old Beatrice diary had been discovered, Scalfero became convinced that Annie had told Marcus the secret too.

It had been Scalfero's plan to deceive Marcus by getting Segolene to play the part of his deceased daughter. Surely Marcus would reveal to his daughter the secret told to him by her mother? But Segolene was now sure that Marcus knew nothing of the revelations, other than that he had heard from Father Fidel Rocher. Either that or he was a good actor and she knew he was not that.

Now she stood to take advantage of Scalfero's desire to own this revelation. Now she would avenge the child so disregarded by a callous father. Now, she would dare to deceive the greatest deceiver of them all, and dare to gamble the life of Tom Royal and possibly her own too.

26.

ROME, ITALY

Tuesday unwrapped the picture of a perfect dawn. The sun rose to the glory of an empty sky. It softly and tentatively fingered its way through the leaves of the plane trees and poured its light onto the dark shadows of early morning. A silence held the soft chill air in heady expectation. The solitary car horn, the breathless optimism of the songbirds, the gleeful bark of a small dog at the chance discovery of some small mammal to chase into the undergrowth. An unseasonal light dew covered the low grass in a damp silvery hue and all around the stir of morning slowly ambled to its inevitable crescendo.

He had slept awkwardly and had left the his palazzo on the Vende Settembre to stroll the Villa Borgese to clear his head and focus his mind. There was business here in Rome that had been broken and would take time to repair. Arrests of amouri at the Café de Lyon were a concern to him. Trials were due and good men would be lost to his operations here in the city. His thoughts dwelt on his resentment of the Lieutenant who had orchestrated the raids on his operations. Lieutenant Costanzo, yes there would be time for retribution he told himself.

Scalfero needed greater and more efficient distribution to cleanse the money he was making in the south. Here were prosperous businesses capable of legitimising large amounts of money but now the operation had been uncovered it might be difficult to operate in Rome. He needed a plan that would allow the conversion of his wealth to legitimacy.

History had taught him from the age of the Medici how money could be turned into permanence by the act of patronage. Civilisations thrive not only on the manners and courtesies of men, not on literature and art alone but by the vigour, vitality and confidence to build a permanence. Reputations are built like edifices not won by one quick throw of a dice. He would find some just cause to promote, some popular complaint to appease. He would be the champion of the people. He thought of the adoration that might be his if he held an event for a charity of some sort. Scalfero the patron, the champion of freedom. He smiled indulgently as his thought twisted through in his mind.

The early sun now shone bright in the July sky as Scalfero walked down the steps to the Piazza del Popolo. He walked alone. To be unaccompanied was to fail to draw attention to himself. Here in Rome he was unknown and there was a peculiar sense of freedom in walking her streets unrecognised. Here he would become a patrician known for his patronage. He would wear the cloth of respectability. It would be his reinvention. He would appear as people saw him. He would be what people expected him to be.

Now there was something else on his mind. Something that had excited him and engaged his imagination more than the everyday concerns that necessarily occupied him.

He had received an offer to purchase something that was of incalculable value to him. A telephone call to his home from an American telling him that he was to be offered something he long desired. It was a diary the possession of which would give him protection and deny his adversaries the chance to challenge his ambitions. It would allow him to piece together the Marian revelations of Aix en Bearn with those of St Therese L'Enfant that he had craved since he was first told of the prophesy by his wife Elise. Only he beyond the Holy See must know that truth and he would now hold the words that witnessed that knowledge and with that he would have the power to dominate the world.

It was almost 10.00 when Scalfero sat at a small café table in the piazza del Popolo looking out across the street. He was waiting with apprehension drumming his fingers unconsciously on the table. This morning someone would be making a delivery to him.

A voice came from behind him.

'I represent someone who wishes to do some business with you.' It was not as he had expected. Clear English with an American accent. He turned and motioned for the man to join him.

'You have it with you?' Scalfero asked.

'No, but I can direct you to a place not far from here where you can pick it up.

I am instructed to take payment from you and to take you to it.'

Scalfero was used to situations such as this. He did not doubt the authenticity of the diary. He had it confirmed by an agent in Avignon that it had gone missing. It seemed to him that this might be the work of amateurs such was the apparent innocence of the tall young man who now sat opposite him at the table but he remained cautious.

'Is it to be just you and me?' He asked.

'Yes just you and me. You let me take the money, and I will take you to get the goods.'

It almost seemed too simple. Scalfero almost felt that he could politely ask the name of person behind the theft but thought better of it.

'The money is in this briefcase. You take it and we will go.' He confirmed.

Tom Royal never thought that it could be that easy. He looked startled, then composed himself and got to his feet taking hold of the suitcase from under the table.

'This way' He instructed.

The tall Canadian and the small Italian strolled together in silence the short distance towards the Chiesa San Marco. Just inside the door Royal put his hand behind a small statue and retrieved something hidden there.

'Here' He said passing a large envelope to Scalfero.

As Scalfero took the envelope in his hand looking down momentarily, Royal was already several strides towards a small crowd of tourists. Neither goods nor payment had been examined. It had been a curious transaction. Brief, impersonal but for Segolene exceedingly profitable.

Segolene saw the tall Canadian coming towards her grinning from ear to ear. He held up the case and shook it victoriously.

'Have you checked to see it is all there?' She asked.

'No, You said it would be.' He had trusted her instinct.

'Did he check the goods?'

'No, he didn't get time. I just shot off'

'Here swap!' She instructed placing a second suit case in his hand. They then ran back to where the transaction had taken place seconds before and swiftly checking to see that Scalfero too had left, placed the second suitcase behind the statue.

'Just in case we lose it.' She explained.

' We will come back for it by taxi later.'

They laughed at the absurdity of it. They had received a substantial payment from the head of a Mafia clan and he had not stopped to examine the item.

As they cantered along the Via Margutta neither saw the motor bike until it was at his side. It was all so swift. A shot in the back of the head and the briefcase snatched from his dying grasp. Segolene moved instinctively to one side but it was not necessary. The motorcycle was already some distance away the pillion passenger holding onto the briefcase he had snatched from Royal. Passers-by looked on in horror unable to comprehend the violent assassination before their eyes.

Segolene knew she had little time. She turned as a small crowd gathered around her fallen accomplice and headed back to the Chiesa San Marco with its small statue behind which they had their hiding place. What if someone had discovered it she thought. How dumb would she feel but it had been her only chance. In seconds she arrived at the door of the church. She could hear the sound of a police car siren as it drove toward Royal's body.

She reached behind the statue. Yes it was there, Scalfero's case. She knew now that he had filled it with cash as she had imagined he would do, as clearly he would otherwise have let them go unhindered to discover his deception later. Now she knew that the cash was in the suitcase and now she was striding confidently, her heart beating rapidly, along towards Ponte Margherita looking for a taxi.

She had booked a room at a small hotel along the via del Corso opposite the taxi rank by the smart clothes stores. Not too far to travel, plenty of tourists to hide among.

She was sure that Scalfero would establish Royal's identity and where he had been staying. She could be sure too that the organised apparatus of the Ndrangheta was already in motion and she had to move swiftly to be ahead of it. There would be a lot of cash to hide.

Her taxi was outside the hotel she had directed it to in minutes. She entered hurriedly and waited until she saw it drive off. Then she exited and walked around the corner to the small Hotel she had booked into earlier that day in the names of two English women Mrs and Miss Beck and asked for her key.

'Room 37' She spurted to the receptionist unable to slow down her racing energy.

It was only when she had flung the suitcase onto the bed and opened it did she actually believe she had pulled it off. It was stuffed with more euros than she could ever have imagined. As she gazed in disbelief at her prize she sat down to think through her deception. Had she overlooked anything? She had brought a suitcase of clothes for both her fictitious hotel guests and had rehearsed her performances as each. She had ensured that the photographs in their passports were particularly poor representations such that a swift examination of them would raise no suspicion. She had made the booking for four weeks and certainly did not intend to stay in Rome for as long as that. Even now the Ndrangheta would be interrogating taxi drivers to find out who picked up a fare with a suitcase near the Piazza del Popolo. They may even have seen her with Royal and be looking for a young woman. That thought made her uneasy. It was time to dress as the elder Mrs Beck.

She looked nervously down to the street. Would she identify them easily enough? A certain type of man. A ridiculous mixture of arrogance energy and stupidity. She had seen them many times before, but she knew too how dangerous they would be to a thief like her. Someone who had the audacity to steal from the Ndrangheta.

This would be a nervous night but she had to stay in Rome until tomorrow morning. To leave now with a suitcase full of Ndrangheta money would run the risk of capture and certain death. She concealed the suitcase in the wardrobe, dressed herself as the elder Mrs Beck and left the room being sure to leave her key at reception to avoid suspicion.

'My daughter is feeling a little unwell.' She confided to the receptionist.

'She will remain in our room for the time being.'

It was the best she could do to post a guard but she felt sure that by doing so, there would be no staff entering the room in her absence. She could play the part of a middle aged English lady and enjoy supper in a Trattoria close by while she planned her next move.

It was only then, while she sat down to eat that she thought of something else. Her erstwhile companion and collaborator, Tom Royal. She had not even given him a moment's thought till then. While her mind was bent on her survival there had been no time. He had sacrificed his life to give her what she wanted. She allowed herself to feel a slight remorse but it was a feeling she found easy to put to one side.

Scalfero had spent some time the evening before the exchange watching his men load the cash into the suitcase. First it had been counted carefully bound in bundles of 10,000 euros. One hundred bundles, stacked neatly into the dark blue suitcase with leather straps and corners. This was why he could see straight away that the suitcase that was now delivered to the room at his palace by the motorcycle pillion was not the same as the one that he had passed to Royal.

'There has been a switch he said rising from his chair and not bothering to look further at the bag. Somewhere there has been a switch.'

The two henchman looked nervously at each other to question whether it was them that were being accused.

'No, No. I can see that it was not you. You are too stupid' He shouted in anger.

'That lanky American was cleverer than I gave him credit. He has duped me. Did you see anyone with him?'

It was following a brief interrogation of the two motorcyclists that Scalfero had got an idea of the deception. The suitcase had been switched almost as soon as he had made the exchange. But why did they allow the American to walk down the street. He had to be a decoy. While he walked down the street with the dummy suitcase someone was making a getaway. Where to, how?

'I want to know who got into a taxi by the Piazza de Popolo at around 15.00 carrying a blue suitcase and where they went from there. Pay what you need to for the information.' He instructed.

Segolene had been right in her assumption. The machinery for the recovery of the money had been set swiftly in motion. Tomorrow she would deposit it in the English bank account she had taken full details of when staying at Avignon and she would ensure that the owner of that account would soon be arriving in Rome. Soon one million euros would be safely in the bank account of Marcus Graham and she would see to it that that bank account would be in her control.

27.

ROME, ITALY

Father Simeon had spent a good deal of his time grooming his brother as to how to take on the role that Scalfero had ascribed to him. At times he became uncertain as to the outcome, but he had made his recommendation and given his endorsement and he now felt that by his own hard work and by the promise his brother had made to him that there would be the reward of success.

Father Simeon recalled the days of his own captivity in the hands of Scalfero. A captivity that he now recognised had been necessary to recruit his compliance in perfecting the part Jacopo was to play in the greatest deception of all. Consanguinity is not inconsistent with incarceration. Blood imposes duty, engenders envy and expectation as well as affection and love, and it is these qualities that caused father Simeon to reflect upon the service he owed to the order while alone in a dark cell surrounded only by brittle grey stone walls. He had reflected on the prophesy that Scalfero had assured him told of the role they had to play and seen the potential for its success.

The deception would be made possible by Jacopo taking the position of the American cardinal Raphael who would receive the election of the conclave and was to take his position following the death of the present pontiff. The likeness of Jacopo to cardinal Raphael was striking and his linguistics contemporised in the facility of English and Italian to which Father Simeon would add the basics of Latin.

The plan was that the new Pope would contract a chronic illness requiring the presence of the stipendiary Cardinals Tratavelli and the aged Dominic Dufour at his side for much of

171

his time. Among crowds he would be seen only from a distance and at close quarters he would largely be among the cardinals that were sworn to support the order.

The principal obstacle to Father Simeon's efforts seemed to him to be the over confidence and insensitivity of his charge. More than once the declaration had been made that there would be no problem with the deception. It had forced the uncharitable assertion in the mind of Father Simeon, that his brother was susceptible to a misguided apprehension that others were limited by the same level of intelligence as was he.

Father Simeon had spent his early years at the Vatican and was familiar with its rituals and respected its providence. For him life had been one long preparation for its departure. One long pious process of making arrangements for the journey. Now he had been allocated an earthly role that was to be his greatest challenge and purest privilege. He would provide the false Pope to its centre and to be the conduit to his direction. The Vatican would become the mouthpiece of the Order when as the prophesy had held that it would rule all matters temporal and spiritual within the Holy Roman Empire.

Father Simeon held his brother's hand to emphasise the importance of what he was about to say.

'The prophesy is contained in two revelations. First the revelation of Aix en Bairn to the children that included the young Oblate Beatrice and then 100 years later to that day there had been the revelation to the children at St Therese L'Enfant. Few knew the outcome of these prophesies but it is rumoured that they are just one prophesy in two parts. It is necessary to know of both in order to understand the meaning of their message.'

'Ok so what is this message all about?' Jacopo enquired with a note of disinterest.

'Few know that message and as much as I have in the past sought to find it I have been unable to do so. Now however the true destiny of our order is defined. The knowledge of both revelations is in our hands. The Padrino had been entrusted with the knowledge and he must now play his part in the deception that it inspires.' Father Simeon wondered whether his explanation had made any impression at all.

Jacopo snatched a glass of lemon juice and threw the liquid back down his throat to quench his thirst. Father Simeon watched uncomfortably as he reflected that the transformation from convict to Pope would take all his best efforts.

'Dignity Brother.' He said simply.

'It will need dignity'

'I got it, sure I got it. You won't see the difference.' Jacopo assured him smiling broadly.

Father Simeon sat back and looked at his brother studiously. It was as if he was watching a comedy. Cardinal Raphael was certain to become the next Pope and the part of the Pope would be played by a hood from Toronto who showed little understanding of ceremony and dignity and far less of divinity. He almost seemed to believe that it was a part in a film where to look the part might be sufficient, but whenever he looked at Jacopo he was struck by how much his brother resembled Cardinal Raphael. It gave him the hope he needed to be sure that his efforts would succeed.

'This whole thing will be busted if you don't get Raphael elected anyhow' Jacopo jibed seeking affirmation.

'We have seen to that brother. Cardinal Dominic Dufour the elder Cardinal of the conclave is stipendiary to the order he is able to take the confidences of all voting cardinals and is their trusted advisor. Cardinal Dominic Dufour has informed us that the Holy see praises the work of cardinal Raphael, he is the choice of the majority were anything to happen to his Holiness. Our plan is opportunistic, daring even but God has given us the chance to make it work'

Father Simeon knew well the documented file on the activities of the eldest in the conclave, Cardinal Dominic Dufour. Since he had joined the order of St Denis en Seine and throughout his service to the church he had revelled in buggery, rape, theft and sale of its valuables. His attempts to conceal his weaknesses had resulted in the murder of a local woman in Perpignan and he had been privileged to witness a greater effort made in concealing the truth rather than establishing it.

It was a past that an old and tired man wished earnestly to forget that had made him the servant of Scalfero and the principal stipendiary to the order serving in the Vatican. The scant remains of his honour and the silence of those who held the truth was the stipend paid for his service.

'It is the plan brother. Not every plan eventuates but we have to do our best to see to that it does. Sometimes it seems that there are many cats to herd but we never give up. It is the will of God.'

It seemed to Jacopo a fair summary and anyway he wanted to believe it. He had to believe in the prophesy too.

'You can rely on me. I won't let you down.' he said again.

'I know brother for you are aware of the penalty for failure.' Father Simeon answered coldly turning his head to look Jacopo squarely in the eye.

'Failure would be to dishonour our order and to dishonour our order can only mean death.'

'You will not dishonour the order?' Father Simeon questioned again.

'I have sworn to the sacred flame of St Michael like everyone else brother. Of course I will not dishonour our order.' Jacopo spat out, resenting the question that had been put to him.

For Father Simeon it was the confirmation he had been seeking. His uncertainty had never been as to his brother's honour but of his ability. He had recommended Jacopo to the role but there remained much to do to convince him that his decision had been a wise one.

28.

FRANKFURT, GERMANY

The Gecko bar in the centre of Frankfurt was buzzing at around 18.30. It was just the place to meet up for a drink and brief exchange and popular with the office workers from the tall buildings that surround it. Peter Beck placed a large glass of Steinfest bier on the table in front of Swartz taking a sip from his own glass to avoid it overflowing as he sat down at the small table in front of the police officer.

'The Strojnica is a Croatian machine gun based on the famous Israeli Uzi.' Swartz began.

'It holds about 20 rounds of 9mm and there were two of them. Enough fire power to cut down seven people effectively in an instant I would say. There are plenty of these weapons available in Europe following the Balkan wars and we know that organised crime has acquired a fair share. There are all the hallmarks of a gangland killing here. We are certain now that this was some kind of Mafia feud.'

Swartz sucked the cool bier with clear appreciation.

'Mafia?' Peter questioned.

'Seems our dearly departed friend was no angel. He worked as director of Drexel Hesse bank but we knew that there was more to it than that. Now it seems there are investigations going back years into their activities. Financial crime mainly, fraud, extortion, theft but our friend also had a few interesting enterprises on the side.

'Like what? You mean he ran his own loan book?'

'Not quite a loan book. Meyer ran a prostitution ring, and narcotic distributor as well as some pretty creative money lending.'

'That sounds like there might be a motive. Any idea who killed him?'

'It was pretty clearly a rival gang. Our information is that as Meyer came here from Calabria. Well, we have suspected for some time that Drexel Hesse was laundering cash for the Calabrian mafia.'

'You don't say.'

'The killings have all the hallmarks of gang wars. Someone else wants to take over the business here. We are talking Ndrangheta wars.'

Peter Beck looked up. He did not catch the final sentence.

'We are talking what?'

'Ndrangheta wars. These guys are from Calabria in the toe of Italy. There is this Mafia called Ndrangheta they say they were originally Greek settlers. The word Ndrangheta is Greek, it means something like man of honour or some shit like that. The whole system works through brotherhood, families that don't dare tell, all of the same blood. That sort of stuff. Two rival gangs of the Calabrian mafia are about to slug it out in front of our noses. The winner will control the business in Frankfurt.'

Peter sat thoughtfully for a moment.

'Has this anything at all to do with the tiny dancer killings. The public are more concerned about those than gangsters?'

'I would be surprised if it has. We really have no lead on those although I can assure you that we have people working on it night and day.' Said Swartz anxious to assure the journalist that everything was being done that could be.

'It just seems to me a strange coincidence that they died on the same day' Peter questioned rhetorically.

'But these bankers had just returned from Italy. Why were the executions not carried out there if it was mafia?'

'I guess they wanted to show that they were in control in Frankfurt. That was the point. To eliminate the opposition and take control. My guess is that there is a change of command. Like when a lion takes over another's pride. He kills off the cubs and seizes the pride and the territory.' He laughed at the metaphor.

Peter Beck was taking it all in to his head. The idea of organised crime in his city was new to him. Strange really for a journalist but he just had not come across it before.

Swartz sucked on his beer again before continuing.

'Time was they kept themselves busy with a bit of extortion, prostitution, protection and kidnap, pretty well on a local level. Well now days these clans have been making so much cash importing cocaine from Columbia they need to launder the money through legitimate businesses. Clean it up so to speak. We think they had been using this bank in Frankfurt for some time. There could have been some sort of fall out among them and that is what we have seen here' He took another long draught of the beer now before adding.

'These guys don't seem to appreciate healthy competition and are not the type to take prisoners.'

'So what do you suppose the police will do about them?' Peter asked beginning to feel that the situation presented quite a challenge.

'Well there is a problem. A change of personnel like this means we don't really have a true handle on who is involved. We are almost better off with Gustave Meyer still in place at least we knew him, his home, family that sort of thing. Now we will have to do some more research. We can't exactly arrest every Italian in Frankfurt. We would run out of pizza.'

'So Meyer rang me just before he died. He was going to tell me something. You think he may have known who killed him.' Peter asked.

'That seems very likely. We are checking out his offices for evidence. The movement of funds has always been a strong indicator of commercial and political strategies now it seems that they may give us some background to this criminal organisation too. Merchant banks are uniquely placed to read the signs. Since the days of the Medici one of the roles of foreign based merchant banks has been the gathering of intelligence. Drexel Hesse is in a powerful position within a dynamic financial centre. Hell Meyer is the eighth death on the Drexell Hesse staff in just a few days. Our people are crawling over the place'

'Has his family said anything?' Peter asked.

'Seems they knew nothing heard nothing. The assassin walked straight in the house strangled Meyer in the next room and they heard nothing. I don't think they really knew he was involved in this sort of stuff. Thought he was just a banker. Families can be very disinterested so long as the bills are being paid '

Peter had felt cheated of a story but as he sat listening to Swartz he began to feel that he may be better off getting the details second hand. Too much knowledge may well be dangerous in such a situation. His piece would now be retrospective and that evening he sat at his lap top and began to write.

'*The Drexel Hesse bank in Frankfurt is housed in a small and undistinguished modern building close to the Palmergarten. To all appearances this is a typical local bank dedicated to the commerce of the district and working within the strict financial limits of the savings of the hardworking local people of the state accumulated within it. This is a business model that can be easily understood by any one versed in commercial undertakings and their requirements for funding and financing facilities.*

It seems that Drexel Hesse however had been more than an innocent private bank. A whole strategy of business that redefines conventional banking and took its activities to a more sinister level altogether has emerged. The bank's business included the habitual foreclosure of mortgages following any breach of its banking covenants and the onward sale of such property at distressed values to its real estate subsidiaries. It acquired distressed debt and acted in the enforcement of debt recovery in innovative ways, often finding it easier to collect from the family of a deceased debtor than from the debtor himself.

It has now been revealed that the bank invested money from organised crime in the south of Italy into real estate and was a significant purchaser of distressed real estate debt bringing its recovery skills in to ensure the maximisation of upside. The Drexel Hesse bank was the principal financial laundering operation for much of the Calabrian mafia.'

Peter paused and read over his piece. It was much as Swartz had told him. What suddenly occurred to him now was that he had written it in the past tense. It almost gave the impression that now things were about to change. But the city had changed its easy style and fluid pace. Out there now roamed a band of killers more ruthless than any he had heard of before and somewhere even darker the demons who had slain two innocent girls in a macabre ritual.

29.

ROME, ITALY

'Of all the gifts that God has given to mankind, the most complete of these is Italy.' The taxi driver spoke good English and grinned widely as he delivered his patriotic statement and he turned to look at Marcus for a response.

Marcus smiled silently in the passenger seat in the rear of the car feeling good to have arrived in the city. He recognised in those words something similar that Father Fidel Rocher had said to him.

'Rome is the jewel that sparkles brighter than all others in the Mediterranean sunlight. She is the city whose bounty leaves replete all the appetites and urges of mankind.'

He remembered too his corollary to that sentiment.

'She is my friend the beautiful mistress who tempts us with the sensuous backward glance over her naked shoulder, and leads us to enjoy the cherished warmth of her embrace, only then to destroy us. Remember my friend the words of Tacitus. All things atrocious and shameless flock from all parts to Rome.'

Now Rome, whose beauty hides the sins of two millennia, was parading herself before his eyes as the car was now speeding south along Via del Corso. Marcus looked out at the magnificent architecture of the Monumento a Vittorio Emanuele standing grandly looking over the Piazza Venezia. He saw the statue of Marcus Aurelius astride his horse. The Emperor soldier and philosopher looked out at the eternal city with a certainty and permanence that had defined it as Italy's capital since 1870. Here was the hero that Marcus wished to emulate. For Father Fidel Rocher had told him.

'Man must never long surrender to the comfort of subordination. He must meet life's challenge with the body of the soldier and the mind of the philosopher.'

He had come to Rome with a mission that had been bestowed to him by the weakened old friar. A mission he had been told, would fulfil a destiny preordained for him by an accident of circumstance. No longer was he an anonymous Architect, apprehensive of the women in his life and controlled by others. To him had been entrusted the role of the messenger to warn of an event that would create the change of one world order to the next for change is inevitable and here in this eternal city, life was about to change for Marcus Graham.

The taxi had pulled up outside a small hotel on the Via Droco. Marcus tipped its driver generously and strode in to the reception feeling comfortable that he would carry out the plan that he had set out with Father Fidel Rocher to warn of an impending perturbation.

First he planned to spend two days in the city as a tourist. To get the feel of it know where the various landmarks were situated and how best to travel around. It might then be possible to understand how best to approach the Vatican to convey the message that Father Fidel Rocher was so desperate to communicate to them before returning to Avignon to continue his work.

That evening he strolled around acquainting himself with the city. He marvelled at the baroque architecture of the Trevi fountain. Its architect Nicollo Salvi had won an architectural competition organised by the then Pope. He thought again of 'the winning' and felt again the warmth of a pride tinged with guilt of his having discontinued with the project uncertain that he would be able to fulfil it. He felt better to reflect that Salvi had not completed every part of his masterpiece. Some details were the work of others.

Legend has it that the ancient Romans were guided to a source of water some thirteen kilometres from the city by a young virgin. An aqueduct was constructed to bring the water into the city which served its needs for 400 years. It was called the Aqua Virgo after the young girl who had led them to the water source. That one young girl had saved Rome Marcus reflected by the source of water. Now it would be for him deliver the message that would be its salvation.

The Architects of Rome were so often Sculptors and many of their buildings look as if they are carved from their stone like individual pieces of art, unlike the regimented style of a city like Paris where a conformity of planned design is apparent. Here buildings compete with each other and at every turn there is wonder.

As he stood marvelling at the Fontana del quarto fiumi in the piazza Navona the small figure of a man no larger than a dwarf staggered towards him with an unusual gait and stood by the fountain taking in its beauty. His wide face was dark and his head crowned with long unkempt hair but in his eyes was a lively brightness that gave an impression of intellect.

'Few sculptors can rival Bernini' The man said in a heavily accented English in a strange whining voice shaking his head from side to side.

'But there is in his Damned soul more of beauty than in his Blessed soul, and in his Rape of Proserpina there is more excitement than his Ecstasy of St Theresa.' He laughed at this in a way that was like the cackle of a goose.

Marcus acknowledged this observation with a light smile. Is this, he thought the conflation and co-existence of opposites that Father Fidel Rocher had so often spoken of? Is there a symmetry of good and evil in art that life itself imitates?

'You are in Rome to see our great art for yourself?' The dwarf asked as if he intended to make conversation.

'Indeed I am' Marcus responded unsure whether a more truthful response would be easily explained or reasonably believed'

'Then you must go to the opera. The ruins of the Caracalla baths by the Appian way outside the old part of the city of Rome are one of its splendid sites of antiquity. They offer the most delightful venue for the best performances. During the summer months the Teatro dell Opera takes over this historic setting for a summer of its most popular shows set against the backdrop of the ancient stone buildings. Ah, you will not be disappointed' It was a suggestion that Marcus felt inspired to act upon. His hotel receptionist was successful in booking a ticket for the performance the following evening.

Marcus was looking forward to seeing Rigoletto for the first time. The music he knew well but despite frequent visits to Covent Garden and other Opera houses he had never seen the story of the court jester who has a curse cast upon him and the death of his beautiful daughter caused by his own blundering intrigue. Now Marcus was to see Italian Opera performed in Italy.

He had left his hotel and been walking now for some 10 minutes towards Termini where he would take the bus to the Opera. It was an indirect route he had chosen to take him there that would incorporate some of the delights of the side streets that led from his hotel. It was thereby unlikely to be a route chosen by others and therefore easy to become under the impression that he was being followed.

Marcus looked over his shoulder as he turned the corner. There were two of them and they did not appear to be too concerned to conceal themselves. A second quick glance behind him as he turned into the Via Baca confirmed it. Perhaps they were following him to the Caracalla but there was something in their movements that told him that they were not going to listen to Opera. At once he concealed himself in a side doorway hoping that they would move on thinking he had run ahead. Shrinking in that doorway he realised how foolish he was. They only had to come by and check the doorway and he would have lost all advantage. There was nothing he could do now.

To Marcus's relief the pursuers seemed anxious to move on to follow their quarry. Perhaps he had shaken them off – if indeed they had been intent on following him. Perhaps a pair of robbers who had spotted a foreigner in their mist. They would move on to do their mischief elsewhere. Perhaps they had no mischief to perpetrate and it had been merely his imagination.

It was still early that evening when he took his seat in the audience next to a group of vibrant and vocal Romans. It was a pleasure to see how involved they were in the show and how proud they were of this Italian opera. Marcus reflected how when in Venice, Verdi had written the music for Rigolleto, the city had been under the auspices of the Austrian empire and this opera had been banned from public performance. It was only since 1870 that Italy had been united under the Risorgimento and all things Italian and especially its opera are now celebrated around the world.

As a group of actors passed by him on the way to the rear of the stage, one dressed in savage black and darkened eyes could be identified with a high level of probability as Sparafucile the assassin and what a splendid assassin he looked. Now he, Marcus thought to himself is a believable assassin, not the imitation that poor Segolene had been reduced to in the Felebrigian play. The memory of that travesty still haunted him.

He watched the first act of Rigoletto and found it enough to provide distraction from any preoccupation. The lecherous Duke's opening piece feigning his inability to choose among the many beautiful women of his court and the wonderful limpid music to the court's dance that inspires ones humour aware of the sycophantic courtiers gracefully engaged hand in hand moving back and forward to the front of the stage.

At the interval Marcus got up to stretch his legs. There was just time for a cold drink too and he bought a cool cup of lemonade and drew it to his lips. It was then that he saw them. They had been sitting not so far away to his rear. Two heavily set men in dark clothing looking somewhat out of place among an audience predominantly of couples. They looked as though they were about to attend a business meeting rather than settle down to Act two of Rigoletto. He was unsure whether they were the pair he had felt were following earlier but there was something in their presence that made Marcus feel uneasy. They were almost unnaturally not looking his way yet some instinct told him to be cautious.

He returned to his seat uncertain as to what the presence of the pair meant and while he was able to convince himself that they probably had nothing to do with him he was determined that just in case he would devise an exit that would give them no opportunity to prove him wrong.

As the crowd got up to leave after the final curtain Marcus heard two young American voices just over his shoulder. He turned to them.

'What did you think of the performance this evening?' Marcus asked determined that he should get involved in conversation so as not to be seen leaving alone.

'Real cool.' answered the girl smiling.

'We are in Rome for just four days, Travelling throughout Europe. It's been amazing, so exciting.'

Marcus could see the two men out of the corner of his eye. They were not looking his way. Perhaps he had been mistaken in his preconception. He sought anyway, to continue a dialogue with the young Americans.

'Where about in the States are you from?' he asked knowing that that was the prime point of conversation made by all Americans abroad.

'Oh we're all the way from Cleveland, Ohio.' Came the response.

He had successfully engaged the conversation of two quite willing participants. It would be easy to stay by their side while exiting the building and then to move among the crowd and loose the two men who were now attempting to appear themselves to be making a casual exit but at the same time moving towards him.

'Excuse me but you sound English.' The American observed.

'Oh yes, yes English. From London.' He confirmed not wishing to lose the flow of conservation and contriving to depart alongside the young couple but as they turned it was clear that they were heading toward the two figures. Marcus moved in the other direction and felt his pace quicken as he looked over his shoulder to see the two figures looking firmly in his direction. He had now to lose them. He turned the corner to see a doorway set back from the frontage of a small house standing at an angle to the main road. He could feel the frenzied beat of his heart its sound almost audible as he crushed his body against the door to conceal himself from his pursuers. It was a moment that felt like minutes. He squeezed tight his eyes not daring to observe the two figures moving swiftly past him shooting searching glances from side to side as they went. They had missed him. Marcus eyes now followed the path of his pursuers to an empty horizon. Triumphantly he turned, looking now behind him uncertainly for any sign of them.

Just at that point he saw them again. They had clearly decided that they had missed him and were hastily returning towards him. Marcus toyed momentarily with the idea that these two pursuers were not looking for him at all but his instincts told him otherwise.

The door in the hoarding around the construction site was indented sufficiently for him to conceal himself by spreading his body and pushing himself against it. Then a small miracle happened. The lock had not been fastened and the door swung open with his weight against it allowing him to step back into the building. Quickly he forced shut the ailing door feeling that he had escaped for the time being from his pursuers.

Looking behind him into the site was less encouraging. It was small and enclosed all around by a high wall. The façade of the building on the site was shored up and reinforced concrete floor beams were in the process of being positioned by a tower crane positioned in the centre of the site. At first he felt there was nowhere to go. Nothing to do but wait until he could exit the site through the door.

Then that he saw an opportunity. The jib of the crane had been positioned over the roof of an adjoining structure. This was possibly intentional as something may have been lowered onto that roof as the last operation of that day. Before he had thought it through Marcus was climbing the steel rungs of the crane's ladder to undertake his escape in the half-light along a crane jib and then to lower himself onto the neighbouring roof.

Looking down below into the side street he saw his chance. The girl had simply disembarked the small scooter and entered a door by the side street its engine still running. It was an open invitation, a lucky break. He would be a fool not to take it. He swiftly lowered himself down from roof to roof one storey at a time till he had reached the street. Marcus took hold of the handlebars of the scooter almost before he had sat on the seat and wound back the throttle. The small engine whined and he could hear the young female voice behind him shouting in Italian. She would understand he assured himself. She would see that his life was in danger. He turned the corner to the exit the narrow street and onto the highway and sped off weaving unintentionally as he sought to master the controls of the scooter. The traffic was slowing as it approached a junction and Marcus saw his chance a side street that seemed to offer the opportunity to escape. He turned the scooter left along a narrow alley and emerged at a point where a car was parked by the junction.

Suddenly his progress was halted and he saw in front of him the broad figure of a man. It was dressed in the black and purple medieval costume he recognised at once as being one of the actors in the Opera. He stood blocking the way and on his countenance was a malevolent grimace. In his right hand was held a small pistol which was pointed purposefully at Marcus chest. Only a short time ago Marcus had been watching the figure on the stage, but it was not the Duke nor the buffoon himself who stood before him. It was Sparafucile, the assassin.

He could not recollect what happened then. A blow perhaps to his head from behind him. What he remembered was how night and day were blurred by his confinement and concealment in the rear of a succession of at least three different vehicles that were taking him on the road to somewhere that he reckoned could be south of the city. He sensed a crossing of the river and thought he felt the glare of the morning sun on the left side on one of the vehicles. He had been drugged inconclusively which had the effect of his waking for brief and incoherent periods that captured little in his recollection but the most momentary of sounds sights and smells. The sound of the engine murmured in his mind. A continuing drone that drove out all other sounds. A smell of fuel and the shouts of voices outside the truck as the diesel was pumped in. The sick feeling the motion of the vehicle had caused him and the hard ride on the steel floor caused him confusion.

He did not know where he was being taken nor why. He did not know what the outcome would be, but what he felt certain of is that he was a prisoner of the Ndrangheta.

30.

EARLS COURT, LONDON, ENGLAND

Emma Dreyfus busied herself in her flat in Earls Court around three activities simultaneously. She was cooking a light supper, taking a shower and washing her hair, while the flat screen on the wall in the bedroom was showing a collection of the short news clips she had downloaded from the internet onto a CD. Just about every electrical appliance in the flat was on. Lights blazing, cooker heating, telephone charging, bathroom fan clearing a fog of vapour and TV playing. She felt better when the centre of action. It helped her think, and this evening she knew she had some thinking to do.

Emma dried herself in her bathrobe and wrapped a dry towel around her head folded into her hair with a dexterity that resulted in a secure towel turban. She grabbed at the remote and sent the screen into rewind, plumped up three pillows and prepared herself to sit back on her bed and watch the screen. Supper would be another 10 minutes or so. Just time to catch up with the range of news items she had selected from YouTube.

All the items were in Italian. However there was little dialogue and it was easy to work out what was taking place. The first showed The Café de Lyon in the Via Veneto in Rome. A convoy of cars from the Caribinieri was taking suspected criminals from the building. A serious faced athletic looking officer was being interviewed for the camera. Lieutenant Costanzo reported how organised crime was running this landmark restaurant as a base for activities in Rome. There had been arrests and shootings in the capital and he declared that he would see to it that the Caribinieri would route out organised crime in the city.

Emma remembered having been to Rome, and she recognised the Via Veneto, a smart tree lined street of Hotels and Restaurants just south of the Villa Borghese. She recalled that one of its beautiful buildings houses the American embassy in Rome. It was not somewhere she would have associated with organised crime.

The next clip was a report from Italian television into shootings in the German city of Frankfurt am Main. It showed bodies being taken from the airport building. It reported the fear that there was an increased presence of organised crime on the streets of this city.

Finally a story of an unidentified naked body had been found dead in a remote part of Calabria in the south of Italy. He had been shot in the head in a manner the report suggested, typical of executions carried out in the area by members of Mafia crime organisations.

The short videos she had been watching were the result of some internet browsing. She had been researching something for Marcus. He had asked her to find out more about the image of St Michael slaying the devil which he had seen on a tattoo on Luc's arm. What was meant by the tattoo? Who used it and why? For Emma the answer was just a swift Google search away, but it had resulted in a protracted browsing of a subject she had found increasingly fascinating.

She had established that the tattoo was intended to represent St Michael the archangel slaying Satan. The depiction of St Michael found in the Church of Santa Maria Della Concezione dei Cuppuccini in Rome fitted the description. At first she had thought this a strange subject for a tattoo but her research seemed to be pointing to an answer. It was not one she had felt very comfortable with.

Emma paused the screen and plated up her supper; a hot ready meal of pasta and chicken with a toasted baguette and a large fresh tomato. In the short distance from the kitchen area to the table she had scooped up two mouthfuls of pasta. She was not one for ceremony at mealtimes, and she was in any event distracted by the increasing pile of papers and photographs that she was assembling in a file marked Marcus on the dining table.

As she finished her meal Emma methodically drew her evidence into chronological order starting at the back of the file so that she could add easily to it as things proceeded. His latest email had reported to her Luc's poisoning of the old priest and his theft of the diary. Without reading it Emma printed it swiftly and added it to her papers. She carefully highlighted the date of each of the emails she had received from Marcus. It was a varied combination of items and comments that when understood would start to throw some light on the events that Marcus was experiencing there. What she had not noticed was that the most recent email she had printed did not include the final paragraph. The paragraph explaining Marcus intention to visit Rome was missing simply because her printer had run out of paper.

Emma paused as she came across his email that revealed the remarkable news of the appearance of his daughter, Segolene. The truth is she could not bring herself to accept that Marcus' daughter had simply turned up and announced herself. Perhaps she resented the chance encounter that seemed to have resulted in a redirection of his allegiances. She worked as personal assistant to him and Fitz and while her relationship with the latter was on a basis of taking and executing his grandly announced instructions she was much closer to Marcus. She regarded him almost as a father figure; he was always interested in her personal life though not intrusively. He was often complimentary on both her dress and her execution of tasks, understanding that occasionally these required much extra effort outside hours, whereas Fitz would see only that this additional effort had been made out of wholehearted enjoyment of working with FHF. Marcus was far more appreciative and understanding.

She knew that this was a reaction that was not logical nor was it fair to Segolene, but nevertheless it was the reason why Emma Dreyfus was inclined to question the authenticity of the daughter who Marcus had rediscovered.

She was muttering to herself as she walked towards the door on hearing the bell ring. She hardly acknowledged Rick who entered with a smile on seeing her questioning herself aloud in a disjointed manner. While Rick looked at her with affection, he was a little uncertain how interested he should be in her rambling self-questioning.

'It is quite extraordinary.' She was saying.

'It appears that Marcus daughter long believed dead has just turned up at the very place he was working. Did she know that he was going to be there? If so how? Had Segolene researched Marcus whereabouts in England? Her grandparents knew that he was training to be an Architect at the time of their daughter's death. Perhaps she traced him through his profession. I am at least uncertain as to the identity of Segolene. We should look into her background to discover as much as we can about her.' I am sure that Marcus' child died in the car accident and I am certain that we will prove that by the death certificate I intend to obtain.'

'Perhaps she's a cuckoo' He observed half-heartedly.

'You mean laid in Marcus's nest for him to feed' She humoured. I hardly think so.

'Not to feed. She may have been placed there for some other reason' He said with more seriousness.

'Brood parasitism is practiced by several species in nature. I did a term paper on avian brood parasitism at Cambridge. The best known example of the avian brood parasite is the Clamator glandarius or Great spotted cuckoo. The male will fly near the nest of a chosen host parent so the parent flies at it to scare it off and in that short time the female lays her egg in the host parent's nest. Often she will kick out one of the eggs in the nest so that the host parent is not alerted. The cuckoo's egg has a harder shell so when laid on the side of the nest it can roll in and crack one of the host's eggs' Rick had helped himself to left over baguette and begun to eat it.

'I have definitely lost you Rick. Why on earth are we discussing Cuckoos? I am trying to get to the bottom of the situation that Marcus is in' Emma pleaded.

'I am even wondering whether the Mafia are somehow involved. The tattoo on her boyfriend's arm is definitely one used by some Mafia clan.'

'Well that is an interesting point Emma. The Clamator glandarius employs what are known as 'Mafia tactics' to ensure that the host parent does her job. First they will frequently visit the nest to ensure that the young cuckoo is being looked after and then if it is not do you know what they do?'

Emma was now curious. She felt that this might be leading somewhere.

'What do they do?'

'They depredate the nest. They ransack it and kill the host's parent's chicks.' He looked at Emma's shocked expression. He had ended his explanation as if he had answered the question but fascinated as she was by this fact, she remained confused.

'So what are you suggesting? Segolene has been planted as Marcus's daughter by a 'Clamator' of some kind. She is there to get something out of him?' she questioned rhetorically.

'There is something else that may be relevant' Rick continued.

'The brood parasitic bird will often choose it's host parent. Often this will be the same species as she was brought up in. Certain types of avian brood parasites mimic the eggs of the host species so that they will not notice the parasites egg. So there is a reason why the parasite is placed in that nest and not any other. Are you with me?' He paused.

'Yes I am starting to see just what you are saying. You are saying that Segolene did not choose to claim to be Marcus's daughter randomly. She had a reason for doing so.'

'Exactly Emma. The question is, What is that reason?'

The notion had not occurred to her before and it made her feel a chill of discomfort. She Googled the phrase 'brood parasitism' and came up with an image that intrigued her. The avian brood parasite was a cow bird chick surrounded on each side by its host parents, a pair of scarlet tanagers. The pale almost white colouring of the chick contrasted strongly with the scarlet plumage of the host parent birds. Their wings like capes around them put her in mind of an image she had very recently seen but could not recall what it was. She retrieved the Sunday paper and its colour supplement and there it was, the photograph on the front of the colour supplement. It was of the Pope standing between two cardinals. What had struck her was how the image and its colours were so similar. If that image was to stay in her mind it was also to prove portentous.

'We do seem to have a number of interesting facts here.' Emma said thoughtfully.

'This diary that Father Fidel Rocher told Marcus of' said Rick. 'You say it has been stolen? It reported a series of revelations by the Virgin Mary given to Beatrice in 1892 when she was a child living in a village in the south of France didn't it? The revelation speaks of the antichrist placing his servant in God's temple to wear the Fisherman's ring. Isn't this prediction similar to one in the book of Revelations? The most intriguing reference seems to me to be to a second edition expected one hundred years in the future, that's 1982. Is that right?' Rick questioned.

'That's right and according to Father Fidel Rocher a second revelation has taken place in a small village in the Pyrenees in 1982 when the virgin apparently referred to first revelation one hundred years earlier. Father Fidel Rocher had said that the two revelations each gave part of a secret prayer that when written together gave protection to their bearer.' Emma confirmed.

Emma looked through the email from Marcus thoughtfully.

'In both these revelations the Virgin Mary appears to give an omen to three small children. In both She states that two of them will die shortly thereafter and she gives an event that occurred on the same date. In both she says that the earth will pour forth a red rage and many will be destroyed. (This is assumed to be an eruption of Vesuvius, apparently Nostradamus said something similar.) Beatrice was the child who survived the first of these revelations and who went on to become a nun living in the very chapel Marcus is working on.'

She must have left the diary to explain all this in detail so that someone could piece together the secret prayer. And now that diary has been stolen by Luc. I wonder when she died.' Rick said suddenly.

'What do you mean? Emma questioned.

'Well after 1982? No not possible she would have to have been about 110 years old. So she didn't write the diary up after the second revelation. Just checking, he affirmed with a mischievous smile.'

Emma was determined to be sceptical about this although she was becoming more fascinated as she read on.

'He says no one knows what happened to Maria Anna the surviving child given the second revelation. Isn't that curious?' she murmured thoughtfully.

Then suddenly she sat up with a start. She had gone to write down Annie's maiden name and realised that she did not know it. It was then that something occurred to her in a flash of inspiration.

'Hey I have had a thought' Emma suddenly announced victoriously.

'What if Annie had been Maria Anna? What if she held part of the secret prayer given at St Therese L'Enfant. Her parents had taken refuge in Eyragues to extinguish her notoriety and in doing so had altered her name to Annie. Marcus never said anything to me about this but it was quite possible that he knew nothing about her past. If Maria Anna the surviving child at St Therese was Annie who married Marcus then she would have the second part of the secret prayer.'

'It all seems pretty far-fetched to me Emma but there are certainly some serious unanswered questions' Rick responded.

'Well someone believes there is something in all this' she stated.

'Why do you suggest that?' Rick questioned.

'I think someone stole the diary because they believe what it says.'

'Well could just be someone wanting an old artefact that may be of value' Rick answered.

'I hardly think so. They poisoned the old priest and that could have killed him. No, someone sees something significant in all this. These revelations corroborated each other as they were intended to.

Rick looked thoughtfully for a moment and said.

'Marcus never knew what caused the accident that killed Annie. Could someone intent on keeping the revelations secret have killed her? I mean what if they have assumed that Marcus's wife had told him of the revelations and that Marcus had come to Avignon to examine the Marian revelations of 1892 in order to complete the prayer?'

'My thoughts exactly. The arrival of a girl who cannot possibly be Marcus's daughter. The discovery of an old relic that reported the first revelation. The possibility that Marcus wife had been the surviving child at the second revelation at St Therese L'Enfant. An attempted murder of an old priest and the possibility that Annie's death was not after all an accident. There is also the sinister prospect that some kind of Mafia organisation might be involved in all this.' Emma summarised.

She studied again the mark of St Michael. With each inquiry one word had kept coming up on her search engine. It was a word that she had not come across before until it had been quoted repeatedly on the news items that she had watched earlier. It was a word that was difficult to pronounce and difficult to remember. But it was a word Rick recognised straight away from the telephone call he had overheard in Meyer's office at Drexell Hesse bank in Frankfurt. That word was Ndrangheta.

31.

AVIGNON, SOUTHERN FRANCE

The TGV to Marseille eased out of Lille station for its journey south. It would take just over four hours to reach Avignon. Emma Dreyfus sat back in the seat she had reserved, looked across at Rick and smiled.

'We are on our way then. I am pleased that you had some leave due. I feel that it is time we went to look for ourselves and it would be good to surprise Marcus.' She observed as if to remind Rick that she had needed to persuade him to take the trip.

'I can't wait to get this piece of the jigsaw to fit and I just know it has to be there.' She said as if she was booking an 'I told you so' when she would be proved right.

He smiled at her as if he was humouring her obsession though he was himself finding this all very intriguing. There was something of a puzzle before them and Emma's intuitive sense had flushed out some interesting facts that needed to be put together to provide answers.

'Wake me when we get to Avignon Emma' he said and closed his eyes.

She looked at him quietly and saw straight away that he was not sleeping but thinking. She felt glad to have him as her companion on this journey. Not only was it delightful to have a partner for any trip abroad but while Rick seemed a source of knowledge on just about every subject, for this trip that made him the ideal companion.

Emma had brought an English language newspaper with her. She opened it and appeared to read it. She was actually reading the page that always interested her most. Her horoscope. It spoke of an exciting time with a close companion much as she had expected it would. It was when she read the Virgo, the one she habitually read for Marcus that she became intrigued.

'A visit to a foreign city causes you to lose your way'

Was Marcus about to lose his way in Avignon? It had been some days since she had heard from him. Emma imagined that it may refer to her finding him somewhere. She looked up from the paper and changed the subject.

'The standard fare on this trip is cheese French bread and wine. I bought some at Lille. Better let me know if you get hungry.' She suggested watching him settle down for a relaxing journey and feeling that he would not be travelling the whole distance without sustenance. For her, sleep would be impossible. Her mind was turning over with the possibilities that might explain the circumstances that she would soon encounter in Avignon.

'I had thought that we should first go to surprise Marcus but I feel that we should go straight away to the burial ground. I really need to know what name Annie was buried under so that we can perhaps find out where Segolene was bought up and what name she had. I have to know whether Segolene is who she says she is before I see Marcus. We may just find out some clues there.'

Emma wondered if her words were heard as her companion was soon enjoying the exceptional comfort of the rail car seating and appeared to be going to sleep.

She had brought with her the catalogue of the Cimetiere Saint Veran that she had obtained on line which gave a full description of the cemetery they were to visit and she read from it.

'It lists some of the people buried there. John Stuart Mill has a tomb at Saint Veran. He was an economist and philosopher who promoted utilitarianism. I have no idea what that is.' She said dismissively.

'It suggests that the morality of an action is determined according to its effects rather than the motives which underlie it.' Rick responded while still appearing to be asleep.

'That sounds a bit ominous doesn't it? Justifying an action by its outcome. Why you could get away with anything.'

'Mill was a disciple of Bentham. You know, the greater good for the greater number of people.' Rick answered trying not to sound too knowledgeable.

'Hey listen to this one.' Emma added excitedly.

'Here is buried Mademoiselle Maurille Virot de Sombreuil who begged the executioner to save her father on the scaffold and was granted the request if she drank a glass of the blood from the previous beheaded victim.'

'Did she?' Rick enquired, roused by the novelty of the revelation.

'It doesn't say. I would guess she did. It seems a ghastly but small price to pay.'

'You don't know. She may have been scared she would spill it on her dress and stain it.' He suggested with a smile.

'How would she have got it off?'

Emma ignored his remark.

'Hey look!' She gasped. 'Here too is buried the ashes of Mademoiselle Beatrice Belfiel the Nun who in 1892 witnessed a revelation of the Holy Mother in Artix en Bearn. So she was buried there. I don't suppose they knew who she was when she was buried, they must have added her to the list after the diary was discovered.'

She put down the catalogue and volunteered an additional notation.

'I am certain that from what Marcus has said that it is also the last resting place of Annie Graham, a local girl who died in a car crash on the road to Saint Remy de Provence. The question is, is it also the resting place of Marie Segolene her infant daughter? Or is she still alive having been raised by her grandparents, and currently residing with her father Marcus Graham?'

The analysis, delivered so emphatically caused her to sit back with some satisfaction. She had set out the objective before them and was sure that she knew what the outcome would be.

It was a bright day without the true heat of August when they arrived at the gates to the cemetery at Saint Veran. It lies on the outskirts of the city of Avignon, a tranquil setting renowned for its beauty and as a place of ultimate rest it cannot be rivalled.

Many of the old tombs are works of art, laid out under the dark green leaves of trees that provide a cool shade and a refuge for the wide variety of song birds that populate their boughs.

The serenity and beauty of Saint Veran takes the mind away from the bitterness of death. Here death plays out its mystery. A mystery that holds the past in a protective custody. The mystery of silence, of secrets buried, of guilt forgiven, of wild indiscretions forgotten. Truths now buried, that will never surface to dispel the myths that feed the imaginations of the living.

They had spent some time enjoying in the unanticipated conviviality of its surroundings. Strolling among the graceful trees that throw their shadows upon planted walkways broken by splashes of quiet sunlight.

She reached for his hand and held it lightly perhaps for comfort, perhaps in anticipation, or perhaps it was the feeling of contentment in their togetherness. A feeling of incipient discovery among the beauty that death had so unexpectedly created.

Then suddenly there was a discovery. Here it was. A less enchanted space within all this beauty and serenity but nevertheless a place of rest and remembrance.

Emma read the inscription on the headstone.

'Maria Anna Temoin Graham. Much loved daughter.' She translated. So Annie was Maria Anna just as I thought.' Emma said triumphantly.

'It says nothing of 'wife' as you might expect.' He commented flatly.

'No nor mother.' I suppose they did not want to emphasise that. Something to do with the shame she had brought to them.

'There is something over here that you might just be interested in' Rick said with a slight confidence that suggested understatement.

Emma went over to where he was standing and stared at it. She could not believe her eyes.

It was a simple inscription. It was a surprise to her that he had noticed it at all, but it confirmed in a few short words what she had suspected. She read out those words aloud.

Marie Segolene Temoin Graham. Enfant.

So it is true she whispered. She died in the car crash with her mother. So who is the woman who has convinced Marcus that she is his daughter Segolene?'

'What's more' added Rick.

'Why?'

'Pour le Palais' Emma directed to the driver as they clambered into the rear of the taxi parked outside the gates of the cemetery.

As the car pulled away to gather speed she sat up with a start.

'Rick, the brood parasite. It's the brood parasite.'

He looked at her as if he was sure that she had become possessed. 'Remember I showed you the picture in the magazine when you were talking about brood parasites. You know the cow bird between two crimson birds was on Google? Remember I said it reminded me of a picture I had seen of the pope between two cardinals? Well that's it.'

'I am not with you but feel that I should be' He replied.

'He shall place his servant in the Holy church to wear the fisherman's ring. Don't you see the same people who placed Segolene in with Marcus are going to place someone into the Vatican to take the place of the Pope. It's another cuckoo.'

'Wow!' Rick responded 'Now we are on to something. We must get to see Marcus and exchange notes with him. Maybe he can throw some more light on this'

After a short taxi journey they arrived at the Palais.

'It shouldn't be too difficult to find. He said it was a cottage close to the Palais itself.' She confirmed confidently.

Hurriedly they searched the side street for something that looked as if it was the cottage but were soon outside the chapel building instead.

'Let's see if he is here. If not he is bound to be in his cottage'

At that point the young priest who had escorted Marcus to Father Fidel Rocher walked by.

'Monsieur Graham the Architect? No he has left to undertake a mission for Father Fidel Rocher Mademoiselle. He has left for Rome and will not be back for several days.'

Emma was alarmed by this news. He had not mentioned in his last email that he was going to Rome. Marcus would usually keep her advised of his choice of breakfast. It was most out of character for him to take such a step without letting her know.

Instinctively Emma concluded that there was something wrong. 'We could stay here or go back to London Rick but I feel that Marcus is in trouble. She remembered the horoscope for Virgo. A visit to a foreign city. Marcus was going to get lost in some way in Rome. If only she could contact him to tell him of her theory that the Ndrangheta planned to place someone in the Vatican to take the place of the pope. She thought for a moment. Surely that would be absurd they would have to make the Pope appear in his regular public appearances as if nothing were happening. That would be impossible. Then she thought, maybe it is true and Marcus was already aware of it. Was that why he had gone to Rome?

They stayed the night in a small but comfortable hotel outside the city of Avignon. Over a perfunctory breakfast of rolls and coffee Emma set out the position.

'So we are convinced that Segolene is not Marcus's daughter. He has gone to Rome. It is quite likely that he has been taken to Rome by her. We think that she may have been planted in his care by some sort of Mafia organisation. Why? Because he knows something about these revelations that we have been told about. His wife Annie was indeed the child who was given the secret prayer so they think he knows too much.'

'So what do you think she has taken him to Rome for?'

'To get him out of the way. If they plan to place one of their people in the Vatican to manipulate the pope they need to have him out of the way I mean they see him as having the two parts of the prayer. The one given to him by his wife and the other discovered from the Chapel. It has to be something like that' She suggested.

Rick looked at her quizzically. This was all sounding improbable but somehow he could not deny that it had a certain logic.

'I think that we should go to Rome and find him'

'How an earth do you expect to do that?'

'Simple, we just go to the police and tell them everything.'

'When do you plan to go?'

'I don't think that we have anything planned for today do we?'

Emma Dreyfus had got down to business in her usual efficient manner. She had telephoned the Caribinieri in Rome and explained that she suspected that the Ndrangheta had abducted her friend and that she wished to come to Rome and speak with them about it. She had been surprised to receive a call back by an officer fluent in English who confirmed that arrangements had been made for her to meet with a Lieutenant Costanzo.

'It is all arranged for first thing tomorrow morning she confirmed to Rick.

The offices of the Caribinieri were situated by the Via della Magliana under what looked like two apartment blocks. The taxi pulled up outside among a fleet of police cars parked by the side of the wide street. Rick squeezed her hand by way of reassurance.

'Be prepared for a few yawns. They're not going to believe all this easily.' He cautioned.

As Emma went into the building she was regretting having made the call. Clearly Rick was right. She would be dismissed as a crank.

'Miss Dreyfus?' asked a female voice presently.

'Lieutenant Costanzo will see you now.'

The officer was an athletic figure with dark complexion and strong alert eyes. She was unsure where she might have seen him before and then recalled that he may have been the officer who appeared in one of the news reels she had downloaded from the internet. He greeted them briskly.

'Miss Dreyfus?' He asked expecting confirmation.

'Yes and this is Mr Brown'

He waved at a chair in front of a desk covered with papers by way of an invitation for her to sit ignoring Rick as he did so.

'You say that you suspect that the Ndrangheta are involved in the disappearance of your friend?' Asked Costanzo sounding a little disinterested.

'Yes. My friend Marcus Graham. He had met a girl in Avignon in France who claimed to be his daughter. We established that she simply could not be. His daughter is long dead. This girl was accompanied by a man who bore the mark of Saint Michael which we understand is the mark of the Ndrangheta. Well now Marcus is missing.' She stalled at this point thinking that she sounded a little absurd. What on earth would this Lieutenant be making of this. It was at least rather circumstantial.

Costanzo looked at her as if he was not interested and then he said: 'Let me take down a few facts'

Emma decided that facts to an officer of the Caribinieri probably did not include horoscopes and wild theories about avian brood parasitism. She had better stick to what she knew.

'Well there seems to have been some interest in the work that Marcus was undertaking at the Chapel. It was as if he might discover something there that someone would find valuable.' Better not to say that it was a relic that contained Marian revelations she thought.

'The Ndrangheta or at least the branch of the Ndrangheta operating in Rome seem to be involved in mysticism. Do you know anything about that?' Constanzo asked unexpectedly.

Emma was taken aback. He had now given her the opportunity to reveal details of the revelations and the diary and her theory regarding the identity of the Antichrist and his placing his servant in the Vatican. It was being received far better than she had hoped. She explained the emails that she had received from Marcus, she assured the Lieutenant that he would be unlikely to have travelled to Rome himself without informing her. Her theory was that he had been coerced.

After about an hour they left feeling that there was every chance the Caribinieri might investigate the disappearance of Marcus. It had been a great deal more successful than she had anticipated.

Lieutenant Costanzo sat back in his chair behind the crowded desk and contemplated. It was certainly not the first report that he had had of a person abducted by the Ndrangheta. The police files were full of such reports. What was of particular interest to him in this case was that they were using a beautiful young woman to attract the victim. She had claimed to be his daughter and therefore must know something of the circumstances of the real daughter's death. He had written down the name she was using. Segolene, he murmured to himself softly. To pass herself off as Marcus Graham's daughter she would have the appearance of a woman of 25 years of age.

He looked through the file of information he had accumulated on the desk in front of him and thumbed through until he came across something that intrigued him. It was the report of Scalfero abandoning his daughter to an institution claiming that she was mad shortly after his wife died. She would now be in her mid-twenties.

'Magdalena? He questioned aloud on reading the notes again. I wonder if this could be Magdalena.'

32.

CALABRIA, SOUTHERN ITALY

The dark dungeon in which Marcus awoke had held its heat like an oven. The stone floor had the smooth surface of a washed pebble and the wall against which he lay entirely in contrast, the sharp brittle surface of volcanic rock. Above him in the ceiling was a small opening where Marcus could make out the small patch of bright blue sky that told him it was morning. His eyes were slowly adjusting their sight to the darkness and he could see now a single tap fixed to the wall. He reached out aching as he did so and pulling himself forward with his hand around the tap could tell straight away by the welcome cold wet metal that it was connected to a water supply. Eagerly he turned it on and bathed his face drawing mouths full of the cold liquid, almost laughing as he did so in exhilaration. Refreshed, he had exhausted himself and found himself falling to sleep again.

Some days passed in this way, without sustenance or the moderate dignity of basic sanitation that had compelled him to evacuate his bowels in the open drain that took away the waste water under the tap. This had inspired him to the an obsessive occupation of ensuring disposal of his faeces first by dissection and next by flushing with the reluctant flow of the tap water that brought with it a coolness that had had become his indulgence.

Marcus felt a fatigue in his limbs that disabled him to a point of seizure and a dull sleep settled on him. His eyes were blurred and his mind uncertain and confused. He saw her dressed as the comedic cardinal in the felebrigian performance, the role that he had detested for her. He stood up despite his weariness to stop the performance to the surprise of the players who all turned to look at him.

'No I will not see her dressed that way.' He protested in an act of pompous defiance.

He was remonstrating now for all to hear, demanding almost threatening as he thundered his objection and turned to the audience hollering his protest. Then one by one the audience rose and nodded their agreement with him. She should not be forced to play the part of the assassin she is indeed too beautiful they all seemed to be agreeing. She must play someone beautiful. Then started a slow handclap as the audience jeered the players shouting at them to recast the beautiful young woman as someone beautiful. He heard them chanting beautiful, beautiful, beautiful.

The actor centre stage held up his hand to silence the protest. He took Segolene's hand in a theatrical pose and led her off stage. Minutes later he returned leading her in triumph. The crowd now roared their applause and Marcus, weary with it all felt the delight of the moment for Segolene was now dressed in the long blue and gold striped dress with the lace bodice. Her hair flowing, her head crowned with the cute peasants cap. He recognised the part she was to play straight away as the beautiful daughter of Rigoletto in the Roman opera performance. She was Gilda and he delighted.

Marcus woke with a start. The suddenness of his waking kept the dream alive. How absurd he reflected. He had clearly been so affected by his daughter's performance as to recast her in his dream. Surely there were better dreams to occupy his mind. More useful dreams perhaps or maybe happier dreams.

Regrets can dominate the idle mind and his enforced idleness gave him plenty of time to regret. His failure with women, his lack of ambition in his vocation, and now his very fate was uncertain. He thought of what Father Fidel Rocher had said to him. That even God cannot change what had passed and he proposed a pact with God that if He would free him from this place then he would strive for a more fruitful future. God must get offered so many deals he thought, He could not accept them all.

He was sure that he was being held for some reason but he could not think why. A kidnap perhaps for a ransom. Perhaps merely mistaken identity. It would have been as night fell on the fourth day of his confinement that he heard the sound of the door to his cell being opened. There stood the figure of Sparafucile. The figure now dressed in the contemporary canvas trousers and an off white shirt open to the neck was the Albanian, Scalfero's henchman. While he was not dressed as the medieval assassin he had played the part of, his more contemporary appearance offered little comfort as Marcus was sure that the Albanian retained the threat of his elimination.

He was taken to a room along the corridor where light shone in broad rays across the floor. At first Marcus almost did not notice that he was not alone in the room. In its corner on the floor was a cage measuring about eight feet by four feet. He noticed at first a bright blue bowl on the floor and what appeared to be a pile of rags. The rags moved and Marcus could see the face of a small girl among them. Her pale and pretty face the countenance of abject misery.

Marcus heard a voice call from outside.

'Bring our guest out to the terrace.' It commanded in an Italian Marcus could understand and he was escorted up some narrow steps smarting at the bright sunlight that assaulted him.

Scalfero stood on the terrace of this fine home high on the hillside his back turned on the most splendid view of the bay of Naples. He was dressed in white dinner jacket and black bow tie against a starched white shirt which was fastened at the cuffs with gold cufflinks that bore a motive that was not visible. On his feet were a pair of shinning black shoes in pleated leather.

He studied Marcus in a quiet look of contemplation. Yet there was a fierce determination in his eyes that told of a savagery and his voice while clear had a thick and heavy accent. He thought he caught Marcus' eye looking over his shoulder to the sea.

'Oh yes, one is never tired of that view. I have owned this house for 15 years and spent a good deal of that time just looking at that view. There is history, beauty and power out there. A wonder to behold.' He gestured to a table by the terrace on which were arranged a number of cocktail glasses.

'You will join me? We can provide fruit juice if you prefer.' He smiled as if he had made a small joke.

Marcus was not clear at first from his accent whether he was German or Italian. He fostered a charm mixed with a tangible determination and it had clearly resulted in great wealth. He was lean and tanned a man perhaps in his late fifties. There was too, an air of malevolence about him in the manner and sound of his cultured English and the articulation of its delivery.

'You will know that so many of the events of this world are out of our power to control. We are not victims of these events. We must accept them like we accept the blessings of God or the travails of the seasons. Nature does not intend to bring blessings nor travails, only consequences. She is impervious to human preference, yet mankind interferes with nature out of pity.' With this he broached this dismissive understatement with a small smile.

'There is no mercy for the meek Mr Graham. Man lives on the meat of sheep, chickens and rabbits not on lions or wolves.'

Marcus could not help being reminded of Father Fidel Rocher in Scalfero's expounding of his philosophies but here he had an uneasy feeling that he was confronted by something quite different from the homespun philosophies of a friendly friar.

'I saw that I was not the only prisoner you have below' He hesitated, realising that his speech was circumscribed by a small injury to his lip which he drew his hand to instinctively.

'A young girl in a cage?' He questioned as if to prompt the confirmation of madness before him.

Scalfero nodded as if he knew that he owed his guest an explanation.

'You are aware of the art of haruspicy practised by the Etruscans?' He paused and looked enquiringly at Marcus and he walked across the terrace to the open drawing room as he spoke reaching for a small bronze object from a side table.

'I cannot say I am.' Marcus declined.

'Etruscan haruspicy involved the divination of omens by the examination of entrails. This bronze is the Liver of Piacenza cast in about 100 BC. It guides the Haruspex in the divination and I

Mr Graham have the privilege to be one such Haruspex. I have however added one refinement to the art. I have established what entrails better inform us and serve our purpose. Those of the innocent are for me the most revealing.'

Marcus examined the bronze passed to him. It was marked as if to section it into parts.

'You don't mean that you can look into the future by simply examining the liver of an animal?'

'Not an animal Mr Graham. He turned to look at Marcus straight in the eyes to contradict him.

'A human being.' He paused to give effect to his pronouncement.

'The torture of a beautiful young girl is the entertainment of many. It appeals to the carnal and savage urges of man while igniting a paternal indignation that extinguishes the sin of participation.' He looked into the distance to compose his exposition.

'Brutality is an ancient and enduring indulgence, a pleasure much prized by all classes and creeds. Its roots lie long before the antics of the colosseo. In the way that urchins hold a puppy by its tail over the camp fire at night to delight in its helpless whelp, so is the pitiful cry of the defenceless virgin the sound that will rock to sleep the spectator. For there is no outrage to shout, no mercy to administer, only the blunt detachment of pity and the cover of the night that clears away the feast to the freshness of a new dawn.' He paused at this as if to consider.

'We live in an age of spectacle. The age of the internet Mr Graham. Mankind would rather witness gestures than listen to reasons. we reach out to a desperate world of perversion that hides its face among humanity. Medieval torture is a culture that inspires many followers. They will pay handsomely for the privilege of its observation without the burden of participation. This young girl is far more valuable to us than you believe. Her beauty is her currency, her innocence her cross. We do not sin who bring her sacrifice to the eyes of those whose desires are sated by it.

His cold eyes fixed on Marcus. There was a certainty in these impossible words that had been delivered in the manner of a tea time conversation. The cultured voice, the suave delivery, the nonchalance of his manner. Marcus felt the thrust of a knife in his words. The horror of a hideous threat was at that moment lifted to a reality.

'And afterwards Mr Graham, the entrails of the Virgin excited by her distress, yield to us the map of our future.' Scalfero turned as if there was a further explanation he needed to make.

'I, Mr Graham am able to read that map for the benefit of mankind. You are aware of the credo of Nietzsche Mr Graham?' He posed expecting confirmation.

'Nietzsche's concept is of rule by the best, an aristocracy of excellence that will lead humanity to a higher plane rising to superior fulfilment to become Ubermensch. That is the goal of human evolution.'

'For Neitzsche has told us that "Only in the savage forests of vice can the new domains of knowledge be conquered."'

'It is unlikely to be popular with the people' Marcus observed lightly, uncertain how to respond to this extraordinary and chilling perception.

'Ah now that is a pertinent point Mr Graham. But the desire to be popular is a weakness in mankind not found in the Ubermensch. Democracy is a ball and chain holding mankind back from highest achievement. We do not believe in such shackles. We have seen that a regime that compromises brutality will be hostage to anarchy.

Mankind's leaders should live by a master morality above common concepts of good and evil. It is the goal of human evolution to be the Ubermensch the 'artist genius' who is to ordinary man as ordinary man is to a monkey.' He paused at this point. It was as if he had been quoting from some neo Nazi diatribe.

'But do you not believe as a Christian' Marcus interrupted.

'Christianity a sop for the weak the meek and the poor. Our task is self-fulfilment not self-denial. We aim to shake off the chains of tradition and the burden of history. We support the rights of the strong over the weak. Hope offers mankind only torment. It keeps him waiting for salvation that will never come.'

211

'You are an Architect Mr Graham. Architecture provides the construction of reality and the Architect has the ultimate mind of wisdom and artistic creativity. You must understand how important it is to our world that the Ubermensch is given reign to rule over the disparate proclivities of mankind? He is the artist master of mankind who must rule to further knowledge and maintain order, for what is intellect without ambition? A bird without wings. It is the eagle that flies highest. The raptor, not its prey.'

Scalfero crossed the room to where stood a second bronze bust on a marble stand.

'Look at this Mr Graham. Do you see any likeness?'

Marcus could see straight away that the bust was that of Scalfero.

'Well yes. I do, it's you isn't it?' Marcus suggested.

'Exactly! And yet I must tell you that it was sculptured over 50 years before I was even born. It is the Ubermensch by Rodin.' He looked at Marcus for a reaction.

'Do you not see Mr Graham. It is I who am the Ubermensch.'

Never had Marcus before been aware of such a combination of ambition cruelty and narcissism. It cut the air with a clarity of shone steel. Here was not only evil but the power influence and conviction to see that evil materialise.

Scalfero then showed him into a room adjacent to the terrace and pointed to the doorway on the opposite side.

'Do you recognise that Mr Graham?' He asked.

'Why isn't it a sculpture with the carvings of figures within the architrave? 'Marcus stammered. He had recognised the sculpture partly from a previous reference Scalfero had made to Rodin.

'It is, well it looks like Rodin.'

'Rodin's sculpture The Gates of Hell' Scalfero finished in his slow gravelly tone.

'It was modelled on the Last judgement painting in the Sistine chapel. I acquired the plaster cast and had it set in bronze. You will see that Rodin shows his starving man devouring his own children Mr Graham. That is what is called humanity. What humanity? Half of it have it stripped from them at birth by the indignity of poverty the rest exploit them, use them, cheat them abuse them. The Ubermensch sees that this is the reality of the human condition Mr Graham and seeks to rise above it.'

'Life cannot exist without death nor death without life. The book that has no ending is without value but darkness and light are of equal value, Mr Graham' He finished with an emphasis of Marcus name as he turned towards him eyes focused and his head lowered.

'But Mr Graham let us come to the point of why you are here. I understand that you have sought to discover the secret of the diary found at the Palais Chapel at Avignon and that you have had revealed to you the revelations of St Therese L'Enfant? You are minded to hold the secret prayer in your possession.'

Marcus looked at him in genuine bewilderment. First he did not immediately connect with the tale told to him by Father Fidel Rocher and he responded instinctively.

'I simply don't understand what you are saying' He started partly relieved to feel that this was some genuine mistaken identity.

'But wait do you mean this diary of prophesies that was found yes, I heard about that but I don't know what it was all about and I don't know who St Therese is'

'Oh come now Mr Graham. I cannot believe she did not tell you'

'Who? who did not tell me?' Marcus protested in his confusion.

'Your wife Mr Graham. Your wife told you the second part of the secret prayer revealed to her at St Therese L'Enfant that is why you, when hearing of the nun's diary, came to the Palais to examine it for yourself. Why else would you do so but to piece together the secret prayer. Do not take me for a fool Mr Graham.' Scalfero directed raising his voice.

Marcus was now more confused with this explanation than he had been before. His only wife had been dead for 25 years. He tried to recall what Father Fidel Rocher had said about the diary found at the chapel and about the second part of the revelations had been made at a village called St Therese L'Enfant.

'I really do believe that you have jumped to some extraordinary misunderstanding. My wife died some 25 years ago and she certainly never spoke to me about a secret prayer.'

'I have perhaps underestimated you Mr Graham' Scalfero said thoughtfully.

'I had wanted to reach an agreement with you so that you might share in the prosperity that is to be mine. You must know that the boundaries of creativity lie well outside the comfort zone. You must be prepared to set aside conformity. The architect has it in his grasp. He is the ultimate artist artisan. He stands alongside the sculptor the painter in the creation of art. It was here in Italy that the Renaissance changed our world through these arts. It was in Rome that sculpture and architecture have combined to give us the greatest achievements and monuments. Surely Mr Graham you understand that this comes at a price to mankind. It is a price worth paying.'

'You think that the death of a child is a price worth paying for your ambitions to be realised?' Marcus stabbed losing patience with him.

'The masses have always lived for spectacle. Such it was in ancient Rome to watch death in the Colloseo, the thrill of feeling alive while another dies to the agony of torture before your eyes. You could have shared with me that feeling Mr Graham. But you have disappointed me Now I see that you are regrettably unwilling to cooperate.

He looked at Marcus with eyes that seemed to penetrate into him.

'It appears Mr Graham that you will have to return to your room for further contemplation before we achieve a meeting of minds'

With this he nodded to the Albanian who took it as a cue. He seized Marcus roughly and took him back down the steps to the dark dungeon from which he had come. Marcus felt now that this dungeon might be the last place he ever saw.

33.

CALABRIA, SOUTHERN ITALY

He could not sleep in the cell that night. The muffled sound of the exhausted screams of the gipsy girl's torture, recorded for perversion under a callous camera, could be heard from the dungeon next to his own. Marcus ached with his inability to intervene. Her innocent pretty face etched in his conscience from her desperate momentary glance. The silent empty captive bird in that prison cage in that dark satanic cell. Somewhere, excused from participation and indifferent to pity, were those with the sunken morality, who watched the lurid spectacle by internet from the comfort of their ordinary lives.

He did not know what time it was that he heard the rapping on the water pipe but he was at once sure that it was a message. He regretted that he did not know any Morse code but swiftly became aware that the sound had no trochaic quality and was made by someone who would not know it either. It was a rapping to make him aware that there was someone there. A pleading for help perhaps or even, he dared to hope, the harbinger of rescue. The pipe he was sure ran outside the building where the soiled water would run to. Swiftly he found a piece of torn rag and a lump of charcoal stone with which to write a brief message.

Praying for the possibility that someone might be outside willing to help him he scribbled just one word, Help. Carefully he wrapped the rag around a piece of pebble and forced it down the drain pipe where he had extinguished his soil. He prayed that the drain itself was not attached to any soak away outside but merely drained to the open ground. His prayer had the most remarkable response. Within minutes a piece of paper appeared in the drain pushed from outside by a stick. He realised that someone was outside and that outside was not far away from him. He read the scribbled note written in English.

'Souterrain under floor leads outside. Lift floor slab.'

Marcus needed no more prompting he began to feel around the smooth paving stones on the floor to detect where there might be a gap that would indicate which of the stones would provide an entrance to a souterrain. It had to be one of the larger stones he reasoned. He would start from the centre and work his way out. It was a small cell and he had plenty of time.

Just then as his fingers felt the edge of a large flat stone he felt a small rush of the sandy grit that filled the joint as if it had fallen into a hole. He brushed it fiercely. More grit was falling under the stone or perhaps he was imagining it. The more he brushed it became clear that the grit was falling down into a void under the stone. This was it, this was the entrance to the souterrain.

The removal of grit and dust from around the stone took Marcus much longer than he had first supposed but it was now clear that all he had to do was work out how he would lift a large stone of this size. He reflected that it had certainly been done before. He was not the first captive who escaped through this route. He had broken off a piece of the rock wall that was proving very effective in the task of clearing the joint around the stone. Carefully he tried to lever the stone with the sliver of rock but to no avail. Further clearance of the sandy grit was required. Suddenly his sharp levering movement caused the remaining grit on one side of the stone to fall away into the void all at once. He could now get his fingers under the stone and begin to rock it in order to free it from its position.

It had taken hours, but Marcus felt an excitement as he pulled the stone across the floor using all his strength, to reveal a hole some half a metre or so wide that was clearly an entrance to a souterrain. It was an entrance that offered no immediate prospect of freedom, rather a dark and damp route to a subterranean burial, but Marcus felt that he was being given a chance and clumsily edged his way down into a narrow damp dark chamber that would surely he felt lead somewhere.

Marcus could feel a solid floor beneath his feet and he felt around him to discover a void ahead. It had to be a passageway. Slowly he moved crouched within a space no wider than his body and rather less tall. It seemed like hours but it was only minutes before a shaft of light became visible in front of him. He wanted to move towards it faster but it was impossible for him to do so but finally the light grew stronger and he could now see his hand in front of him as he shuffled forward.

At last he felt the passageway rise and the light bathed him in its brightness. He looked up to see a figure and a face looking down at him and with arms extended willing him to make the final effort to exit the passageway.

As he pulled himself out onto the hot ground of freedom and rolled over gasping and sucking in the fresh clean air, his eyes focussed on the face of his saviour. It was a face that he thought that he would not see again. The face of his daughter Segolene.

'What. What are you doing here?' Marcus asked clearly astonished to see her.

'I am rescuing you from certain death.' She answered coldly as if slightly offended to have been questioned.

'We will have to get moving quickly before they discover that you are gone. We get away as far as possible as we cannot trust anyone here, they will return us to the Ndrangheta without hesitation. You can be sure they will follow us. I brought you some change of clothes, water and food.' With that she thrust at him a small loaf of bread cheese and water which he ate ravenously. A swift change of clothes was effected and he now felt an energy and determination to escape.

'We have a motorbike.' She explained.

'Come this way.'

By a copse of trees was a small motor bike that Segolene started with an accomplished kick that set the engine off to high pitched whine of its revving engine. They were now on their way. He shut his eyes and lent on her shoulders as the machine let off an excited pace in a direction he knew not where.

34.

SOUTHERN ITALY

Outside a small abandoned house in the pitch black darkness a wounded wind whined and moaned in unresolved discontent. It burst upon the windows in short sharp gusts and rocked the door as if to seek admission. It hurled among the trees and howled in the eaves the sound of pain. For them the waiting grew their fear. The fear that they would be found there hidden. It was almost Marcus felt, as if their early discovery would be a comfort. A certainty to end this cold unbroken game of chance. He felt the possibility that to reveal themselves and plead for mercy might be their better hope, but deep down he knew, there would be no mercy for the meek. They were the quarry their role was to run, to hide, to wait. They had to escape.

Day breaks early when you are on the run. Fear rises earlier than the cockerel at dawn. He sounds the alarm and seizes the viscera in a vice like grip in the silent dark of that cold hour before daybreak. He plays with the imagination with his images and sounds. He questions logic and distorts reason. He enervates the body that must flee. His torment will emaciate the soul.

It was the sound of a shower that woke him. It was as if he had been hearing it for hours. She appeared with only a thin towel around her head and quickly began to dress in the clothes she had been wearing as she slept. Marcus turned to her, heavy with fatigue.

'It was cold but it was wet.' She said as if he had asked her a question.

'We have to get moving north, they will be close by now.' She added with certainty.

'Do you think we should get out now and take the road?'

'We won't get far without some food Marcus' Segolene answered.

'We ought to see if there is anything to eat here. There could be some cans of something in the kitchen.'

A search of the kitchen revealed only some tins of artichokes. Tinned artichokes shared on a cracked plate was a lean breakfast but enough for the time being.

It was a slow ride through the woodland to the road up a rough track at an incline. From the top they could see to the north a small village nestling in the valley.

'Let's keep off the road Marcus and take that footpath to the village. We will just have to see when we get there what happens next.'

His loss of weight was serving him well. Even with a loss of strength he was feeling good as he gripped the seat of the small bike that wove its way across the uneven ground. Their small breakfast had been supplemented en route with the soft fruit of an orchard hanging full on low bushes by the track and the fresh air and early sunshine had injected an energy in him.

It was around 11.00 when they saw him. As they looked down to the main road they saw the black car heading north and Segolene recoiled on seeing it as if its driver might spot her from the distance.

'Just as well we stuck to the track' he suggested.

'It's definitely him' she confirmed. 'I've seen the car before. That is our assassin.'

It seemed at first as if her casual confirmation of this fact was an acceptance of her fate.

'We have the advantage though' she looked up at him enquiringly.

'How on earth do you come to that conclusion?' He asked.

'Well first we know that he will stop at the next village and ask if we have been through. When he is told we have not he will wait for us there.'

'And we simply go another way?' He reasoned.

'No, he will have thought of that and besides, there is no alternative route we can easily take. No we go in disguise'

He was dumfounded. Did she mean that she was prepared to risk her life playing some sort of tom foolery with this thug? To dress up in full view hoping to deceive him?

'Are you serious?' He asked. 'Are you suggesting we just ride in there in some form of disguise straight into his arms?'

'It is exactly the opposite of what he expects us to do. First we will separate. He is looking for two people not one. For a man and a woman, not a solitary woman. Then we will walk in there. He is expecting us to go in by motorcycle.'

He had to admit to himself that he was feeling rather anxious at this idea. There was some comfort in her being his companion in this predicament. She seemed to have an instinct as to what to do next. So why should he not now trust her judgement. There was too the feeling that his life had been extended, its ending stayed, and that somehow risk was more acceptable now that it was in extra time.

'It's our only chance Marcus' She added seriously.

'They will have all routes north covered one way or another. If we can get through just where we know they are present it is better than our believing we are free only to discover that they are on to us.'

It seemed a reasoned proposal.

'So how do we approach this deception?' He asked resigned to its inevitability.

She smiled a wide grin.

'Well my idea. My idea is that we ...

'A pantomime horse?' He suggested feeling that the idea might be no more absurd than the one she was about to present.

Segolene laughed.

'Good thinking but no. First we hide the motorbike. I thought that I might take one of those donkeys over there and lead it into the village right up to the bar where he is drinking. I can cover my face a bit and throw something around me to look local.'

'That is incredibly daring' He suggested.

'What do you plan to do when you get there? Get another motorbike?'

'There is the motorbike or perhaps his car. We could have a choice.' She suggested optimistically.

Marcus watched incredulously as Segolene led the donkey down the slope to the village wearing a costume that she had contrived from some sackcloth she had unearthed. He laughed quietly at the sheer daring of it. Two bullets from a gun and they were gone but what was there to lose at this moment but the agony of apprehension that choked every defensive move they made. Now they were on the attack, this was their initiative and he felt strangely better.

Her entrance into the village had raised no suspicion. An old woman leading a donkey it appeared was a commonplace sight here. What Marcus did not know was that she had a mission to fulfil that commanded the huge risk that she was to take, for Segolene had seen the face of their hunter and it was a face she knew well.

Now she froze as she saw him through the window of the Trattoria. The large fat man sitting innocently by the window quietly sipping a drink of soda. It was him for sure. The brutal face its thick set jaw and thin lips. The large square head crowned with jet black hair. The Albanian her father's henchman came from one of the arbereshe villages in Calabria populated by refugees from Albania during the ottoman invasion of that country in the fifteenth century. It was curious that he remained known as the Albanian but he was part of a community that had long held on to their roots.

She felt sick at the thought that to others he would appear quite normal, pleasant even. They might engage him in conversation and laugh with him in the manner one might do with anyone. Yet there was something about him only she knew that disgusted her to the point of abject hatred. It was something that crystallised in that moment in her mind a resolve that had fermented in her for much of her life.

It was someday in February 2006 when the large black saloon car pulled up outside the Scalfero mansion just four miles from Reggio Calabria on a day the small scudding clouds broken into pieces like cotton wool moved low under a bright blue sky. The Albanian descended from the vehicle uneasily and stood by the door clenching his fists as if anticipating some physical confrontation. This he did out of habit probably before any assignment. He knew that today this job was not to entail anything of the kind. A small girl to be chauffeured. An important child was his charge today. Perhaps his clenching fists gave him some ease from his apprehension.

The Byzantine liturgy is still strong among the Albanian people. Their Greek orthodox faith and their language still survive today in the village of Lungro where the Albanian came from to serve the Scalfero clan. To serve but never to be accepted as one of them, merely a servant and it was a role that he understood fully and executed well. He was in effect Scalfero's trusted lieutenant and obeyed his master's instructions whatever the results might be.

Presently a nurse appeared from the door dressed in a pale uniform escorting the girl with an arm around her narrow shoulders. The child was taller than he imagined. Looking down to the ground, frail, unsure. The loss of her mother had been a devastation to her but the loss of a family member was commonplace here. Perdition scalded this earth like the sun's heat. Death followed life like night followed day. Some darker some brighter, some longer some shorter the Albanian reflected as he opened the door of the car and held it for the two passengers. The nurse smiled at him quietly as she ushered the child onto the back seat.

After a silent journey of no more than 40 minutes the car drew up outside a large ornate building surrounded by poplar trees and with a small area of grass to the frontage. This was to be the child's home the Institutio Santa Christina. An asylum for lost and mentally disturbed young women. It would be the making of her, her father had been assured. She would conquer her distractions, strengthen her resolve soften her temper. Most of all it would keep her at distance from a Father who had never loved her, one who could now claim to have cared by introducing her to the opportunities for conformity offered by the Institutio Santa Christina.

If there was an enforced silence around the Institutio Santa Christina. It was not the silence of observance nor of penance or contrition but a silence born of fear. It was the fear of retribution for the almost inevitable catalogue of sins and that every inmate accumulated without effort, omission or intention. Small and minor contraventions that would deserve a calculated humiliation among peers, the fear of solitude that served the sanction of reprehension. Here would be salvation through obedience hard work and prayer. Here the angry child would become assuaged, to become the docile woman who would serve without question and whose faith would be restored.

The Albanian was to visit the girl during her stay here to check that she settled in. A perfunctory duty imposed by her father as an afterthought in one last brief direction. The child would not speak to him nor look him in the eye. The Albanian was her father's agent. The trusted ally there to carry out a duty too distasteful for a father, but his words were without warmth or compassion and she smelt on his breath the stench of her betrayal.

Over those early years the child became a woman. The long wiry legs filled out to a slender but shapely form. The hair was combed out and a silent confidence borne by soft eyes shaped her face to an extraordinary beauty. His visits were more frequent now. The Albanian had found his gaze fixed on the small round breasts that rose from her blouse like delicious fruit. Her scent now had the fragrance of lemons derived from the secret gift of a bottle of Limon di Capri from a departing Nun. Her skin the colour of pale coffee had the smooth shine of wax. Those last few visits had not been the duty nor the burden he had expected and he now looked forward to taking the short car journey to the Institutio Santa Christina. Her intense beauty had aroused in him a lust that had been driven further by the expectation of her solitude away from the attention of the silent sisters.

It was Saturday when he visited her for the last time. A fine day in summer. He had shaved his wide chin with unusual care and splashed a palm full of cheap after shave about his face. He had snatched some flowers from the stall run by Senora Ellora Rattan by the ladies store at weekends to provide a gesture of affection that might ease the passage of his desires and make his sin the less gratuitous. He had sung out in his strong boisterous voice the Ave Maria intermezzo from Cavalleri Rusticana as he drove to her in the car.

He had imagined her quiet murmur as his lips would suck at her flesh. Her hot anxiety on his fingers as he drew his tempting touch up between her soft thighs. He would feel the grateful grasp of her youthful expectation on his firm hide as he drove himself into her. The sweetness of her breathless caress in the finish as he delivered to her the joy she had craved.

The Sister smiled as she let him in, in recognition rather than affection. She showed him to the door of the room with a casual gesture as she was aware that he knew his way. He opened the door and looked in quizzically as if only half expecting to see her. She was sitting on her bed with her knees drawn up to her chin and she looked at him with cold distaste.

He stood there motionless looking directly at her as if to decide on his tactics. He had dreamt of her complicity, her desire even, but had known in his heart that this would be impossible. Instead he reached out to grasp her with a swift clumsy movement. Her stiff resistance surprised him, a hard blow and a bite to his hand. It had strengthened his resolve, he seized her at her waist and struggled momentarily to hold her down to the bed. Gasping with excitement he pulled off her skirt in one rough move. She kicked out at him aiming low below his belt in intense and wild anger.

It was a battle now, a battle only he would win. There was no retreat possible now that he had committed to the engagement. The Albanian held her with all his weight on the bed wrenching her knickers from her hurling legs in desperate expectation like a child unwraps a parcel. Then it was easy. He felt the loss of her strength under his weight, her unwilling submission excite him even more, as he dislodged his clothing in clumsy violent impatience. He mounted her savagely and his beastly bulk now held her to the bed as he spread her legs and penetrated her, moving inside her with impulsive and disjointed thrusts, taking his pleasure with impossible grunts, improbable saliva and prolific perspiration.

His enjoyment of her body completed, he looked down at her weeping silently as if he meant in some way to compensate her for her humiliation and suffering. He saw it was not to be. Her submissive frailty silently begged him to leave. He left her without a word of remorse or gratitude. What would be the point. To find some use from something cast aside by its owner was surely not a crime. It was the consequence of paternal dismissal, the reward for his loyalty.

As he pulled the car away from the drive he resolved that he would end his visits now. She would become just a memory. But the assault of her young body was no vague memory to her. It burned into her soul as only the deepest injustice can and it resolved a retribution. One day she would avenge that usurpation by a fatal blow.

The black car was now parked in the piazza Cocodelli under the shade of a small tree. There was a simple explanation as to why at 13.30 the car had been parked outside the Trattoria. It was lunchtime and the driver was looking forward to an indulgence. She surmised too that during his lunch time he would perhaps be less astute to the vengeful quest to which he had been assigned. She could see his bulky shape now seated by the window that gave him the best view of the piazza. She moved cautiously and crossing the Piazza around the rear of the buildings she entered the restaurant kitchen by the side door.

A lady cook was facing away from her toward the cooking range muttering as she worked on a dish.

'Excuse me' Segolene waved. The cook pointed directly at the door to the restaurant on hearing her voice at which immediately a young waiter appeared with a wide smile on seeing her.

'You do me a favour?' she asked.

He looked receptive to the request.

'My uncle is in the restaurant by the window on his own, well I wanted to buy him a drink to surprise him for his birthday, a bottle of wine. Could you do that for me?' She scrambled for some Euros from her pocket.

'Yes of course' the waiter answered having expected a more demanding request.

'Red or white? '

'What has he ordered to eat?' Segolene asked considerately.

'Ah yes, some delicious Oysters. I'll get a bottle of white for him. He said he would not be ordering wine so you will be surprising him.'

'Yes that's right. I want to surprise him. Don't tell him I sent it over. I want him to be surprised.'

As the waiter went to fetch the wine the cook spread a plate with ice and Oysters and placed it on the pass right by where Segolene was standing. She seized her chance at once as the cook turned back to her range pouring from a small vial she had hidden between her breasts onto the seafood. She then scribbled a note with lipstick on a spare plate and swept the food onto it in one deft movement. She had acted so swiftly that the few more moments she had to wait for the waiter's return seemed minutes.

'Call it 15 euros for the wine. We have a special wine for birthdays. I had to go out the back to get it' He explained clearly wishing to embellish the surprise with a little contribution of his own.

'Oh thanks a lot, that looks lovely he will really be intrigued by this.'

She had the waiter on side, and conscripted to the intrigue. She could see him approaching the Albanian's table. She heard him explaining to the Albanian with contrived formality how he was under important instructions to serve a special wine to his customer.

The deception had been perfectly executed. The Albanian had assumed that the authority had come from the restaurant's proprietor out of respect for Scalfero's lieutenant. He could hardly refuse such a gesture. He could relax in the knowledge that his host understood the importance of his task and would not have sought to undermine it, only to make more pleasurable his execution of it.

He was already pouring his second glass of wine when the oysters were served to him fresh on a bed of ice and lemons. The Albanian started ravenously to feed his hunger swallowing the delicious seafood from their shells without ceremony and pouring a third glass of the cold straw coloured white wine.

It was only as he finished the dish that he could see that the pattern on the plate under the ice was actually an inscription which appeared to have been written in some haste. Curiously he turned the ice to reveal the inscription. As he read the words, slowly making them out under the melted ice he felt his curiosity grow to outrage as he comprehended their significance. For scrawled into the glaze in a thin red line of lipstick were a number of words he could only just pick out, but words that he knew well,

'La vendetta e un piatto che va mangiatto freddo.'

The Albanian stared at the plate in disbelief. He felt his stomach churn and tighten, his head dizzy. He clutched his throat as if he might misplace it. A panic overcame him as he searched the room with frightened eyes. He raised himself to his feet not sure whether to go outside or stay in. He then turned to the men's room uncertain of his next move as he felt a swelling in his throat. His napkin trailed from his bent figure as he moved across the room in panic. It was all too late, he clutched his gut at the pain that began to overwhelm him. He was staggering now as he tumbled into the men's room door and fell into a cubicle onto a latrine with the dull thud of a fallen goose.

His last meal may not have inspired artists like that of our saviour at Emmaus. No painter would be inspired to paint the bloated fallen figure slumped over the cold porcelain where the Albanian ended his days Yet if one ever wished the scene of death to record the life led, the corpse that lay there offered that picture to perfection.

Segolene had left the Trattoria as swiftly as she had arrived. She did not want to be around to see the consequences of her action and knew that she would now be a fugitive from justice as well as injustice. No judicial authority would pardon her for retribution. The Belladonna would be easy to detect. She had no doubt that she would have to leave Italy but she had contrived one strong ally. Her identity as Segolene Temoin Graham and her English father, Mr Marcus Graham.

Marcus had been waiting for her sitting on a stone wall by a small well as she arrived putting on a casual air.

'I just needed to see someone about the bike' she lied. It was the first thing that came into her head and she felt uneasy that she had not thought to think of how to explain her short absence. It was nevertheless accepted by him readily.

'It's alright then. We get to hold on to the bike for a while?' he asked with tangible concern.

'We do' She answered unprepared to say more.

Their journey was now taking them north along the beautiful Amalfi coastline. He detected that she was now more relaxed, content to cruise rather than race the small machine. Pointing out some sights of interest and laughing at the sight of an open bus teeming with waving passengers. Perhaps she felt that they were finally near to escaping their pursuers. His confidence in her grew, but nowhere in his head could he see her as his own. She had nothing of him about her. No sign of conformity, nothing of his habitual reservation. She was a free spirit daring impetuous and outrageous. Hers was the spirit he admired perhaps that he had wished for himself.

It was early evening when they reached the small village of Curso. He could not tell what it was exactly that had inspired it but there was some celebration in the air. Some of its residents had returned from abroad and this was the cause for celebration. After a simple supper of pasta and salad there was dancing. Segolene did not hesitate to show off her abilities in her suggestive movements with several of the menfolk who were clearly enjoying her participation. How could she dance like that Marcus thought. She had rescued him from certain death, they were being followed by an assassin and yet, now she was dancing.

Marcus smiled contentedly sipping on a glass of local wine. He recalled the inscription over the door of the café Zizi Jeanmaire where they had first met.

'We should consider every day lost that we have not danced'

35.

THE MEDITERRANEAN SEA

As a crisp dawn broke over the Mediterranean Sea off the northern coast of Libya, a sailing boat sailed west with the sunrise on her stern. Boats have sailed under these westerly winds for centuries to trade along the coasts of the Mediterranean Sea. Egyptian Minoan Greek and Roman have in their times traded a wide variety of goods along this shoreline.

This boat can comfortably make twelve knots at full sail with only the tremor of tail wind. She lies low in the water keeled gently to starboard. She is seventy five metres in length and with a beam of over fifteen meters. She is the world's largest sloop she is a most graceful sight against a calm sea sparkling in the sunrise.

She is the Ubermensch. Her single mast rises to 90 meters bearing her giant main sail and jib. Her crew numbers fifteen including sailors and catering staff and in addition to her grand lounge, sun decks and sumptuous accommodation, she has luxurious suites for twelve passengers. Today she sails with just one, her owner Michelangelo Scalfero.

For Scalfero it was not only the tranquillity and the sight of the open sea that mesmerised him. Not only the joy of its smell as the early light sparkled on the boat's wake nor the peace that brought his mind to rest. His heart beat to an equal temper. The cruel uncompromising temper he understood so well. The bleak indifference to the fate of those who sail her was his too.

The sea is not partial to good nor evil. She is the ultimate predator. She will take without mercy, and judge without favour and she will wash the souls of men from them without regard to their righteousness, just as she has always done. Hers is that same power, that cold heart that deep indifference that defines the ubermensch, and the boat that bears that name will sail on her a journey to inevitable glory.

The ubermensch is moored in the small harbour at the Scalfero villa and frequently sails westward to Tangier where his order has an N'drina that keeps alive the old established businesses of gambling and prostitution, but his interest was the profit to be made from the importation of cocaine from Columbia and the making of necessary arrangements for its onward journey to the port of Geoia Tauro.

In the trading port of that beautiful white city, corruption is the only reliable means of commerce. It had never failed him, he understood its operation, its motivations, its rules. Here was a machinery of commerce driven by self-interest, poverty, greed and contempt for authority and indifference to ones fellow man. Here there are no questions asked and all is possible at a price. Here the ubermensch thrives on an ancient and trusted blend of reward and retribution.

It was almost mid-morning when Scalfero looked about him as he heard the sound of jeers and cries from the crew below him. Cries of:

'Let's sink them'

Scalfero moved swiftly to the forward deck.

'What is the commotion?' He demanded of the steward girl standing there.

'They have seen a boat of clandestini on the port bow sir' She answered and she passed to him a pair of binoculars she had been holding.

'Take a look sir. Heading for Lampedusa I imagine. That is if they get there in that tub'

Scalfero adjusted the lens of the binoculars to look at a small boat crammed with black faces that all seemed to be looking at the Ubermensch with a mixture of awe, uncertainty and trepidation as she sailed by.

'Do we pull up to assist Sir?' The girl asked feeling that she knew the question was naive.

'Man interferes with nature through pity.' Scalfero sighed. 'I have no pity. They are the victims of circumstance that is all. There are many like them. To pity one is to open the heart to pity them all. No heart is large enough. The heart beats for one being only. It cannot be shared.'

It was as he passed the binoculars back to the girl the sound of a gunshot was heard from below. Someone from the crew was firing at the small boat and he could see that one bullet had been on target as distress could be witnessed among those on board the hapless craft. The boat had either been holed or perhaps the passengers had moved scared by the shot, to upset the balance of the craft.

Scalfero moved swiftly to the lower deck to apprehend the gunman. The deckhand looked around to see him standing silently behind him and instinctively put down the weapon.

'I do not employ you to take shots at illegal immigrants' He complained with a venomous whisper.

'We do not waste our time on such amusements. Return immediately to your stations'

Out at the port bow the makeshift boat was clearly taking on water and they could hear cries and wails from the stricken vessel which was now lilting to its starboard side as its passengers were catapulted into the sea. They could see clearly the desperate choking heads upon the surface of the water. The pleas of drowning souls, of mothers grasping for their children, the desperate struggle of those condemned to die.

There would be few survivors, those who might find something to hold onto might have themselves washed ashore but for most, that beacon of hope would be extinguished by the cold caress of this beautiful sparkling sea. The cleanest seas in the Mediterranean would be again polluted by the rotted corpses of those who did not belong there.

Order returned to the Ubermensch as if nothing had happened. The crewmen returned to their posts. The stewardess watched it's master return to his bridge and overheard him as he answered his cell phone.

'We are making good headway' she heard him say 'No, nothing to report. All is as expected. An unexceptional but beautiful voyage.'

The white city lies at the doorway to the Mediterranean Sea. It has seen more cultures than just about anywhere on earth. Greek, Roman, Arab Portuguese, British, French and Spanish have all brought with them some part of themselves, language, literature, government, architecture and cuisine all thrown into a melting pot of culture and trade. Its people speak Berber, Arabic, French, Spanish and English. It is a city known for its tolerance. It has been home to murderers, drug takers, paedophiles; a city that knows the power of corruption. Here morality is a commodity for sale just like any other in the souk and away from the colour of the souk the commodities for sale are those made to order for a price.

In the narrow teeming streets of the Medina a small figure of a man lurched between stalls laden with a riot of coloured fruit vegetables and clothing. He walked with an unusual gait swaying from side to side as he made his way with determined swagger. His stature no more than that of a dwarf weakened by time and fate. His wide face was hardened by the elements and seasons and his long unkempt hair swung from side to side as he shuffled his uncoordinated ambulation. He was Scalfero's man and his mission was to purchase innocence so pure that it would confirm for his master a future that would be his. Two young virgins to be slaughtered in the name of the Ubermensch were awaiting his purchase.

The dwarf swung his body with awkward athleticism across a low wall and down a flight of stone steps to a heavy wooden door and rapped upon it in what was certainly a code and the door was opened.

'You have the goods? My master sails tonight he is anxious that there is no delay' He questioned in a voice that was no more than a thin whine.

'They will arrive here soon. I am to check the money' Came the response.

The dwarf thrust him one million dirhams which the vendor could see there was no need to count. Immediately he pulled back a curtain to reveal the goods. They were two young girls of about fourteen years old standing silently, the fear in their eyes a tangible sparkle in the half light.

'They are pure?' Demanded the dwarf. 'My master requires only the purest.'

'They are as you directed. Untouched and pure as honey' Confirmed the vendor.

'You will deliver them to the harbour at midnight' The dwarf instructed.

That night in the harbour a delivery was made to the Ubermensch that concluded a transaction among the darkest hidden in the history of that city.

The Columbian consignments travel south through Brazil to Europe via Africa to Gioia Tauro the largest container port in Italy. Here vast quantities of Cocaine are offloaded from the ships that arrive with a wide variety of goods for distribution around Europe. Scalfero had established himself as the sole distributor of the commodity and his control over the port ensured that there was only the most infrequent opposition to his dealings. When opposition had arisen he insisted that only a sole distributor could ensure that the quality of the import could be maintained and that it was his moral duty to ensure its purity. This morality had been enforced with the veracity of medieval observance so severe and successful, that this curious morality of monopoly was now widely believed.

He had seen that in North America the demand from many distributors allows for the product to be diluted and soiled. Here in Europe there would be quality assured, customers' content, and the business continued for the benefit of all. Business indeed it was. The import of Cocaine through Gioia Tauro had made his operation immensely wealthy and he now had control over the whole of the trade.

The proceeds of the trade in cocaine is transferred to a bank in Frankfurt where his accounts are preserved with rectitude by the most respected of bankers as had been approved by Scalfero himself. Such wealth facilitates the funding of Real Estate investment and development and the operational activities associated with Real Estate. Hotels in many of Europe's cities are run by his trusted lieutenants. Prestige restaurants run under the names of recognised chefs, breweries and drinking establishments, fashion houses and stores all the means to spread the vast wealth of his dark empire in Calabria to the enlightenment of commercial legitimacy.

For Scalfero it was ambition not avarice that drove his ardour. His mission was to spread his influence to create the edifice of enterprise a Pontifex of power. For he had seen the future and was certain that soon, the Heavens would roll a thunder of distant dice. Power alone will rule the fate of man. Fortunes will fall, lives will be lost. Countries will crumble under the storm to come, cities and thrones and powers are ephemeral and fade like flowers in times eye.

But there will be one who bathes in the tumult of tears and feeds on the bones of the fallen like the lammergeyer, the baleful bearded vulture of doom that sucks the very marrow from the bleached bones of the dead. He will be the one who has grown from the seeds of a small lemon grove outside Reggio di Calabria.

36.

ILLINOIS, USA

The lectern set up on the stage at the end of the great hall in the University of Southern Illinois was draped ceremoniously with a heavy cloth coloured crimson and gold. The figure that stood behind it had all the authority that such a tribute could announce for he was a Cardinal of the Church in the full robes of his office. He was a man in his early fifties with the strong even features one might more expect of a screen actor, a full head of dark but greying hair, a firm well set jaw line and blue eyes that conveyed an alert but friendly demeanour. He spoke without any impression of pomposity that might derive from the importance of his position. There was instead an enthusiasm and companionability in his warm tones and comforting well-chosen words.

'Miracles are the rarest jewels of our lives. They endow us with the sparkle of delight, they bring the brightness of hope and inspire the richness of faith.' He began.

Cardinal Richard Raphael paused to allow his audience to digest and think through his words. The concept of miracles had become one in which he was justified to believe in wholeheartedly. His life had been blessed by the intervention of timely answers to life's complicated questions. Divine interventions had always provided solutions to complex problems. He believed in the ability of mankind to forge his own future and make his own fortune and that in so doing, God lends a hand. This inspirational spirit combined with his personal charisma and strong even features, made him the most popular Cardinal in America and a figurehead known around the world within the church and beyond.

He spoke to a congregation that hung on to every word in a speech carefully contrived to convey his beliefs in a manner that would be remembered.

'Blame never fails to find herself a suitor.' He was saying.

'She smothers truth and distorts reason. She is the easy answer that eschews complexity. She will be the whore of the bold or the mistress of the meek. Her kiss is their betrayal. Yet no man dare deny her for to do so brings the certainty of their guilt.'

He could feel the power of his well-rehearsed words resonate around the hall. This was a performance not just for his congregation here today but for the whole of Christendom, for it was being televised and would be reported around the world and as he stood on the stage in the great hall of the University of Southern Illinois he could feel the warmth of this congregation. For here was a symbolism that would find a place in the hearts of this nation.

'We must live our lives without blame. For to blame is to distract ourselves from all that is positive, all that we believe we can be, all that we can achieve with our sacrifice, our faith and our labour.'

He was finishing his address now. He looked across the hall at his audience and saw that every one of them was waiting for his final words with wide eyes and full attention.

'Events are not predestined. They are in our hands to bring about as we would wish them through our efforts, faith and sacrifice.'

A small smile appeared on his lips as he knew he had delivered a most compelling speech.

'I will finish with the words of William Jennings Bryan.'

'Destiny is not a matter of chance but a matter of choice. It is not a thing to be waited for, it is a thing to be achieved.'

As a wild applause reverberated around the great hall, he turned to the man standing beside him and shook his hand warmly to the louder cheer and of the audience.

'Welcome Mr President. Today our nation is united in this great state of Illinois and God will bless our church and God will bless America.' It was a simple symbolic statement made between two of the world's most influential men. The President of the United States and a Cardinal who it was generally believed, would one day become the head of the Catholic church and this event today would cement that belief.

His speech had put an end to one episode in his career that had defined his tolerance probity and foresight. When a nation had been ready to believe that ruin was the only outcome to be expected it was he who had seen the challenge as an opportunity to prove the overwhelming power of faith and of fraternity. He who had not just seen the answer but carried it out.

It had centred on the Sisters of Philomena, a group of nuns who had been led by a vociferous minority determined to move the church to a more feminist agenda. The Vatican had strongly deplored the notion but whatever the opinion of Rome the feeling in America was greatly more sympathetic to such equality. The President himself had been in the difficult position of appeasement to those around the world who found it difficult to understand why the cradle of freedom nurtured a tolerance of the minority view, irrespective of the view of the majority. Cardinal Raphael had proved himself to be the gentlest of persuaders. He had started with compassion had ended with compromise.

Today President Edgar Allen was here to enhance the standing of his host. For he knew that humble words are wasted. It is the words of great men that are heard and it is sometimes expedient to make great the men who utter those words in order that they be heard. This was to be the fate of Cardinal Raphael.

It was not apparent on that occasion, but some part of that fate was to be inextricably linked to that of Maria Braganza Martinez. She was certainly, one of his most fervent and enthusiastic supporters. She held to her faith beyond the usual requirements of observance. She believed in the miracles that Christ himself had executed and saw that everything is possible in the eyes of God. For Maria Braganza Martinez had been given the blessing of clairvoyance and it was a blessing that she had employed with some success.

It had been six years since she had moved to Carbondale from Pittsburgh shortly after the death of her husband. She had known extreme poverty with her husband's disability. Equality is open to all in America, but it is sometimes gained only by the throw of a dice. In the life of Maria Braganza Martinez that dice had fallen resolutely foul, to afford her a life scarce of comfort or advantage.

Now, these years later, when having to face the world alone, her clairvoyance would transform her life. For her the sole reason for her gift was something she understood without question. Her blessing was endowed to her by God to promote the progress of her idol, the priest she had followed all her adult life, the priest she had witnessed advance his position within the church and whom she had seen would one day be the Holy father himself. She was now devoted to his cause and convinced, not without reason, that she would play her part in his advancement.

It was a morning just weeks after she had arrived at Carbondale when she first met him. He had spoken directly to her and this had made the impression that would change her life. He had comforted her on the death of her husband at that time and spoken of the life she would now lead. How perdition can alter lives for the better. How she might now progress her life unbound by service to her husband and find a new service to God.

'The withered wind brings no change.' He had said to her.

'The word of God is heeded best when carried in the tempest. Only in the storm, does man see God clearly.'

She knew then that only adversity would convert the unbeliever to see God. Perhaps forgiveness needed reciprocity to truly heal the soul. She had knelt to kiss his hand and recalled that subtle moment often. The lightness of his touch and the fine line of his fingers. She had remembered the small blood red blemish on his ring finger in the shape of a teardrop. He had caught her eyes examining it and said.

'Yes. I have but one tear of sadness for humanity. The rest I cry in joy. For the Lord is good and He sees everything.'

It was his words that inspired her to play a part in the reshaping of lost souls. It was her privilege to watch the arrogance of men brought down by cruel adversity and then to offer them hope. For she saw their future and could describe what faith would mean to them.

Such fate struck the life of Kevil Tye one day while he was on his way to work at the auto parts factory in Greenville. It was a day like any other until a phone call came at 10.34.

'Telephone for you Kevil. Says it's personal.' Said the foreman. He didn't remember much else. The shock of the news drained him of recall. One hour later he was in the hospital staring at the body of his young wife, lying on the bed with tubes driven into her body and nurses surrounding her and hearing those words.

'Nothing more we can do. I am so sorry.'

That was three years ago now and time had been his physician. Time and the counsel of Maria Braganza Martinez. He had never forgotten what she had told him one day before the death in the convenience store.

'You will experience tragedy soon, but when you do be sure to turn to God. For when you do life will get better for you'

It did. Kevil met his new wife shortly after and he felt reborn. There was a greater bond between them than he had with his first wife. His fortune had not just been restored but improved.

The same could be said of the pound man. A vagrant who lived an existence by the highway on what he could beg from the passers-by. Food, cash, rags and cigarettes.

'Your future is waiting for you' she had told him. 'I have seen it. Go and grasp it God will help you.'

She had pointed him to a better life through God too and now he was the handyman in the church. Well-fed with food and purpose and charged with dignity.

Maria Braganza Martinez had a younger sister living in Cincinnati. She was now resolutely of the catholic church though she had been married to a Calvanist who had passed away quietly over a number of lonely years. The bond between the two widowed sisters was as strong as for Maria Braganza Martinez,Valentina was all the family she had now and the two women were as close as any two people could be.

There was always a feeling of excitement before any meeting up with her sibling and much planning as to a short stay in Chicago, a shopping trip for something contrived to justify the visit and a drive to a lovely lakeside location to share its beauty and to talk. There was always so much to talk about and neither ever tired of their conversation.

One night as she lay awake listening to the silence, Maria Braganza Martinez had a nightmare. What she saw was the death of her sister at the hands of an assassin. In her mind troubled by the confusion of this nightmare was the image of the nave of a church. At first she considered her preoccupations prior to retiring, the church service she was determined to attend as Cardinal Raphael would be present and of course her thoughts for her sister. Perhaps she thought, the two had become dreadfully conflated and had emerged in her nightmare. It was something she did not wish to contemplate but it was a nightmare that was to reoccur with greater colour and detail as time went on.

With each terrifying vision Maria Breganza Martinez had seen the event with more clarity and had even been able to search the apparition as it came to her for the detail her rational mind had sought. She had seen the place where the atrocity was to occur, she had seen the swiftness of the blow that struck her poor sister down, and she had seen the face of the assassin.

She had awoken with a start. She had seen again the stark nightmare that had haunted her nights since she had last seen Valentina. The point at which she had awakened was the same each time. The brief vision of the assassin's face as he turned towards her to look straight into her eyes and as he crossed himself as he hastened to leave. To leave the dreadful corpse on the floor in front of him the guilt clear in his eyes.

Now that vision of his face was clearer than before. Clear as to those guilty searching eyes, the desperate mouth half open, its breath hot with malevolence. It was the vision she had now seen several times in her dream. She could see that he was an elderly cleric and she was now sure that he was a Cardinal.

She had called Valentina yesterday. The same news, the conversation that recounted every episode of her day and all that she felt about each of them. Conversations that took longer to recount than the episodes recounted. As always she was happy. Happier still to hear her Valentina's voice. It was on that occasion that the first news of an ambitious excursion was relayed to Maria Breganza Martinez.

Valentina's choir group was planning, only planning at this stage, to visit St Pietro in Rome. There had been excitement among the choir members for some months but it had been resolved not to discuss plans until they had been better developed. What had been an ambitious notion had now transformed into a workable concept with dates, delegates and a list of excursions that were to be undertaken within the five days of the visit, shuffled and changed daily in between telephone conversations among the various choir members.

Accommodation requirements had been discussed in detail and hotels thoroughly examined until one had been selected that was not only reasonably priced but seemed upon the repeated examination of city maps to be close to the river and within a short distance of the Vatican, yet still close to some of the tourist hot spots that had been advised to them from many differing quarters. Valentina could not conceal her delight that day when she rang her sister to inform her of the arrangements.

'The choir has been invited to sing in Saint Pietro.' Valentina had announced with pride.

During that conversation Maria Breganza Martinez was filled with enthusiasm and it was only afterwards that she reflected on the recurring dreams she had had and the portended fate that might befall Valentina. However, her clairvoyance had brought her to the dilemma of choice. She could not alarm her sister by advising her of such a prediction at the height of her enthusiasm. Why it may not be true at all or be assigned to take place at a very different time in her life. Valentina could well interpret such an intervention as envy, when in practise Maria Breganza Martinez could not wish more fervently for the joy that her sister anticipated from this trip.

Should we share with the victim the spoils of the intuitive mind when it can challenge reason to warn of a death foretold? Maria Braganza Martinez had paced upon this ground with agonising discomfort and in the end had decided to say nothing. If that were negligent, she was supported in that decision by the absence of any reoccurrence of the dream from that day till that of Valentina's departure.

37.

VESUVIUS, ITALY

In a hotel room in the west of Rome Emma Dreyfus was listening to rather than watching the TV tuned to an American news channel. The presenter spoke enthusiastically as he glanced to one side to look at a middle aged bearded man sitting by him.

'Now more on the story that is taking place in southern Italy. The increased level of seismic activity in the area around Naples and the possibility that this might mean an eruption of the Vesuvius. We have volcanologist Federico Otto from the university Oregon to give us his view.'

'Now Mr Otto there was of course an enormous eruption of Vesuvius a very long time ago, in AD 24.8.79 that wiped out the cities of Pompeii and Herculaneum. We are not envisaging anything like that are we?'

It was a question many would argue was put to the wrong person. Federico Otto was known as a scare-mongering volcanologist. His were the reports issued from time to time warning of the potential of destruction in all corners of the globe but his main preoccupation and fascination was the most potentially dangerous volcanic region in the world, the Vesuvius and the Campi Flegrei caldera known as the sunken volcano to the west of the city of Naples.

'The wholesale destruction that would result from the eruption of the Vesuvius or the Campi Flegrei would create the change in the climate of Europe and up to three million refugees.' He started is if eager to lay the foundations for wholesale alarm.

'Explain the cause of an earthquake like this Dr Otto.' Invited the presenter carelessly.

'Well eruption technically, but it's like an earthquake in a way, the African plate is pushing under the Eurasian plate …'

'Now just a moment Dr Otto. We have a direct link to the National Institute of Geophysics and volcanology control centre Observatoria Vesuvio and to Doctor Enzo Calanici.' The presenter confirmed enthusiastically.

It was a deliberate act on the part of the television station. The two men disagreed on the Vesuvial point regularly. Calanici sometimes wondered if his view was just optimism as Otto's arguments were often the more forcibly made.

'One day you will be right. Only thing is, I reckon we will both be well gone by then' Calanici had once said in a manner designed to reduce the impact of Otto's prediction on an anxious television audience.

'You've seen the seismic results for the last five months? Otto asked rhetorically.

'That's one hell of a pattern. We have seen some gas fumeroles.'

'Yes I have to admit Dr Otto there is some activity there. We have seen that sort of thing constantly though.'

'Yes sure' Otto interrupted but not as prolonged as this. We are now possibly only weeks away from a major eruption. I still say that something will happen and it could be bigger than the '79. The point is we are just not prepared. The '79 was reckoned to have wiped out 20,000 people or so, we know that with increased population this one could be two million 'Heck you're living next door to a serial killer and you take no notice.'

'Yes, Dr Otto's reference to the '79 was the known quantity. The first volcanic eruption to be recorded step by step by Pliny and often termed the Pliny eruption. It is true that Herculaneum was buried under 23 metres of ash, but we consider that the Volcano ended a cycle with the eruption of 1944.The worst case scenario would be a 1631 eruption. We can cope with that with current evacuation plans.' Replied Calanici in a tired voice.

'Sure you just about can. But what if it is greater than that. There are eighteen towns in the red zone. Vesuvius is a complex Volcano. There is an extensive assemblage of specially temporally and genetically related major volcanic centres with their associated lava flows and pyroclastic flows. Just 10 kilometres under its surface lies some 400 square kilometres of molten magma.'

'Now hold on' The interviewer complained.

'We are now getting a little too technical. What you are suggesting Dr Otto is that we are just weeks away from witnessing a massive, and I can call it that, eruption that could wipe out up to two million people if evacuation plans are not in place. Is that right sir?'

'I believe that we could be about to see a Plinian eruption. It will change climates and weather patterns across the whole continent. It could wipe out everything on the Sorrentine peninsula heck it could be a lot worse than that it could wipe out the whole of southern Europe.'

'And deaths Sir. Will the lava destroy that many people?'

'It is the intense heat of the first surge after the pumice fall that cause deaths by asphyxiation prior to any lava flow.' Dr Otto replied.

'It is not as if you have the option to run away from it '

'But we are prepared for evacuation.' Protested Dr Calanici in a tired voice.

'That all sounds rather ominous to me gentlemen.' The presenter interrupted.

'But we can be sure Dr Calanici that the evacuation plans will allow the local population to escape whatever is in store can't we?' He suggested seeming anxious to conclude the debate on a superficial level.

Dr Calanici confirmed that he thought that was so.

'And I am afraid that is where we will have to end it. Cleary there is debate but we are assured that evacuation plans are in place should an eruption occur. We now go over to Victoria Rainey who is outside the Westminster cathedral in London.

The young woman presenter smiled briefly into the camera.

'Now we have a different opinion on this story not from scientists but a more controversial source. Rosa Minto is an expert in the history of the Catholic church, tell me Rosa is there not some sort of prediction of this event though. Is it not right that certain people are saying that many people from Nostradamus to the Virgin Mary have predicted a huge eruption of Vesuvius?' The interviewer questioned.

'There have been several prophesies that indicate that the eruption will be the sign of something greater such as the second coming or the coming of the antichrist. Predictions like these have been with us since before Christian times and indeed exist within other religious philosophies as well.' The expert informed her.

'But there was one, a particular revelation that spoke specifically about the eruption of Vesuvius and the coming of the antichrist is that not so?'

'Indeed yes that did occur though of course we have to be aware that such things are sometimes inaccurately reported' She answered attempting to dismiss the suggestion.

'So do you believe that something of this nature is about to happen? Does anyone in the church think this might be an omen of some kind?'

'I think most people are realistic about this. An eruption of this volcano was always likely and I think it is more likely a natural event than a supernatural one'

'Well we shall have to watch this very carefully' Cautioned the interviewer seemingly without conviction 'Rosa thank you'

Emma listened to the debate with interest. There were clearly two different opinions as to the severity of the eruption and it was quite possible that the program had tended toward some scaremongering. That was not however what had grasped her attention. It was the reference to a prediction that Vesuvius would erupt. It sounded very much like what she had heard about in the revelation that she had heard from Marcus.

What if the effect was catastrophic? It sounded as if evacuation plans had been made on the basis of a lesser eruption. There was at least one expert suggesting that it could be a great deal worse. What if there was something in the revelations, that the eruption was part of some change in the world order and that the events predicted in the revelations reported by Father Fidel Rocher would come about.

She turned to watch the screen. It seemed that in the final analysis the possibility of a volcanic eruption was soon to be subordinated by a piece of far greater interest. The wife of the prime minister of Italy was seeing an American rock star and lurid reports of their spending the night together in a hotel in Rome had surfaced. Details of the affair were of much greater interest that a mere volcanic eruption wiping out a large area of Italy and effecting the climate of Europe. Emma switched off the television and turned to her phone to read the emails that had accumulated.

'Rick' she said later as they sat quietly together.

'Did you hear anything about the possible eruption of Vesuvius? There were two guys talking about it on the television. It seems that there is the possibility of a huge eruption. Was there not a huge explosion of some kind predicted in the revelation that Marcus referred to. Something about a red rage?'

'Perhaps. Though we could be talking of Betelgeuse, the red giant' he suggested.

'What is Betelgeuse?' She asked.

'It is a huge star in the Orion constellation. The point is that it is due to explode soon.'

'Soon?' She exclaimed sounding concerned and thinking she had missed something.

'You mean that there is this huge star out there that is going to explode and wipe us all out? When do they say soon will be?'

'Oh, it could be anytime, tomorrow or a million years from now' he was finding this amusing.

'Sounds like an exact science to me. What happens if it is tomorrow will it wipe out the earth?'

'Well, the effects of it will take about million years to reach the earth and well no it really is too far away to affect the earth. The point is that Astrologers have often seen its demise as something significant. It could well have been foreseen by some ancient civilisation as an omen of some kind. That's what we are talking about aren't we, omens?'

'I guess so. Omens, let's see, an occurrence or object regarded as portending good or evil' She was reading from a large dictionary spread out on the table.

'It seems strange in a way that events have to be portended'

'Well they don't' he said.

'Look at 9/11 no warning there. It didn't even come up on old Nostradamus radar apparently.'

Emma was looking through her Marcus file.

'It's here somewhere. The exact wording that Father Fidel Rocher had given him from the 1892 revelation. Here it is.' Emma read aloud the transcript of the revelation that had been translated by Father Fidel Rocher.

'There will come a time soon when two of you will join me in Heaven. That time will be the day on which the Antichrist took the Western Schism. And there will be a thunderous eruption south of the eternal city and the red rage will announce the coming of the Antichrist. He will place his servant in the Holy church to wear the fisherman's ring and he will seize for himself the Holy Roman Empire from which he will rule the world with a wisdom of lies. By his cursed divination he will know that coming and the blue eyed child will lead the way to freedom.'

'You say this was corroborated in the later revelation? The one to Maria Anna' Rick asked.

'It appears it was at a small village in the Pyrenees called St Therese L'Enfant. Remember too there was the two halves of a secret prayer, one given in the first revelation and one in the second.'

'Yes the secret prayer? What did it say?' Asked Rick.

'Secret means, hidden, kept quiet usually Rick'

'So, if we are to believe in a volcanic eruption heralding the coming of an Antichrist we could soon be seeing him come into view as it were?'

'I guess that is so. Let's see someone pretty ghastly I suggest. A politician probably.' He surmised.

'You don't suppose?' She had spoken before actually thinking through what she was about to say.

'Suppose what?'

'Well all our research keeps coming up with one organisation that could easily supply us with an Antichrist, the Ndrangheta.

'Of course, yes organised crime seizes advantage of disruption and fear following a widely predicted omen like this and looks to take over the world. They place their 'cuckoo' in the Vatican and seize power through some politician or something. It's not that unlikely Emma.'

Emma looked at him studiously, as if she was still piecing it together in her mind.

'When I did my research on these guys I discovered that the Calabrian mafia's income is greater than that of McDonalds and Deutsche Bank put together. They are the world's most powerful crime organisation and control some significant percent of Italian GDP. That seems to me like they are wealthy enough to seize power somewhere. If we do see this eruption of Vesuvius it could mean more than just the disastrous effects that volcanologist spoke of. What we could be witnessing is the end of the world.'

38.

CALABRIA, SOUTHERN ITALY

By the Church of the Crucifix in the small Calabrian town of Sarorio Bintou Diabarte feeds her child a small meal of soup and chicken. Within the fine features of her face and under a dark black skin is a smile of hope. Her body is athletic through hard work and narrow with a lack of sustenance. This one small meal is all she has and this she will give to her child. The last she can expect until some fortune smiles on her, some act of generosity, some small discovery, some payment for any favour she will give in her desperation.

The child is about seven years old. She is much lighter skinned than her mother and has a thick mat of curled hair falling to her shoulders. She is dressed in a single piece of faded white fabric covering her whole body and she has no footwear. The child pulls away from her and runs around in a circle moving her limbs in an involuntary dance routine that gives off the frenetic vibrancy of a lit sparkler. Even in this place of unmitigated suffering with all its broken promise and wholesale grief, the darkest hours can be lit up with impromptu joy. That momentary irrepressible reaction to life itself.

''Nyeleni!' cries out her mother aware that to separate here could bring danger.

'Nyeleni.' Stay by me she adds in a hushed tone in an accented West African French.

In the palm of her soiled hand the child holds a tiny gilt coloured plastic crucifix on a thin chain. She smiles and without speaking, she opens her hand to show it to her mother looking deep into her eyes. This token of her faith has become her one treasure. It is as if she knows that by that token the treasure of her faith will be maintained. With that the small girl falls into her embrace and there is an exchange of love.

The broken sheet metal factory buildings outside the town are their home. These are open to the elements, without windows, absent doors and with roofs that leak in the rain fall. They sleep on concrete floors on whatever they can find for bedding. Sheets of cardboard, straw and beds made up of polythene wrap. There is no running water to the single tap that serves the building now. No payment has been made for its supply and only the most basic sanitation in two barely serviceable latrines is shared among hundreds of them.

Here live the Clandestini. They are packed in with little space to call their own in small groups that share the most basic facilities. They cook their meals on fires of driftwood gathered from the streets and shoreline, outside in the open air and argue for advantages and trade what they can to get fed.

They have been moved here to the mainland from the island of Lampedusa where their numbers have grown so much the government had to act to move them from the holding camps that were busting at the seams. The island of Lampedusa has a population of 5000 people with 35,000 immigrants. More arrive daily on small vessels of every kind from the African mainland. They have paid dearly for this hopeless journey. Smugglers charge thousands to arrange this short and perilous boat ride with its promise of a new life in Europe. Today the 'Clandestini' the illegal immigrants now over whelm the town of Sarorio.

It is the first morning of the working week and just as in ancient times when the sick would stand in line to bathe in the healing shadow of Saint Peter as he passed, so do lines of clandestini wait in some form of order that only they recognise waiting for the call to work. Their mouths are dry from the hot night and stale air, their joints scarred and aching from the makeshift beds on concrete that are their only reprieve from the grind of work and boredom. In their hearts is the disillusion of hopelessness but their eyes search in desperate expectation for the passing of the overseer the nod of his head that is the call to work.

The overseers, will come soon, in small vans and open trucks to select them for the work on the citrus farms where lemon and oranges are prepared or juiced for the fruit factories further north where they will be turned to crystalized fruit and candied peel delicacies for the privileged. They will earn miserable wages if they are lucky to be selected and luckier still to be paid.

Much of the citrus growing and production is controlled by the Ndrangheta and the Scalfero Ndrina dominates production here just as it does everywhere in this area. Here is the harshest of masters, the most brutal of overseers. Here the clandestini know the small reward for success and the painful penalty for failure. Here is tolerated no word of contradiction. Here the poor are judged, the rich beyond reproach. Here fear rules these tattered lives and blind obedience the only currency they have.

Today as the harvest is of lemons, it is not likely to require large numbers of workers and there are many among this army of hopeless expectation who will know that there will be no work for them. These are the west Africans. Those that by the colour of their skin are the last selected, they know that only after all other paler shades have been exhausted will they be called for work by the fruit growers.

They are those that know that they will have to beg for a meal tonight or get lucky. They will remain in groups of four or more to avoid the attacks by local vigilante who will ride by them on motor scooters and beat those found to be alone.

They are economic migrants from west Africa who dream of a life in Europe. A dream that has eventuated in their being beaten on the streets cheated of their wages when they earn them and left to eke out an indigence in any makeshift shelter that can accommodate them. It is a dream that has ended in slavery and prostitution for many young women. It is a pitiful sight this waste of labour this destitution, this waste of life.

Enrica Postilana watched the television in her home while she prepared a simple meal for her son Luciano. She took pleasure in its preparation as he always praised her cooking, even though now he was himself a professional chef, working abroad in an hotel in Provence it was her cooking he praised the most. He was her only son, home for a short stay and she would enjoy spoiling him. She took pride in the admiration that women seemed to have of his good looks and had even fallen in with the trend of calling him by his French name of Luc.

Enrica was a woman of 57 years of age. In her younger years she had worn a simple southern beauty under her thick dark hair, wide eyes and sugar brown skin, a pretty face and even smile. At that time she had shown the rebelliousness of her youth. She had tried to stand for what was right in a world of wrong, and she had not listened to the collective wisdom of her elders. She had resisted the requests of the Ndrangheta to allow the distribution of its imports in the youth club she had run in the town, but when a bloodied head arrived at her home in a gaily bound box on the morning of her forty first birthday Enrica Postilana became a convert to the reciprocity of accommodations that are met daily between those who live in fear and hopeless poverty and those who dispense it. She had chosen then to run with wrong rather than to stand alone by righteousness in a brother hood of misery where there were no prizes for dissent. Where morality receives no reward other than perhaps an inscription on a wall somewhere obscure or a mention in a daily newspaper, something soon forgotten. She had learnt that day that complicity is easier and more profitable than dignity.

She had seen her son Luciano grow into the clan and prosper. He was happy to be among others like him and he was secure so long as he obeyed its rules. She had the status attributed to a mother of a clansman too which gave her safety and security in this community, though she knew its fragility. Protection was the small stipend she received for compliance. Due only day to day and subject to instant withdrawal. For Enrica Postilana knew, that the reality was that she was living on the edge of obliteration.

Honour is the foundation of the clan. It binds brothers by rigorous ritual to a ruthless code that justifies a darker conduct. It feeds prejudice with fear and envy and it was most certainly the spark of it all. It was all about honour, though it had emerged from an unlikely source. An unknown northern politician had appeared on television that afternoon to speak out about filthy dead bodies floating in the clean seas around Lampedusa and stated that the Government should not allow the refugee boats to land nor to allow the problem to come to Italian shores.

These were feelings held in the hearts of many but feelings that had not yet been exposed to expression. They now became inevitably the subject of heated discussion in every home especially those around which the refugee problem had descended.

'We must' The northerner had declared.

'Defend our country from this invasion. We should fire upon the boats and drive them back to the north African shores. We cannot allow these people to take our jobs our homes our lives.'

He had spoken with all the emotion and accuracy of one who is detached from the day to day complexity of the refugee problem but for those who had watched the TV with growing anger, it was impossible to discern the rhetoric designed for political advancement from the sympathy they felt and the outrage they expressed on behalf of the poor residents of the south who had to contend with this unwanted influx of economic migrants.

Outside in the street, groups of young men had armed themselves with air rifles, metal bars and anything that would provide a missile. It was all rather a hesitant affair at first but some interchange of sentiment encouraged them to a resolution. This evening they would confront the Clandestini and bring blood to the streets of Sarorio.

The police had read some of the signs and had moved many of the immigrants back to their accommodation fearful that riots may break out between them and the increasingly resentful local population.

It was early evening when the sky looked very black and lowering and the wind rose and it started to rain in torrents. The mob had mobilised and was moving toward the clandestini encampments through the downpour along the wet roads on foot and the inevitable scooters sounding horns of encouragement. The violence of the ensuing storm seemed to stir them to a fever and there were more shouts of retribution and revenge for the insults that had been brought to their town.

At the encampment the first news of the mobilisation of the mob was arriving. Men were looking around them wide eyed with concern for anything that would defend them. They realised that they had nowhere to run. Some had family, wives, mothers, children to defend.

It was after 19.00 when the mob arrived. A wet seething horde determined to restore the honour they had felt to have been stripped from them by the clandestini and it was instant. Volleys of anger swinging clubs, firing air rifles pulling the hair of screaming women, tearing their clothes from them and brandishing them like ragged trophies. The battle came and went in just over one hour as the rain came down upon them.

A deathly silence weighed heavy in the chill air of early morning. As the damp leaves shone on the fruit trees in the first frail rays of sunlight, all around lay scattered the corpses of the dead. The mellow silent tragedy of the dead who would not answer the call of morning. There was no dignity for the dead. They lay crumpled and distorted in heaps, some half clothed some fallen grasping wounds, lay in dark pools of blood and puddles of rainwater that saturated the clothes they died in. They were defending their lives against the savage wave of hate, but that wave overcame them the more they defended the more that hate raged. There was no way out for them but to be the victims and to accept death. Now the incipient stench of death began to pollute the air. All sympathy was to be abandoned to the gruesome job of their removal.

A small child looked on in disbelief at the overwhelming scene. Nyeleni knew to hide when evil came. She had sought the darkness that had so often been her comfort in the past. The stinking crack between the rocks in which she could barely conceal her small body was her refuge as she shook in fear to hear the wild cries of avengement and the pitiful screams of the dying. Now she witnessed its outcome and she looked for her mother among the dead lifting the limbs of the fallen corpses to look under them, and waiving away the large black flies that were beginning to settle on the scene.

Bintou Diabarte was not to be found among the dead that morning for she had survived that terrible episode. She had been selected for special work too important to allow the local youth to slaughter her. For the Scalfero clan had selected her to play a part in the packaging despatch and distribution of cocaine throughout Europe.

In the souterrain, deep pitch black all enveloping darkness surrounds them like prison walls and holds them like a jailer. Here there is no need of chains for the darkness shackles the limbs to impede the slightest movement when they sleep on the damp floors with only a rough blanket to cover them. Here the cocaine is packed for distribution.

In these underground tunnel factories favoured by the Ndrangheta for their secrecy. The captive workers are selected from the clandestini for their docility and desperation. They are young women who stand at wooden benches sorting cutting and packing the drug ready for distribution.

They work in the intense heat unclothed, not for any consideration for their comfort in the heat of the confined area but so that they are not tempted to conceal within their clothing any of the drug that would force their overseer to beat them to death for the transgression. It is this merciful ruling that sees lines of naked young black women standing at the benches busily and silently processing the white powder in the half-light with an urgency and a silence driven by fear.

Those nights spent in the darkness on the hard floors of the workspace hearing the cries of the weak until the sound of their complaints was silenced by the harsh brutality that despatched them to the mercy of God had been hard for her. But Bintou Diabarte cared not for herself but for the daughter she had been forced to leave behind in the camp. She worked the long hours without complaint for to die would be to terminate any chance she might have to see her daughter again.

The dull hours before work commenced, when a shipment was awaited from the dock, could be filled with some form of conversation between them. A brief breakfast of fruit and bread and cheese was fed to them and for some this was more than the scavenging life they had led hitherto. Bintou Diabarte heard of the life that some had led and for the first time counted herself, even with the hardships she had endured to be one of the lucky ones. It was in these exchanges that she heard a name that was only ever whispered in fear. That name was Scalfero.

It was Scalfero who controlled the trade in produce from fruit to drugs, of services from prostitution to protection. Scalfero who controlled the operations in the port of Giouro Touro and the construction projects that sprung with relentless disharmony from the landscape of dilapidation. Scalfero who selected from the hapless immigrants those who were to work for the clan. It was Scalfero who would decide ones fate, whether one would live or die.

Bintou Diabarte had only her dreams for comfort, and in every dream she dreamed of Nyeleni. She felt through her faith that her child was safe and in her dreams she heard the words of the old fortune teller in the market at Bamako.

'You will find happiness in Europe for your child. There is nothing here for her but misery and servitude. The world waits for your child in Europe. For she will achieve great things there.'

As one more bright dawn rose away from the darkness of the souterain it was the turn of Bintou Diabarte to remain asleep. Never to work the dark distressing hours again. To follow her faith to heaven's welcome. To rest with her dreams forevermore.

39.

VESUVIUS, ITALY

On the same morning that her mother died Nyeleni was woken from a deep sleep on the floor of the shepherds cabin where she had found refuge to hear an enormous explosion. It was the loudest sound she had ever heard. She had looked out from the makeshift shelter that had played host to her that night across at the magnificent mountain that she had only last evening stared at with such awe.

She had never imagined that the earth could be so angry, that like a fractious child, it could belch so and throw its playthings into the air and inspire in those who watched it an apprehension, and uncertainty that would cause them to stand their distance and gaze. In her desert home the quiet monotony of stagnant heat and the hot dust of the desert were what she had had to bear. Here among the opportunities for aspiration and promise of freedom the very earth shook and thundered in remonstration.

It was just after 6.00 in the morning when the narrow wisp of smoke that had been rising from the top of the volcano like an umbrella pine surged into a column increasing its height and splitting off the hot rock around its crater causing the crust to unravel the sides of the mountain as if a banana was being skinned by an invisible hand. The eruptive column surged to a great height that was probably miles into the sky and its great shower of dust, rock and pumice was shed to the ground.

Where it landed, a chaos and panic of activity was in progress with the desperate evacuation taking place. Pumice and rock was showering down on the fertile farmland and settlements around the volcano itself and where it fell, it did so like a shelling from a badly ordered military battery crashing through roofs of buildings destroying vehicles and making the narrow roads impassable. Many residents had already left seeking refuge outside the town that followed the evacuation plan and they must now have looked on and thanked God for the blessing of their caution. It was a spectacle so horrific that to the observer, watching from afar helpless and uncertain, it appeared unreal and like a filmed staging of some ghastly inferno.

For those closer to the imbroglio it was a reality uncircumscribed by notions of cinema graphic interpretation. There were the screams of victims, the barking of frightened dogs, the hopeless revving of car engines going nowhere on the broken roads.

Marcus had felt that they had by good fortune found themselves at a sufficient distance but now he looked at Segolene and for the first time saw in her measured eyes a terror at the spectacle before them. They could see now the pumice mounting up in layers on the ground and on the roofs of farm buildings. The sky was beginning to darken with the huge eruptive column now spread for miles south west of the volcano.

'We keep going north' He directed 'If we go south the sea will cut us off.'

In a second and more dramatic surge, the rock fall now spread towards them. Fragments of tephrite fell in front of them puncturing the soft soil and springing wildly from hard surfaces. The intense heat could be felt on their skin and the air was dry with the hot dust that had now become tangible and they could hear the coughing of victims caught by the asphyxiation. They ran towards a group of low trees to pause under their canopies but the further surge made him think better of pausing and more of running as they could.

Segolene tore at the door of a small shed swinging it partially open. Inside was the old dukati.

'Here let me' He volunteered but she was already pumping her foot down on the kick start muttering a small prayer as she did so.

Suddenly the engine roared to life although its sound was now drowned out by the crescendo around them.

'On the back' she directed without needing to. Marcus held on tightly as they sped away down into the valley. Skilfully she took a narrow pathway that cut between the hairpin line of the highway in order to avoid the chaos of vehicles descending in disorder. As he hung on to her he could feel the hot sweat from her torso strong and confident under his grateful grasp. The small engine of the motorbike gurgled its protest amiably and turning to look to one side he could see that their escape from the danger zone might soon be accomplished.

It was over an hour travelling across country, north towards Nola. They had kept away from the roads that were full with lines of traffic slowly struggling to escape the eruption. Marcus felt good that they had been fortunate to be free to travel by motorbike rather than by car. It was almost at the point when his confidence was highest there was a sharp cracking sound from under him and he found himself lying on the ground some feet away from the bike.

'Are you alright?' He shouted to Segolene who was draped over the front of the bike.

'I am alive Marcus, but the bike is not. Are you OK to walk from here?'

They could see now that the bike had certainly done its job. It had taken them well away from the volcano and the traffic on the roads was now thinning. They were able quite quickly to reach the road leading to Nola and the vehicles moving north at a slow pace all carried additional passengers clinging on where they could and talking excitedly to one another questioning the whereabouts of those known to them as they did so.

It was a short hitch on a small fruit truck that took them to the small village of Pantanto.

'I can't imagine that they will be looking for us here do you?' Marcus asked her dismounting from the back of the truck.

'I wouldn't put it past them' She responded unconvincingly and with a smile.

'No, I think at least that is one thing we don't have to worry about.'

Progress is slow when you feel as if you have been cooked, pelted by rocks and thrown from a motor cycle. He felt the swell of pride in the way in which Segolene had handled their escape.

First from his prison cell, then the pursuit from an assassin and now again from a volcanic eruption. It was a cause for huge gratitude.

The village was full of evacuees and they had to walk away from the centre some distance to find somewhere to put down for the night. It was not long however before they came across a small stone building that appeared to have been a shepherds hut. A group of three or four young people were debating whether to rest up there or to move on and appeared to have decided to the latter.

'We rest here' She said.

'A sleep will do us some good if we are to travel north tomorrow.'

The door had been left ajar as the young people had left and they ducked as they entered the tiny dark room. Then they became aware that they were not alone. Lying on the floor was a child who had made up a bed of cloths to sleep on just as a dog might on the dusty floor. She had been awakened by the eruption but lay in her makeshift bed as if to ignore it.

On the wall of the room on a patch of discoloured plaster, she had drawn a sketch of the figure of a woman with a cake of soot taken from the back of the fireplace. Marcus could see that the figure drawn to perfection was that of a slender black woman sitting on a what appeared to be a throne, and she was looking down at the child while she slept.

The detail of the image was extraordinary. She had coloured the flowing white robes in chalk and drawn over them in red brick dust a cape that covered the woman's shoulders. It was not only the dark black skin that caught his attention. The drawing showed the woman's right eye coloured bright blue.

I think it is a drawing of her mother. She clearly has no mother with her. Perhaps she lost her in the eruption.' Segolene surmised.

'Perhaps the blue eye is the eye of the virgin. She wants it to watch over her as she sleeps. Let's stay here with her, perhaps her mother will watch over us as well'

As evening drew in they left the child to sleep in the cabin and stood outside in the warm air looking down at the coastline. The sunset threw a strange and eerie beauty across the bay in burnt orange, soft strawberry red and charcoal colours half stirred together like some delectable confection. To the south the volcano dust covered the sky with a curtain of darkness, and as if to remind them of its perturbations the volcano sent out missiles of the stuff high into the air that exploded in the distance with little more than a puff sound showering the sea with dust and sparks like some extravagant firework.

The air was warm and in the sticky heat the fine dust clung to the skin and it was impossible to avoid it in the mouth and in the fine creases in sweated skin. Looking to the shore they could see on the beach the small camp fires of evacuees who had set up in tents and bivouacs unsure where there next night might be. Families were cooking meals from cans and towards the rear of the beach a cooperative effort was in place cooking large numbers of light meals on a professional looking barbeque with a determination that was as admirable as it was energetic.

Segolene looked out to sea in disconsolation.

'Don't look like that' He said 'We have done really well. First the great escape from captivity now this, the escape from a volcanic eruption. Well I mean we are still alive.'

She turned to him and smiled the briefest hint of a smile.

'I have known what it is to have my own father look me in the eyes and not recognise me' She started dramatically.

'Good Lord no' he began to protest believing she planned to chastise him.

'No Marcus there is something I have to confess to you. I am not Marie Segolene. I am not your daughter. She died shortly after that car crash and is buried in the cemetery at Avignon just like you had always understood.'

Marcus looked at her in disbelief. It was a disbelief not of what she was now saying, that the extraordinary coincidence of her being his daughter was not true. He had felt that possibility all along. It was more that she should have in the first place led him to believe that it were.

'Then why on earth did you say you were?' He asked plausibly.

'It was my father, my real father who asked me to do it. He suspected that Maria Anna had told you the second part of the secret prayer and that was why you had gone to Avignon, to piece together the prayer from the Beatrice revelation. He saw you as a threat to his plans.'

'Good Lord no. Who is your father?'

'He is the man I rescued you from Michelangelo Scalfero. He is the head of the Ndrangheta.' Marcus looked at her unsure how to respond.

'He believes that this is a prophesy, the key to the ordination of a new breed of super being who will take over the world' She looked at him for a reaction before realising that she had probably sounded absurd.

'That may sound extraordinary to you but it is a belief that makes him a very dangerous man.' She looked at him seriously.

'Power, intellect, money and madness are a dangerous cocktail.' She confirmed.

'Scalfero aims to seize minds through knowledge, souls through faith, beings through wealth. You Marcus, hold the key to that knowledge. At least that is what he believes.'

Marcus stood back feeling the disappointment of her deception and the naivety of his complicity in its perfection. It was good to be able to remind himself that she had saved his life on two occasions. It somehow made him feel that his trust in her had not been entirely misplaced.

There was a stillness in the air now as the darkness grew punctured by the camp fires and the insistent bursts of hot dust that lit the sky on its southern horizon. The heavy heat was causing him to feel exhaustion.

It all somehow seemed unimportant now. From the pain and deprivation of his captivity the assault of rocks from a volcano, the threat of death from the mafia, her deception, he was still alive surely that was what mattered.

'So what do I call you now?' He asked simply.

'Segolene if you don't mind. I prefer it to Magdalena. That was his name for me.'

Marcus smiled happy his illusion had not been totally destroyed. Now he thought of the mission that had been entrusted to him. Somehow now it was the only thing that made real sense. Here among the debris of destruction he resolved to complete the mission that Father Fidel Rocher had asked of him. For who could tell what lay before them now.

A pale violet mist hung heavy on the morning till the sun broke through in small patches in the blackened sky. There was a silence all around, the collective wonder of human beings set in trance by the overwhelming miracle of their preservation.

The child had woken early after her long rest, oblivious to the discomfort of her makeshift bed. She looked at him in a way that conveyed a sadness but one that was resigned to her fate. He could see now the extraordinary pair of eyes different in both colour and intensity. Together they combined to convey a maturity and a wisdom that had accepted the loss of the person most dear to her without the absence of love for what little she had left. That lone blue eye shone like a tiny patch of July sky caught among the grey clouds that will not allow the rain to fall.

There was a joy in her laughter that touched his heart with the briefest of regret, that felt for her the loss she had suffered, but rejoiced for the gratitude that laughter expressed for the small blessings that were left to her.

They said nothing. More due to what appeared to him some form of autism than his inability to converse freely in French but there was nevertheless an easy understanding between them and he was sure that she could detect this as she passed to him a small scrap of paper on which was written her name and pointed to herself.

Her generous mouth smiled as if she understood his mind and he saw for the first time in her a most intense beauty. Her features entirely even her skin smooth, coloured a dark brown the richness of tobacco. Her perfect white teeth were even and unmarked and her unmatched eyes held a brightness and a wisdom way beyond their years. She was at once remarkable and delightful to behold.

Marcus looked into her eyes and suddenly a realisation came to him. Didn't the revelation say something of a blue eyed child?

He had when he read that somehow imagined blond haired blue eyed children as those being referred to but here in front of him surely was the child referred to in the revelation. Nyeleni was the blue eyed child.

The following day they travelled north, following a stream of refugees towards Rome taking shelter where they could sometimes sleeping under the stars. As the days passed, Nyeleni's confidence grew discernibly. She had the attribute of anticipating the next move and being there to assist in its execution. She had a smile that acknowledged remarks that she could not possibly comprehend and yet it was as if she had understood every word.

They had discovered a small game for their amusement, that simply involved her identification of items in the dark. It amused them greatly to discover that she would always succeed in retrieving the smallest of things on the darkest of nights. Then there were her artistic skills. She could draw objects to intense complexity from memory having seen them only in the dark.

'Is it just your blue eye that you do that with?' asked Segolene.

The child shut the eye and nodded her head as if she could not now see anything smiling as she did so, enjoying the compliment to her ability.

'There is danger ahead' Segolene confirmed 'When we reach Rome the Ndrangheta will be waiting for us. I do not think that we should risk Nyeleni. We will need to move swiftly to avoid them'

'But we have to travel to Rome. We have to warn of the Antichrist. It is my promise to Father Fidel Rocher that I do so' Marcus confirmed.

There was regret at having to leave the child but they were sure that she would be well cared for among the nuns of the Santa Agnes convent who had accepted her in their small school with the promise of a small payment for her keep and the confirmation of her strict adherence to her faith.

Segolene smiled with satisfaction. Tomorrow they would arrive in Rome and for her Rome held one million euro's in a bank account in the name of Marcus Graham. She would need to persuade him to make a withdrawal.

40.

VESUVIUS, ITALY

There had been a further eruption of the volcano. A Pyroclastic current of dust had swept south during the night and the region around Vesuvius had become uninhabitable. Around the Campi flegrei fumeroles of carbon monoxide were seeping into buildings and the earth itself moved as if some invisible hand passed under its surface with malevolent intent.

Scalfero watched the sky with several of his trusted illuminati with awe and satisfaction from his villa one hundred kilometres south. In his eyes what he saw in the sky north of him was the prodigy, the omen that signalled the fulfilment of a revelation. The revelation of the Holy mother that fate had decreed would be his to prosper from.

He would now place his servant to wear the fisherman's ring. He would expand the activities of the Drexel Hesse bank to dominate the financial world and he would ensure that the ubermensch, those gifted with intellect and ambition would take the positions of power to reign over the Holy Roman empire.

A figure of a manservant entered the terrace hurriedly as if in panic. Scalfero looked at him malevolently.

'You have come from the Osservatoria what news is there?' He asked sharply.

'The evacuation is still in progress there are expected to be over a million people disrupted from their homes from Misena right round to the Sorentine peninsular. The scale of the disaster is something that has not occurred since AD79. Thousands of victims have suffered death by rock fall, asphyxiation, and now that the lava is beginning to flow there will be more.' The man reported in distress.

'It is the signum, the omen' Scalfero confirmed with satisfaction his voice trembling with emotion.

'But there are tens of thousands of dead.' The man protested.

Scalfero turned to those who surrounded him as the sky darkened with the cloud of the volcanic eruption, and a thin band of sunlit sky to the west on the horizon could be seen over the sea. He raised his hand to gesture towards it and turned to announce theatrically.

'They make way for a new beginning. A beginning that will herald the reign of the ubermensch. We cannot interfere with nature through pity. Theirs is the sacrifice that will bring mankind to a new level of existence. This is nature's principle of Eugenics. In our quest to breed a superior race, a master race, we must first witness the reduction of populations by catastrophe or wars. We must prepare to accept enslavement of those who do not die to serve the master race.'

'The world is overflowing with a scourge of humanity. We have seen this reach our shores to seek our pity and offer us nothing in return. It is our duty to control the spread of this infestation. There are populations that must be reduced, races that must be destroyed. We will arm those in conflict who wish to destroy each other for they play no part in our philosophy.

New superior races will be bred with heritable intellect. We will educate the young to believe in the superior being and the rights of the ubermensch to rule.

We will raise the aspirations of mankind to live beyond his comfort zone. Man will live by his instincts, his intuition, his creative abilities and desire for aesthetics. We will relish a world where the winner takes everything including, the life of the looser. A world of competition that rewards the best and expunges the mediocre.

Tomorrow heralds the ascent of the Ubermensch and those gifted the sign of the archangel have been granted the discretion of Judgement.' He announced before declaring.

'It will be for us to decide who will live and who will die.'

41.

ROME, ITALY

The late afternoon sun in the narrow streets of Rome still heated the air defying the shadow cast by the fine buildings that lined each side of a small street by the Pantheon. Marcus sat with Segolene at a small café table overlooking the activity of people dashing to and fro creating a vibrant hubbub of sound and activity.

They were resolved to be thankful for their preservation, but the arrival of celebratory cocktails was quickly followed by the presence of a number of small wasps. They appeared on the scene to assault the drinks as soon as they were placed before them. It was then he witnessed something he found intriguing. Segolene did not wave the insects away or even comment on their presence but simply removed the cherry from her glass and placed in an ashtray. To Marcus's surprise, the insects lost all interest in the drinks and set about the cherry. It was as if a deal had been struck.

'You know how to handle them.' He remarked with surprise.

'It's part of the culture here' She replied stirring the ice in her drink and looking down at it pensively.

'All blessings are to be shared, they are never yours alone. For everything there is a small price to pay. A toll, a tax or a tithe. A small ransom that will allow the enjoyment of that you have earned or paid for without the curse of envy. Nihil est ab omni parte beatum Marcus, nothing is an unmixed blessing.' She added with a light smile.

'That sounds like the 'pinch'. Is that not the principle of the Mafia?' He commented jocularly.

'I think it was Horace actually, but yes, the Mafia will leave you to get on with your life and your business for a cut and you are encouraged to succeed so that you can pay them. It is the same as a toll for the highway, a tax to the state. A tithe to the church is surely something you pay in the same way'

'Though not quite the same obligation I would suggest. The penalty is less severe' Marcus pronounced.

'You don't think that eternal damnation is a threat?' Segolene gasped and fell back in her chair in laughter.

'Surely, there is little to distinguish the Mafia and the Church. Both love their ceremonies, swear their oaths, enforce their silences and both deal in judgements and retribution.' She added provocatively.

'What do you think they want of me?' He asked suddenly exposing his preoccupation.

'Not a small toll, tithe or tax I imagine' He added.

'Perhaps it is not you they want.' She sung in her intriguing inflection. She turned her head to one side and looked at him as if to invite him to follow her implication.

'You mean it is you they want?' He gasped.

'I don't know, perhaps.' She was not prepared to say, although he began to feel the she knew more or at least suspected more than she was letting on. It seemed at least reasonable to ask her what their next move should be.

She spoke softly as she looked down at the table, as if to study it gave her some inspiration.

'How can we stand when our toe is rotted? How do we breathe when our air carries the stench of corruption? How can we speak when our words are silenced by a curse? This is the reality of the Mezzogiorno. The Ndrangheta is like God. It is everywhere, but it is invisible, hidden in the souls of men. It is the parasite that feeds on the fear of the poor and the greed of the rich. It is the salt in the tears of its widows, the silence in the oath of its code and the blood in the veins of its brethren.'

Then she turned to him and said.

We say 'Noi siamo il pasato il presente e il furturio.' Whispering these words with her eyes now fixed firmly on his.

There was a cold moment that swept the air of uncertainty and left it crisp and clear. Marcus felt the realisation swipe him like a blow.

'You mean, that you are one of them?' He asked not wishing to believe what he now knew to be true.

'Of course. I was born into them. It is in my blood like that of my father, but like my father I have sought to find my own way in life, to look out for myself. I have seen a brotherhood of misery, a landscape of dereliction, a population in poverty through corruption and contrition. An obedience and service that pleads only the mercy of the most wretched existence. Yes, I have abandoned the order to find my own way in life and for that there is no forgiveness. Only the brief retort of the assassin's gun. Yes it is me they wish to kill.'

Marcus was silent for a palpable minute. Around him the waiters shouted to each other, the customers carried on their conversations a pair of small children argued with each other for the shade of an umbrella, the couple on the next table ate without words an early supper of melon and thinly sliced ham. For Marcus her words conveyed a heavy truth that he would later dissect to reveal much of the mystery that had surrounded him ever since he had arrived in Avignon.

His mind raced to piece together, her deception, the poisoning of Father Fidel Rocher, the theft of the diary that held the secret of the virgin's prayer.

'They are here in Rome today, now. They plan to kill me in revenge and to extract from you something that I now believe you do not know.'

'My mother Elise was linked to the Basque separatist movement ETA.' Segolene smiled as she recalled her mother.

'She was described posthumously as 'angry, her motives uncertain her allegiances various.' She was rumoured to have been involved in many attacks on the establishment in Spain but also elsewhere. I lived my early life with her and the intermittent presence of my father in Calabria. After my mother had been executed on a street by the Guardia Civil my father stated that I was mad and had me committed to a lunatic asylum. He then deserted me. I guess that I have always felt the absence of a father figure. Perhaps that has led me to seek the security of older men.' She smiled at him suggestively.

'Then my father's henchman contacted me. He told me that he had a job for me to undertake and that I would be well rewarded and that it was the duty I owed by my blood. He said that I must pose as your daughter to extract from you the secret that he was sure you held for why else would you have arrived at the chapel in Avignon.

You see your wife Annie lived her childhood in a small village in the Pyrenees and as a child was known as Maria Anna. One day the virgin Mary appeared to her and revealed to her something of great significance. She was sworn to secrecy by the church but she told one person, my mother. They were teenage friends and, well teenage girls share secrets.'

Marcus was listening intently to this unsure what to believe.

'Where does your father come into this?'

'The revelation is something my father is obsessed by. He has always believed that the destiny of mankind is preordained and he has tried many ways to discover what is in the future. The revelation is something he feels holds a secret that combined with power will make him ...'

'The Ubermensch?' Marcus finished.

'I did not know of this revelation before Father Fidel Rocher mentioned it to me.' Marcus said emphatically.

'Annie never said anything to me about it. I wonder why not?'

'Perhaps she was in love.' she suggested with a teasing smile.

'Would you have fallen in love with a girl who talks with angels? Anyway, clearly my father believes that you know more than you do.'

He studied her for a moment as he felt not for the first time, her betrayal.

She looked into his eyes to see a hurt. It was the hurt that a younger man might display on his discovery of his girl's indiscretion. A visible reaction to dishonesty.

'I have a room in a hotel near here.' She confirmed avoiding his question.

'We will be safe there and we could do with some rest.'

He thought about asking why she would have a hotel room reserved here, He was sure that she had not booked it since they had been together on the journey from the south. He decided not to ask. She had perhaps revealed as much as he could digest for one day and besides, it would become clear in time.

Room 37, the twin room at the small hotel at Corso was a useful retreat and he was grateful for its modest comfort.

'We can wash up and change clothes. I had some new ones brought in before I left Rome to pick you up. I think you will find that they fit.'

He was again surprised. She had clearly prepared to rescue him and bring him here. It crossed his mind that this was some further kind of deception and that he might soon be passed over to her father's men.

He was now feeling a selfish satisfaction in the disappointment he had shown her as he sensed that there might be compensation to be received that would heal the wounds he felt from her betrayal. He watched the way she stood and stripped by the open window in view of who knows who. The intense look in her eyes that locked onto his as she came towards him. Suddenly he was pushed down to the small bed with a quick emphatic punch of energy. His head filled with the smell of fresh white sheets stiff with the scent of vetiver.

'Some rest Marcus. I think you need some rest.' She confirmed.

The soft waft of the city air from the open window cooled his body as she pulled off his shirt from his thin torso and left it naked. She smiled almost kindly as she pulled herself into his caress. It was something he had not seen in her before. He had seen her confidence, her beauty and her boldness. He had witnessed her intellect, her understanding and knowledge but kindness had not been something he had yet seen in her.

She looked into his eyes suggestively.

'Do you think that now you know that I am not your daughter you might do to me what you wanted when you first met me in the Café Zizi Jeanmaire?' The suggestion was complete. It needed no augmentation or translation.

She weaved her head around his in playful tease and sucked on his mouth lip by lip with hungry deliberation. Her soft breath was warm on his face with the hint of vermouth. The close touch of her tanned limbs, the invitation in her eyes, the scent of her warm body fuelled the heat of his anxiety. It was all too much to resist. Temptation is more easily resolved by acquiescence than resistance. His silence in response implored her first advantage. She spread her fingers wide across his chest pushing deep into his pectoral muscles. Her mouth toyed with his jaw as if to taste the rough unshaven line of bone and skin sticky with the sour cocktail of sweat and dust that had stuck to him for days. Her hand went to his belt fastened tight around his slender belly. Her practiced fingers jerking the buckle to open the waistband of his faded jeans.

'We are almost there' she joked.

'You can stop me now if you want.' She invited knowing she had gone beyond the point of return.

The fingers drew down his zip with alacrity grasping his anxiety with a warm hand and a squeal of triumph as if she had located it unexpectedly. Marcus lay back as if to resign himself to an inevitable assault for which he would take no responsibility. She was the instigator, the perpetrator, he would not invoke the delight but allow her to do so and enjoy its implementation. As she stripped him of his clothes and sat astride him, mounting him purposefully, he lay back on the bed and she took him inside her perfect moist body with a small tremulous gasp. Was this some form of apology for her deception? Or was this the incorrigible lust that he had witnessed in the small parlour when she serviced her two friends in one triumphant exhortation?

For Marcus Graham the prospect of spending an early evening skin-to-skin with a beautiful young woman was not something he had dreamt possible only a short time ago and it gave him a purpose and a confidence he had not felt before and the soothing nurture of her rhythmic motion charged him with a new energy that was the purest pleasure.

He turned her onto her back and entered her body again, feeling for the first time in command of her, and with a masculinity that had for too long been dormant he felt his limbs steady and in control, his mind clear and his will strong. The enjoyment of her young body gave him a fresh feeling of confidence and power. Marcus smiled as he heard the words of Father Fidel Rocher echo in his head.

'It is written that to everything there is a season and a time to every purpose under heaven. The time has come my friend for you to bear that which God has ordained for you.'

42.

ROME, ITALY

Jacopo picked up the rifle and looked along the barrel for no reason other than to familiarise himself with the object that was to be his companion for the next three days. He had taken it apart and reassembled it for the same reason though do to so was some kind of rehearsal for his escape after making the shot.

He did not need to familiarise himself with the weapon. It was an AK 47, the Kalashnikov assault rifle, the world's most prolific killing machine that he had known before in the heady days when he helped to control the Toronto suburbs and where he learnt the craft of assassination. He had retrieved it himself with the key to locker 920 concealed in the packet he picked up in the back of the limousine that had picked him up from Millhaven.

He was an expert in its use and had never been caught for that crime and he was sure that his luck in that was due to his well-planned retreats in the minutes that followed the shot. This would be no different. The single shot to the head if he was lucky and plenty in reserve if he was not. The confusion among bodyguards and attendants when the blow was struck. The distress among the faithful when it was realised what had taken place.

His chance to escape was always within those first minutes that followed the shot. The wiping clean and concealment of the gun. The swift exit to the street at the rear to join the concerned rush of pilgrims to the place where the fallen Pontiff fell. No one would walk away. They would crowd the scene of the fallen and they would look in disbelief and horror. He too would join them and look on in that horror.

Raphael was to be the sure-fire-bet as successor to the deceased Pope Eustace. Father Simeon had told him so. He was admired throughout the world. A number one guy. Italian American, plain spoken guy. Raphael had good looks too. He must have, he was Jacopo's double. Jacopo smirked.

'You will wear the Fisherman's ring.' Father Simeon had promised him. 'Reach out with that same hand to net the fruits of the Sea. These are the words of prophesy my brother. The words of the Blessed virgin.'

He slumped down on the floor beside the window with its open view across the street. He had studied that view so many times. Distances, obstructions, weather constraints the likely speed of the convoy as it slowed to pass the corner. The positions of pedestrians and onlookers, the presence of security, the line of fire. He had painted every picture in his mind of the fifty seconds he had to aim and fire one shot that would lead to the death of a Pope and the fulfilment of a prophesy. He was in position, he was ready and he was waiting.

It was almost two days later when the papal convoy entered the piazza on its way to Ciampino airport. Jacopo had been in position for three days just waiting. The elderly Pope stood in the back of the vehicle waving to the crowds that surrounded the route. That was until he stumbled almost unnoticed, as if he had merely fallen backward into his seat. The shot had been unheard in the hysteria that had surrounded the car. He had been seen only to stumble and it took some moments for the driver realising that something was wrong, to come to a halt. As the onlookers strove to see what had happened pushing forward towards the car there was one among them who knew for sure. Jacopo looked on incredulously at the scene with tears in his eyes.

Later that day there was nothing on the radio other than the news of the assassination of Pope Eustace. Speculation on who may be responsible, enemies of the Christian church perhaps, terrorist's, a group located in Peru who had vowed to take some form of revenge on the Catholic church was running as favourite possibly due to the colour of such a story. The gun had been found in a nearby building. An AK47 high calibre rifle capable of the single shot was reported. The type that might be used by a professional assassin it was speculated.

Jacopo felt that he was in the clear. No one had any clue as to the motive for the assassination and it would soon be impossible for them to piece together the audacious plan to which he had been assigned. Soon the newspapers would begin the speculation as to which cardinal would take the position of Bishop of Rome. Of who would be the next pope.

Jacopo threw the newspaper to the floor and looked at his brother with a resolution in his eyes.

'What now?' He asked sure that now he had taken the first step in his transformation.

'The papal conclave is steeped in mystery, elaborate ritual and veils of secrecy.' Father Simeon advised in a quiet tone as if he was thinking through his response as he spoke.

'These are fundamental to its mystique and the glue that binds the worshippers in faith. It is the mystery that guides not politics. The mystery of the Holy Spirit. Mystery is a big idea in the Catholic faith. Its deepest meaning is that parts of faith are unknowable through reason and intellect alone. There will be the grief and regret at the passing of our Holy Father but intrigue and expectation as to the succession will take its place and the suppositions and political debate will consume the conclave but with one inevitable outcome.'

Father Simeon spoke with the confidence of one who believes in an outcome through the horror of contemplating its alternative. So often such belief can be self-fulfilling.

On the day the conclave met, Scalfero had to admit to a measure of uncertainty such as he rarely experienced. There was just one cardinal who he had been informed would be preferential but he would play no part in his election. His whole plan had been premised on the appointment of cardinal Raphael to the position of the Holy Father. Failure to achieve this would mean failure of his plans and yet this was to be one decision that was totally out of his hands.

He waited as the white smoke emanated from the chimney of the Sistine chapel and allowed himself a short prayer. Would his plan come about? Would Cardinal Raphael be the elected pope? He had laid his plans and done everything in his power to ensure that this would be the case but the conclave was closed to his influence beyond the endorsements given by the two stipendiary cardinals Trataveli and Dufour.

It was Father Simeon who came hurriedly towards him now. Scalfero looked at him unable to conceal his expectation. Father Simeon smiled broadly.

'Yes' He confirmed simply. We have our Pope.

What followed had been carefully planned some months previously. The stipendiaries had their instructions and it would take little time to smuggle Jacopo into the Vatican to take up his role. The sooner it was accomplished the fewer people would become acquainted with the speech and mannerisms of new pope and the more likely they were to be deceived.

That evening Scalfero answered his cell phone to the voice of Father Simeon.

'Cardinal Raphael is now our guest at Castello Rocca. The new Pope has chosen his name. Pope Michelangelo will wear the fisherman's ring.'

43.

LONDON, ENGLAND

Emma Dreyfus had arrived early to the office on a Tuesday morning in August following a return flight from Rome that had arrived late the previous evening. There had been extensive delays from Leonardo da Vinci following the eruption of the volcano and the large numbers of additional passengers arriving at the airport wishing to flee the country.

There were some telephone calls to make in order to catch up. Routine calls chasing up instructions and she would need to offer an explanation for Marcus absence and perhaps promise someone to take over the work if it was urgent. The first two calls were simply unanswered. Emma suspected that the high net wealth clients had more interesting things to do than concern themselves with the alterations to their London homes. They were no doubt away in the Caribbean and only on their return would ring to demand immediate action. It was the third call she made that was quite different.

'Is Mr Tate there? Mr Gordon Tate.' Emma asked.

'No he isn't here.'

Emma detected some reticence in the voice that answered.

'Is that Mrs Tate?'

'Yes'

'Oh It's Emma Dreyfus from Fisher Holt and Fitzroy architects. I was just ringing about the refurbishment work on the property in Dulwich.' She paused as if that were a question.

'Oh yes.' She answered flatly.

'Well we obtained planning permission some three months ago now, the conditions are satisfied and I wondered if we should be preparing working drawings?'

The voice at the other end seemed now more relaxed. There was something in the altered tone that gave Emma the impression that Mrs Tate had been expecting a call regarding something else, almost certainly something more important.

'I haven't seen him for two months now. I just don't know where he is.'

Emma could immediately hear that the woman was distraught and instinctively held on to the phone to prepare to offer some assistance.

'You are not expecting him back then?' She tried cautiously.

'No.' She muttered.

'He is in some sort of trouble I know he is and I can't get hold of him. He mortgaged these properties with a bank in Germany and they have been on to me about the repayments. He wouldn't have just left things like that. I know that he is in some sort of trouble. I just don't know what.'

Emma could hear that Mrs Tate was at her wits end trying to decipher the cause of her distress. Mr Tate would not be the first husband to disappear into the arms of another woman leaving his wife to put together the pieces, but there was something in her distress that told of something different. There was not the suspicion nor any allegation of desertion. There was only distress and concern. Emma felt that she needed to console Mrs Tate and was sure that she was not about to ring off.

'I am awfully sorry to hear that Mrs Tate. Do you think that he might have had an accident or something? I meant, maybe a loss of memory' She added by way of retraction.

'He was going to Rome, I had thought, to see an engineering company but it seems that he went there to get a mortgage on these properties. He must have needed a lot of money but I don't know what for.' She was crying now. The opportunity to speak to someone to release her anxiety had brought out her tears.

Emma did not know whether to continue speaking to this woman she had never met or to somehow end the conversation. It was then that Mrs Tate said something that convinced her she should continue.

'Have you heard of a bank in Frankfurt called Drexel Hesse?'
She asked.

'Why yes' Emma answered surprised that she should.

'Why only the other day someone mentioned the name to me.'
Emma was trying to remember what Rick had said about his
work for Drexel Hesse.

'Why do you ask that?'

'Oh I know nothing of business at all. I just wondered why
my husband went to Rome to mortgage his property portfolio
with a bank in Frankfurt. It seems a strange thing to do to me.'

'His mobile phone. Have you had the police check that out?
If it is switched on they can trace it' Emma suggested.

'Yes someone else suggested that. It seems he turned it off in
Rome' 'Look' said Emma.

'I will try to find out more given what you have told me and
get back to you.'

'Oh I am so grateful. If you can find out anything I just. Well
I just want to know.'

It was a voice of a woman who had resigned the fact that something terrible had happened to her husband. Emma felt herself
driven by sympathy to her but also she had to admit to herself
that she was addicted to this kind of intrigue. A puzzle to solve,
a riddle to work out. As she assured her and rung off Emma instinctively tidied the notes that she had made while in conversation with Mrs Tate. 'Has not seen husband for two months Went
missing in Rome. Frankfurt, Drexel Hesse bank.'

It was then that she remembered what Rick had said. It was
when he was in Frankfurt visiting the Drexel Hesse bank he had
heard the word Ndrangheta. It had been the only word he had
picked up when overhearing a conversation in German. It was
now clear to her that something sinister surrounded the name
Drexel Hesse.

Emma decided to look at her notes later and filed them away.
Her thoughts were wandering and that was perhaps why she did
not realise that she had inadvertently slipped them into the file
on her desk marked Marcus.

44.

ROME, ITALY

Cagnaccio twisted his head to look up at the window on the first floor of the hotel. It was a habit now, ever since he had looked up at that window to see her swiftly undressing her fresh youthful body by its glass his eyes had been drawn to its promise. The possibility of 'encore' to feast his prurient gaze. Yet while he had not witnessed much more than a momentary glance, it had been enough to intrigue and take his gaze each time he turned the garbage out to the yard around the back of the Hotel kitchens that were accessed from Crociferi.

He pulled the back of his rough hand across his stubble chin, its thin mouth leaking a nicotine stained saliva into the sweat and dirt on the nut brown skin. She had become the creature of his fantasy. It was not just the beautiful body that had so injudiciously revealed its self by the window. She had tormented his furtive gaze with an illusion to him far more alluring than his sight of her naked body. She stimulated his imagination to dream of a prize that might have been his. A prize he now knew to be lost.

It was two weeks earlier that the call had gone out from the Albanian that the Ndrangheta were looking for a young woman just like this. Cagnaccio's imagination had raced around the improbable chance that had he seen this young woman earlier he might have discovered the very quarry of their search. How would it have been if he Cagnaccio, had discovered her, reported her and been applauded and rewarded for doing so? For him money always imputed morality. There is no need to question he who will pay.

It was surely too late now. He had heard that the Albanian was dead, killed in a vendetta. Perhaps he himself had suffered the inevitable fate of failure.

To fuel his fantasy Cagnaccio had been careful to make discreet enquiry about the young woman in room 37. He had established that the Hotel register made it clear that there were two women in that room mother and daughter. They had booked in for four weeks while they toured the city. The vision in the window was not, he concluded with regret the young woman who was sought by the Ndrangheta. She would now be far away in some foreign land enjoying, so he had learned, the proceeds of an audacious theft from the Capo Criminali himself. Some people, he reflected, had no respect.

He unzipped the fly in the stained corduroy trousers that he wore and began to piss against the wall of the yard. It was just then, as he relieved himself that he looked up at that same window that he saw a man by that same window. Surely that was nothing unusual. A relative perhaps come to visit. He could be the father. Perhaps he worked in the city and he would be the reason why the ladies were spending four weeks here. He dismissed any thought he might have had of anything that might give an opportunity to profit from his observation.

It was only later that evening as Cagnaccio ordered his beer at the bar in Picolo that he heard there had been further news. Information that would be paid for handsomely. Half a year's wages with the guarantee of payment in cash. How he yearned for the opportunity to find and to yield up that information and now his excitement grew. It seemed that the young woman being sought for the theft was now accompanied by an older man. She may well be in Rome and his imagination was reignited with the possibilities offered by room 37.

At the hotel the following morning he checked again the details. Room number 37 had been booked for four weeks. There was certainly a young woman and perhaps it had been booked in the name of her mother rather than her father by mistake or perhaps deliberately. Cagnaccio was careful not to ask too much of the receptionist. Although he wanted to sound out his theories with someone else he could not. He did not wish to share the prize and could not risk someone else claiming it. He would have to work it out himself.

The two English women staying in the room went by the name of Beck the receptionist confirmed and yes she was sure there might have been a visitor. Cagnaccio weighed up his chances. It sounded too uncertain, too unlikely. The Ndrangheta would not appreciate a false alarm, the information they paid so handsomely for needed to be reliable.

Cagnaccio searched his mind as he sat on his own in the bar that evening. If he made no report and let the opportunity pass he may miss his chance. If he was wrong he would have to explain himself but surely they would understand. Besides, if he were right he would secure for himself the prize that he longed for. He swallowed another beer and came to his conclusion. What had he to lose?

45.

ROME, ITALY

Maria Breganza Martinez spent much of her spare time keeping up with the events at the Vatican for her sister would be arriving tomorrow in Rome with her choir on what they had planned to be the trip of a lifetime. Today she was looking intently at a video of the new Pope Michelangelo filmed outside St Pietro as he appeared on the balcony overlooking the square. It was a joyful occasion blessed by a clear sky and sunshine with much adulation and his blessing of a large crowd.

The camera scanned to his hand, presumably to display the fisherman's ring, as that is what many see as the symbol of his recent ordination. It was then that she stopped in disbelief, stunned by what she saw. It perhaps was what she did not see that had affected her. For she knew that Pope Michaelangelo when a less exalted cardinal Raphael bore the blemish on his right hand ring finger that resembled a tear. She remembered clearly how he had said to her.

'Yes, I have but one tear of sadness for humanity. The rest I cry in joy, for the Lord is good and He sees everything.'

What could be the explanation for this? she asked herself. Perhaps the Vatican was zealous in its preparation of the Pontiff for the cameras. It had to extinguish any blemishes in favour of its portrayal of perfection. She was not persuaded by this and searched her mind frantically for an explanation. It was then she was able to catch a glimpse of his eyes. Those kind eyes so full of wisdom that had smiled at her and conveyed the grace that her sister had always said one is either born with or one is not. Now here was something very different, something sinister and cold.

Maria Breganza Martinez at once became sure that this man was not the priest whom she had followed from his humble beginnings to the most exalted in the church. This was not the pope she was sure. What she saw was an imposter.

Her observation had flung her into confusion. What was she to do? Who would believe her? In an instant she knew she had the answer. Perhaps indeed it was God's will that her sister Valentina was at that time in Rome and close to the Vatican itself. She decided that she would call her and instruct her to speak to the most senior member of the church she could find and tell them of the imposter.

Valentina had taken the call from her sister without questioning the truth or importance attached to it. She was quite literally to go to the nearest church and ask for the most senior cleric. She was then to inform him of the existence of an imposter posing as his Holiness himself. It was a tribute to the closeness of the two sisters that this she did without question and without hesitation.

As Valentina entered the Chiesa San Nicolo she could see the ceiling open up to a magnificent trompe l'oeil, a di sotto in su of a ceiling that was painted as if open to the sky with angels and a number of people painted at its edges as if hanging their limbs over the upper walls. Valentina marvelled at the wonder of its deception. She lifted her head to view the heavens under the dome and was rewarded by a vision of blue sky and angels. Never before had she seen it in such perfection. The splendour of this illusion caused her to stand transfixed in awe and she was almost unconscious of the figure standing beside her.

'Good morning sister' came a soft voice in English. It was a thin faced cleric dressed in a habit that she could not identify.

'You have come to admire our church I imagine?' He questioned.

'The di sotto in su were painted in many Jesuit churches in the 16th to 17th centuries. This is one of the finest in Rome. Beauty so effectively conceals deceit doesn't it? She offers us a spectacle to seduce us, but look closely and you will see that it is the death of Ananias and Sapphira that is portrayed. You are indeed fortunate to have stepped into our church. We do not see many Americans here.'

He was pleasant in his conversation but Valentina felt him to have something of a lack of sincerity about him. A shiftiness, was the only way she could describe it, an untrustworthy demeanour that she could not explain. She certainly felt that she could not reveal to him her sister's message for he would not be likely to act on it and to act on it was clearly essential.

'I wish to see someone of high rank in the church' She began. 'I have an important message to deliver from my sister.'

These words had no impression on the clergyman who looked at her with suspicion.

'My sister is from Chicago and well known to his Holiness' She added.

This seemed to get the response she was seeking but clearly she would have to explain precisely what the message was to have any opportunity of delivering it to a suitable person.

She began again.

'You see my sister knows the Pope is an imposter.' She declared. 'The true Pope has a tear mark on his ring finger.'

The thin faced cleric looked intently at her for a moment and then said simply.

'Wait here, I will call someone to see you.'

Cardinal Dominic Dufour trembled as he took the call. If this was to be made widely public it would have so many of the faithful looking at Jacopo's hand for the tear the absence of which would reveal him as an impostor. He had to act. He knew that he would answer for the oversight. There was no forgiving treachery nor crass incompetence. He could hear the verdict now as he faced the certain death that would follow his failure to recognise the one distinction between Cardinal Raphael and his imposter. He called for a car to take him to the Cheisa San Nicolo.

'Swiftly' he directed the driver. 'It is a matter of great importance.'

It was 10–15 minutes of agony as he was driven to the Cheisa San Nicolo. He sat impotent in the car as it battled the traffic around the city. He imagined the American woman speaking to others, spreading this rumour in her garrulous and swarthy accent and as he did so his anger and resentment towards her grew. How could she challenge the work that had been put in to create this great deception? How could she threaten the favoured position of Cardinal Dominic Dufour in the last years of his life? A life dedicated to service to the church.

The car drew up outside the church and Cardinal Dufour alighted with as much grace as his elderly bones could bear.

'Where is this woman?' He asked of the thin clergyman standing by the door waiting to receive him.

'Your grace I have bade her wait in the vestry for you.'

'Tell her that I must hear her confession' Dufour instructed with some presence of mind.

'Show her to confession. I will await her there.'

With that the thin clergyman directed Valentina to confession such as she might make her allegations as if she may be guilty of some mortal sin. As Valentina sat down and composed herself Dufour addressed her.

'You have asked to see me my child. Tell me what is it that you have imagined?'

'Your Grace I speak with humility to you but I cannot question the observation that my sister has made of our Holy Father for she has declared him to be false. An imposter your grace. He does not bear the mark of the tear borne by the Holy Father on his right hand.'

'How have you seen this my child?'

'It was my sister. On a television broadcast. She has met the Holy Father and knows him to bear the mark.'

'You must know that much can be done to extinguish such marks for ours is the promotion of mystery not of spectacle. I am sure it is that that answers your concern.'

Valentina was not to be deterred. She innocently believed that the Cardinal who received her message as if he were taking her confession in these most unusual of circumstances was simply unaware of the significance of what could be implied by the absence of a birth mark. She continued with determination sure that her sister could not be wrong.

'I am sure that he is indeed an imposter' She found herself denouncing while starting to question in her mind the very words she uttered.

Cardinal Dufour knew at that point that he had to act. To fail to do so would be to fail the order that kept him free from incarceration and to fail would mean certain death. It was either this woman or himself. He signalled to the thin clergyman and spoke to him briefly in Italian.

'Escort her to the vestry. We will see to her there.'

As Valentina entered the vestry Cardinal Dufour turned to her swiftly.

'You have witnessed too much to remain on this earth.' He announced with savagery as she stood shocked at his demeanour.

'The world is not intended for the meek. Soon the ubermensch will rule and I am their servant.'

With that he lunged at her clumsily swinging a heavy candlestick he had snatched from the table behind him at her head and knocking her to the ground where Valentina lay motionless. A pool of scarlet blood started to flow from her head onto the fine stone floor.

As he moved away from the scene towards the door he looked up into the eyes of the Madonna that looked down at him from the portrait on the wall as if somehow they had borne witness to his act and he crossed himself unconsciously. It was exactly as Maria Breganza Martinez had seen in her vision. The death of her beloved sister at the hands of a Cardinal.

46.

FRANKFURT, GERMANY

Jens Swartz was inelegantly eating something in a bread roll wrapped in a paper napkin as Peter Beck approached him standing under the statue of the hammering man, as had been arranged.

'We have something else on the Meyer murder' He started eagerly without greeting Peter.

'When we searched his house on the Leiter Strasse we found that he had been throwing runes just before they got him' He looked at Peter as if he was suggesting something.

'Runes?' Peter questioned 'You mean like dice?'

'Well not exactly. Runes are small wooden tablets marked with letters in ancient Nordic script. The Nordic runes are marked with the Futhark alphabet said to derive from the Etruscan alphabet. They are letters on small tablets of wood. It is said that the wood must derive from a nut tree and the letters be red, the colour of blood.'

'So what of it?' Peter asked.

'Well the Futhark alphabet is not just an Alphabet. It is known as the Alphabet of mystery. Each letter has a meaning and the runes are cast in order to divine a message. A sort of horoscope.'

'Ok you mean like Tarot cards?'

'Yes exactly. In fact both are apparently supposed to work by reading the subconscious mind of the dealer.'

'So what has this got to do with his murder?'

'Well, we got an expert in from Gothenburg University to read the runes. There is no doubt that they made pretty uncomfortable reading for Meyer.'

'You mean they foretold his death?' Peter exclaimed.

Jens passed some photographs to Peter. They showed the runes spread randomly on a white cloth.

'Let's see what I made a note of' He said taking his notebook from his pocket. This is what his casting of these runes reads.

'All the letters have an esoteric meaning used in divination. This is Uraz the ox. It speaks of violence. The giant, Thuriaz is danger or evil and Sowilo here is the sun shows the wrath of God. There's a lot more but you get the picture.'

'You seem to be well up on rune reading all of a sudden.' Peter remarked surprised at Jens knowledge of the subject.

'The runes are supposed to read the subconscious mind.' He said again.

'I get it, you mean Meyer felt that he was going to die?'

'Assuming he could read his runes yes, he sure did. Well I found it quite fascinating and I will possibly learn more later. I'm seeing the professor again for dinner this evening.'

Peter smiled widely. His image of the Swedish professor of Norse mythology had suddenly changed from the wizened bespectacled troll he had assumed, to the attractive Scandinavian beauty he was now certain she was. He knew that Jens eye for the ladies was a discerning one. His interest in Norse mythology had not been entirely professional. It was likely too, that Jens would be aiming to expand that knowledge during the professor's stay in Frankfurt.

'Why not join us at the Kat Kat for a drink. I'll introduce you.' Jens said perceiving his clear curiosity and perhaps wishing to show off his putative conquest.

It was 19.30 when Peter arrived at the Kat Kat club. It had not been an invitation to turn down. First he had a curious interest in seeing for himself the lady that Jens seemed keen for him to meet, but also the subject of Norse mythology itself was proving something of a growing fascination.

Professor Ingrid Jensen was everything he had imagined from the level of interest that Jens had shown in her subject. Her long blond hair hung almost in ringlets down to her shoulders and her face was wide with an alert and pretty expression. She wore dark rimmed glasses that gave her the look of an academic and her figure was slim and beautifully shaped. She greeted Peter smiling expressively.

'This is quite fascinating, quite a story, a guy who predicts his own death shortly before it happens.' He summarised while taking a seat in front of her.

'So you Professor, are an expert in Mythology?'

'Well yes, the history of Mythology and the similarities and distinctions that existed between civilisations and cultures that were geographically separated before Christianity came to Europe.'

'It is surprising to think that people still believe in these methods of divination.' Peter observed.

She smiled briefly and prepared herself to answer his question.

'Divination is as old as humankind itself. Mankind has always sought to believe that cause can follow effect determined to invent all the evidence that does not exist. The pendulum that answers yes or no, the tarot cards that guide the unconscious soul, the reading of bones and the runes of Norse mythology. All are used for divination.'

'Does this have any significance to who may have killed him? Some other gang of these Ndrangheta has been suggested.'

'I doubt that they will tell us that.' She laughed.

Jens's mobile was buzzing.

'I'll take that. It might be something.' He said in expectation, and with that got up to go to the door for a clearer line to answer the call.

Peter looked out through the window to see that Jens was looking a little as if he was on the defensive as he took the call. A raised hand, the shrug of shoulders, the impression that he was unable to finish his sentences. Could this be simply be a call from the office or a domestic confrontation? The confirmation came as he returned to the table.

'Look' Jens said awkwardly.

'I've sort of got to go. Really sorry.' It was the kind of apology that gave away the essence of the call. It was not the demands of the police force that had broken up his evening, for such could be set to one side with some light excuse. The call he had re-

292

ceived had been driven by a suspicion from someone who well understood the motivations behind his extracurricular liaison and the ultimatum was one he could not avoid. He sort of had to go.

'It's OK I understand.' The Professor confirmed eagerly. We are OK to stay on here for a bit.'

She looked at Peter and smiled to gain his confirmation as Jens left hurriedly.

'I didn't come here to start an argument.' She confirmed with a light smile after he left.

'So tell me more about these runes' Peter asked with genuine interest. You say the alphabet was Etruscan. 'Was that not in Italy?'

'The Etruscan Civilisation was in Esturia. An area around to-day's Tuscany. The runes are marked with letters from the Etruscan alphabet. They were called the 'people of the book' but there is not much of their literature that survives today as they became part of the Roman Republic and the Romans were pretty efficient at extinguishing all evidence of past civilisations that they conquered.

Jens told me that there were two other murders?' She questioned.

'Yes, there were actually several gang members that Meyer was going to give me information about.'

'No, I didn't mean them. There were two other murders the same day.'

'Oh yes you mean the tiny dancer killings. No one has any leads on them. Seems the kiddies murderer will get away with it. Do you think that they may be connected then?' He asked becoming aware that there may be a theory.

The professor looked at him in silence for a moment as if unsure how to put to him what was in her mind.

'It's silly I'm sure' She started.

'It's just that the nature of these killings indicates some sort of ritual.' She looked at him starkly to see if he agreed.

'Yes, that has been suggested.'

'Well they were not slaughtered where the corpses were found were they and certain parts of the viscera were missing. In both cases the liver.'

Peter looked at her intently. The professor was about to give a theory and he was anxious to hear it.

'It was the Etruscan letters on the runes got me thinking Peter. It got me thinking of the 'tiny dancers' With that she looked at Peter as if to invite comment.

'These girls were killed in some form of ritual, their livers were removed. Do you know what Etruscan haruspicy is?'

He shook his head in silence.

'Well the Etruscans believed that every natural phenomenon was an expression of divine will and contained a message which could be interpreted by their priests. Haruspicy was the art of derivation of omens by examination of entrails of animals. The libri haruspicini was Etruscan, the first book of the Disciplina etrusca it gave all the details necessary for understanding the art of haruspicy. They even had a college dedicated to the study of it as an art. The image we have today of the sorcerer with his conical hat is derived from the ritual costume of the Haruspix. He would wear it for the ceremony. The Etruscans would usually divine from the liver of a sheep but ...'

'But what?' Peter questioned in agitation.

'Well, Esturia became part of the Roman Republic and the art was continued well into roman times. There is at least one recorded event in Gaul where a sheep was unavailable for the ceremony.'

He looked at her anticipating the words she was about to say.

'The Romans used their prisoners. Two young virgins.'

'That is horrific, they must have hated the French.'

'Mainz was in those days part of Gaul Peter. It was the roman stronghold of Mogontiacum, the northern military town of Gaul. That event happened not far from here where the river Main meets the Rhine. Not so very far from where the tiny dancers were found.'

For Peter the details of Roman history had left him feeling a discomfort that silenced him. His mind was racing to understand the implication of her words.

'I wondered if there may be some connection here.' She invited.

'You mean this Meyer guy is mixed up in some cult. Hey Jens said he was involved with something, something to do with the Calabrian Mafia. Does that tie in to your theory?'

'Not to my knowledge. Calabria is a little out of my territory.' Ingrid Jensen had brought the conversation to an abrupt halt. Peter Beck's mind was churning.

'Holy shit. You think that those kids were murdered so that someone could have their fortune read?'

She sat back in her chair seeing his discomfort.

'Do you believe that certain events can be predicted by examining the condition of present circumstances? If you starve your dog he dies right? You eat too much, you get fat, you smoke so you get disease.' She was looking over at a rather large couple at a nearby table who had momentarily diverted her attention as if to illustrate her assertion.

He smiled at her observation. She had an authority in her pretty face that made her the more desirable. An intensity in her eyes, a gravity in her voice and its slight delicious accent.

'I guess that's true but it seems a bit farfetched to see omens in someone's liver.'

He reflected that he already had a story to publish and it had all the elements of mystery that he needed for now with its reference to runes. It would not need to include any speculation about the murder of the tiny dancers. This fascinating theory was for tomorrow.

She looked at him for a moment more sternly.

Do you have far to go? I am staying at the Steigenberger Messe hof. I have a very comfortable room. We could perhaps go back there for a nightcap.' She urged quietly.

He felt an instant gratitude to Jen's wife at this point. She had clearly ordered Jens home and now Peter had been left the open goal to take up this delicious opportunity.

In the taxi to the hotel they sat for some minutes in silence until she said.

'How long have you lived in Frankfurt.'

'Twelve years now. I was brought up in Swegwick Holstein. Practically Scandinavian.' He joked.

'I came to work on the Frankfurter Allgemeine Zeitung. Reports on exhibitions mainly. It got a bit dull so I switched to Hesse Heute. It's a bit more varied a brief.'

There was a moment's silence as she appeared to be thinking of what next to say. Then she leant over and kissed him on the mouth. A small laugh followed and a long look up to his face from her lovely eyes portrayed a longing. It had been a declaration of intent.

'Now, you are not married are you?' She asked lowering her voice rhetorically and wishing to make clear her disavowal of Jens.

He laughed.

'No, not me. Unwanted, intolerable something like that.'

'It leaves you pure.' She suggested, a word he had never imagined would be applied to him.

'Just what I like in a man.'

She stroked his hand in confirmation and held on to his arm as they entered the hotel. There was a warmth that had developed between them in that brief time that saw them embrace on entering her room as if they had known each other for much longer. Her mouth found his in hungry anticipation and he kissed the soft skin on her neck delighting in the sweet scent of her hair. There followed an easy pattern of unspoken exchange that saw him peeling off her clothes and her yielding to his touch without resistance.

Peter felt the warm taut flesh of her belly as he spread his fingers across it to enjoy the beautiful body that now wrestled unambiguously in his arms. Her eyes focussed and determined invited his strong touch. The firm muscle in her athletic arms pulling him closer as he mounted her nakedness. The soft mouth that sucked at him and the warm moist caress as he gently entered her.

Yet within this sublime moment his mind was now occupied by discomfort. Something that could not be dislodged. It was the growing realisation that somehow her theory was right.

47.

FRANKFURT AM MAIN, GERMANY

It was as if the whole Meyer story had taken place without a hint of suspicion on the part of the authorities. If indeed there had been, nothing had been reported over the years. For Peter Beck it was a missed opportunity he had started to regret. The guy had run a bank that was almost a crime organisation right under the radar of suspicion for years. It had been a news story that was only now surfacing. What was clear was that Meyer's competitors had been alert to his activities and had now taken steps to intervene. Now there would be the task of tracking down the new criminals and finding out why they had come to Frankfurt. It was almost certain that the reason why his city had been targeted was the ease in which the proceeds of the drug trade could be so easily laundered in the financial centre of Europe. As Peter went over his thoughts the phone rung from reception.

'Something new on the Meyer case? I have Hans Klempner on the line.' Said Mizzi.

'Hi Hans' Said Peter abruptly.

'The whole Meyer empire is coming apart Peter. It seems that the police had raided one of his brothels last night. Found women working there as forced labour. The papers will all be screaming sex slavery this morning. We need to do a feature on this Peter. Find out a bit more about slavery in our society. I want you to get hold of one of these anti-slavery charities and get some information from them. I've been given the name of one you may like to get in touch with Peter. They do a lot of work in west Africa, Mali and Niger. They are called Maliberation'

It was that direction that had brought him to a small hotel close to Via Corso in the eternal city. Peter Beck unpacked the small suitcase he had purchased hastily for the trip and carefully placed his personal items on the desk opposite the bed. He looked out of the window across the light well onto the featureless bare wall not two metres away that was its view. A call to Maliberation and now only a few days later he had taken the plane from Frankfurt to Leonardo da Vinci to follow up the assignment that Hans Klempner had given him. He had been given an address along with a time which he had hastily written on a small crumpled sticker that he drew from his wallet and read out loud.

'Palazzo Pontinia Vende Settembre. Sounds pretty important.' He said allowing himself to imagine somewhere a good deal grander than the hotel he was now staying in.

His invitation was to meet a Madam Gigency of Maliberation, the French charity that spoke for the rights of women in Mali and their liberation from servitude. The charity was to have a party held in its aid by a its new benefactor, a businessman and Philanthropist in the courtyard of his palazzo in Rome. Madam Gigency had no doubt suggested that he join her at the party as it gave an opportunity to demonstrate the status of Maliberation. She had arranged to meet several members of the press and Peter was privileged to be included.

'Our benefactor is to hold a Roman carnival to highlight the plight of the African immigrants in Italy.' She had confirmed rather grandly.

'We could meet there.' She had suggested in an enticing manner during their phone call just days ago.

It was to be a masquerade ball with the theme that of a Roman carnival. Peter had accepted enthusiastically. The idea of a trip to Rome and the fun arranging the mask and costume that would transform the humble news hound into a glamorous Duke was certainly appealing.

The Roman carnival portrays the inversion of society. Rich becomes poor and poor rich. Black becomes white, good, evil. The master becomes the servant, and in years past the carnival offered the opportunity for the oppressed to vent their feelings with satire and free expression against the oppressor. This was the theme that supported the ultimate underclass, the slave, a theme chosen by the charity's new benefactor Signor Michaelangelo Scalfero.

Perhaps it had been no more than instinctive inspiration that had caused Scalfero to choose the supreme deception. A deception that fulfils fantasy with its innocent illusion. That disguises itself in the most outlandish of costumes of cynicism and hypocrisy and hides it face amongst revelry and celebration. The roman carnival was for Scalfero the perfect deception.

It was early evening when Peter Beck arrived at the Palazzo Pontinia. It was a tall and beautiful building on four floors. Its rendered walls were painted a terracotta red and its heavy timber windows were crowned with carved lintels that were of different design on each floor. All the windows bore shutters to seal the privacy of its occupants. Wide Stone steps led from the street to its front door around which rose two large columns that were crowned with a sumptuous balcony with carved stone balustrade which could be accessed from the first floor level. The building retained something of its historic austerity from the days when rival merchant families inhabited this city and fought each other through their commerce for patronage and in arms.

Through the entrance doors was a large hall that broke out through further elegant doors to the most splendid courtyard within which were placed stone carvings of classical figures and grand planters filled with exotic shrubs. It was surrounded by beautiful buildings, their stone and warm coloured render baring the patina of age and painted doors opened to decorated metal balconies that were lit from behind in a subtle glow that revealed an intrigue of occupation.

The guests were arriving now in numbers alighting from chauffeured limousines and taxis. All were dressed in the most elegant and colourful of costume of a variety of historical periods, many strictly associated with Rome, but some bearing the flair of Florence and vitality of Venice. The great and the good of this city here to endorse the generous patronage that Scalfero was to offer. The support of a charity that had spoken out against the worst excesses of mankind. A patronage that would build a reputation that would endure.

Peter had been ushered to a corner of the courtyard to meet with Madame Gigency who was herself looking most striking in a heavy red dress decorated with gold braid. He detected that she was a woman in her early fifties. She was certainly slim built and was probably attractive as he could see that her eyes were bright and she spoke as if there was a smile behind the gold mask that she wore.

'Isn't this absolutely marvellous?' She questioned excitedly.

'This is an event that will make everyone sit up and take note of what we stand for. Signor Scalfero wishes to publicise the plight of the African immigrants in the part of Italy he comes from. They come to the country looking for work of course but are often abused by those who employ them in the fruit picking industry there.'

'What part of Italy is that?' Peter asked feeling that perhaps he should have known the answer.

'Calabria. It is on the toe so to speak of the country.'

Peter reflected that he knew something of the plight of these people and had heard a good deal about the area of Calabria. It was the area from which Meyer had come and the area from which Jens was sure those that killed Meyer had come from.

'Oh 'she said excitedly addressing the assembled press upon the arrival of a neatly dressed dark man who had spoken briefly and quietly to her and appeared to be a guide of some kind.

'Signor Scalfero has invited us to look around his art gallery. He has of course shown me around personally and while he is not available to do so for you I do urge you to view the gallery it really does have some wonderful pieces of art.' She signalled to the guide who had spoken with her and added.

'Yes do show them around. They will see for themselves the works of art that have made signor Scalfero so sensitive to the suffering of others.'

'Where is signor Scalfero?' Peter asked looking around expectantly.

'Oh did you not hear?' Madame Gigency questioned loudly for all to hear.

'Signor Scalfero is at dinner this evening as a guest of His Holiness with the American president Mr Edgar Allan.'

The story was embellished by one of the other journalists in the party.

'Yes it seems as if the White House had second thoughts on him meeting up with the Italian prime minister following this scandal regarding his wife and the rock star who had spent some time in a U.S jail. Seems they arranged for Allan to pop in for pizza with the Pope and our host instead' He laughed.

The guide smiled a thin smile at the revelation and nodded ready to lead the way for the small group of press who were to enjoy the privilege of the inspection. Peter Beck took a glass of sparkling wine and orange juice and joined the party. He was not exactly a frequent visitor to art galleries but reminded himself that he was in Rome, and 'when in Rome' it was customary to do as Romans did.

They were taken down a wide flight of stone steps to a cool basement its walls lined with brick. He noticed the scent of lemons as he walked in wafting through a sophisticated air conditioning system clearly designed to take out the usual musty smell of a basement. It was a beautiful space well lit around the extraordinary pictures that were hung on its walls.

'In this gallery' The guide began in a heavy accent. 'We see some of the less well known works of the renaissance artists. Here is a painting by Cimabue called the Last judgement. It was for years part of a private collection in Milan before Signor Scalfero acquired it.'

Peter thought to himself that it was a less than original subject for a renaissance picture and frankly to him while it was beautiful, it looked pretty much like any other renaissance picture. He was pleased to hear that some members of his press party were showing a great deal more enthusiasm than he was.

'Now here is a picture by someone you will definitely heard of. It is a painting oil on canvas by Michelangelo. Signor Scalfero is particularly fond of this artist. Perhaps because his own name is Michelangelo.' The guide permitted himself a small laugh that was definitely out of character.

On entering the main gallery Peter was struck by the most magnificent and enormous painting that was lit on the end wall that rose up for two storeys. It showed a biblical scene of a man kneeling as if in confession to a group of roman soldiers. The colours were astonishingly bright under the light of the high window at the gable end. The guide gestured to the picture as he began to introduce it.

'This picture is a fresco. It is painted straight onto wet plaster which helps it retain the brightness of colour that it has even after the centuries have past. The plaster is put onto the wall every day by the artist. Each day's work is known as a gionato and sometimes it is possible to see how many gionato it took to paint a fresco by the number of joins in the picture. We do not know who painted this fresco but we are sure that it was painted in the renaissance period. We do know that it is called the Deception of Judas. I believe that this fresco is the favourite of Signor Scalfero and one of the reasons why he bought the palazzo.'

There was some murmuring among the party at the sheer splendour of the fresco. Such a picture would have been painted for a private benefactor for his personal enjoyment and for him to show off to his guests just like Scalfero himself was now doing.

'The next chamber is one of interest but one that you would not have wished to visit in medieval times' Announced the guide with confidence.

'It is the torture chamber. Such chambers were used to extract confessions of witch craft, heresy and apostasy in medieval times. This is a rack where you can see that the victim was stretched by the wheel until his joints were pulled apart. It was very popular but not with the victims.'

He smiled a thin smile at his joke which he had no doubt used many times before.

'The iron maiden contains the body of a victim so that sharp knives can be slotted through piercing the body at certain points. You can see that the position of the slots where the eyes are located gives a particularly unpleasant effect '

While the party of journalists were squeamish at the descriptions they chose to take the instruments of torture as humorous given their obsolescence and the ability to detach oneself from something that had no doubt been unused for centuries.

The party were shown into a third gallery full of sculptures that at first reminded Peter of his visit to the Louvre in Paris. The gallery was filled with statues in marble and bronze.

'Some of the sculptures in this gallery date back to the Etruscan period prior to the founding of the Roman republic.' The guide began.

'Signor Scalfero is particularly interested in the art and culture of the Etruscans so much of which was suppressed by the Romans. I feel that he has an empathy with the people of the book as he is himself particularly learned.' He added with sycophantic embellishment.

The guide paused to allow the visitors to look at some of the exhibits themselves and Peter found himself looking with minimal interest at the variety of stone statues that to him appeared very much the same.

It was then that he saw something that seized his attention. It was a bronze of the liver of a sheep marked into sections. The inscription below the bronze was clear. The liver of Piacenza.

Peter remembered what Professor Jensen had said about the practice of haruspicy by the Etruscans. How they would extract the entrails of animals and dissect them for divination. Here was an example, here in the private art collection of a respectable roman philanthropist was a relic of Etruscan art that bore witness to this practice. He began to take an interest in the exhibit as since his night with the professor, he had developed the suspicion that the tiny dancers were killed in order to satisfy a desire for divination. It seemed an incredible concept. Perhaps here he would learn more about this practise and establish whether this could possibly be the cause of their deaths.

He turned to speak with the guide.

'This seems a curious subject for a bronze.' He questioned innocently.

The guide smiled his thin smile.

'This is an artefact of Etruscan haruspicy. The liver of Piacenza dates from the late second century BC when Piacenza was already part of the Roman Republic. The Etruscans practised haruspicy in order to divine the future. The omen was the direction from which they perceived the strike of lightning to fall. Signor Scalfero is an expert in the arts of haruspicy and is well able to conduct the rituals himself.'

Peter was taken aback by the confirmation that Scalfero was a haruspex. A macabre picture was starting to come together in the most extraordinary of ways. The Calabrian connection, the haruspicy. Next, he thought he would discover Scalfero to be associated with the Mafia and then he stopped momentarily to consider. Perhaps such an assumption was not so farfetched. An individual of remarkable wealth from Calabria, surely he could well be associated with its crime organisation. He made a note to speak with his contact at Reuters to see if he had any information. The evening at the palazzo Pontinia had turned out to be a great deal more promising than merely an introduction to an anti-slavery charity. Here could be the answer to the slaying of two young girls that had as yet gone without any leads.

Breakfast at the hotel made up in variety what it lacked in quality. It did little to inspire his appetite. Peter Beck's eye was instead taken by the pretty young woman two tables away. She appeared to be English and was arranging with the waiter a tray of food that she could take up to her mother's room.

'No that's no problem.' He heard her say.

'I will take it to her when I go up myself.' She seemed anxious not to trouble the staff in a way that seemed to him to be so typically English.

His cell phone buzzed, a text arrival.

'You are kidding Peter. How did you get invited into his home? I have been following this guy for over a year now I never knew that he opened his house up to the public.'

304

The message was from Steil, a Reuters contact journalist and someone who had apparently been tracking the activities of the Calabrian mafia. Peter took a quiet chair in the hotel reception and dialled Steil's number. The voice at the other end was incredulous.

'I have a file on this guy half a metre thick. He is one of the most notorious members of the Ndrangheta there is. How the hell did you get into his home?'

Peter toyed over his response. He was minded to claim something more praiseworthy than merely to say that he was invited by a lady from a charity to attend a party there at which the host was absent. However he decided not to embellish the story. To do so might lead him to be required to undertake something for Steil and he would soon need to be making arrangements to get back to the airport.

'Listen Peter, we have to get together as soon as you return to swap information. I am sure I will have something to interest you and well, now you're a house guest ...' Steil laughed at his comment.

'Ok will do. I will contact you when I land at Frankfurt this afternoon.' Peter confirmed.

'There had been no time to alert Steil to his theories on the tiny dancer killings. That would have to wait for his return and besides he didn't want to give the story away.

As he walked back to his room through reception the Receptionist smiled at him and made a curious comment.

'I hope that la Signora is soon feeling better' she said.

Peter acknowledged her without thinking. Perhaps she had thought that he was with the pretty young woman whose mother was sickly. He did not wonder why she should have made such an assumption and could not possibly have known the very simple reason why she had indeed done so.

It was mid-morning when the two motorbikes pulled up outside the small hotel at Corso each with a rider and pillion. It was poor timing from their point of view. Segolene was returning from a brief shopping trip to find an English language newspaper and was able to swiftly conceal herself outside the building upon seeing them arrive. She had immediately identified them as manovali, Ndrangheta men. They were of a type well known to her for their broad heavy features dark complexions. They were all the same and she despised them. Only Luc had been different, his slender but muscular body his thick dark hair and cruel eyes. How she had loved Luc, he had been irresistible to her she thought but even he, while different, was just as deadly.

The two manovali entered the front door of the hotel purposefully the later looking over his shoulder instinctively to see who might follow. They walked up to the receptionist.

'You have a Signor Beck staying here? 'He questioned.

'We wish to see him on business. Is he in the hotel at present?'

There was something about the appearance of these two men that made the receptionist apprehensive. She cast her eyes quickly from side to side to assess the space around her but found herself alone.

'One moment. If you will wait here I will call him to see if he is in his room 'She requested as she, in an attempt to stall for time typed the name Mr Beck into the computer on the desk to one side of her. The screen showed Room 42 Beck Peter.

The man had seen the screen and mumbled something to his accomplice who made for the stairway leaving the receptionist in no doubt where he was heading. She could see now that there was likely to be trouble of some kind and picked up the phone dialled the room number and prayed that her guest would not be there.

'Hello' Came the voice in English.

'There is a gentleman on his way up to your room to see you.' She began nervously.

'I am sorry that he did not wait in reception as I asked him to …' Her voice trailed. It was easy to make out the sound of two gunshots on the end of the telephone and imagine the scene in room 42. She held the phone in shock and disbelief as she heard the bulky assassin now run down the stairs and across the reception area to the door of the hotel to where the two motor bikes awaited him and the second pillion.

Segolene entered the hotel reception a moment later to the sight of staff in panic. Explanations were being made and directions being given in loud agitated voices and gasps of sheer horror were audible.

She had to keep calm. Marcus was still out shopping and momentarily she felt irritated by his absence and then reflected, had he been here he would possibly be the corpse lying on the bedroom floor. Swiftly she composed herself. How long would it be before the Ndrangheta would find out that they had hit the wrong man? How long did they have to make their escape?

She went to the room to pack a case. She felt glad to have paid the cash into Marcus's English bank account. He would have to answer questions from the British revenue about this but he would merely say that he was caretaking it for someone. Any way it was better to explain to the British revenue the deposit of one million euros than explain to the Ndrangheta a why suitcase full of it, taken from their capo crimine was hidden in her hotel wardrobe.

It seemed that the innocent victim of the shooting had been a German reporter. She felt guilty to have read that his name was Beck, the same name as she had quiet randomly chosen for herself and her fictitious mother. It certainly confirmed to her one thing. The intended victim had been Marcus. They had assumed that he too had been booked into the hotel room and was using the same name. Perhaps too they had come for her knowing that she had played a part in his escape from the cell and that she had killed the Albanian. Perhaps they had also worked out that it was her who had stolen the money from Scalfero.

There had to be an informer in the hotel she thought. They would be making arrangements to leave as soon as possible and be sure to give the Receptionist a fictitious account of where they were heading.

For the refuse collectors who cleared the bins outside the hotels and restaurants that backed onto Crociferi there was an unusual and unwelcome addition to the stench of garbage. The legs of a man clad in grey corduroy trousers hung over the side of the bin, feet dangling in worn shoes and a body leaking blood that lay across its contents eyes wide open in disbelief were attracting the blue bottle flies that circled the bins. Cagnaccio's hunch had failed, his information judged inaccurate, and the Ndrangheta had delivered its verdict.

The news of the death of Peter Beck had shocked the staff at Hesse Heute. He had been a popular and dedicated reporter on an assignment to report on the modern slave trade. Mizzi felt devastated by the loss. She knew him to be a true professional and it was to her that the task of going through Peter's emails fell. He had sent drafts of his report to his email for collating on his return. She read each one. Details of the Maliberation organisation and their operation. Details of the party at Palazzo Pontinia. It was then she saw something else, something she had to discuss with Hans Klempner.

'They were just notes but it was clear that Peter had found something else. It was something about the tiny dancer killings. The notes seemed to describe how an ancient civilisation called the Etruscans carried out ritualised slaughter to see into the future. She recalled that he had mentioned this theory before after spending some time with the Professor from Sweden. Now he had witnessed the evidence of this in a private museum owned by a guy he thought might be Mafia boss. He now suspected that this ritualised slaughter was carried out by some members of the Ndrangheta and that the gangland killings and the tiny dancer killings in Frankfurt had something to do with this. He confirmed that he had spoken with Steil at Reuters and was arranging to meet with him on his return but had said nothing about the theory he had regarding the tiny dancer killings to anyone.

'This is pure gold.' Said Hans Klempner forgetting himself.

'Peter was certainly on to something. We are hearing that he was probably killed by the Ndrangheta. Now we know why. Clearly they could see that he was on to something.'

The first instinct of the journalist is to write the story. Here was something that had the violence of a criminal gang the mystery of an ancient civilisation the death of a local journalist and the solution to two notorious killings. Hans Klempner could see the potential in a story to run and run. He had valued Peter Beck as a colleague and as a friend and he now convinced himself that Peter would have wanted him to report all he had in relation to this story. Hesse Heute would have a scoop on this one.

'Do they know that he sent this email to us explaining his theory?'

'I guess they are bound to check his laptop. They may well come to the conclusion that you have Hans but we got a message from Swartz. The police checked the hotel register. They found that Peter was not the only Beck staying at the hotel. Seems like there were two English women staying there too with the name Beck '

'The plot thickens but I can't imagine that there was a case of mistaken identity. I mean there was a clear motive here. Peter had found this guy out.' Klempner replied with some confidence.

'There is one thing that struck Swartz as odd. The women were booked into the hotel for four weeks but were absent for the second and third of those weeks. '

'What are you implying by that?'

'No idea' Said Mizzi 'But it is a little unusual.'

'I guess there will be an explanation and the Caribinieri will no doubt question them'

'That could be difficult. The Caribinieri told Swartz that the two English women left the hotel within half an hour of Peter's murder paying in cash. They deliberately gave a false forward address as the Caribinieri cannot trace them.'

'Maybe they were just so shocked they just had to leave. If they were due to leave within a few days anyway. It is probably difficult for two single women like that to find themselves in an hotel where the Ndrangheta murder the guests.' Klempner ventured.

'The police are clearly looking into it. They have provided Swartz with one or two facts about the women. First one of them was ill for most of her stay and spent most of the time in the room. Next the two women spent no time out of their room together, either one or the other would leave the hotel. One would take a tray of food up to the other The police wonder whether they were hiding something or someone in the room.'

'That doesn't sound unusual to me and listen, it seems to me quite obvious. Peter discovered that this Ndrangheta guy is some crazed murderer they find out he suspects and so they have him killed '

'But that does not answer the question. How did they know that Peter had arrived at the supposition that Scalfero was a murderer? It seems to me that they could not have known.' Mizzi answered thoughtfully.

'He confirmed that he had not mentioned it to Steil only to us' Just then another email arrived on screen.

'Another email from Swartz. They found another body at the Hotel. One of the kitchen porters shot in the head.'

Hans Klempner was sure that the solution to Peter's murder was straight forward.

'Ok so the kitchen porter found out what Peter knew somehow and they had to finish him off as well.'

'Well' said Mizzi sure that the explanation was missing something. 'We will all know more in time. I think that someone should meet Steil and get the low down on this Scalfero guy. He is clearly key to a bigger picture on all this'

'I'll get across to Reuters myself' Klempner volunteered.

It is never a good idea to commence an investigation armed only with a preconception but that was what Hans Klempner arrived with later that day at Reuters offices in the European central bank building. He would establish information on Scalfero and embellish his theory with a little fact. It is a curious truth that where guilt cannot be traced innocence can provide a reliable substitute.

Klempner looked out of the window of the European Central Bank Building onto the city he had known since he was a boy. Its skyline is formed with many of the highest buildings in all of Europe. It is a place of commerce, trade and enterprise. A financial centre and airline hub. It was his city and one he felt proud of. He knew how Peter Beck felt. To have been invaded by foreign criminals organising crime and murdering young girls in the most horrific ways possible made his blood boil. Now they had murdered Peter Beck himself when they found out what he had discovered. Klempner would go to Rome to find out more.

48.

ROME, ITALY

It was just 09.00 when Lieutenant Costanzo of the carabinieri was standing at the edge of one of the most beautiful swimming pools he had ever seen looking into its crystal clear water able to pick out the finest detail on the blue mosaic tiles that patterned the floor. It was a pool of perfection, some 30 metres in length and 2.5 metres in depth at its deepest. It had been split into lanes by floats anchored each end to accommodate six swimmers abreast. It was a pool perfect for the day ahead. The final of the police department's swimming gala, an event organised by Costanzo and he felt particularly proud to have secured for the final, the use of the pool of the five star Imperiali the grand hotel on the hill overlooking the eternal city to its east with its spectacular views, sumptuous grounds and spacious terraces.

Elegant sunbeds were laid out to one side of the pool and spectacular shrubs planted on the other. By the corner the poolside café sported a cute shaded terrace with large pots of coloured plants surrounding it. Here a club sandwich would cost Costanzo a day's wages as an officer of the Caribinieri on a normal day in the height of the summer but today was no normal day.

It was around 11.00 when the first competitors started to arrive. They were the heat winners from around the city and Costanzo took great pleasure in their gasps of awe at the scene they encountered. It was almost as if he was receiving them in his own home and he found himself playing down the opulence to avoid any question of his boast.

'Have you seen those changing rooms?' Gasped one highly impressed contestant.

Costanzo tried to subdue his pride in his achievement.

'A little grander than we usually use aren't they?' He commented modestly.

'You're not kidding, this place is awesome.' Came the response of the competitor clearly overwhelmed by the venue.

'We are running three races for each event 'He found himself saying trying to sound business-like.

'How did you fix this Costanzo?' An athletic young woman officer asked.

'Well, the Hotel management has been pleased to accommodate the city's Caribinieri for this event. I guess closing the outside pool area to guests was a small price to pay for the goodwill it will create and it's up to us to make the event something special for the guests to watch.'

It was clearly an ambience that generated a good feeling among the competitors and it was around 10.30 when the event started. Under a full sun and in those sparkling waters some fifty competitors strove for success in a succession of races. It was a friendly but competitive event well supervised by its organiser and results were efficiently recorded following a succession of the first of the races.

It would have been around midday when the sound of the engine was first audible. It could have been a plane or a bus at first but as it grew louder the swimmers looked towards the sky to see where the Helicopter was flying. Just then it came into view as it rose from beneath the hill from the east close now to the pool, its engine noise drowning out the sounds from the ground its blades creating a swirling current on the pool water over which it hovered.

As suddenly as it had appeared the sound of the rotor blades was overtaken by another sound, the sound of gunfire. As the swimmers looked up at the helicopter a hail of gunfire rained down upon them. Two gunmen holding Kalashnikov rifles let go a stream of bullets into the swimmers below them. The clear water turned red with blood, corpses of swimmers now motionless floating on its surface, others draped over the sides of the pool where they tried to climb out to escape the massacre. There was carnage. Death had been instant and comprehensive. Over a dozen officers of the Caribinieri lay dead.

Then the helicopter rose into the sky and headed for the horizon leaving the screams of onlookers to break the silence of disbelief. It was all over in just a few minutes and yet there in and around the pool lay the bodies of some of the city's finest police officers. A macabre message had been delivered.

Costanzo had watched the episode in horror as it occurred. Now he looked on in rage. He was sure that this audacious attack was the evil work of the criminal organisation that he had played a part in clearing from the streets of the Rome. The Calabrian mafia that he had publically sworn to eradicate from the city. What's more he was sure that this was an attack directly on him, something personal. It would be impossible to prove but he was sure too who had given the order to attack his swimmers. One name and only one name entered his mind. That name was Michelangelo Scalfero.

49.

ROME, ITALY

The news that the state prime minister's wife was having an affair with a prominent American rock star had been reported all over the evening news. It had been subject to the usual salacious suppositions, assertions and overreactions. What was well known now was that US President Edgar Allen was due to meet up with the prime minister and his wife with his first lady. The complication that arose was that the whole idea was founded on the long term marital relationships that both couples had enjoyed and it was to be portrayed as an endorsement of marriage and the concept of union. This was now looking a little fragile for the White house aides. It seemed that an alternative engagement had to be found for the President's brief Italian visit and the suggestion had come from the Edgar Allen himself.

'If I can't meet the prime minister how about the Pope? Allen had asked.

'I have met him before at Chicago. What's the point of having an American Pope if we don't make use of him?' He joked to his Press aide. It was a suggestion swiftly taken up and his aides had been pleased with the enthusiastic response shown by the Vatican and indeed His Holiness himself.

'It will be great to meet him again. We can talk football just like last time' The president joked to his aide.

Father Simeon was in his instructive mood. Today he sounded the teacher and in his nervousness he sought confirmation that each of his points had been understood.

'You met him when you addressed the University of Illinois. He confirmed to Jacopo. He was a speaker there. He won't ex-

315

pect you to remember what was said but he will certainly expect you to remember you met him'

'Ok Ok yeah I got it. Didn't we go and get some pussy together?' Jacopo swiped back.

Father Simeon was not amused.

'You say as little as possible. Cardinal Dufour will explain your illness has led to some loss of memory.'

It was frustrating speaking to someone who refused to acknowledge his understanding of what was being said but the truth was Jacopo had presented a perfectly believable pontiff and he was sure there had been no questioning of his role. Perhaps one day they would laugh at this together.

Father Simeon had good reason for concern as to the authenticity of his charge in portraying the role he had been ascribed as his performance this evening would be observed at very close hand. For it had been announced that the benefactor of the significant anti-slavery charity Maliberation, would be present at the Pope's invitation. Scalfero was seeking to raise his legitimacy as the patron of his charity and it was both an excellent opportunity for him to do so and to witness the success of the work of Father Simeon. What was also possible was that it was potentially the opportunity to witness his failure. Father Simeon was anxious to secure the former.

It was indeed an anxious evening for Father Simeon. He had first thought to contrive his own presence at the gathering but thought better of it. Jacopo would need to learn how to conduct himself when Father Simeon was absent anyway. He would have to suffer his anxiety on his own.

It was a call on his cell phone early the following morning that gave him the confirmation he had sought.

'Brother Simeon' He knew the voice of Scalfero.

'Why our Pope had me believing in him last night. You have done wonderful work. This will make our task so much easier.'

Father Simeon gasped a wholesome relief at the words of his mentor.

'It is an honour to serve in this way' He stammered.

'My charity held the most marvellous event at my Palacio last night while I was with his Holiness and the president Scalfero confirmed without irony as if to be in their presence was something to be expected. He seemed to have convinced himself of his transformation from Mafia padrino to charity benefactor.

'Both his Holiness and the president praised the work we are doing '

Father Simeon reflected how fantasy is so often more comforting than reality. It lacks complexity and is thereby more easy to believe. It follows aspiration and bends to preference. It was the willingness of mankind to embrace such deception that had always fascinated him.

He smiled contentedly. How could he have doubted that Jacopo would triumph?

50.

ROME, ITALY

It was early evening when Father Simeon moved quietly around the Chiesa San Marco tidying the artefacts of his ministry in deep thought. He was expecting a visit from the senior Cardinal of the Holy See, but his was not an apprehension as to the seniority of his visitor but more the potential purpose of that visit. It was the aged cardinal he knew well. The cardinal whose life had been stipendiary to the order and who had been supported by it throughout that wretched life. A life that had known well a commitment to the sins that answer greed, lust and narcissism.

Cardinal Dominic Dufour arrived at the main door and shuffled towards him hunched and looking distressed.

'Be seated Cardinal. We will fetch some water for your thirst' Father Simeon instructed.

The old man leaned over to Father Simeon and looked into his dark eyes.

'I am persuaded by your clemency and goodness to implore you Father Simeon that I might be released from the duty you impose upon me.' He started in a tired voice.

'I have washed away my sins Father by service and confession. I have received forgiveness from Almighty God. Those sins are buried now. I have served the order and given it opportunity. I have delivered to our order the revelation of St Therese L'Enfant passed to me in great confidence from Father Etienne Petit. I equally commend for your consideration my honour and reputation and plead to you my declining age and bodily indisposition. Surely an old man deserves freedom to live the rest of his life in some peace?'

Father Simeon looked at him with quiet distain.

'We are but vassals of our times brother. Circumstances paint the colours of our lives and find us favour or failure beyond the rhythm of rhyme or the edge of reason. We must follow the stroke of the brush that shapes us and colours us to blend with the composition, to be as the spectator wishes to see us, but we must act to seize control. To stand still in time, our hours ceded to disenchantment is not our philosophy. Genius lies in understanding and original thoughts but riches only in their execution.

A gift confers no rights. To whom who knows your secret you surrender your freedom. Freedom is not free. Its price may be measured in the vigilance of nations, or the temper of mankind, but so too is it measured by the sins it sanctions of those who abuse it.

Our order is not like the church. It does not deal in forgiveness. Here we have cleaned your sins only for safekeeping that we can store them that we might from time to time review them evaluate their currency examine what has past and place upon them the price of your duty to serve us. To preserve your dignity you will continue to serve with obedience until we place in your mouth the ferryman's coin that will take you to the rest you speak of.'

Cardinal Dominic Dufour narrowed his eyes as he played one last card his voice faltering as he spoke.

'You forget Father. You have placed upon me the highest duty. To mentor your brother in the ways of a Pope. To stand by his side, his counsel and confidant. In my hands are held the reigns that will steer the success of our order. In my being the blood in which the words upon the wall are to be written. All I ask is that I should in time be free of my duties and if you cannot agree to this I am prepared to reveal the American woman's observation.

The old man was shaking now as he delivered his final threat with a recklessness of desperation that defied the reticence of his heart. Father Simeon was shocked by the words of the old Cardinal and looked across at him alert to his threat. Dufour had indeed been placed in a highly responsible position and Father

Simeon had believed him to be trusted in this role. He stood up and paced about the old Cardinal deep in thought, his dark eyes searching the room for his response.

'We are bound by the pledge we give at baptism. Ours is not the option to yield but the obligation to strive, for the sake of our order. You have received the grace of your position in the church by the patronage of our order. You will not desert us, for to do so will bring upon you the ultimate punishment. The fate worse than death that will visit you with pain, dependency, deprivation and humiliation. The fate reserved only for those who betray the trust that our order has placed upon them.'

The old Cardinal was silenced by these chilling words. He had seen only once in his long life the reality of retribution upon those who had been found guilty of betrayal. The amputation of hands and feet and the blinding and castration was a worse fate than death its victim placed into uncertain and resentful care from those who would despise their charge. There was no dignity in betrayal. Cardinal Dominic Dufour inhaled the deep and thoughtful breath that when exhaled brought with it a calm considered response.

'You are right Father Simeon. You are right of course. You must forgive an old, frail and foolish man for his temporary absence of mind and lack of resolve. I will see to it that our mission will not fail'

Father Simeon watched as the old man left to climb into the car that waited for him outside the church. Could he be trusted? Father Simeon asked himself. If he reported this interview to Scalfero it could result in the hideous retribution that was known as the ultimate punishment. For it had been said of Scalfero that to stand in the shadow of his vengeance it is only a matter of time till you feel the cold blade of his wrath.

For Father Simeon, conscience could not allow that. He must trust that the plans he had put into place would be carried out, but he should be aware that to serve his order, he must be prepared to take swift and signal retribution against those who would fail him.

51.

ROME, ITALY

Lieutenant Costanzo of the Caribinieri poured a cup of dark Lavazza coffee. He had but one focus in his mind. Twelve days ago some of his finest officers and friends had been slaughtered at a swimming gala organised by him at the hands of the Ndrangheta and now after he had attended the burial of each and every one of them and paid his respects to their relatives he was to pursue the vengeful quest of his life. A quest to capture the leader of the criminal organisation that had undertaken this outrage.

The dispute had been set several months ago with his arrest of members of the criminal organisation who were using the Café de Lyon in Via Veneta to launder money generated by operations in Calabria. Several arrests had been made by Costanzo's men and he was sure that this was the reason why his swimming gala had been targeted. It was a warning to him to lay off but Costanzo was not inclined to give up. He felt the anger that only a police officer could feel at the loss of other officers and he was going to capture those who did this.

First there would be the collation of information. He wanted everything that was known about Scalfero and his operations. There were the fruit farms of Calabria, legitimate operations in themselves but businesses that opened contacts in the north to the transfer of illicit funds. Farms that were employing hundreds of immigrant workers under duress. The construction activities employing local people that provided infrastructure housing and commercial buildings built following planning permissions granted by corrupt officials. There were restaurants and hotels throughout Europe many that ran gaming and prostitution as part of their service, but principal among these activities were the operations in the ports of the south of the country that played host to the shipments of cocaine from Columbia via Brazil and Tangier.

Now was confirmation from Frankfurt Germany that Scalfero had taken over the Drexell Hesse bank and all the wealth of financial operations and investments it held. This was his principal vehicle to launder illegal money. Costanzo Googled that name to see whether it came up anywhere in Rome. For the time being nothing showed up.

It seemed that Scalfero had become the benefactor of Maliberation, an anti-slavery charity that worked in Mali and Niger. It sickened Costanzo that such a cynical appointment had been made for someone who used slaves to work on his estates in the south.

What was missing however was the evidence, not to show that any of his operations were breaking the law, but that he had broken the law and this angered Costanzo more than anything. How was he to trap a villain who operated outside but above the law? He needed evidence.

It was a routine call at the Via Crociferi. The body of a man had been found in a dustbin to the rear of a small hotel which had been the site of the murder of a German journalist in his hotel room. Costanzo had been asked to accompany the investigating officer, the possibility of an Ndrangheta connection had been put forward. Now there was something more interesting. On arriving at the hotel he could see that the investigating officer was interviewing a well-dressed German man seated in the reception area.

'He says, that Herr Beck sent him an email just before he was killed sir. Seems Beck attended some kind of charity function at a Palacio in Vende Settembre. Guess who owns the Palacio?'

'Palacio Pontinia, you don't have to tell me it's Scalfero's lair. What did he say about it?'

'Well it seems that the deceased was shown around a basement art collection with a group of journalists. He seemed to get really excited by the Etruscan art Scalfero had collected.'

'I don't follow you'

'Frankfurt police have been investigating a strange murder, a ritual killing. Beck reckoned it had something to do with Etruscan haruspicy. That's divination by dissection by the way. Anyway, it seems that he had found out that Scalfero was involved in this black art. Thought he might have been responsible for the murders. Sent a short email to his office just before he died.'

'Well we sure know that he is capable of that' Retorted Costanzo.

'The question is, did Scalfero know that Beck knew something and did he have him killed to prevent him talking.' The officer went on.

'You got a copy of the email Beck sent to his office?'

'Sure. It doesn't make much sense to me but if it's true, it could be that it makes a case directly against Scalfero and not just one of his Manavali'

Costanzo felt good. Perhaps here was something to pursue directly against his enemy. It was clear that the Frankfurt police had information on the crime and no doubt some circumstantial evidence. Now all he had to do was to prove it. If the guy was some kind of ritualistic killer there would be previous killings recorded and someone who would talk.

Perhaps thought Costanzo, it was true that the German journalist Peter Beck knew too much. That was why he had been killed.

Costanzo was sitting opposite Hans Klempner astride his chair resting his notebook on the back of it and looking deep into Herr Klempner's eyes.

'So Peter Beck, your journalist was sent to Rome to write about anti-slavery yes?'

The question was translated to Klempner by a young female officer.

'Sure' Klempner answered.

'He attended a roman carnival at Palacio Pontina the home of Michelangelo Scalfero at the request of the charity Maliberation. You requested he do this?'

'Sure' Klempner answered again.

'When he was there he seems to have witnessed something that led him to believe that Scalfero was an active haruspex and that he may have been responsible for the killing of two young girls in Frankfurt '

'That is about right' Klempner confirmed.

'So Scalfero somehow finds out that Beck suspects him and has him shot. Do you believe that Signor Klempner?'

'I do. I can't think there is any other explanation'

'How do you think Scalfero found out about his email to you alerting you to his suspicions?' Constanzo asked.

'Well I heard that there was some sleaze of an informer in the hotel. Must have overheard something I guess.' Klempner submitted.

Costanzo was less sure. He suddenly felt that there was a weak link in the theory that until then he had shared with Klempner. No this was not the truth behind the murder. It was going to be difficult to put a clear allegation together. Surely there had to be something else.

'The two English women went by the same name? Was that coincidence?' He asked the receptionist.

'We think so' She confirmed tearfully.

'Only I didn't see much of them together. The younger woman had an older man with her whenever I saw her. It was as if the elder lady had been replaced by the man. He could have been her father. But I do not think there was any relationship with the unfortunate German gentleman'

Costanzo thought of what Emma Dreyfus had said about the abduction of her friend Marcus Graham. She posed as his daughter to gain his trust. Instinctively he produced the photograph of the couple seen getting into the taxi at Via Tritone.

'Is this the couple? 'He asked the receptionist feeling now that he knew the answer.

'Yes. That looks like them. I am sure that is them.' Confirmed the receptionist looking surprised that the Carabinieri were astute to a lead.

He smiled widely at the response. So Segolene was in Rome. The question was. Is Segolene Magdalena?

Costanzo was looking at the screen on his desk with a frown on his brow. The body of a middle aged woman had been found by the Tiber. It had been confirmed that she was an American tourist who had been reported missing. She had been visiting the city with her choir from Illinois. Somehow she had left the party she was with and ended up bludgeoned to death by the river bank.

Costanzo instinctively sensed something curious about this. The woman's purse had been found in a money belt around her waist. It had over 300 euros in it. Bludgeoned to death but not robbed of cash. It seemed unlikely to him. Had she been killed by the river bank or had her body been placed there? The answer to that question was soon reported to him.

'No likelihood of having been killed where the body was found sir. No the body was dumped there after death.'

'There is a report on this murder sir. Seems someone has spoken with the deceased's sister in the states. She says she knows who did it '

Great, that's a help. Someone known to her was it?'

Not exactly. It is a little stranger than that. Seems this sister claims she saw the death in some vision she had. Knew her sister was going to die and where she was going to die. She says that the woman was killed by a cardinal in a church in the city.

'Ok so she is a crazy or perhaps the grief got to her 'Costanzo suggested.

'Well possibly sir but listen to this. She says she knows exactly what the murder weapon was. A silver candlestick like those that stand on the alter.

'So we check every silver candlestick in Rome for blood stains. Better cancel all leave'

'There is something else. She said that she feels that the cardinal who did it is Dufour. She saw him on the television standing next to the Pope when his Holiness received the US president. The report was all over television in the states.'

'So we really do have a deranged sister. She sees a cardinal on the television and attributes a murder to him. I guess she expects us to go and arrest him. What else did she tell us?

'It happened in a church. Probably only yesterday sometime.' Costanzo was getting impatient with this theory.

'Look I really don't think …' He started.

'I hope you don't mind sir but I checked Cardinal Dufour's timetable for yesterday. His chauffeur confirmed that he visited the Cheisa San Nicolo around 18.00.'

'Well I suppose that narrows down the number of candlesticks to check out. Do you think that we should all go and take a look?' Costanzo asked with some sarcasm.

'I have already got someone over there sir' The officer confirmed with a serious expression.

It was just after midday when an Alfa Romeo gazzella was screaming down the Via Corso heading for the Cheisa San Nicolo its siren wailing for a clear passage through the steady stream of traffic. Costanzo sat in the rear looking forward through the windscreen in some sort of expectation in his anxiety to reach the destination. The initial investigation had indicated that one of the altar candlesticks in the beautiful Jesuit church was stained with blood. Costanzo had not hesitated. He was on his way.

As the police car drew up outside the church Costanzo leaped towards the door.

'Where is it?' He barked at the young officer standing by the entrance.

He examined the implement and looked around the church instinctively.

'You said the sister saw the murder in some sort of dream. Where did she say it happened?'

'Right here by the altar sir. It was although she was standing behind that picture in the way she saw it' Confirmed the young officer gesturing at the portrait of the virgin on the wall behind the altar.

'Almost as if she were behind the picture 'repeated Costanzo his eyes now fixed toward the portrait enraptured by its beauty. It was a portrait so life like that as he looked at it he felt that he was looking into the eyes of a human being.

'Looking out of those eyes.' He added mysteriously.

The blood match was confirmed and within the hour the aged cardinal Dufour had been apprehended.

The news of the arrest had reached Father Simeon and his concern grew. The old Dufour had shown weakness and an unwillingness to continue his role in the deception. What if he were to become an informant? Action would need to be taken and taken swiftly.

It was no doubt the reputation of a Cardinal supported by the Pope himself that that secured an easy grant of bail. Cardinal Dufour would be detained at a lodging close to the Vatican and for the time being relieved of his duties until his name was inevitably cleared and the clear attempt to blacken his spotless reputation revealed.

Father Simeon considered carefully the possibilities of a weakness in the edifice of his grand deception and the potential resolution of such a risk. It may be that an old man who had enjoyed such a career might choose to end his life perhaps by means of poison rather than face the ignominy of investigation. It needed to be arranged, with care of course.

Cardinal Dominic Dufour had received his visitor with the quite acceptance of the condemned man who knew his time had come. Father Simeon brought with him the judgement of the Archangel that was sure to be his angel of death. The dark determined face the strong brown eyes the few words that he uttered. He brought with him too, the rest the old man craved, an end to the pain of inquisition, the comfort of certainty.

'The time has come.' Was all that was said and the small file of cyanide passed to him without expression. It was soon after that the old cardinal ended his life, avoiding the ignominy of his guilt in the revelation of his sins.

52.

ROME, ITALY

Segolene had settled the bill for the hotel room in Corso for her two invented English women on making a hasty departure following the assassination of Peter Beck. It was therefore, only later, as she put the bill away in her bag, that she noticed it had attached to it an email written in German. It was a message from a newspaper in Frankfurt.

She could see straight away that she had been handed the invoice made out to the murdered news reporter rather than her own. The invoice would be paid by Peter's office in Frankfurt but it was not that that attracted her interest but what was attached to it.

It was first of all a message addressed to the hotel simply expressing shock at what had just been reported to them and confirming that the payment of the invoice would be made by them. Below that email however was the message that Peter Beck had sent to his office shortly before his death. The respondent confirming settlement of the hotel bill, had no doubt in distress at the news and with the intention to trail the emails for filing, simply readdressed Peter's earlier email to the Hotel. Either he had not read the incoming message or he had not appreciated its significance.

Segolene struggled to translate the email and read her version to Marcus.

'I attended the Roman Carnival hosted by Maliberation the freedom and anti-slavery charity. Quite a night and a splendid palace owned by an important benefactor who has all sorts of artefacts around his palace.

The benefactor has an interest in Haruspicy and is said to be some sort of expert in the art. I have come to the conclusion that the Tiny dancer killings and the gangland killings are connected. I spoke with Steil at Reuters just now who tells me that this guy is about as high up in the Ndrangheta as you can get and that rumour is that he is moving into Frankfurt having taken over the Drexel Hesse bank. This is the break we need. Will discuss on my return.'

'So Scalfero is possibly involved in some macabre ritualism as well as everything else' Marcus observed.

'What do we know about these Tiny dancer killings and the Drexel Hesse bank?'

A Google search in an internet café revealed several articles in the Hesse Heute written by Peter Beck himself. Segolene's attempts at translation were aided by a translation of the text on the screen.

'So these were two young girls slaughtered in some ritual killing on the same day that several members of the Drexel Hesse bank were gunned down. Question arises. Are the two connected? Looks like Peter Beck felt they were.'

'He believed that this ritual killing is something to do with Scalfero? I think that somehow we should get inside the palace and take a look' she suggested.

'What. How on earth do we do that?' Marcus asked plausibly.

'It shouldn't be too difficult. If Peter Beck simply sauntered in as a guest of a charity. Perhaps we could claim that we work for the charity. I don't know but if we can get in and look around it could answer a lot of questions.'

It was a bright clear morning when two representatives of the Royal Academy of Arts in St James, London arrived at the door of the Palacio Pontinia. They were there to examine the art archives within the basement of the Palace at the request of a Signor Scalfero.

'Dr Fuller Green and I are in Rome examining several of the better private collections' Segolene assured the pretty young woman who had come to the door, showing her an identity card written in English.

'I believe that Signor Scalfero is anxious that the artefacts be catalogued.'

It appeared that the young woman was aware of how Scalfero would feel privileged to receive such a visit as this, as she was not concerned to examine the identity of her visitors merely giving them a fleeting glance. She seemed pleased to show them down to the basement. It was clear to them that it was unlikely that she would know anything of the true identity of her employer such was her enthusiasm for their quest.

'Just help yourselves' she invited.

'Signor Scalfero is always very happy to share his interest in art with those who have an interest in his collection and will be pleased to have had professionals from England visit us.'

It had been easy to persuade the young woman to leave them to look around themselves. They viewed the striking pictures on the walls and lifelike forms of sculpture positioned skilfully to maximise their aesthetic impact. They walked between the chambers each displaying its own art work and eventually found a smaller chamber containing Scalfero's collection of Etruscan art.

'What does this mean?' Segolene asked looking at a script which was supposed to serve as some form of explanation.

'It seems to refer to the end of the world'

Marcus remembered enough of his theological studies to be able to supply the information.

'Eschatology is that part of Theology that deals with the final events of history. We could assume that this means the end of the human race but in practice Etruscan eschatology believed that history is divided into ages that end, with new ages beginning.' He confirmed reading through the script.

'These ages were called Saeculas and the Saecula was a period of one hundred years. At the end of that period signs or omens informed mortals of the completion of the period. So as one age ends another begins. Often there is some disaster that predicates the change from one age to another.'

'You mean like a large volcanic eruption? 'She asked rhetorically.

'They say that the saeculas lasted for 100 years so the dates are not precise but if Scalfero believes that we are about to reach the end of a saecula and these revelations are the signs? The revelations were themselves 100 years apart weren't they?' Marcus questioned.

She looked into the distance as if she saw there the conclusion.

'He sees this as the prodigy or omen that heralds the coming of his vision. The reign of the ubermensch. That's it isn't it.'

'He will put in place the fulfilment of the other two revelations, the placing of his servant in the Holy church and the seizing of the Holy Roman Empire'

'Father Fidel Rocher has said that the Antichrist gaining access to the Holy church is predicted in the Bible as being something that happens just prior to the second coming of Christ, but how will he place his servant into the Church?' Marcus questioned.

'In the same way as he placed me into your care, deception. My father has long practiced deception as a means to his ends. He directed Luc to have me gain your trust by declaring that I was your daughter. He will no doubt be planning a way of deceiving the very Vatican itself. If the eruption of Vesuvius is the disaster that predicates the event then he could be planning something right now.'

Suddenly she turned to him.

'Look' She directed.

'It looks like a torture chamber. I wonder if this is well used.' She was gazing at a small recess housing a collection of instruments of torture used in the medieval times.

'Frankly it doesn't look like it is. It's not as if it's swimming in blood. I guess that we shall just have to acknowledge that it is merely a macabre artistic interest.' Marcus answered.

He was standing by metal jacket in the shape of the human form that stood some six inches less than him.

'It's an iron lady.' He commented.

'The prisoner was placed in this metal jacket and knives slotted in through the holes while he was held in there.' He observed.

'And this is the rack where prisoners were stretched so that their bones came out of their joints. Not a healthy interest I suggest but one Scalfero presumably finds of value'

As Marcus moved around the hideous implements of torture arranged around the chamber he became aware of a cold draught coming from the right of where he stood. It was a draught that told him that there may be an opening nearby despite there being no evidence of one. He examined the wall of the chamber carefully but there was nothing.

Then he realised that the draught was coming from the iron maiden. Carefully he opened the front of the device to reveal the spikes he expected to see lining the instrument. He knew now that there was some kind of opening to the rear of it. He grasped the spikes carefully one by one. It was the highest spike that was the lever and lifting it up allowed the rear of the instrument to swing open.

'Look here' he shouted to her.

'It's a an entrance to a passageway'

'This is a typical of an Ndrangheta hideaway' She said.

'The Ndrangheta conceal themselves in underground bunkers when they are being sought by the law. They seem to compete with each other to provide the most intriguing concealment for the passageway.'

'No lights in here' Marcus confirmed 'Do we ought to go in?

She did not answer but pushed her way into the darkness. The air was still with a damp smell as they entered.

'It's not a bunker. It's an entrance to the subterranean catacombs. There are several around the city leading to the underground passages and chambers that contain the ruins of the ancient city.'

'Do you think it leads somewhere.? I mean do you think it is used to access somewhere particularly.?' He asked.

'Maybe. Let's take a look' She suggested boldly.

Carefully they eased their way forward along a narrow passageway bending low in places where the ceiling was uneven. It was slow progress in the pitch dark and Marcus could feel the wet walls on each side brush against him as he moved forward and he could smell the musty stench of damp in the heavy air.

At first it was just a murmur, a broken sound that was only just audible and then lost for a moment before returning.

'What was that?' He whispered placing a finger across her lips to that bade her not to answer but to listen. As they moved forward the murmur sounded almost like the sound of voices in the distance but a strange sound that was low and constant. Soon they could hear that it was a rhythmic chanting of a number of voices and as they moved further towards it sounded louder.

Eventually the narrow passage opened to a space lit with frail lighting on each of its walls that threw shadows long and low across the chamber. It was a subterranean cavern within which high stone walls surrounded the space and upon which there were lit torches of firelight striving to light the space in a low glow. They could see upon choir benches at one side of the space a line of robed figures chanting rather than singing into the darkness and in the centre of the space there stood three figures robed in blood red cloaks and wearing the conical hats of sorcerers.

'Look' he whispered.

'These must be the haruspices'

At last the chanting stopped and they could see a child brought into the cold space by three hooded figures, her frightened eyes moving from side to side in the half-light searching for answers. She was a child of about 13 years of age, narrow and athletic, her golden skin looking dark under the half-light. With silence and the deliberation of exaggerated ceremony the child was stripped of her gown and laid naked onto the stone table in front of the haruspex. She was bound by the assistants with woven cord to the table, her body frozen stiff with fear unable to resist. Her eyes pleading now for mercy her lips trembling, unable to utter her plea.

As they watched they could see that one of the figures held a knife with the curled blade. Slowly he lifted it into the air in some symbolic ritual and held it above his head. The haruspex looked up skyward his conical headdress pointing to his rear. He would have looked rather absurd were it not for the slaughter he was about to undertake. He murmured a short prayer in some indiscernible tongue and raised his second hand in some kind of salute.

Then quite suddenly he plunged the dagger down into the child's abdomen. There was a violent scream of agony fear and disbelief as the haruspex cut away the child's liver with the skill of the butcher carving the carcase of a lamb oblivious to the screams of pain and distress. There was with the sound of pain, the vised sucking sound of blooded viscera. A heavy suspiration of a last breath and the twitch of nervous agony that convulses the body and limbs. There was the indignity of the death in the hands of the slaughterer. The cold indifference of the perpetrator to the distress of his victim.

Marcus looked on speechless with shock at what they had witnessed. The death of a child slaughtered before their eyes for the sake of an ancient and distorted ritual. There was the feeling that they should intervene but to do so would be useless as they would only submit themselves to capture. They could only lay low and watch the ritual trembling with frustrated anger.

Delicately the entrails were laid out on a stone slab and the robed figures gathered round to carefully examine them with an avid scrutiny, searching for the signs that will guide the Haruspex in his divination.

After what seemed like an hour, Marcus looked across to the door and saw to his horror another small figure being led forward by the robed figures. He could see that it was another child somewhat smaller than the last and he could see her dark skin on her frightened face as she looked in confusion at the fate that awaited her. To his horror he could now recognise the face of the child by her vivid blue eye, It was Nyeleni.

Marcus turned to Segolene and uttered one brief instruction.

'The flaming torches on the walls. You go for the one on the right I will go for the one above the Haruspix'

He knew that he had but one chance. If he could only extinguish all light Nyeleni would have a chance as she would be able to penetrate the dark to lead them to the exit.

It was the element of surprise that secured their success. Swiftly they raced to the flaming torches and extinguished them feeling the blackness surround them as the light was lost. Marcus felt the small hand in his within a moment and he gripped it as she led him first to Segolene and then out along the narrow passageway.

'They must have a torch with them' Segolene suggested.

'We will have to move quickly before they find it.'

They had made considerable progress before they became aware that they were being followed by a thin flash of light that was probably a torch. Clearly they had managed the element of surprise successfully and their ability to move swiftly through the pitch black had confused their pursuers. They were well ahead and as they found their way into the catacombs it was easy for them to choose a route that was unlikely to attract the pursuit.

At last Marcus could see that they were coming to an exit by a thin shaft of light from above. It could be anywhere in the city. One of the entrances used by the tour companies or another private access from possibly one of the city's grander houses. As they approached they could see that there were steps leading from above which they climbed with relief feeling the exhaustion of their escape. In minutes they had emerged into a small courtyard that faced a narrow street the end of which to Marcus relief, he could see two taxis parked, awaiting hire.

'Here jump in' Marcus directed and bellowed to the driver to take them to Barberini.

As they sat back with relief in the rear of the car, Marcus caught sight of the taxi driver looking into his rear view mirror. It was a face that was curiously familiar and at first he felt that it had to be the same driver as he had met when he first arrived in Rome who had so grandly praised his country as being God's greatest gift. He looked again and saw the tousled hair the small frame behind the wheel. It was then he realised that their driver was the dwarf he had met at the fountain in the Piazza Navona. Marcus sensed danger and cursed himself for not realising it before. This was the man who recommended the Opera where he was followed and abducted. He had to be part of the clan.

'Do you recognise our driver?' He asked Segolene curious to know if she too knew of him.

'No' She answered looking confused.

'But I do know we are not heading for Barberini'

As she spoke the car accelerated going east away from the traffic. He was sure now that they were being taken somewhere and that soon they would be in the hands of the Ndrangheta.

It was the child who sensed the opportunity to act. As the taxi turned the corner at speed she pulled on the handbrake forcing the vehicle to spin across the road out of control its rear wheel hitting the kerb and as it did so its rear door flung open. Marcus and Segolene were quick to escape before the car could pull away but it was all too quick for the child in the front seat.

Shattered by exertion and fright and breathless with relief they were left by the side of the street watching helplessly as the taxi sped away with its lone passenger to who knew where.

53.

ROME, ITALY

Fresh information was coming in day by day to help Costanzo build a clearer picture of his enemy number one Michelangelo Scalfero. His task now was to find the simplest route to entrap him. He had seen so often how the foulest of deeds can go unpunished due to an inability to piece together complex evidence while simple transgressions could be more easily pursued to capture and conviction. Success relies on focus, one crime at a time. Start with the one you where have clear evidence, however minor it appears.

If he felt he knew his opponent and what drove him in his convictions and his allegiances it was because Costanzo, like so many of the Carabinieri officers was from the south. One of an irreproachable breed of men that escape the brotherhood of the Mafias for security of law enforcement. So often they find themselves drawn against those motivated by an honour they have themselves denied, those bound by the blood that auspicates their calling.

What had intrigued him was the report of the English woman Emma Dreyfus. She had referred to a young woman named Segolene who claimed to be the daughter of an English architect and whom was certain to be an imposter. Could she be the missing link. Was she Magdalena, the daughter abandoned by Scalfero in a lunatic asylum? Had she reappeared to work with him under the consanguinity of the clan? Had she led the unfortunate English architect she had fooled into believing was her father to play some part under the cloak of Scalfero's deception?

He picked up the report and photographs handed to him that morning. It showed a middle aged man and a young woman entering a taxi in the via del Tritone. The photographs were clear and it would not be difficult to have Emma Dreyfus verify them. The taxi had headed for Via di Grottarossa. They would possibly be staying in that area. It could be a breakthrough. To place Magdalena under arrest would surely cause alarm to Scalfero have him more vulnerable to capture.

An officer entered the room.

'Yes Lieutenant. Signorita Dreyfus has seen the photograph. She has no idea about the woman as she has never seen her but the man, she is sure is Marcus Graham'

The confirmation caused Costanzo to pace the room deep in thought.

'We have a few team members out searching around Grottarossa and asking questions. Hotels, restaurants, banks. She used the name Beck before maybe she will again and hey tell our people to watch out she is bound to have support from the Scalfero clan and will be able to call for assistance.' He directed.

He now had two leads. The murder of the German journalist and the abduction of the English architect. Surely one would lead to the arrest of his enemy. He tapped the desk in deep thought until a casual glance at a bulletin on the screen drew his eye. There had been a vendetta some weeks ago that was almost definitely an Ndrangheta killing. The victim was known to be part of the Calabrian mafia and yes, there it was, part of the Scalfero clan. Costanzo could not read the bulletin fast enough. Poisoned in a restaurant by a dish of iced oysters. A young woman had been involved, the message scrawled in lipstick on the plate.

La vendetta e un piato che va mangiarto fredo.

'Revenge is a dish best eaten cold.' Poisoned iced oysters. The lady has got a sense of humour 'He smirked.

'Can we email a photograph of Magdelena over to the local police?' He yelled across the room sounding victorious.

'It's her, I know it's her. Magdelena is working for the clan'

He remembered her from their one encounter. It was strange he felt to have spent so many hours in front of her and yet not one word had passed between them. He shrugged in discomfort as he remembered too the name that his colleagues had ascribed to her. Magdalena Scalfero, the black queen.

It had been a cold crisp air that resisted the warming rays of a low pale sun early one morning some five years ago. There was no sound of voices in that air, just the rattle of footfall on the concrete platform. The sound of leather soles on solid ground and the eerie undefinable murmur of motion in the air. Speechless, resolute, hasty motion blended in a low muffled chorus.

It had amused him to feel himself the imposter. He looked like any other commuter dressed in a smart suit its jacket worn unbuttoned his hands thrust firmly in deep pockets, his silk tie swinging as he moved to the rhythm of the rush. Yet for him there was no need for the distraction of the free paper to scan, the lap top to tap furiously nor the mobile phone to study continuously for texts and emails in expressionless desperation. He remembered how he had been the one enjoying the excursion. His was a very different objective. These were people to pity not to envy. No grey silent routine gripped his life. Today he was just an imposter and it felt good.

Today it seemed his was the only smile among the resolute rush of commuters and he alone had time in front of him and behind him. Well prepared, shoes cleaned shirt ironed hair washed. Breakfast enjoyed with leisure, that set a positive frame of mind. A day to look forward to. It had been a long time since he had taken a train. Daily travel would be insufferable but it felt good that day travelling among the grey sea of commuters.

He had arrived at the Palazzo Comunale at 08.45 following a short walk to his destination. Costanzo had always been a competitor. His swimming had earned him several medals as a youth and it was something that he still pursued with enthusiasm. If his swimming maintained his body he had found that the game of chess somehow improved his mind. It developed the faculties he employed as a police officer. The analysis of your opponent's position, the limit on one's resources that is imposed on the public servant, the obligation to make a move following the opponent's weak or strong. It all fascinated him and as a result of that fascination he was one of the strongest boards in the Carabinieri's chess team.

It was this that had brought him here and if he was intrigued to have been drawn against an unknown competitor from the south for the three games he would be playing that day it had less to do with the ability of his opponent and more with her occupation. For Sister Magdalena was a postulant of the convent of Santa Maria.

The room in the Palazzo Comunale had been laid out with the chess boards furnished with fine Staunton pieces, those recognised for the most prestigious competitions. Costanzo recognised with some satisfaction a player he had beaten in the last round representing a government department he could not remember. What would his competition be like today.?

He remembered seeing her entering the room. A striking looking woman much younger than he had expected and while she was dressed in a black robe of the postulant, the headdress covering her hair was drawn back over her shoulders and it was quite possible to see her astonishing beauty. Her dark eyes had picked him out straight away as her likely opponent and she had smiled at him a cute pirate smile that was as unnerving as it was endearing.

The matches were pretty even as he recollected. She played black in the two games she had won but had lost to him the one she played as white.

'Huh, they were right' He said remembering his colleagues' taunts and managing, in retrospect, to appreciate the humour.

'Magdalena, the black queen'

He could not remember who had told him the true identity of the black queen, how she had spent her formative years a captive in an institution, but it had always brought a tremble to him that this black queen was the daughter of the head of one of the most notorious clans of the Ndrangheta, Magdalena Scalfero.

54.

ROME, ITALY

It was a quiet moment in that hour of indecision that follows an early breakfast on a day when nothing has been planned. Fruit bread toast and honey and cups full of strong coffee brewed on the small ring of the cooker were eaten in silence in the small flat that was their temporary base.

'Tell me about Magdalena Scalfero' Marcus invited at last, his voice rich with the early hour.

'There is not so much to tell.' She answered instinctively.

'A childhood mainly spent with my Mother who preferred to play the rebel from El Bocho and a Father who couldn't wait to get rid of me when my mother was killed. He had me incarcerated in an institution for fallen women until I was 18. It was intolerable, I was denied any contact with the world outside. Luc was the only friend I managed to keep in touch with. He remained loyal to me despite working for my father.

It was Luc who persuaded me to deceive you Marcus. I was ideal for his plan. The right age, the same background. He reminded me how my mother and your wife were once friends when they were young in Avignon.' She looked disconsolately for a moment.

'Look I really feel bad about this now. I know I was wrong. I can't think why I did it.'

It was an admission that entreated forgiveness but he did not respond changing the subject to retrieve some further facts.

'What did you do before emerging as a guide for the tourist office in Avignon?'

'After I left the Instituto Christina I became a postulant at Santa Maria convent. At that time it was a natural progression for me, almost set up for me and you know I almost got used to it. Not such a bad life. Nothing like the Institution I had left. Eventually I felt that there had to be more to see in the world than a convent so I left. They were kind about that so I remember. Maybe they thought that I did not fit in.'

She looked at him now with an unmistakable affection and followed her look with the short sideways smile that punctuated her speech. He had none of the aggressive confidence she had been used to in men. He would never wish to deceive or to seize advantage. He was a different kind of man, diffident, unsure but veritable. His was a cultured manner that inspired in her a longing for his affection and approval. She had offered her body to him as some form of compensation for her betrayal but now she was sure that she wanted it to be something more. Now she could feel more than just an affection for him. There was a bond between them that she was eager not to sever.

He smiled as if he had unravelled her thoughts. She had touched him with her contrition. He had felt flattered at her wishing to be his daughter and dreamt of her as the unblemished heroine his life had never had. She had saved him from the hell that was Scalfero's lair and carried him away from the anger of the Vesuvius. Then her deception had been compensated by the soft touch of her flesh and his enjoyment of her young body.

The beauty of a woman can inspire a man's forgiveness as it does a woman's envy he reflected. Life would move on now, together they would pass on the prophesy that Father Fidel Rocher had sought him to do.

They would never know how Nyeleni had found them. Hidden supposedly from the revenge of the Ndrangheta and the reproach of the Carabinieri they had been discovered by the instincts of a small child who did not know the city, understood little of the language and spoke not a word. A child who they had last seen being abducted in a taxi by a member of the Ndrangheta.

Hers was a most extraordinary presence. A child who said nothing but saw everything and understood the communications of birds and beasts. She could capture images it in her head in an instant and reproduce them in her astonishing drawings in extraordinary detail.

One night while they lay naked on their bed, moist with the perspiration of their exertions Marcus thought he saw the child's faded image in the mirror on the wall. She was standing by the open door outside the room looking in as if she was about to enter but not wishing to intrude. He supposed that this was one of her nocturnal walks. Then when morning came he saw the picture on the kitchen table etched in a thick lead pencil. From that brief glance at their reflection Nyeleni had drawn them as they lay together. It was image that can last a lifetime, captured to perfection in a moment in the solitary darkness of a hot night.

It was when Marcus spoke to her about her drawings, mesmerised by their astonishing detail, that she passed to him another drawing. It was of an elderly man, his face bearded and his hair overgrown. He looked the image of a captive just as Marcus had himself been in the cell in the Aspromonte.

The child's drawing showed her man lying on a bed staring upwards into the ceiling of the room his hands clasped vainly together as if in prayer. So precise was the drawing that Marcus could see when looking at it more deeply that the man was thin with neglect rather than age. He looked at her confused for a moment and she pointed towards the ground to indicate where the subject of her drawing was located.

'Does she want us to go with her and see?' Segolene asked.

The child shook her head wildly and pointed to her chest.

'No, it seems that wherever they took her to she has seen this man captive. We could assume that she escaped through the tunnels.' Marcus confirmed.

'The child nodded at this and smiled widely. Then, to their astonishment Nyeleni drew another drawing. It was of a Pope.

'Good Lord' Marcus said.

'She seems to be telling us that this captive is the Pope. Perhaps they mean to capture him.' He volunteered.

'No. I think that she is telling us that they already have. The Pope in the Vatican is an imposter. He has been placed there by the Antichrist just as the revelation said. She is telling us that she knows where the real Pope is. What's more I think that she plans to rescue him.'

It was then that Marcus remembered something drawn to his attention by Emma Dreyfus from the photographs he had sent her of the panelling in the chapel. It was an inscription made under a carving of one of the eyes in the head of the panel. They had assumed it to be Sister Beatrice who had coloured the eye blue and inscribed those words in Latin. Memento minima maxima sunt.

'Remember the smallest are the most important.' He said in no more than a murmur.

'Now we know what she meant' He said, and he laughed with satisfaction at the extraordinary blue eyed child.

55.

ROME, ITALY

In the Castello Rocco Cardinal Raphael was accommodated for his internment in a cell of the barest of appointment and frugal facilities. The basement cell was walled with ancient stone that revealed it having derived from the old city upon which the Castle itself had been built in the sixteenth century. It appeared so perfectly constructed for incarceration that it was almost certain to have been intended for that purpose from its inception. It contained only a narrow bed and thin mattress over which two blankets were thrown, insufficient to any probability of delivering him from the brittle cold that crept through his flesh and into his bones.

He had been unsure of the reason for his abduction and captivity but time to consider his plight provided for him an insight as to the motives and objectives of his captors. He was now certain that they had substituted his office and put in place a replacement who better suited their mission. He had been uneasy about the elderly cardinal who had seemed to encourage his appointment but was somehow too zealous an ally. He suspected that the elderly Dufour was indeed less than trustworthy. Had he secretly wished for some alternative appointment? He even wondered whether the death of Pope Eustace gunned down on a street in the city was the work of his captors? It could well be that those who now held him were responsible. They would surely have been disappointed to have killed his predecessor only to see the wrong man elected in his place.

He had wondered how his absence had been explained. Would there not now be a general search for him throughout the city?

Perhaps that was why he had been confined to the cell that held him.

Among all thoughts, memories and possibilities that turned in his mind one kept returning to him. It was the words of Maria Braganza Martinez a faithful supplicant from his home in Illinois. She had believed that life is preordained for one and she could see into the future of those who suffered misfortune to bring them hope. It had never been something he had himself believed in. To Cardinal Raphael it is the way we live our lives that delivers the outcome of our destiny. But he now felt the tenor of her words sound in his being.

'It will be you who will wear the fisherman's ring. You who will serve our Lord in the highest house, but the future speaks of a time of solitude before that service comes, a time of contemplation, a time of temptation from the very devil himself.'

He had answered her that it is wrong to submit one's future to the uncertainty of prophesy but now it was these very words that provided him with an explanation for his incarceration. That he like Christ himself be given a time of contemplation and temptation at the hand of evil.

The cruelty of his captivity for him was the darkness. The deep pitch black darkness to which he was subjected broken only by ten minutes of artificial light each day. It mattered not to Raphael the frugal diet delivered to him daily. He had existed on less than this and been grateful for it. The cold that cut to his bones did not cause him resentment. It was for him the absence of literature and his inability to read it that was his torture. Day after day, night after night and no way of knowing which was which. The stricture of contemplation and prayer made weak by weariness, the tedious repetition of time. When would it end?

He could not tell what time it was when he awoke with a start, but it was the faint sound of movement in his cell that woke him. Carefully he studied the darkness his eyes narrowed for closer examination. A rodent perhaps searching for the crumbs of bread that had fallen as he consumed it. A fractured water pipe somewhere near leaking to the floor. But no, the presence he felt was more than that. It was, he felt the presence of a being. The soft sound of breath and his instinct that someone or something was watching him and in his cell with him.

Instinctively he reached out his hand into the darkness and held it there as if to invite a touch. It was answered by something that could itself have been divine. Something that was a shock to him, for in an instant a small soft hand took his into its light grasp and held it in a gentle embrace. Here was someone in the room now watching him and holding his hand in affection. It would have been easy for him to believe that it was something spiritual but somehow he felt certain of a temporal presence.

A figure now stood in front of him and he could make out the features of a child. Her height no more than four feet tall. Her slight frame covered only by a thin white dress, grey in the darkness, her hair thick and dark and her right eye now glowing a brilliant green.

'My child?' He said as if to question her presence.

'Have you come here to save me?'

The child said nothing but pulled at his hand and motioned towards the door. She swung it open and as if anticipating his question she showed him that she held its key with a light touch on his cheek. She tugged again at his hand leading him along into the darkness without a word. It was as if she could see her way clearly as she moved swiftly along the passages that weaved in different directions turning to one side then another confident that she knew her way through the pitch darkness.

She was pulling at his hand and turning direction as she did so until finally she halted. Stretching out his arm again he felt what seemed to be a heavy wooden door. He smelt a draught of air that carried the scent of dampness as the child opened it. She tugged at his hand again pulling him forward into the darkness.

It was a journey though the tunnels now more open, less restricted, as he followed her blindly gripping her hand firmly in a desperation not to lose her. His feet were bruised by the hard uneven floor of the tunnel and his legs felt weak from their lying dormant for so long but still his instinct drove him on to follow the small hand that led him.

At last he saw a light above them that threw a fine ray of sunlight down into the darkness and his heart warmed at the thought of freedom. There were steps leading to daylight above them and Raphael staggered wearily up towards the light before him.

They emerged into the daylight by a sign that read *Entrance to the catacombs*, a public access that was used by tour companies in the city to explore the underground of Rome. Raphael found himself standing by the street and as he blinked his eyes and raced to focus his vision in the daylight and he turned in gratitude to speak to his diminutive liberator. But when he looked down to his side he saw that she had gone.

56.

ROME, ITALY

The church of Santa Augustina welcomed her with a cool embrace of sweet scented air as Segolene nervously entered it through the door that was open to the Via Augustina. She felt in her heart, an apprehension but she knew that the sacrament of penance would allow her to clear her soul of her sins and relieve her of the guilt she felt for the way she had treated Marcus for now she knew she loved him and her heart needed to confess.

It would be simple, just as she had been taught to do when a child in the Institutio Santa Christina although she acknowledged, there was a good deal more to confess than when she was a child. It made her uncomfortable to think of her betrayal but for her the sacrament of penance emptied her soul of sins and made space for the small indiscretions she was inclined to make.

She had stolen from the room of Father Fidel Rocher the diary of the nun Beatrice that had in it the first part of the secret prayer that blessed its bearer with protection. She had poisoned the old priest who had become a close friend of Marcus with the hemlock potion she had persuaded Luc to buy for her from the apothecary at the Son et Lumiere. Most of all she regretted her role in the deception of Marcus Graham, for now she felt a love for him that she could not assuage. Now she would clear her soul of sin to embark on a new life with him.

Slowly she sat herself down in the confessional and covered her face with a light scarf and looked down at the floor as she spoke.

'Bless me father for I have sinned. It has been some year now since I have confessed. I am an unmarried woman and I have fornicated with many men. I have deceived men, I have stolen an artefact from a priest and I have poisoned him in order to do so.'

She detected some hesitation from the priest on hearing these multiple mortal sins but finally she was relieved to hear him say:

'Do you now honestly and earnestly turn back to God my child?'

'I do'

'God sees everything my child. What is the deception you are party to?'

'I have deceived a man by pretending to be his deceased daughter so that I could obtain his trust as I believed him to hold a truth that he did not hold' She murmured apologetically.

'And the theft you speak of, you have said that you stole an artefact from a priest, one of God's servants. This is indeed a mortal sin.'

'It was an artefact that had no value save for the man I stole it for, my father. He is head of an honoured society under the patronage of St Michael. I deeply regret, the theft and the manner in which I took it. I poisoned the priest Father and I confess that sin.'

'Do you accept the penance that God will ask of you?'

'I do accept that Father'

'May God give you pardon and peace. You must pray to God to ease your lusts, you must use the article that you have stolen to the benefit of the church and you must seek out the man you have deceived and confess your deception to him. I absolve you of your sins in the name of the Father the son and the holy spirit.'

The priest watched to see the young woman leave the church. He could not see her face but he caught sight of her elegant figure and the manner of her walk on the high heeled shoes she wore. It should be no surprise that she was pursued by many men he thought to himself. Surely to women of such beauty sexual indiscretion is a well-rehearsed art, practised routinely and instinctively.

He wondered whether his counsel had been of use to her. He was not naive enough to believe that it would all be heeded. That was not the purpose of the sacrament. Surely it was to bring sinners back to focus on God not to mend their ways.

He turned to the elderly woman who had arrived carrying a basket that indicated that she had come to undertake some cleaning of the church.

'Senora Rosina. The church is all yours, I will be leaving now' He said thoughtfully.

'Yes of course.' She replied.

'Have a restful evening Father Simeon'

As the priest returned to his lodgings he could not clear his mind. There was something in what the young penitent had said that made him dwell on her words. She had confessed a number of mortal sins. This was to Father Simeon of less surprise than the penitent had perhaps thought. The most unlikely of women confessed their indiscretions to him. Sexual indiscretion was commonplace and he had on more than one occasion been told of murder. What interested him more was that she had spoken of an honoured society under the patronage of St Michael. Surely she could not mean the same honoured society that he had been born to.

Father Simeon's had not slept well that night. His mind was churning over the possibilities of the words he had heard from his beautiful penitent who had come to his church the previous day. His mind had searched for something from long ago. He had recalled how Scalfero had a daughter who had lost her mind when her mother had died, a daughter who had been institutionalised. How Scalfero had spoken of obtaining the secret prayer, part of a revelation given to a young girl by the Holy mother that was the very prophesy that he had acted upon to mentor his brother to the role of the Holy father.

He whispered to himself the facts that turned in his mind.

'Her father a member of an honoured society, an artefact stolen from a priest, the deception of an innocent man she believed to hold a truth she later found he did not hold.' His deliberations now led him to one conclusion. The beautiful and promiscuous penitent was the daughter of the one man he feared most. The man he served, Michelangelo Scalfero.

In the quiet of that evening and by the low candlelight in his chambers, Father Simeon contemplated his dilemma. He now had

351

to decide the priority of the dual faiths he held. Which would he follow? The Seal of confessional to the church, or his oath of allegiance to the order. Each demand the silence and obligation of those who swear to them. To breach the seal of the confessional that is so central to the sacrament of penance, the silence for which death itself cannot brake he would suffer discommunication from his faith. To fail his obligation to report the confession and dishonour the honoured society to which he was sworn to would mean certain death at the vengeful hands of the order.

It was a decision that he would not make swiftly nor lightly and it had troubled him deeply since he had pieced together the truth behind the young penitent's confession.

Father Simeon did not know if he trusted the young man who undertook the most discrete of services for Scalfero. Perhaps it was the fear that he felt as he looked into the cold eyes in the handsome face in front of him. Steel grey eyes that fixed upon him with the rigid determination of affirmed allegiance.

'You think she might be Magdalena the daughter of our Padrino.' He was saying.

You say she wore high heels like a whore? He said bitterly.

'She would not have walked far in those. I suspect that she is residing locally and I suspect too that she is sheltering the English architect who has poisoned her mind and is privy to the sacra secreta. I do not suppose it will take us long to find them'

Father Simeon was restless in his uncertainty. He was now regretting reporting the details of the confession to the order. He had been so heavily conflicted but last night he had chosen the expediency of reporting the incident to his order. Now he shivered under the cold grey eyes of the assassin that told him he had made the wrong choice. Now he felt having laid upon her the curse of death that he wished it to take place as soon as possible as if in this way it would relieve him of his guilt.

That evening Father Simeon permitted himself a short prayer for her, but it was a prayer not for her salvation, but for her nullification.

57.

ROME, ITALY

Costanzo woke with a start. It was a sharp sound he was sure that had awakened him but as he looked around his room he could feel only the stillness of the empty hour before dawn in the half light. It had been his nightmare, fresh now in his mind. He wiped his brow of the sweat that wetted his hair and felt the jolt of its recollection. How he had been captured by the beauty of Magdelena how she had smiled at him her cute pirate smile and beckoned him with her dark mystic eyes. He had been too frail to resist her, too eager to want her. Her sultry invitation to him to reach out to touch her breast. He had been dreaming of the soft tanned skin under his investigative fingers. Teasing the full flesh of her naked breast. Then in sudden outrage she had torn apart her blouse to reveal her breasts in a shocking revelation. The third nipple there in front of his very eyes. She had thrown her head back and laughed like a demon at his innocence, his naivety. In her mouth the twin fangs of the hell hag. Now he knew she was the witch who succoured demons from her breasts.

Hot with fear he had then awoken. Now the black queen coloured his vision in dark reality. Now she ruled his reasoning. Now he was fixated on a vendetta to find her and destroy her.

Luc did not need to spend long looking for her. Magdalena had not changed. She would gather fruit from the street stalls as she had always done. Fresh lemons to squeeze over crushed ice and sugar. She would take her coffee in the café in the mornings she would buy a French language newspaper just as she had always done. He knew it would not take too long to find her, but he knew too that Father Simeon's fears were far from his mind.

She would never die at his hands. She was far too beautiful to die. She was too precious to him. She was his past, she was to be his present and she would be his future.

He saw her first at the crossing by the Panetteria. He was surprised that she had not seen him as he almost stumbled across her but on seeing her concealed himself from view. How could such a beautiful woman hide herself he mused. It would be easy to follow her and later arrange a visit to eliminate the English architect he was sure she was concealing and who had so clearly and cunningly seduced her, and put together the two revelations that Scalfero alone must possess.

Luc followed her at a distance. He knew her from her movement and he supposed that had she caught sight of him then she too would recognise his shape and movement. She had turned into the pretty front garden of a small low rise block of flats and swiftly ascended the steps on the exterior of the building that led to the first floor. He made a note of the number and began to think about a time to return.

It was early evening when Luc skipped up the steps to the first floor flat. He had waited patiently for her to leave and when he had seen her turn the corner in the street he reckoned that it would be some time before she returned.

He drew his gun as he turned the handle to the door and entered quietly but it was too small a flat for someone to enter without being noticed. Marcus looked up from his newspaper to see in front of him the muscular figure of a young man moving towards him carrying a gun in his right hand. As Luc raised his hand to fire Marcus could see clearly the tattoo on his arm, the mark of the Ndrangheta that told him without doubt the identity of his assassin.

Marcus must have stood up on seeing him perhaps to try and escape but then he froze as he felt a force push him to one side as the single shot from the handgun sounded, a violent pain gripped his arm and a bullet ricocheted on the wall behind his left shoulder. He felt a moment of surprise almost as if the bullet was an unexpected consequence of the gun fire. Then a second shot followed and this time it caught him directly in the chest sending him backwards with a cruel jolt.

He fell to the floor clutching his chest and coughing wildly. He could see that Luc was reloading the gun and at that moment Marcus was certain that death was only a moment away. As he lay on his back on the ground he could see her looking down at him. She was shrieking to Luc and shaking him wildly seizing his tattooed arm and pushing him back towards the wall in a frenzy.

Marcus looked to the door his eyes glazing over as an unconsciousness overwhelmed him. Now he could see the two men in dark blue uniforms with crimson stripe down the leg, and the Baretta sub machine guns held in front of them. The shuffle of hurried motion and the cries of chaos. Then the brief retort of gunfire and the hollow thud of bodies falling to the floor, and then all was silence.

The three carabinieri galettas parked across the road outside the flat in Grottarossa were a clear signal to those who passed that some incident had occurred. Three bodies were now being carried out on stretchers through the pretty front garden as the officers looked on keeping onlookers at distance. Costanzo had arrived late on the scene just in time to see the result of his officers' engagement.

'So who have we got here then' He asked.

'Two dead one injured Lieutenant. You may be pleased to know' said the young officer finding it hard to conceal a smile.

'We've just taken the black queen'

58.

VATICAN CITY

The officer of the Vatican's Swiss guard looked at the Carabinieri officers with deep concern. What he was hearing was the most unbelievable story, though one that would perhaps answer the questions that had been posed about the death of the elderly cardinal Dominic Dufour who had long been suspected by the Vatican of unsavoury connections.

'Yesterday evening' Constanzo had begun as he seated himself in the elegant leather chair in front of the guard.

'The Carabinieri shot dead two members of the Ndrangheta in a small flat in Grottarossa. We recovered there a captive, shot by the criminals. He was an English architect who had been reported missing. Just before he passed out he told us how the Ndrangheta have placed an imposter in the Vatican.'

The guard composed himself to enquire further.

'An imposter? He questioned.

'Have you any idea who that might be? There are so many people employed here it would be difficult to know'

'Oh yes we know precisely who the imposter is sir.' Costanzo interrupted. He had been waiting for his moment, aware of the shock his revelation was about to make.

'You see sir, the imposter has been implanted here to take the place of the Pope.'

The guard looked at him in disbelief. Unable to find any words to question or contradict him.

'You mean' He uttered fumbling for a response.

'You mean the Pope himself?'

Constanzo looked him straight in the eyes.

'Last night we had a visitor at headquarters' He began almost mysteriously.

'We were visited by Cardinal Raphael the elected Pope. He explained to us how he had been abducted from the Vatican shortly after his election and kept captive in a cellar in the city. Cardinal Raphael had been rescued by a small child who had apparently led him through the dark tunnels and passages under the city to safety.

'That is most extraordinary, so the Pope we have here now has been placed here by the Ndrangheta?' The guard was finding it difficult to digest what he was being told as his mind lurched between disbelief and incredulity.

'This is indeed a supreme embarrassment to us Lieutenant.' He exclaimed shaking his head in clear shock at the revelation.

'The reputation of the Church will suffer greatly. We will be laughed at to have been taken in by these criminals if this becomes known.'

'We have little choice sir' Costanzo confirmed.

'The church has the head of a tape worm in its gut. The worm will grow fat if it feeds on the dignity of the Vatican' Costanzo volunteered in his best attempt at a metaphor to emphasise the gravity of the situation.

'Indeed Lieutenant, but I wonder if this matter has to be made public. It would surely be possible would it not to apprehend this criminal and to replace him with our true Pope without alerting anyone other than those in the Dicastery who need to know.' The officer looked at Costanzo in an enquiring manner that was now calmer and thoughtful as he added.

'We would of course afford you suitable recompense for your cooperation and silence Lieutenant'

'It would be straight forward enough for the transfer to be made for while the Pope has lost considerable weight he is now recovering well in a safe house close by, but even if I were to find your proposal acceptable sir, what of the imposter himself? He would spend time in prison telling of his crime. It is bound to become public knowledge.' Costanzo protested.

'Then it will presumably be necessary, Lieutenant for you to ensure that the imposter does not have that opportunity.' The Swiss guard officer was looking at the Steyr machine pistol resting on Costanzo's lap. It was clear that he felt that by one swift burst from its barrel a good deal of embarrassment could be avoided.

'Where is the imposter now?' Costanzo asked as if to avoid the suggestion and eager to bring his mission to a conclusion.

'I will take you to him so that you might place His Holiness under arrest?' The Swiss guard officer questioned cynically hoping that he had already made it clear what outcome was expected.

'Thank you sir' Costanzo said lightly simply rising from his chair.

In the Pope's private office Jacopo was speaking with Cardinal Tratavelli the one surviving Cardinal stipendiary to the Scalfero order.

'We are arranging for the Drexel Hesse bank to have greater control of finances for the Prefecture.' The cardinal was confirming.

'There will be complete management of property held by the Vatican and access to funds to ensure all management and maintenance. All staff will be suitably vetted. We will ensure that our own people hold all positions of power directly answerable to the Padrino himself'

'And the tithes we collect from convents of the southern seas. These are to be paid into the bank for the payment of government officials for public contracts ...'

Suddenly the door to the office sprang open. Jacopo turned swiftly looking towards the door. It was his instinct that told him it was over. Two officers of the carabinieri stood in front of him, their Steyr machine pistols cocked in front of them.

Costanzo looked the Pope straight in the eye. It was a countenance that froze him. Surely only yesterday he had looked into those eyes, that face, the worn face of Cardinal Raphael. He had seen the caring eyes the acceptance of suffering the innate kindness of one who serves his God and his people. What he saw now was the same face but not the soft and cerebral look of the cleric. The hard suspicious stare of the imposter had turned that face to a demonic mimicry.

That moment of hesitation might have cost Costanzo his life for as he started to speak he found himself looking down the barrel of a machine gun. Instinctively he moved swiftly to one side and was too quick for Jacopo as two bursts from the Ak47 tore into the panelled wall behind him. Jacopo ran to the door pushing aside the two officers as he exited the room with a further burst of fire to make his escape.

Tratavelli shook with the sudden violence. It was not the officers of the Carabineri he feared but the brother of the imposter who had just fled. He, Tratavelli had been entrusted the duty of governance following the unfortunate suicide of Cardinal Dufour. How would Father Simeon react to hear that his charge had been captured or even slain by the caribinieri? He would likely meet the same fate as Cardinal Dufour?

In mad panic Tratevelli lunged at the sototenente seizing his gun and turning it towards Costanzo. It was futile, he clearly had not the experience of handling the weapon for he seemed uncertain how even to hold it and it was easy for the sototenente to relieve him of his grasp. It had however given valuable seconds to the fleeing felon.

As Jacopo threw himself down a flight of stairs he realised that his robe was not only conspicuous but would impede his progress. Desperately he searched around the small lobby he found himself in to be rewarded by the sight on a black habit hanging on a rail on the wall. Without hesitation he found himself changing into the habit of a priest and concealing the white cassock and zucchetto under a low bench.

He was on the run now and he would need all the skill of that well-rehearsed escape that he had made after every assassination. Always it had been he who had set the chase. Now he had been taken by surprise, there was only the gun that he carried that had stopped his pursuers from catching him but now he thought, perhaps it was his gun that he had to dispose of.

They would expect him to take the Passetto di Borgo, the ancient passage that lead to the Sant Angelo castle reputed to be the means of escape for past Popes pursued by attackers. They would expect to see him armed with his gun but he should not be. For Jacopo's instinct was deception. A deception that might succeed under the cover of the very cloth that he wore. With luck the foolish Tratavelli would alert Father Simeon to mount a rescue but he could not rely on that. It was for him to complete his escape.

Swiftly he headed for the Sant Anna gate the business entrance to the Vatican to make his way out into the city. Here the guards would be kept busy moving on tourists and attending visitors. Jacopo gambled that the guards would not apprehend a lone priest and prevent him from exiting the gate and besides he had to take the risk. Once outside the gate he would be free to mingle with the crowd.

The two caribinieri officers were chasing down the corridor searching from side to side for the armed fugitive.

'The Passeto di Borgo. He is sure to have taken that route' Suggested the Sototenente with confidence to Costanzo.

'We will have officers waiting for him there.'

As he made that call to recruit the officers to attend the Sant Angelo Castle, Jacopo was making his escape from the Vatican.

The minutes past and as the officers looked at each other sure that they had lost their quarry, Costanzo's radio crackled to inform him of an incoming message.

Lieutenant a priest has just stolen a motor cycle in the Piazza Risorgimento. Looks like he headed east toward Ponte Margerita.

'That's our man. We think there is a safe house near Twenty Settembre he could be heading there. Let's make sure we have officers on every corner. A priest on a motorcycle in a hurry should not be too hard to spot.'

Just then the radio crackled again.

Suspect just crossed the bridge right in front of us. Do you want us to apprehend him?

'No. No. We need to know where he is heading not to catch him.

There was then three minutes that seemed like an hour. No reports.

'Do you think we've lost him?

'He is somewhere south of Piazza del Popolo. Come on someone call in' Constanzo agonised. Just then it crackled again.

'Our man has just passed into Sistina. He is not speeding just taking it real easy.

That's what we want. He doesn't know we are onto him. Costanzo confirmed with satisfaction. If they could follow his progress through the streets of Rome without his being aware perhaps they would find the Mafia safe house and perhaps even find something that would link Scalfero to the grand deception.

Jacopo had at first found the small motorbike difficult to operate but now it seemed so easy. He was cruising effortlessly along Sistina and enjoying the ride. He was sure that he was not being followed. The Carabinieri were like the police everywhere, when they followed a suspect there were claxons sounding cars screeching and general mayhem. There was no sign of this today. He was free to ride, but as he drew up at the traffic lights at Cappuccini Jacopo turned to see something that made him freeze.

The blue and white fiat had pulled up alongside him. There was no doubt that the theft of the small motorbike had been reported, but he had reasoned that such a minor crime would be of no interest to the Carabinieri. His pursuers had far more important things to do, but he had not considered the Polizia di stato. Vehicle thefts were reported to them regularly and there was the possibility that the Polizia would recognise the bike as stolen. He tried to avoid looking into the car for fear of catching the eyes of its occupants. Jacopo was fearless but this was a little too close for comfort.

As the lights changed Jacopo instinctively yanked back the throttle, The bike leapt forward, its front wheel coming down on the blue wing of the fiat. Jocopo groaned with dismay. He who had assassinated Pope Eustace played his part in the abduction of Cardinal Raphael and deceiving the Vatican could find himself apprehended by the local police for scratching a police car.

The Police officer was smiling as he signalled the priest over to the side of the road. There was little damage done but it was enough.

'Well Father. You have to be a bit more careful on that bike of yours he said genially'

Let's just have a few details from you and get you on your way.

'I do apologise officer. I am in such a hurry to visit an elderly lady who needs my blessing and counsel. I do not have my identification with me and I'm afraid I was in too much of a hurry. My hand must have slipped inadvertently on the throttle' Jacopo began.

The officer looked down at the hand and looked puzzled. For what he saw was something he had not seen before but he instinctively knew well. It was no ordinary ring that shone with the brightness of pure gold on the priest's finger. What he saw on that hand was the fisherman's ring.

Nyeleni had escaped the Sahel and servitude for the city and freedom. Yet in her desert home, freedom knew only the prohibitions of danger and distance. It was the wild desert where life was frail and without permanence but where mankind moved from place to place a transient existence unfettered by territory and title.

Here in this eternal city where there was freedom for all, there were the limitations of ownership. Walls of exclusion, gates of segregation, buildings that housed secrecy, but somehow, as if by some divine magic, this small child could find her way past all such obstacles to roam unrestrained by boundaries and barriers.

She had found her way into the most beautiful picture gallery she had ever seen. Walls and ceiling coloured with images of saints and sinners painted as if in motion. Some were rising and some falling and in the centre a picture of Christ. She promised herself that she would one day draw these pictures for she had captured them in her mind. As she left the chapel she saw under a low arch the figure of a priest dressed in a habit of black and white and bent with the frailty of age. His face was lined above a white beard and in his eyes burned an intensity of intellect and wisdom. Father Fidel Rocher turned to look at the small dark child shrouded in only a thin white dress and smiled lightly and he spoke to her as if he knew her.

'Now my child the world awaits the second coming of our Lord to sit in judgement of mankind. The righteous will rise and the sinners will fall. Dark will become light just as evil will give way to goodness. The servant of the Antichrist is banished just as the creeping thistle is plucked from amid the roses of yellow and white. Our mission is complete.'

Then from within a pair of small clouds there came a beam of light that found Nyeleni like a searchlight does an actor on a theatre stage. She outstretched her arms and looked up towards heaven as her body levitated slowly into the air.

It was Costanzo himself who had devised the spin. The story of how a deluded intruder dressed as a Pope had found his way into the Vatican, was pursued by his officers through the streets of Rome on a motorbike until he had ridden into a police car and had been arrested. This version of events had been accepted readily by those charged with Vatican security and the suggestion of some donation to the relatives of the Carabinieri officers murdered at the pool of the Imperiali had proved a welcome one.

The Pope himself had not been disturbed by the event and was at no time in danger. Cardinal Raphael was informed that he would upon recovery from his ordeal be taking up his position as Pope Michelangelo. The Vatican had been obliged to put out a press release that the Holy Father had been unwell but was making a swift recovery.

In the bar Piccolo the following evening it was a night of celebration for the Carabinieri officers gathered there. Costanzo was enjoying the role of a minor celebrity among his peers who were sworn to secrecy, and while they would not reveal details of the conspiracy they were none the less freely discussing the success of the mission while drinking beer and eating plates full of calamari, artichokes and smoked ham.

'They looked identical. How did you know that he was not the true Pope?' The young officer questioned Costanzo suggesting perhaps the monumental error that would have arisen had the victim not been an imposter.

'When he pointed the AK 47 at me and fired it at my head, that's when I reasoned he might be an imposter.' Costanzo confirmed nodding his head in mock severity.

They laughed together triumphantly. The Pope had been found and his imposter dead and two members of the Ndrangheta gunned down including the black queen. This evening would be one of celebration. But Costanzo still had one thought on his mind. He had to impose the retribution due to his enemy. Would he one day witness the death of Michelangelo Scalfero?

59.

TUNBRIDGE WELLS, ENGLAND

Heavy snow had fallen in the night. A deep blanket covered the village in the soft beauty and the still silence of a winter morning. It brought an eerie quiet to those short hours of frail light that visit the winter solstice. Here in an English village, peace and dignity bury a life with the deepest of respect and the simplest of formality.

The parish of St Giles stands back from the centre of the village on raised ground accessed from the High Street along a cobbled driveway. Its spire rises high above the sandstone cottages that line the street in quaint regency terraces and the older timbered buildings that were once home to shopkeepers and artisans. By midday all around the small sandstone church narrow paths had been cleared. They led through the Churchyard to a freshly dug grave.

It had been the most perfunctory of services. A single eulogy by a clergyman who had not known the deceased, who had little to do with an earthly life past and more with the potential of eternal life to come. Now, small groups of mourners cautiously made their way along the paths to stand by the graveside, exchanging glances but few words between them.

Silhouettes stood in long black overcoats, some wearing hats. Solemn black figures stark against the whorl of white that surrounded them and as the snow then started to fall again, they drew their collars tight against their motionless faces and looked towards the sky as if to watch where it was falling from. First, tiny fluttering flakes, falling slowly in the cold crisp air. Then as the coffin was lowered into the grave, heaven cast a fresh tumult of the stuff twisting and turning in a bitter breeze laying a bleak blanket over the grave, as if to erase all memory of the committal. The few fragile flowers, laid to freeze and whither upon a hard and unforgiving ground now wore a white of innocence and were all that was left of memory.

The clergyman spoke quietly to a young woman standing alone wrapped in a long black overcoat.

'I would appreciate your conveying my condolences to Sir Clement on the loss of his friend.' He ventured to her in a clear and cultured tone that conveyed a practised sympathy.

All arrangements for the funeral had been made on behalf of Sir Clement Ambrose Fitzroy the well-known architect from London and the body was flown back to England from Rome. The burial in this small churchyard to be attended as he had directed, by a small number of carefully selected 'acquaintances of the deceased as appropriate.' A special flight had been laid on for Marcus from a contact at Bell Air Charter. Fitz never needed to know all the details in order to instigate preparations nor to orchestrate plans. Just a few phone calls from Sir Clement made to the right people got the job done.

Emma quietly acknowledged the condolence unsure how she should respond.

'Thank you. I shall see to it that he is informed. I am sure that he will appreciate your condolences. He regrets very much that he cannot be here today.' She heard herself sounding unnatural in her response but she found herself unwilling to venture further with any exchange of condolence. She was today Fitz's chosen representative as a requirement to be out of the country had 'made it awkward' for him to attend.

Emma stood back from the graveside alone not wishing to engage in any conversation with the other mourners. She would have been here in any event, she reminded herself. Marcus would have wanted her here. He had involved her in his extraordinary story from the outset, and she had played her part too in the unravelling of its mystery. He had told her to tell no one, not even

Fitz. Now, perhaps that story had ended here in a graveyard in a village near Tunbridge Wells.

Here, had been laid to rest deception, danger and death. Here in this frozen earth as winter laid its white blanket to cover the ground. All the world around her was at peace and in silence and the chill fresh air seemed to her to carry the clear scent of a new beginning.

She walked alone back to the lynch gate hearing the sound of packed snow scrunching under her feet until she reached the large black limousine that Fitz had arranged for her. She turned to look back for just a moment. The small group of mourners were departing in pairs in unhurried silence.

It was only then she saw him. Standing alone by the lytch gate well away from the grave, clearly anxious to remain apart from the mourners. A man of about the age of Marcus. A short, dark and slender figure well dressed in black with a dark complexion and she noticed the conspicuous gold ring on his right hand. He was a figure she felt somehow out of place in this English village churchyard, and she could see that he was crying.

Emma allowed herself to look for just a second before feeling sure that she was intruding into his grief. A tangible grief that, as she turned towards the car, made her feel that she was witnessing a deep sorrow. She knew that his alone, among these mourners, was not the casual pity that was being buried under one brief snowfall of winter. For while she had never seen him before, she knew precisely who he was and why he was there. Perhaps she alone knew his loss and she could comprehend its gravity. For even the most dispassionate of fathers will mourn the loss of his only daughter. Now she witnessed Michelangelo Scalfero cry tears imbued with guilt from a heartbroken with regret.

In a room in St Thomas hospital on the south bank of the Thames, Marcus lay motionless on the stiff bed on his back looking toward the ceiling. He could hear nothing feel nothing but was somehow aware of the brisk and efficient activity around him and the fierce pain that had been subdued by tranquilising drugs.

His mind trailed back to the sick room of his boyhood. He had liked being ill then. There was his mother to wait on him fussing over him more than usual, asking how he felt, what she could bring him and making him feel so important. He remembered how he had lain there for days looking at a wide blue sky during a bout of measles and how he had counted the silent planes high in that sky their vapour streams behind them first two straight lines then scribbles in their wake before disappearing into blue emptiness. Where did he imagine were they going to? They were the manifestations of the stories he read in the pile of Readers Digests beside his bed. They may be sent to rescue a research team in the frozen Artic or be naval bombers on some wartime mission. Then there were the ships on the river on a still night sounding deep dismal horns as they headed to the estuary.

Now, he could close his eyes and rest and return to that blissful time of ease but as he did so he heard the voice that had guided him. It was as if he was standing there by the bed speaking directly to him in a voice both distinct and hollow.

'In that hour when we first met my friend I saw your fate was predestined. You had lost your white queen early in the game and you felt the hopelessness of continuing without her. The failure of that loss weighed heavy on you and you believed that your life was a game that you were destined to loose. But you have played valiantly on.

The black queen deceived you with her beauty and her false guises but she has been struck down in the penultimate move, lost to you like the passing joy that one can never bend. The black king my friend will never die. Even in defeat he will survive to fight another day. Fate has played out the game against you and now that game has ended.'

As he heard the voice of Father Fidel Rocher, Marcus felt himself drift into a sleep uncertain whether he would awake.

As the wind gathered and the snow fell heavier now, Emma Dreyfus stretched herself on the leather seat in the back of the car pulling around her legs the long black overcoat to keep her warm. She was rehearsing how to tell Marcus that Segolene had been buried in a churchyard in Tunbridge Wells in a clumsy attempt by Fitz to do the 'right thing' for his friend. She spoke briefly to the driver as the car's wheels spun in the deepening snow in pulling away.

'Fisher Holt and Fitzroy in Chelsea please' She instructed.

End

HERZ FÜR AUTOREN A HEART FOR AUTHORS À L'ÉCOUTE DES AUTEURS MIA ΚΑΡΔΙΑ ΓΙΑ ΣΥΓΓΓ
HJÄRTA FÖR FÖRFATTARE UN CORAZÓN POR LOS AUTORES YAZARLARIMIZA GÖNÜL VERELIM SZ
CUORE PER AUTORI ET HJERTE FOR FORFATTERE EEN HART VOOR SCHRIJVERS TEMOS OS AUTO
SZÍVÜNKÉRT SERCE DLA AUTORÓW EIN HERZ FÜR AUTOREN A HEART FOR AUTHORS À L'ÉCOL
CORAÇÃO ВСЕЙ ДУШОЙ К АВТОРАМ ETT HJÄRTA FÖR FÖRFATTARE Á LA ESCUCHA DE LOS AUTO
AUTEURS MIA ΚΑΡΔΙΑ ΓΙΑ ΣΥΓΓΡΑΦΕΙΣ UN CUORE PER AUTORI ET HJERTE FOR FORFATTERE EEN
YAZARLARIMIZA GÖNÜL VERELIM SZÍVÜNKÉRT SERCE DLA AUTORÓW EIN HERZ FÜ
HART VOOR SCHRIJVERS TEMOS OS AUTO CORAÇÃO ВСЕЙ ДУШОЙ К АВТОРАМ ETT HJÄRTA FÖ

The author

The Fisherman's Ring is a debut novel by
Denis Minns.
Born in the UK, Minns lives with his wife in the
Kentish Weald. He has a Masters in Law and is a
chartered surveyor.

Minns writes features about the housing industry
for magazines and local papers. He is fascinated by
mankind's desire to predict the future which is a
central theme of this novel.